WIFE TO MR. MILTON

Wife to Mr. Milton

The Story of Marie Powell

by

Robert Graves

ACADEMY
CHICAGO
LIMITED
1979

Contents

	FOREWORD	vii
I.	THE LAST DAY OF CHRISTMAS, 1641	3
II.	AN ALARM OF THE PLAGUE	16
III.	A SIGHT OF ROYALTY, AND OF ANOTHER	32
IV.	LIFE AT FOREST HILL	48
V.	MUN BECOMES A SOLDIER	61
VI.	I FALL INTO PIETY AND OUT AGAIN	75
VII.	A STRANGE TALE OF SYMPATHY	89
VIII.	I FALL INTO DISGRACE	101
IX.	AN ACCOUNT OF MR. JOHN MILTON	114
X.	I AGREE TO MARRIAGE	126
XI.	MR. MILTON'S COURTSHIP	138
XII.	MY MARRIAGE	150
XIII.	I AM TAKEN TO LONDON	167
XIV.	I SAY FAREWELL TO MY FAMILY	183
XV.	I COME BACK TO FOREST HILL	197
XVI.	THE BEGINNING OF THE WAR	211
XVII.	MY HUSBAND SENDS FOR ME	227
XVIII.	I AM PERSUADED TO RETURN TO MY HUSBAND	240
XIX.	I AM GOT WITH CHILD; AND MY FATHER IS RUINED	259

XX.   MY CHILD IS BORN; AND MY FATHER DIES   277

XXI.   I SPEAK WITH MUN AGAIN   293

XXII. I WATCH THE KING'S EXECUTION   304

XXIII. EVIL NEWS FROM IRELAND   320

XXIV. MY HUSBAND BUYS FAME AT A HIGH PRICE   338

       EPILOGUE   357

       APPENDIX   367

       GLOSSARY   373

Foreword

1942 was the tercentenary of the outbreak of the Civil War, and also of
John Milton's marriage to his first wife, Marie Powell of Forest Hill,
Oxford.* He was thirty-three at the time; she was sixteen. Since this
book is a novel, not a biography, I need not write a learned preface to
justify my conjectural reconstruction of the story—how he came to
marry her, why she left him after a few weeks, why she returned three
years later, and so on—but I have tried to answer all the outstanding
questions plausibly and fairly in the course of the narrative.

Three centuries of English history do not seem an impossibly long
time. The language and the details of social life have changed a good
deal; yet war is still in fashion, the pike still obsolete, the English climate still uncertain, divorce-laws in no less of a muddle, most of the
same stock people with family-faces still about, taxes as heavy as ever,
newspapers as unreliable, the Colleges of Oxford University once more
commandeered by the Government, and few of the political questions
that the Civil Wars brought to a head yet finally settled—there is even
a renewed complaint in the Press to-day of "unwarranted interference
in secular affairs by the Archbishop of Canterbury."

The post-war Cromwellian solution of these political questions,
which Milton endorsed, was drastic and unconstitutional—it would
now be called "undisguised Fascism"; and democratic journalists and
politicians who quote with approval Wordsworth's:

> Milton, thou should'st be living at this hour.
> England hath need of thee . . . .

should read, or re-read, Milton's life and works. It is true that during
the war he had written his famous *Areopagitica,* a plea for the freedom of the Press; but almost as soon as the fighting was over he became Assistant Press Censor for the Council of State and helped to
enforce a most repressive Censorship law. This Council was the execu-

* Modern historians reject the traditional date of 1643.

vii

tive of a minority Government set up by the mutinous New Model Army, after they had suppressed the House of Lords and had forcibly reduced the Commons, by a purge of the conservative majority, to a small party of Independent members who were willing to co-operate in the execution of the King and the abolition of the Monarchy.

A glossary of obsolete words and phrases will be found at the end of this book. In those times the date of any day between January 1st and Lady Day was, in England, given in double notation (e.g. Marie Powell was baptized on January 24th, 1625–26); but in Scotland in single notation, as now. I have here adopted the single notation for the sake of clearness, also modern spelling and punctuation. The documents quoted in the Appendix give a fair idea of what this book would look like in contemporary dress. The value of money was then four or five times what it was at the outbreak of the present war; to a man of Milton's limited income the non-payment of the £1,500 which his father-in-law owed him was a very serious matter.

1942 was also the tercentenary of the battle of Newbury, in which the most sympathetic character of that period, Lucius Cary, the second Viscount Falkland, died fighting for King Charles. I have to thank my neighbour, the thirteenth Viscount (also a Lucius Cary), for his great kindness in helping me to get *Wife to Mr. Milton* ready for the printers.

R. G.

Galmpton, Brixham, Devon.

CHAPTER ONE

The Last Day of Christmas, 1641

I T WAS January 6th of the year 1641, being the last of the twelve days of Christmas, and my fifteenth birthday. My godmother, my Aunt Moulton, had travelled in her own coach from Honeybourne in the County of Worcestershire to pass Christmas at our noisy house (then hung in every nook with holly and ivy); which was the Manor-house of Forest Hill, a little town lying distant from the City of Oxford not above four miles by road, to the eastward as you ride out beyond Headington Hill. She came to me that morning where I sat in the great parlour with my brothers and sisters—for outside it was snowing plentifully—and "Here, Child," says she, "here's my annual gift to you; I had almost forgot."

I sprang up, my cheeks smarting from the blaze of the fire, and made her a low curtsey, for though I had already so saluted her twice or thrice that same morning, she was a gentlewoman whose bearing naturally demanded a ceremonious exactness from children; besides, a birthday gift from my Godmother Moulton was always worth a dozen of curtseys, she would choose it so judiciously.

When I pulled off the paper wrappings I found a book, of middle size, bound in fine white vellum, with a silver clasp that had a lock to it and a little silver key. The title was stamped upon the cover in gold letters: "Marie Powell: Her Book." My younger brothers and sisters crowded round me, and Zara who was next below me in age cried out, very unmannerly: "Let me look! Let me look! Oh, let me unlock this thing and see the painted pictures!"

My brother James, who was next in age above me, and an under-graduate of Christ Church, pulled her away and "Patience, Zara," says he, "your birthday falls not until September. This is Marie's own day: to-day she is all and you are nothing." Thereupon the turbulent children fell back a little while I unlocked the clasp.

I opened the book at the title-page, as I thought, but the paper was wholly blank, as likewise was every new page that I turned over;

3

which at first dashed me out of countenance, though I tried to hide my
disappointment from my Godmother Moulton. She took my face between her hands, whereon were white worsted mittens and a great
beryl ring of silver-gilt, and kissed my brow. Then she said: "Godchild,
I hope you'll take kindly to this gift of mine, which the Queen's own
stationer has bound. For I reasoned that by now you would have quite
wearied of the *Seven Champions of Christendom* and the *Morte d'Arthur* and such-like old papistical tales of slaughter and magic, which
were your constant entertainment when last we met together; but, further, that you would not yet be grown to an age when the gift of a
good book of sermons would content you. Then I remembered your
lively fancies and inventions, which indeed are proper to a child born,
as you are, under the capering sign of Capricorn, and on Twelfth
Night too, when the stars seem to dance running-battle in the sky.
Said I to myself: 'Let the child write her own book, this New Year; but
I'll fasten it with a clasp and lock, so she may keep it private from her
meddling brothers and sisters. She shall wear the key on a ribbon
about her neck.'"

My Godmother's notion, when it was dressed out in this fashion,
charmed my mind. I stammered in my thanks, which she knew for sincere, and presently with a smile she cried: "Children, God bless you
all! I must go and put on my bravery!" With that she withdrew herself
into the little chamber over the kitchen, where she always lodged because it was the warmest, though the window looked out upon the
wood-yard and the stables, rather than upon the orchard and gardens.
After she was gone, my younger brothers, John and William and Archdale, who were lumpish, mischievous boys and hunted together in a
howling pack like beagles, closed upon me again with "Let me see, O,
let me see!"

I assured them there was nothing to see but white paper and handsome covers; so presently they went back to the fire, where they were
playing some idle game with hazel-nuts. Only William stood fast, and
says he: "Sister Marie, won't you write a tale of warlocks and witches
in your new book, and won't you read it out to us every Saturday at
evening, chapter by chapter? You are the best one at the telling of
tales in this whole town. Or won't you write out a history of Knights
and Squires and Ogres in the brave old days?"

I did not answer him for awhile, for though his little petition flattered me, it did not jump right with what my Aunt Moulton had put

into my mind, of keeping the contents of my book private to myself only.

"No," said I at last. "There's no need. I can read tales in the flames of the fire as I sit on my stool before it; so the fire's a better book for your purpose than this would be. You shall have a tale to-morrow about Mother Grime, the Witch of Wheatley, who lived there in the days of King Harry—how she put a curse upon the bells in the bell-tower to prevent their ringing. That's a firm promise."

"And did she grease her broomstick with adder's fat to make it fly the faster?" he asked.

"Phoo, that's nothing," said I, laughing. "Witches always grease their broomsticks with adder's fat or viper's, even the least cunning of them. Mother Grime was no common witch; she would tie three knots in the tail of the little badger-dog, her familiar, to make him invisible and give him a soundless bark."

"Did she brew hell-broth in a great brazen cauldron? Did she throw in toads and puddocks and dead men's fingers and the soot of sea-coal?"

But I told him he must wait until the next day if he would hear the right manner of brewing hell-broth according to Queen Hecate's own receipt and practice. Then Zara, who was at that time a spiteful little wretch, always plaguing me, crept up again and, says she, pretending innocence: "Sister, will you indeed confide your whole heart and mind to the book? Will you write out in plain words what that little scholar of Magdalen Hall, Gregory What's-his-name, proposed to you on Christmas Eve when you were sliding on the ice, and what answer you made him? Will you also copy into it the letter, perfumed with musk, that he slipped into your hand as we went walking towards——"

At this I brought down the book on Zara's skull with a hearty thump and laid her flat among the rushes. Then I gathered up my skirts and ran from the room, lest any new riot might delay my enjoyment of the happy fancies that now crowded me.

I went first to knock at the door of my father's little study, which was also the linen-chamber, where he sat casting his accounts. He worked by candlelight, the whole heaven being dark with snow. Presently he pulled open the door, the handle of which was ready to his hand, and I showed him my gift, that pleased him mightily. We conversed awhile and soon I was bold enough to beg a bundle of goose-pens, an ink-pot and a sand-caster; which he denied me at first. However, I pleaded my birthday and Twelfth Day kindness; and also gave him leave to write something for himself on the title-page, which I could see that his fingers itched to do. To tell truth, I shrank from the hazard of smudging a clean book; moreover, I loved my poor father well and was content that he should write something for me in his own hand. So in return he gave me all that I asked.

When he enquired how I proposed to fill the pages, I put him off by saying that my brother Will had petitioned me to write down tales of the brave old days of Robin Hood and Sir Launcelot du Lac, to read out before the fire every Saturday, at evening before supper. At this my father gazed fixedly on me for awhile and then with a sigh that had something prophetical in it, "Marie, my dear," says he, "I'll acquaint you with something to the purpose. *These* are the brave old days, as no others ever were. Write of them, if you will, and let the record be a solace to you in the sad new days that I fear must soon break upon us with the present alteration of the King's affairs."

He took up a pen and trimmed it well with his pen-knife and then thrusting aside the candle-sticks to give him more elbow-room for his task he very exactly inked me out a lozenge figure on the title-page of the book. In the lozenge he set the arms of Powell, which are a *chevron* (or roof-tree) *argent* on a *sable* ground, with two bloody spear-heads above and one below—"*gutty de sang*" is the heralds' cant for the gouts of blood on the spear-heads. For want of vermilion colour, he painted the gouts with blood drawn from his own thumb, which he pricked with the knife to show his earnest affection for me. Next, he wrote a flowing M, and a flowing P, at the outward point of the lozenge, and below it set the day and the year, and at the foot of the page in fine Italian writing:

> "These Were the Brave Old Days,"
> saith Richard Powell.

With that, he kissed me and bade me begone, since he had now four times miscast the same crabbed reckoning of moneys.

This then was how the book came to me, and how I began to keep a record of my maiden days at Forest Hill, which (as it seems to me now) were truly the brave old days, as no others can ever again be. For this was to be the last year of peace in England, before the bloody Troubles arose which cast us Powells, with many thousands of other light-hearted, loyal and well-to-do families, into the lamentable black mire of delinquency and ruin.

After dinner that day, when eleven invited guests (besides our household of sixteen) sat down to table, began the customary merry-making of Twelfth Night, to which numerous persons of quality, our neighbours, came in their coaches or on nags from all the country round, so far as Thame and beyond: for we kept Twelfth Night more gaily than any other house thereabouts, upon account of my birthday. They came masked and dressed in very rich clothes, or in such grotesque disguises as the skins of wild-beasts, or the foreign garbs of Turks or Jews or Chinamen; or they assumed the characters of rufflers or fools or antics or astrologers or country sluts, disguising not their persons only but also their voices. The Lord of Misrule who controlled the festivity, that otherwise might have run out of hand, was my brother Richard, the eldest of us all, whose profession was the Law. To him all the company must formally bring their charges if they saw through any masquerade, saying that it concealed such and such a person. Then the Lord of Misrule, advancing his long black rod, would march up to the accused masker with: "Sir (or Madam), you are accused to me by this credible witness to be Such-and-Such. Do you plead guilty, or do you plead not guilty? Signify your plea either with a nod or with a shake of your head."

A masker that pleaded guilty was straightway ordered to unmask and pay a forfeit; but if he pleaded "not guilty" with a shake of the head then the accuser himself paid the forfeit unless, pleasantly giving the accused person the lie, he challenged him to discover himself. Then the forfeit would be doubled, falling against the party that was proved to be at fault. Between ladies and gentlemen the customary forfeit was either a kiss or a grovelling abasement; and one gentleman piercing the disguise of another might give him a stroke with the open hand upon his forehead; or he might smudge his nose with charcoal, or gently tug his beard; but if upon the unmasking he proved to be mistaken, then the other might kick his buttocks for his pains. Yet by an ancient law of Misrule, no woman might lay accusation against any other woman; which was wisely contrived, I think.

Our good friend, Captain Sir Robert Pye the Younger, of Faringdon Magna in Berkshire, came disguised as a country-carrier with a smock and whip, his cheeks well smeared with ruddle. My little brothers were tricked out as apes, capering about together and each officiously catching fleas for the others, but since they were all much of a size and shape, it was hard to tell this one from that. Little William won a forfeit on account of false accusation from Provost Tolson of Oriel College, who mistook him for Archdale; and elected to smudge the Provost's face for him with charcoal, which he did with the letter S upon each of his cheeks. The old gentleman, thinking these to be simple smudges, joined in the laughter against himself, until in the little silver mirror which I showed him, he saw himself branded as a Stirrer of Sedition; whereupon a sort of horror overcame him and he wiped off the ignominy with spittle and the sleeve of his gown.

My mother counterfeited an aged and meek nun, which she did to the life. Her cheeks were chalked, her eyes downcast and her voice quavered as she clicked her poor cherry-stone beads; but the character that she assumed contradicted her nature point-blank, for my mother is a hearty, jolly, managing woman and by no means frequent in her devotions. Before long, upon a drunken gentleman's wagering that she was in truth but a sinful old baggage and that she lay every third night with the Devil, she could not refrain, but burst into her familiar baying laugh and so was discovered. Then a gentleman disguised as the Devil, with hoofs and horns and a goat's beard, laughed more heartily yet; whereat he was immediately accused to the Lord of Misrule of being my father; so the waggish gentleman had knocked down two birds with the same stone. Then the little apes, my brothers, swarmed into my mother's lap, making as if to tear her rosary from her, and "By Sulphur and Brimstone, Nan," the Devil cried to the Nun, "haven't I begotten a brave horde of devilkins upon your dainty body?"

Zara was dressed as a Spanish lady of quality, in fine clothes lent her for the occasion by my Godmother Moulton. Her bodice was of yellow satin richly embroidered; her petticoat, of striped gold tissue; her robe, of crimson velvet with a raised pile and lined with white muslin that was spotted over with stars. My godmother had brought these clothes with her for me to wear, but I had outgrown their measure; whereby Zara had the profit of her kindness.

As for myself, I dared that night to assume man's clothing: I affected to be a modern goddame blade, wearing a tall ribboned hat, with a narrow brim and a great plume caught at the ends with silver ribbon, and carrying a frosty-blue cloak over my arm, lined with white. I had fine Greek lace at my wrists and neck, and a tight doublet of willow-coloured satin, very short in the skirt, with breeches of the same colour, shaped like organ pipes, and ornamented at the knee with many dozen of points. The feet of my boots were two inches too long and their lace-fringed tops were terrible large, being turned down as low as my gilt spurs, that jingled like bells of a morrice-dancer. I carried a cane in my right hand, with which I toyed as I straddled down the hall; keeping my two feet wide apart, like a child at his first steps, lest the rowels of my spurs should catch in the lace and overset me. I also wore a little sharp artificial beard at which I plucked carefully, lest it came away in my hand, and fine fringed gloves scented with musk; and I made legs and bows instead of curtseys. My cousin Marmaduke Archdale, who was afterwards slain in the King's service, during the siege of Gloucester, had procured these masquerade clothes for me from a young courtier of his acquaintance; my cousin being always very attentive to my petitions.

That I could so indulge my fancy, though now a marriageable girl, and that I ranged myself in the dances with the gentlemen, and that, when I was at last accused and unmasked, my parents were not vexed with me, nor nobody scandalized, but that all was taken in good part as a Twelfth Night prank—all this, I think, fairly shows both my particular bold spirit and the general kindness of the times. None who was admitted to our house was ever allowed to feel ill at ease in it, unless he were some felonious prisoner that the town-constable hauled in to be tried by my father, who was a Justice of the Peace; or else some snuffling Puritan tradesman, come on an errand, who often by the freedom of our speech must have thought himself in Babylon or Bantam. Only my Aunt Jones of Sandford, my father's elder sister, who was a backward-looking gentlewoman and came to our masquerade wearing her ancient open-breasted grey gown, with her usual starched ruff, and her ancient velvet hat like a wind-blown balloon—only she spoke some few slighting words against me to my father. She asked, pointing rudely at me with her finger, how he hoped that any discreet gentleman with an eye to marriage would choose such stale goods as *those?*

My father answered that this was Twelfth Night, and that if she uttered more scurrility he would accuse her as a spoilsport, and then the Lord of Misrule would put her to the ordeal of squibs and firecrackers; whereupon she begged his pardon and said no more. My Aunt Jones has ever had an extraordinary sneaking countenance and way with her.

In an interval of dancing, as was my privilege, I cut the great

Twelfth-cake, which was rich with raisins, plums, ginger, honey and pepper, and frosted over with Barbary sugar; in the middle of it stood a coloured sugar-work of a wood-monger's wain, heaped with cut timber. There were also various fruits set here and there upon it, as apples, lemons, oranges, citrons, pears, plums, all of sugar and in their colours scarce to be discerned from the natural. Being grateful to my Godmother for my gift, I saw to it that the slice of cake came to her in which the fortunate bean was hidden; for I had been in the pastry-room while the cake was being prepared for baking and had marked the very spot. She drew out the bean with a cry of joy, like a child; and when she was acclaimed and crowned Twelfth Night Queen she chose my brother James as her King and myself as her Page. The Lord of Misrule was her Grand Chamberlain.

As Queen, my godmother laid divers witty obligations on her courtiers. In particular, she instructed Sir Robert Pye to stand before her and preach in celebration of the Divine Right of Bishops. My father protested that she was shearing this sheep a thought too close; for, as we all knew, Sir Robert was of the same Presbyterial way of thinking as his father, Sir Robert Pye the Elder, Member of Parliament for Woodstock; which Parliament was determined upon removing the Bishops, root and branch, from their places of power about the King. My father would not, for the world, see any of the Pyes offended, to whom he lay under an obligation of gratitude for a timely loan of money.

However, Sir Robert was no mean little wretch, but a knight of generous mind, and, speaking in the character which he represented, he swallowed (as the phrase is) bait, rod and angler too. For he extolled the Bishops in a highly ironical manner, likening them to busy country carriers, who, not content with the management of their horses and of the merchandize entrusted to their care, will make it their business to listen to all manner of piddling talk in the courtyards and alehouses of their circuits, and will pump old gossiping women, their passengers, for scraps of parish history. He swore that these spiritual carriers, the Bishops, had become by this traffic in news so very-very knowing and enlightened as to be worthier Lords, or Esquires, of the places where they were but licenced visitants, than the uninstructed laymen who ruled there by mere hereditary right.

This speech vexed two splenetic University Doctors, Dr. Browne and Prebendary Iles of Christ Church, who were hot Prelatists and rightly guessed that Sir Robert was drolling against the Bishop of Oxford, Dr. Bancroft, who had lately in a visitation of Woodstock pried somewhat too closely into the affairs of Sir Robert's father. They pulled their gowns tightly about their shoulders, looked budge, and glowered, and Dr. Browne muttered that there were some *Christmas Pyes* that made his belly ache.

At this my brother James, turning to his Queen with a frown, said aloud: "Madam Queen, there sit two sour-featured subjects of ours who must be reminded of their allegiance!" Which bold observation was well received by the company. James fixed their sconce, or fine, at half a gallon of Scotch ale to be drunk between them "to the health of the Blue Bonnets"; meaning the anti-prelatic Scottish Covenanters who had come out in arms against the prayer-book that our Archbishop Laud would have forced upon them. This sconce the Doctors dared not refuse; besides, they knew that our Scotch ale, the brewing of which I had myself overseen (tunning it in a sweet-wine barrel) was nappy and good beyond the ordinary.

When I brought them the pot to drink, they muttered the required words, but with the saving addition of a prayer that these same Blue Bonnets might presently turn blue all over, from snout to rump, for the peace and security of both Kingdoms. This drew a general laugh, which restored them to better humour. They drank up, turn and turn about, and the ale worked on them so powerfully that they blinked like owls and soon forgot the cause of their punishment.

At about half-past nine, very unseasonably, while we were at supper, came a knock at the door and when it was opened there stood the parish constable, a burly fellow, having a poor man fast by the collar.

The constable asked: "Is his Worship the Justice at home? Has he leisure to commit this felon? I have the necessary witnesses here to swear a charge against him for attempting a robbery."

I had gone to the door, and spoke up, saying: "S'death, Mr. Constable, we have no time for any such ordered sublunary justice here to-night. Know you not that this is the season of perfect Misrule?"

Yet the constable would not take the man away, and protested that the town-jail had no lock to it, from the negligence of our carpenter, and that the villain would doubtless escape away. He begged that the Justice would commit him to some secure place for the night. He continued stubborn in this, and the accused man, drawing courage from the word Justice, cried out too: "Ay, justice, give me immediate justice! I am no felon but an honest man from Noke parish who have lost my road and my horse in the snow, and must return in haste to my wife's lying-in."

A servant acquainted my father with this plea, who replied: "Let the constable bring the prisoner and witnesses to me in the little parlour. Instruct the Clerk of the Peace to be present with a prepared *mittimus* and whatever else he may consider necessary." Then he turned to Sir Robert and "Cousin," said he, "come with me into the parlour and you shall see sport!"

My father borrowed from another masker his long black visor-mask and pulled it over Sir Robert's head. About the same time the Clerk of the Peace came running in from the kitchen, dressed in a suit of black serge with white bones painted on it, and a skull mask, very horrible, over his face. "Give me leave, your Worship," he cries, "to go home and change this disguise for my formal dress."

"Never a bit of it, Mutton-bones!" replies my father. "We must carry this business through in proper style. Be as you are."

The constable led the supposed felon into the little parlour, and he was indeed an honest poor man, one John Ford from Noke parish (which lies a few miles from us along the Worcester road) and my father knew him. He had been thrown from his horse in the snow and was crawling to take shelter in a fowl-house near by, when he was observed by two men, one of whom caught and held him, crying "A robbery, a robbery!" while the other man ran to seek the constable.

The witnesses, bewildered by the many lights and all the hubbub, followed behind and when they entered the parlour, Lord, what a sight was there! The Devil himself, his face smeared with yellow— there is very good yellow ochre dug from a mine on Tyrrell land at the edge of Shotover Forest—the Devil, I say, sat there before them on a chair of state hung with primrose-yellow silk. Beside him glowered a tall grim fellow with a black visor, holding a drawn sword in his hand. At the table a skeleton played with pen and ink, and three little apes squatted on a chest behind, scratching themselves. The candles were shaded with red paper, which cast a hellish glow on the scene.

Of the sequel I cannot speak certainly, for I was not present in the parlour, and my father never omitted to embellish a good tale; but it happened something after this manner.

The constable, who knew of what a fanciful spirit my father was sometimes possessed, held his ground, though a little astonished, I dare say; but the poor man from Noke turned pale and cried out: "O Gentle Satan, your Worship, I have a clean conscience, I swear I fear you not, I defy you! I am no felon, I am John Ford, a poor goose-herder, who never in his life willingly injured any man, and comes of honest parentage."

"Ha, ha, John Ford," quoth the Devil, neighing like a horse, "you speak me fair. But beware lest I catch you, for I know a thing or two standing against your account which, if you do not make amends, will lead you direct into the hottest part of my bonfire."

"That I promise to do, good your Worship," said the poor man, blub-bering—for the chance shot had struck home—"to-morrow at the very latest, though I have to sell my wife's gold ring to raise the money necessary."

"Now, for this other matter, tell me, where are your accusers?" the Devil asked, suddenly very stern. "Come forward, Sirrahs!"

The two witnesses, who were a fell-monger and his son, coming from Watlington (which lies beyond Wheatley) had stood in a sort of horror during this act. But now, when they were instructed to come forward, the son uttered a screech and ran from the room, his father pelting after him; whereat everyone, except John Ford, broke into im-moderate laughter. Then my father cried, gasping, to the three little apes, my brothers, "Hilloo, hilloo, my brave rogues! Seek 'em out, Pyewacket, seek 'em out, Vinegar Tom! At 'em Little Mungo, my beauty! Hilloo, hilloo, and after 'em, all!"

The apes caught up a parcel of fire-squibs, whereof they lighted sev-eral at the candles and flung them down the corridor after the fugitive fell-mongers, who, when they found their way barred by the guests, doubled back and up the stairs, to cast themselves together from a window. They had like to have been slain, but that they lighted upon an old thatched shed, which was broken and fell down under them. They rose up again unhurt, and ran off through the snow.

"Constable," says my father, with as mild and grave countenance as he could command, "since this honest man's accusers have both fled, Esquire Beelzebub and I cannot properly concede you the *mittimus* which you demand, for there is no evidence against him. Let him go in peace; but first see that he has a good warm peppermint caudle prepared for him in the kitchen. And, stay, he shall have a nag from the stable, to take him home to his wife."

When supper was done, the whole company together played a

drunken game of blind-man buffet, and then danced again. The merrymaking continued after this manner until midnight, when Christmas certainly ended. Then the Lord of Misrule rapped on the floor with his rod and commanded us to pull down the holly and ivy from the walls; which we did, and threw it to crackle on the fire, and drank hot sack-posset. We sang a song of "Farewell Christmas"—or all of us who remained, for the elder folk were by now to bed or calling for their coaches. A party of five young gentlemen, having gone out together into the snow to untruss, came back presently to the fire; and being there suddenly overcome with drunkenness, in the change from extreme cold to heat, staggered and fell headlong, three out of the five, and could not rise again. We laid blankets over them, and the servants packed them together on a couch, like pickled herrings, head to foot and foot to head, where they snored horribly until morning.

The musicians declared that they would play no more that night; however, we prevailed on the worst of the three fiddlers to stay, agreeing with him for sixpence, which he required to be doubled each half-hour. We continued thus with our jigs, brawls and galliards for a long time, I having for my greater ease put on woman's dress again, my second-best green satin.

At this time a gricomed young gallant named Ropier, cousin to the Lord Ropier, imagined himself to be fallen deeply in love with me. Since there was now nobody present of greater age or better quality than his own, who might have restrained him, Mr. Ropier behaved very insolently, pestering me to kiss him and bestow even greater favours upon him; and fawning on me complimentally with: "Loveliest Lady, Magnetic Mistress, your denial is a dagger to my heart!" and "How shall your passionately devoted vassal be refused satisfaction, Empress of my soul, and yet live?" etc. All that I consented to answer him was "No, Sir!" and "No, No, Sir!" and "You may speak to me tomorrow, proud servant, when you are something sober, but not now!" I did not venture to deal him a whirret on the ear (as I would have served any other gentleman who used me so ungentlemanly), for I knew his bloody and treacherous temper; and presently he desisted and made his address to Zara instead, thinking I suppose to stir my jealousy, and she proved a deal kinder to him.

At three o'clock in the morning the gentlemen found that their common purse would no longer bear up against the strain of the fiddler's bargain—for by indifferent firking with his fiddle-bow, he had earned from us more than thirty shillings in a space of three hours; and so he proved by simple addition and multiplication. When he would not let us compound for a lesser sum that we named, four young gentlemen took him by legs and arms and flung him into a snow-drift and young Ropier spitefully broke his fiddle upon his head, which I thought was ill done; for a bargain is a bargain, and though he was but an indifferent fiddler, yet the fiddle was a good one.

At last we said our good-nights and good-byes one to another, and I went upstairs and watched through the glass of my chamber-window how the lanterns and torches wavered across the court to the stables, where the cattle all whinnied together to hear their masters and mistresses approaching. Presently I saw the cavalcade ride out through the gate and turn into the road, some going this way, some that, as in the figure of a dance, taking their several ways homeward through the thick snow.

I had carried a lighted candle with me and set it in the candle-stick in my chamber (which lay over the wash-house). Then finding Zara already fast asleep on the bed, in all her clothes, I threw the coverlet over her, and took pen and ink and began to write in my book. I wrote first of the masquerade, covering half a page, enough to refresh my mind with slight particulars when I should read there again in after-times; yet with no least suspicion that before I had turned twenty-one this half-page would read as strange as a history of China or Abyssinia —the pleasant company scattered, the house no longer in our possession, even the Christmas feast abolished by order of Parliament!

The house lay quiet enough, and the chamber was very cold. My spirits, that had been puffed up so high with the wine and the music, began to flag; and I wrote that merrymaking continued beyond midnight, or at the furthest one o'clock of the morning, was no gain to any girl. I added that young Mr. Ropier had done ill to treat the poor fiddler so, and that I would not marry such a poxy beast as he, not though he were worth so much as £1,500 per annum; and that certainly I wrote this not without having been made an offer of his person and fortune. Lastly I confessed myself a fool not to have come to bed three hours earlier. The clock in the hall chimed four as I blew out my candle; and the next morning I kept my bed, with the headache, until past ten o'clock.

CHAPTER TWO

An Alarm of the Plague

OUR stilling-room maid Trunco had at that time been engaged with us for four years, since the infancy of George, my youngest brother: for then, my mother suddenly finding no more milk for him, from a sickness that came upon her, my father was hard put to it to seek out a lusty young wet-nurse for the child. Having business that day at Banbury Hiring Fair, which is called The Mop, he rode thither very early in the morning, his old coach following behind. At The Mop those labourers who have a mind to change their masters stand in their several companies, as woodmen with their axes, carters with their whips, ditchers with their spades, serving-maids with their mops (from which the Fair has its name) and sell themselves to the best master they can, at the highest price. My father had that year taken over, from the Bishop of Oxford, the long lease of certain coppices in Stow Wood and the Royal Forest of Shotover, which has its name by corruption from the French *Château Vert*, or Green Castle, and lies between Forest Hill and Oxford. He stood in need of a handy woodmen or two that could clear away underwood, and saw up fallen trees for carting, and mend broken fences; for the coppices were spoiled by long neglect. Since this lease yielded my father no rights over the large standing timber, but only over fallen trees and the young growing wood, a woodman past the prime of life would suit his purpose and pocket better than a young sturdy one.

Two such lean old wretches whom he had found at The Mop, he plied well with ale and brought home with him stretched along the floor of his old coach. It was there also that he found my dear Trunco standing disconsolate, a little apart from the rest, her babe in her arms. Her husband, a brewer of Abingdon, was lately dead of the plague, which had raged fearfully that year in his town. When his debts were paid, there was nothing left for Trunco's support; and being thus cast back upon the parish of her birth, and having no great skill either with the mop or with the needle, she was sent by the parish officers to the

16

Fair to hire herself as a wet-nurse to some rich family, for she had milk enough for two babes. My father, judging her to be a healthy, honest woman, immediately engaged her and packed her in the coach with the old men; *item*, a turkey-cock with two hens, *item*, a spotted pig, *item*, a dozen of young ducks which he had bought. I remember how he came stamping into the house very late that night, a little drunken, hillooing and swearing he had sprung a rare variety of game at The Mop, from ducks and turkey-birds to young nymphs and old satyrs.

Trunco's child died not long afterwards, of a cough. To me she was thereafter more devoted than to any other soul, even to her foster-child George; for when one day a fellow-servant accused her to my mother of the theft of some trifling braid or ribbon, and my mother was for whipping Trunco well, I interceded for her. I undertook to be a surety for her good behaviour and declared that for certain she was no thief; whereas Agnes (the maid who had accused her) was by no means above suspicion. Trunco's innocence came to light before long and she was rewarded with a position of greater trust, being appointed our stilling-room maid. Then her wages were raised to £3 per annum, for she proved to have a pretty art in distilling simple waters of wild herbs and garden flowers—as also the Snail-water, the Bezoartis, the Hiera Picra, the Mithridate for melancholy, the Aqua Mirabilis, and such-like curious medicinal waters, of which she knew the virtues as well as did any apothecary. She was, besides, given charge of the pewter and the silver, to see that it was kept bright and no piece lost or nimmed. To Trunco I opened my heart freely enough, for I could trust her beyond any of my own family, my brother James alone excepted.

It was Trunco who wakened me, on the day after my birthday, and told me that it was high time to be stirring, for this was a working day and Zara was already risen; and that my mother had missed my face at breakfast and looked vexed. Trunco waited awhile for me to speak to her, and when I said nothing, she began to pump me. She asked me: "Well, my fine lady, and did no gentleman yesterday offer you his heart smoking on a pewter dish? Nor did none even ask leave to speak a few words to his Worship, your father?"

I answered faintly: "One only put the matter to the touch, dear Trunco, and he not the right one, neither. You had promised me four at the least."

"Who then may the right one be, my young lady?" Trunco was saucy enough to ask me.

"I have an headache, Trunco," I answered her. "Do not torment me, pray. My head goes round and round."

She asked my pardon, and went out and fetched me a red-currant cordial which warmed my stomach, and some white bread, with curds in a bowl, which strengthened me a little. I put on my woollen working gown and my worser shoes and came slowly down the stairs. The house had already been swept and set somewhat to rights, and of the three drunken gentlemen on the couch but one remained, who was sitting upright; he looked foolish enough, being dressed like Hercules in flesh-coloured hose and close-fitting jerkin, with a lion's skin fastened around his neck with a brass button. A cart with hurdles laid upon it came rolling into the yard. As I saw through the window, it was no longer decorated with Christmas greenery, except for a little bush of holly, tied to one wheel, which had been forgotten.

"So Marie Mischief, you are come downstairs at last!" my mother bawled at me from the pantry. "I have needed ten hands all this morning, yet have but two. Go at once into the fowl-house and see whether the young chickens and the larger poultry be not starved to death. They are for our eating in a week's time, and if they are not sufficiently fat by then, you know well, my jolly daughter, whose sides will be thumped."

I went out into the yard, where my father, with his back turned to me, stood gazing at the wreck of the thatched shed. He was saying to his bailiff: "It will not serve again for a shed, I fear. Have this old thatch laid aside; it shall be spread as dressing on the piece of ground, below the orchard, where the geese now are pastured."

My head ached so, I did not greet my father, but passed by in silence.

In the fowl-house we had coops, made with divisions, each fowl apart from its neighbour, and not room to turn in, but with means to cleanse their droppings from behind; and for each fowl was set a porringer for food and a pottle for drink. The food I gave them was barley, boiled tender, some days in water, some days in milk, and some days in ale, for variety; but always I mixed it in the porringer with a little brown sugar. In the pottles I poured strong ale by day, so that the fowls were very drunk and stirred not much, for much stirring makes fowls lose flesh, and by night they had fresh water, and a candle burned all night above the coops to keep them from sleep. Then they would drink much because of the thirst that the ale gave them, and eat much because of the hunger that the water gave them. With this course they grew prodigious fat in a fortnight. As for the chickens, of whom I kept six in each coop, they had another diet, which was rice boiled in milk so thick that almost a spoon might stand on end in it, and sweetened with kitchen sugar at sixpence a pound. I would put this before them every day for a fortnight, mixing with the rice a little bran to keep their maws clean; so that their flesh should be white and of a pure taste. Then for five days more I would give them dried raisins, pounded in a mortar, and then mixed with milk and the grated crumbs of stale white bread. They profited at night from the same candle that burned for the fowls, and delight of the raisins made them eat continually. When they came to their height of fat, they were then eaten, for if they lived longer they would lose appetite and fall off; but at the height of their fat they were exceeding good to eat, especially in a fricassee, fried first in butter, with white wine, savoury herbs a d endives. It was now the second day of their diet of raisins and they were about the bigness of a blackbird, yet so fat that they could no longer stand, but grovelled upon their bellies to eat.

When I came to the fowl-house, I found the candle already blown out; and the barley and ale duly set before the fowls, that were eating greedily; and the raisin mess set before the young chickens. This was Trunco's work, and I must thank her for her kindness. I returned to the house, going in by the door of the pantry, where I hoped to find Trunco; but she was not there, and I went to seek her in the kitchen.

There was a stench of stock-fish frying at the fire, and of garlic being bruised, and as I came in at the door I began to feel as giddy as a spinning-top and tottered upon my legs. Then I sneezed twice, and the cook-wenches held up their hands and all cried together: "The Lord preserve you, my young Mistress!" At that I vomited up the red-currant cordial, the bread and the curds, and O, then, what a scurry in the kitchen! A little cook-wench whipped past me and out into the yard; the greasy cook dropped upon his knees and began a long litany of prayers; and I stood there feeling silly until, turning to go, I fell down along the floor.

Now, the plague, that had been so severe in this country in the year before I was born, by which above 30,000 people died in London alone, had returned four years before this and destroyed ninety persons in Abingdon, which lies not many miles from us to the southward. Oxford, with the places thereabouts, is salubrious and has always felt the rage of the plague less than other cities, but we stood not the less in terror of it. This year it was again in London; and two brothers of my mother, Archdales of Wheatley, had spent Christmas Day with us, coming from Moorgate, a parish of London said to be infected; of whom one, my uncle Cyprian, had fallen sick and cut short his visit, being taken back in his coach to his place at Wheatley that he might not be a burden to us over the holidays. Imagine, then, what noise and confusion ensued in the household, when I sneezed and fell down fainting along the floor, and when it was recalled by the cook that, on the morning before, I had come to him for a lump of dried figs to plaster a swelling beneath my arm. It was thought evident, as evident as the teeth of a cur when he curls his lip, that I had taken the plague.

Zara with my young brothers and my little sisters Ann and Bess ran out of the house, to peep in at the kitchen window and gaze on me as I lay there. My father stood in the doorway, perplexed, and crossed himself in amazement, like a Papist, making sometimes to come forward and take me up from the floor, but as often making better thought of it and shrinking back again.

My mother, as it happened, was no longer within doors, and they could not find her. She had run half a mile down the road, after a carter, shouting and swearing that he had not delivered the full measure of flour certified in the bill he brought from Tomlins of the Mill. My Aunt Moulton was ridden to Oxford, my elder brothers were out coursing with their greyhounds towards Elsfield and, besides my father, nobody with any more head than a pin remained in the house, but only Trunco. When they told Trunco: "The eldest young lady is tumbled down with the plague in the kitchen and lies there senseless," she stood not still for a moment of time, but ran immediately and came in and threw me upon her shoulder and carried me to my bed, the servants and others fleeing away before her, like poor villagers before a troop of dragoons at pillage.

Now there was love for you! Yet I cannot have it thought that I would write anything against my own father, for indeed his was a very difficult case. Since upon his continued life and health depended the fortunes of ten others of his children, beside myself, he was unable to justify the first motion of his mind, which was to risk the contagion and take me up in his arms. For my part, I think that it stands more to his credit as a father that he refrained and left me lying there, rather than that, by over-fondness for me, he should have risked to infect himself and so bring ruin on the whole house.

I knew nothing of all this until afterwards; nor of the grand suffumigation of the house with sulphur, which my mother put into motion when she came in again; nor of the hasty messages of warning that were sent out to our Twelfth-night guests; nor of the marshalling of our whole household to be doctored with the plague-water, of which Trunco had distilled a gallon or two the year before, concocting it for the most part of simples which she had set the children to gather in the fields.*

After the hue and cry was raised, that evening the parish officers came with a physician to certify my case. But Trunco had by now pulled off my clothes and made an examination of my body, before she put my warm night-gear on me; and she had something to say to the physician when he came into my chamber (though most unwillingly), smelling a lemon against the contagion and keeping close to the door. "Sir," says she, "my poor husband died of the plague four years ago, and his sister too, and I nursed them to the end and buried them both and I have no fear of the plague; for the Lord, I believe, has made me proof against it. I know the signs and marks of the plague, I dare swear, as well as any physician in England; and if you accuse my poor lamb of being stricken of the plague, that is very false. True, your Honour, she has sneezed and vomited and lies here in high fever, and true, she has a little swelling and a redness under her right arm-pit, where the bubo or carbuncle or what-d'ye-call-it usually appears. But my meaning is: seeing that the swelling rose when she was otherwise in perfect health, for she dressed it with a fig-poultice yesterday morning, after she had ate a hearty breakfast of veal collops and three eggs, why, I judge it to be no true plague-carbuncle, but an imposture of an altogether other nature. I believe, your Honour, that this sickness is no more than a fever that she caught last night, lolling or loitering in a cold place after she had over-heated her body in the dance. As for

---

* These were rue, agrimony, wormwood, celandine, sage, balsam, mugwort, snapdragon, pimpernel, marigold, feverfew, burnet and sorrel; also wood-betony, scabious, brown may-weed, mint, avence, tormentil and the benedict thistle—a like weight of all of these, but of rosemary twice as much, and of elicampane-root half as much only. You mingle them all together, shred small; then you steep them in a good white wine three days and three nights, stirring them once or twice a day; then they are distilled in a common still. This water is held a certain prophylactic against the plague, and an indifferent good cure for the same.

the redness, it proceeds doubtless from the fig-poultice clapped on when it was scalding hot; moreover, as I can show your Honour, the swelling is seated lower and more forward on the ribs than is usual with the plague."

The physician, grown a little bolder, came nearer, and pulled up my shift, and he tried the swelling with a lancet from his bag. He probed about awhile and presently lifted out a little splinter of thorn-wood, which was the apparent cause of the swelling and perhaps also the cause of the fever. This I had got a few days before when, in a chase with my brothers, I had leaped my horse over a bank where a thorn-tree grew; three or four thorns had pricked through my gown under the arm, as I threw up my whip-hand to cover my face.

The physician now had pleasant news to take out with him to my mother, who waited on the stairs, in a distraction, swinging a pot of stinking sulphur. Yet when she heard it, and he showed her the thorn-splinter resting on the point of his lancet, she flew into a passion and cast the sulphur-pot through the window and blessed me backwards, and cried that her good hangings and clothes were spoiled and well-nigh ruined by the grand suffumigation she had given them. Moreover, some of the servants had run off for fear, and were five parishes distant by this time, and what was worse, the cook lay in a fit, with a light froth at his lips, who was a very master of his trade especially for pies and hotch-pots. And what servant or tenant remained to send after the several messengers who had ridden off with warnings of the plague to the gentlemen's houses? And how many of the said messengers would venture to return?

However, by the week's end, all was again smooth and peaceable at the Manor, and I had so far recovered from my sickness that I could sit upright in my bed with cushions set behind me, and take gruel with little sops of bread.

Trunco nursed me all this while and would let none come near me, except once a day my mother, and would not permit even her to stay long, or to chide me for the trouble I had brought on the house. Says Trunco: "Madam, when your daughter was thought to have the plague, all the household fled from her, but only your woman Trunco; who now, by your kind permission, claims a natural right to nurse her through this sickness, with caution and advice from none."

My mother huffed and snuffed at this plain speaking, but she granted

Trunco's plea, on condition that she cured me speedily; which Trunco undertook to do before the month was out. Being armed with this authority, Trunco also resisted the physician when he would have bled me of a pint and a half of blood. She contended that in January, when the forces of the body are weak and Nature hoards her sap, it would be murder to take so much as a thimble-full from me; and she cast at him such a tigress look that he was wise and altered his intentions. She also drove away the curate, the Reverend John Fulker, who would have prayed over me. "Go off," says she, "little Reverend Sir, and pray instead with Molly Wilmot, who I think will presently have need of your best prayers and sermons too." This Molly Wilmot was a tenant's daughter, an airy flirtish piece, and it was commonly said, though perhaps with more malice than truth, that the curate knew her body in a larger manner than he knew that of his own wife. The Reverend Fulker turned red, looked foolish, and left us in peace again. It was my father who paid the curate his £20 yearly; for the rectory went with the Manor.

Trunco treated me marvellous kind, and continued at my side night and day, stroking my head, turning my pillow, laying hot bricks wrapped in woollens to warm my feet if they were cold, and commanding jellies and other delicacies from the kitchen, whatever she thought would tempt my palate. If my little brothers were noisy on the stairs, or in their study (which lay next door), she would fly at them with her fists, and after a while they became exceedingly careful not to offend her. Thus, when my fever had abated, I passed there some of the pleasantest days of my life, and grew plump and merry.

I asked Trunco whether I had spoken wildly in my delirium—was I frantic, had I said what I should never have said, had I disclosed what modesty ought to have concealed?

"O no, my dear," says Trunco, "you were at all hours sweet discretion itself!"

"I mentioned no gentleman's name, did I, my Trunco," I asked, "not in any way that seemed strange to you? I spoke no foul, ugly nonsense?"

"There was nobody here, in any case, to listen but myself," she says, "and what I heard I have forgot. But I swear to you, my little mistress, that so far from my hearing any ugly, frantic nonsense from your lips, it was the prettiest deliration that ever I listened to. Indeed, your ravings were more delightful than many other women's rational conver-

sation. Nay, nay, I have altogether forgotten their purport, except only
that you came back always to talk of sweet primroses and violets."

This was Trunco to the life, for certain I am that I spoke a thousand
foolish things about a certain gentleman whom I have here not yet
named.

Well, in my vellum-book I wrote of him as "M," but here I need give
him no enigmatic alias, but may write his name in full. "M" stood for
"Mun," which was short for Edmund, and Verney was his family; he
was third son to Sir Edmund Verney, of Claydon in the County of
Buckinghamshire, the King's Knight-Marshal and Standard-Bearer.
Some years before this, when he was an undergraduate at Magdalen
Hall in Oxford, he had two or three times come to our house at the
invite of my brother Richard, with whom he would go coursing. Now
it may seem absurd and almost against nature that I, a child of but
eleven years old, should have fixed my affections so steadily on a man
near ten years older than myself; but so it was, and if it were a fault,
yet time mended it.

Mun had the name of a wild young fellow, a naughty scapegrace,
at the University. His tutor at Magdalen Hall was Mr. Henry Wilkinson, a Puritan and a fiery preacher, brother to Dr. Wilkinson, President
of Magdalen College, and Mun and he did not fadge well together.
Mun told my brother once: "Dick, my friend, I am all for God and the
Church, no man more so, but long unnecessary prayers weary me; and
my mind falling asleep, the Devil enters in by the back door." To circumvent the Devil, Mun would stay away from prayers at the Hall
whenever he expected that his presence would not be remarked, and
go out to drink and play skittles at the Greyhound Inn. After a term
or two, he also grew weary of his studies, which seemed to tend no-
whither: the logical problems, sophisms, and disputations, the cate-
chisings, the metaphysical declamations, and such other exercises as
he was expected to attend in the College, were unfit, he said, for any
man of spirit. He abhorred even to read Aristotle, and absented himself from the lectures of the President of the College, spending his time
instead in the company of jolly drunken young noblemen of his acquaintance at the tavern, or at the public bowling green, or at the
Dancing and Vaulting School of Will Stokes. To hold their esteem, he
must dress and be mounted as well as they were, and game with cards
and with dice for stakes as high as theirs, and lay wagers for as great

sums; and this though his father, the Knight Marshal, having many other children to provide for, could allow him but £40 a year for his keep.

Mun's course of living drew him into great debts, as may be imagined, which he at last despaired of paying and confessed all to his father; who rode down to Oxford to take him away and settle his affairs for him. Sir Edmund was, I believe, more than commonly grieved, for he had a particular affection and partiality for Mun. Mun, alas, had fooled him into believing that he liked both his devout tutor and his difficult studies; and that he was going very attentively about his College exercises; and that when he had kept the necessary terms he would easily attain his Mastership of Arts, with high compliments both from the Principal of the Hall and the President of the College.

Yet I would say this in Mun's defence, that he had fallen insensibly into this foolish course, and that the Doctors themselves were much to blame for not having sooner fetched him out of it. Mun was always in hopes that by a lucky wager or suchlike accident he could haul himself out of the mire, and that his father would never discover that he had so much as soiled his boots with it. He rode in horse-matches and wagered high on victory and sometimes won a good sum; but sometimes lost as much or more again. When at last he was stuck thigh-deep, he would rather have died, I believe, than humble himself by begging relief from his noble friends; however, I think he did worse, not knowing where to turn—for he borrowed money from tapsters and College servants and other mean persons who could ill afford to lose even small sums. For myself, I never saw Mun at any disadvantage, for he counted no man a worthy gentleman who, how deeply soever he had drunken, did not show himself as wholly polite and attentive to gentlewomen as if he were stark sober.

I first made Mun's acquaintance on an afternoon in March of the year 1637. He was invited to dine with us on the Wednesday, but had mistaken the day, and as it happened all the men of the house were away, hunting with the Tyrrells, and my mother was too busy in the cheese-press to entertain him. The bailiff's wife, who managed the dairy, had that day miscarried, a month before her account, and nobody but she and my mother understood the art of making little slip-coat cheeses—of which that day from the milk of ten cows my mother made 12 lbs. weight, laying them to ripen in flat boxes of wood.

My mother excused herself to Mun, but when he would have ridden

away, she would not suffer it; for that would have been to put an
affront upon his family, which she held in esteem. So she says: "Mr.
Verney, here is my daughter Marie who, by your leave, will play
hostess until I am at greater leisure. Now, as you see, I am wet to
my elbows with whey, and the cheese-vats are not yet filled. Marie will
show you the library, if you will, and the stables; and you may take
tobacco in the hall—but not, I pray, in the parlours—and the servants
will bring you whatever drink within reason you command." Thus it
chanced that, the very first time that we met together, I was presented
to Mun as a grown woman; and for the honour of the house I entertained him very mannerly and kindly. In so doing, on a sudden, for
the very first time in all my life, I was overtaken by love for a man.

Mun was not of large body, but had a most graceful and upright
carriage; his brow was broad, and below it stood a strong, noble nose
that made compensation for his pale slenderness of cheek. His eyes
were a little over-tinctured with melancholy and his hair thick, silky
and fine, falling to below his shoulders with a constant undulation of
dark curls. He was dressed in a red cloth hunting suit, with buttons of
silver and pearl, and a Spanish montero cap; and he carried a little
riding whip with a stock curiously inlaid with pieces of shell. Sitting
a-straddle on a thrum chair with this whip in his hand, he could each
time, with the tip of the lash, strike a pea or bean laid upon the floor
at three or four paces from him and send it spinning across the hall.

He had ridden up from the University in a dismal mood, which his
careless mistaking of the day did nothing to lighten; but somehow my
innocent presence so worked upon him that, after a few words spoken
on each side upon indifferent matters, his face suddenly grew bright
and he was good enough to say: "Mistress Marie, you have a very fine
head of hair; upon my word, I never saw one that I liked better. It
shines in that sunbeam like thin-drawn gold wire."

I thanked him and said that I wished my features matched my hair,
which I knew was good of its kind; but, truly, my mother's glass told
me I was ill-featured, especially as to the nose.

"Your mother's glass is jealous, I do not doubt," he says, "for upon
my soul I think that, nose and all, you have a face like a fairy's."

"And did you ever see a fairy?" I asked, teasingly. "For, unless you
did, how can you cast the comparison?"

He paused before his answer. "To come to think of it, I never did,"
he said, "though they have been credibly reported, some years since,

from as near to here as the two Hinkseys, not above a mile from Oxford, which have a southern aspect and many gardens and coppices. Fairies, it is said, choose to frequent the warm southern slopes of hills; and *secreta amant, fugiunt aperta:* that is to say "they love close nooks, and open ground they loathe." Old Dr. Corbett, who was Bishop here before he was translated to Norwich, has written that these pretty ladies danced often under the moon in our grandmothers' days:

> Witness those rings and roundelays
> Of theirs which yet remain,
> Were footed in Queen Mary's days
> On many a grassy plain:
> But since of late Elizabeth
> And later James came in,
> They never danced on any heath
> As when the time hath bin.

"Dr. Corbett judges from this that the fairies are of the old profession of religion and that, when Queen Mary was dead, most of them flitted overseas in the same ship with the Queen's confessor, and with the other priests."

I told him that, as I had heard, these angelic creatures might yet be invocated to appear. Old Dr. Simon Forman had so written, who though a rogue in some matters was a man of credit in all that touched his art; indeed, the spirits were so thick upon his staircase that one might hear them rustle by, like owls, as one went up to knock at his door. "But," said I, "Dr. Forman told my father once that it is not for every one, or every person, that these creatures will appear, though he repeat the proper call over and over."

"What is that call?" Mun asked me.

I answered that it began with *"O beati Fauni proles, turba dulcis pygmæorum"*—"O pygmies sweet, children of blessed Faun"—but confessed that I knew no more of it, for Dr. Forman would not sell the secret to my father for a farthing less than £200, which he either would not or could not pay. However, he told my father that neatness and cleanliness in apparel, a strict diet, an upright life and fervent prayers to God are a necessity to those who would invocate the fairies, and especially Queen Micol, their sovereign.

"Then shall I never see any one of them," said Mun, "for, to deal freely with you, my diet is by no means strict, either in eating or drinking; nor is my life at all upright; nor are my prayers to God fervent, for of late a sort of mist hangs between Him and me, through which I cannot pierce. Nevertheless, I have to-day seen a sight, although without invocation or hardship, which makes me very well content: for though you be not a fairy, you are the nearest creature to one that ever I saw; and, to my eye, not much more substantial." He spoke earnestly and without the least smile; then he sighed and cast down his eyes, as one who repents his foolish course of life. I gazed in admiration at him, while with a knife he scraped the mud from his boot-heel.

Now, the eye has a sort of power, like a cold fire, of which the person gazed upon will often become suddenly sensible. It has happened to me many a time and oft, that while I sit in a crowded assembly, I say to myself: "Someone is gazing very closely at my face from the left side," or "Someone at my back is doting upon my hair." I turn my head sharply about and always discover the fact, the person who gazed at me then looking away in confusion. Yet there are two unlike manners in which a woman—for here I can write only of woman—may become aware of a glance directed at her: either with a gross disgust as though someone were taking liberty with her body, or, it may be, with a deep delight as though the eye conferred a lasting benefit upon her, so that, were she a cat, she could cry "purr, purr." I cannot say in what manner Mun felt the power of my glance, yet he looked up sharply and left off scraping his boot, though he had not near finished. Then he smiled full in my face, saying nothing. Nor did I say anything, but continued unabashedly gazing upon him.

I know not how long we thus sat, but at last I remembered myself, and looked away through the glass of a window. After awhile I asked him soberly, how came it that he yet carried such fine long tresses, when at the King's Visitation of Oxford, in the August before, every undergraduate was ordered to cut his hair to the tips of his ears, on pain of expulsion from the University?

"O," said he, "I avoided it, with the help of my loving father. There was a Proctor put in each house while the King continued there, and observing that the chiefest thing that they would have amended for His Majesty's pleasure was the wearing of long hair, I wrote to my father begging him that he would send for me immediately, before I lost mine. I knew that this severity of the Proctors would last but a week, and so it proved. After His Majesty's departure I could laugh at them and flaunt my tresses in their faces—though why His Majesty should have played the Puritan, in this matter of long hair, passes my comprehension."

"And mine too," I cried, "though my mother says that long hair often harbours ill cattle."

"Well, well," said he, rising from his chair, "what say you? Shall we go out and gather primroses together to present them to your mother? A primrose or two is nothing, but a bowl full of them will refresh a fusty room most sweetly."

His offer pleased me, for it was my task to find flowers for the house, and the children either would not help me or plucked off the heads only. I led him out into the coppice behind the stables, where the primroses have long stalks and one may gather nine or ten at a single wrench, they grow so thick. We passed across a little field, where the turf was sodden with rain and hissed under our feet.

"This is a very good field for dancing," said I, "when it is well dried by the sun."

"Command me here in July," he answered. "You will find me a nimble dancer."

We came to the hedge, beyond which was the coppice, and he gave me his hand to help me over; it was firm and steady, but my own trembled. Then we set to work among the flowers. I observed that when he gathered his primroses he laid them very orderly in the basket, in several nosegays, each of them wound loosely about with withered grass, and that in each nosegay he put five or six narrow green leaves to set off the pale hue of the flowers. We conversed, stooping together under the trees, with our minds intent upon the task, yet with our fancies free to bandy nonsense. Then, though we had been perfect strangers a short hour before, it seemed to me that we had been acquainted a lifetime, and ingenuously I told him so.

"Nay," said he, "not a lifetime, but an age."

With that, by an unspoken accord, we left off gathering primroses, though each had a nose-gay half finished: and Mun took mine and bound it to his own, first adding to it several of the large violets, peculiar to our woods and coppices, which have hairy leaves and white rays upon the pale blue flowers, but no scent.

"This nosegay is for your own chamber, my dear," said he.

We sat down together side by side upon the stock of a fallen tree
and Mun asked me: "Have you ever heard speak of Pythagoras the
Greek?"

"That I have," I assured him. "My brother James now studies the
books of Euclid, in the first of which is a proposition which yesterday
he demonstrated to me in the yard. James laid down triangles and
square figures in the muck with sticks and, said he, 'Now is this not
a pretty proposition, Sister? It was found for Euclid by one Pythagoras.'"

"And did you find it pretty?" Mun asked me, smiling.

"Oh," said I, "I told James it was wonderful pretty. But then old
Marten the Woodman passes by, and sees the faggots, and addresses
him very earnestly, with 'Young Master, if I may make so bold, his
Worship your father would take it very ill as he knew you were laying
these heathenish spells in his own wood-yard.' And he says: 'Should
Brown-back chance to set her hoof upon this figure, she would cast her
calf before her time. Have a care, young Master, have a care!'"

"Well, to be sure," says Mun, "that was the same Pythagoras of
whom I would speak to you. He also propounded what he named
Metempsychosis. This is a notion that the soul, when a man or woman
dies, passes not into Purgatory or Limbo or any such place, but into
the body of another person, or indeed sometimes (as a punishment for
mis-doing) into the body of a hog or a lion or a wolf, and continues
in his passage from body to body until the Day of Judgment, when the
score is reckoned up. They say that Pythagoras hit on this notion by
a recollection of his own past lives, two or three. Now, therefore, that
you and I think to have known each other so long is perhaps no idle
fancy, but the very truth. Yes, indeed, I cannot say whether you were
my sister in Aristotle's Athens, or my wife in Cæsar's Rome, or a dear
she-friend at King Arthur's Court whose glove I wore as mantling to
my morion."

"Nevertheless, it is a very strange and lovely notion," said I.

We went slowly back together, with not another word said, and as
he helped me again over the fence I could not help but weep a little,
for joy.

Whether he was aware or no of the deep impression that he had
made upon the young wax of my affections I cannot say, but he kissed
my hand and told me that he had not spent so happy an hour all the
while he had been at the University. Even as he spoke, there came

shouts and a clatter from the road and up trotted my father and my brother Richard, with James following about a bow-shot behind. I slipped off into the house, covertly kissing my nosegay, and had no occasion to speak another word to Mun that day; nor he to me.

As now I lay sick in my chamber, with Trunco waiting upon me, I went back in mind a score of times at least to that day, muttering over to myself the words that Mun had said to me, and the words I had used in answer; and once in my fancy I went for a lover's journey with him into our field at Lusher's Farm, and the piece called Pilfrance, making it June weather just before the hay is cut, when the grass is speckled silver and gold with the buttercups and the great daisies; and he kissed me full upon the lips and called me his honey; and I put these words into his mouth, "Next month is July, when we shall dance together along the turf behind the stables, after the hay is cut. And you shall be my dear darling."

CHAPTER THREE

A Sight of Royalty, and of Another

W HEN a young gentlewoman loves herself so well that she can be at pains to write down small particulars of her life, as I now did in my new vellum book, she begins always, I dare say, by spying and prying and toting at herself in a glass and making the image as it were a frontispiece to her history. With a young gentleman it is otherwise: who naturally begins with a record of his illustrious ancestors and how nobly they conducted themselves in ancient battles and sieges. Or if his father should happen to be a *novus homo,* as we slightingly call mushroom gentlemen, who have made their fortune by merchandizing, then he will begin with his grandfather (a God-fearing yeoman of such and such a place, respectable to his neighbours) and write of him as related by blood to a certain great house; yet he will slip in for his own comfort and honour, that this grandfather was of the elder line of the aforesaid great house, which in the Civil Wars of York and Lancaster favoured the Lancastrians and lost all on Bosworth Field—whereupon they prudently changed their name from de Bolton or de Manny or de Lancaster to plain Hogman or Henman.

When I spied at myself in my hand-mirror, I saw eyes between grey and blue, a narrow forehead, a face more pointed than round, a straight nose, lips that pouted out, two gaps only where rear teeth were missing from my mouth, long narrow ears. My hands contented me when I gazed down on them, as being small and long and regularly formed; and now, after I had lain ten days in bed, they were as smooth and lovely, from idleness, as though they had been washed every day in milk and rose-water. As for my hair—I write not in my own praise, for the growth is natural—this was the wonder of all who saw it, being so long it reached to my girdlestead and so thick it cost me half an hour every morning to comb it well through. Zara had no love for my hair, for hers was of rat-colour, lank, thin, and not over-long.

I am below the usual height for a woman, but my legs are proportionable to my body; I have known women of low height with a body of ordinary size and stumpy legs like a goose—they are called "spuds" in Forest Hill. My bosom is good and has never lolled upon my ribs. My skin, as I saw it in the mirror, was not staring white, but rather the colour of a peach and with the same light down, or bloom, upon it. Whatever I might have said to Mun on the first day of our acquaintance I liked my face and whole person well enough; yet I had been unripe then, my body like a boy's and the bones of my head green and unformed: especially, my nose was not yet grown to its full size. Now these defects were remedied.

My name, Marie, was given me in compliment of King Charles's Queen, whom His Majesty never called by her first name, Henriette, but always by her second, Marie. She was married to him a few months before I was born. Afterwards I saw her often in Oxford with the King, but the first time I set eyes on either of them was at Enstone (which lies a few miles northward from Woodstock), at the house of Esquire Thomas Bushell, when I was ten years old. We Powells had a familiar acquaintance with our neighbour Sir Thomas Gardiner the Elder, of Cuddesdon, who was the Recorder of London, and with his son, Sir Thomas the Younger, who afterwards married Mun's little sister Cary. One day in August the younger Sir Thomas called upon my father and said that in two days' time, namely on August 23rd, there were to be great doings at Esquire Bushell's house over at Enstone, and that Their Majesties themselves would be present. Sir Thomas asked my father, would he not ride with him? and undertook that he would be well entertained. My father excused himself, pleading that the notice was too short: he had neither hat nor doublet nor lace fit to wear in Their Majesties' presence, and doubted whether he could prevail on the tailors to make a gentleman of him in two days. "Besides," says he, "the barley on Picked Stone piece is mown to-day and in two days' time we shall cock it, and I must see that it is well cocked."

However, Sir Thomas said that, early on the day of Their Majesties' visit, his mother and a young she-cousin would ride by our house in a commodious new coach, on their journey from Cuddesdon to Enstone, and he would accompany them on his horse. He asked my father, would not his two elder daughters ride in the same coach, undertaking that they would be welcome and well cared for.

My father was well content that Zara and I should go, for it so happened that we had been bridemaids that very week at a marriage of my cousin, Agnes Archdale, and were provided with new gowns of cream satin, the short sleeves caught at the elbow with gold rosettes; and my mother would lend me her necklet of little pearls and a Greek lace apron. Sir Thomas did not yet inform us of the spectacle that we should see at Enstone, but kept it secret from us.

The day came, we climbed into the coach and after we had passed Beckley by, where we had sometimes ridden on a pillion behind our father and our brother Richard, and passed by the spot, above Noke, where three church towers are to be seen set in a straight line, we came to the town of Islip. We had not visited this place in the summer time for two or three years, for most of our rides were in the contrary direction, to visit our land at Wheatley or to go down into Oxford City; so that it seemed new to us. It was a small town, but with every house, almost, an ale-house, and the rest forges and wheelwright shops. There were two or three drunken men lying face-downwards in the gutters, and others in the grass about the elms at the Church gate; the like of which we seldom saw at Forest Hill, even on a holiday, and never, as here, in the morning, our constable being so terrible to drunkards. The reason of the many ale-houses and forges was that there is great traffic of coaches and carts through Islip because of the stone bridge, which is the only one about for miles, the land spreading marshy and flat on either side. Here is firm land even in February; and a little sedgy stream, the Ray, a confluent of the Cherwell, running under the bridge; and tall aspen trees, very pretty; and great flocks of gaggling geese.

On our right hand, as we drove out of the town, we passed by an old barn and stables in a field, at which the coachman pointed with his whip and "There, my young gentlewomen," says he, "stands the Chapel of King Edward, called the Confessor, a Saxon; and the cattle drink out of his font, and, S'neaks, so they should, for he was of the Romish religion, no true Christian."

Sir Thomas told us, through the coach window, that it was this King who first had the gift, from an angel, of touching those sick from the itching *scrofula*, or King's Evil, and healing them; from whom the gift had been conveyed in a direct line of descent to his then Majesty King Charles, the truth of which we should perhaps see that same day. And he said that it was at Islip, from a quarry opened by King Edward, that the stone was hewn from which was built the Abbey of Westminster in London, being floated in barges down the Cherwell river.

Sir Thomas went off the road to salute some friend at Hampton Gay, and promised that he would be with us again at Enstone. We then passed through Kidlington, where we saw the great hollow elm that was used as a jail, and through other places not remarkable, until we came to Woodstock, an ancient town where they make fine gloves and very good knives. Here were throngs of citizens and their wives in the streets, wearing holiday dresses and hoping for a view of Their Majesties' progress. The house-gables were hung with flags, standards and streamers, and silk hangings drooped from the windows, with abundance of flowers—as roses, peonies, sweet-williams and monk's hood—set in the windows of the meaner houses. The Mayor and his officers in their robes stood at a corner and were continually asking: "Are the outriders yet come? Are they not yet come?"

We baited at the Bear Inn and ate bread and green-cheese, and a pot of quince-marmalade that we had with us in the coach, and sent in for a can or two of small beer. Then, the weather being fair and the road clean, we walked to the town's end, while the coach followed a little behind us; and so came to the house called Chaucer's House and to the gate of the Royal Park. This park King Henry I had enclosed with a wall to be a harbourage for all manner of wild beasts procured from other princes, to run at large; he had camels, and lynxes, and leopards, and lions, but they remained there not long, for they preyed on one another and did not procreate their kind. At last was left only a porpentine, a beast like a great hedge-hog who (they say) rattles his quills and shoots them out at the hunting dogs, and will kill even lions so; but this porpentine was dead many a hundred year, and now there were only buck in the Park, and a few badgers and foxes.

Yet one wonder remained, which was the Echo. We were advised to stand at the corner of a wall enclosing three hayricks, and listen while the coachman holloa'd out some words, facing towards the King's Manor, which stands upon a little eminence above a stream. This echo, we were told, would return by day nineteen syllables and twenty by night. So the old Lady Gardiner says to the coachman: "Hob, get down from your box and cry out something for the Nymph Echo, for these young girls would hear how she answers you back. Nay, take your post at the corner yonder!"

He says: "At your service, good your Ladyship, but what words shall I use?"

"Any words you please, Puddinghead," she answers him tartly, "so be it they are neither lewd nor scurrilous."

Thus licenced, he straddles his feet apart and coughs and clears his throat a little, and at last he bellows out in a great gruff voice:

"My throat is dry, my cheek is pale,
Restore my soul with a pennyworth of ALE."

At once the Echo answers back: "Hobbledy, Gobbledy, Gibble, Gabble—ALE!"

"There, children," says the old Lady Gardiner, "you heard it, did you not? Holloa again, good Hob, but pitch your voice a little higher."

Merry old Hob knew not how to pitch his voice higher, he could only shout louder; and this time he roared to the Echo again·

"My cheek is pale, my end is near,
O save my life with a shillingsworth of BEER!"

But all the Nymph would reply was this:

"Hobbledy, Gobbledy, Glibber, Globber—BEER!"

The old lady was wroth and spoke very tartly to Hob, with: "Get you back upon your box, whoreson, before you ruin us all by your thirst! You will next be asking for twenty-shillings-and-sixpence worth of cream sillabub or good sack posset!"

All this while a gentleman, whose fine bay mare was tied to the park gate, stood a little apart from us observing what we did. Zara had already plucked at my sleeve and said in a low, muttering voice: "Oh, Marie, look at that strange gentleman! Did you ever see the like of him?"

He wore plain clothes, nevertheless not ill-fitting, nor in the offensive "Lord-Thou-cast-me-down" manner of your canting Puritan, who makes short what men of honour and quality wear long, and long what they wear short, and who, avoiding cheerful colours, affects sad black or dun or maggoty grey. These clothes were exceedingly well cut —the doublet of dove grey, with a falling ruff in the Dutch style; light grey silk stockings and a sleeved cloak of darker grey, inclined towards blue; a silver-hilted sword, and a plumeless sombrero hat. As for his person, he was of middle height and well-knit frame, with quick movements like those of a practised swordsman. His hair was sleek, of a light auburn, and as for his face, this it was that had caused

Zara to pluck at my sleeve. It was well shaped and of a pure complexion, the chin and nose long, the forehead high, the dark grey eyes like a woman's, and the mouth small and well formed. Yet there was an inexpressible quality in it, of such haughtiness and conscious power that he seemed to stand there in arrogation of an ancient claim to be rightful Lord of the Manor—yea, even though the whole country acknowledged it to be the King's own. His lips were pursed, his eyes stared unblinking and he tapped with one toe on the ground as though he could scarcely refrain himself from passionate speech. In age he appeared to be between twenty-five and thirty years.

Well, this gentleman, after Hob had with a surly look climbed back on his box, came forward to us, uncovering with a little stiff bow. Says he: "Though I have not yet the honour to be of your acquaintance, Ladies, yet I flatter myself that I can be of service to you. That sottish Auriga of yours has no knowledge, nor so much as the least inkling, of the proper manner to address Nymphs, and by your leave, I will show these young maidens the proper manner."

The old lady was somewhat startled by this unknown gentleman's familiarity in pressing his services upon us, all unasked and in so managing a style; yet she did not rebuff him. She signified shortly that he might make his demonstration, if he pleased, for which she would thank him according to the measure of his success.

"In the first place, then, Madam," he began (speaking eloquently, like a Doctor of the Mathematic; and pronouncing his r's very hard, like a Scot almost), "your coachman stood not at the true *centrum phonicun*, or speaker's place, which (by my reckoning) is about thirty paces below the corner of the wall where he stood. The distance from the brow of the hill whence the Echo answers, is correctly judged for the number of syllables whereòf I heard you speak: for by my measure it is 456 geometrical paces, which, by the agreed allowance of one syllable for every twenty-four paces, allows for the return of nineteen syllables. But, as I say, the *centrum phonicum* is not to be sought at the corner of the wall, which lies not at right angles with the brow of the hill, but a little obliquely: rather it is here where I now stand. Again, Madam, you were right in commanding your man that he should pitch his voice high, for crass and heavy tones do not slide so easily through the *medium* of the close valley air as do light and tuneable ones: indeed, a woman's voice is somewhat better for the purpose than a man's, unless his be a tenor."

Then, holding up his hand for silence, imperatively, he called out a
Latin verse (the words of which I have since verified for this relation)
in very clear, strong, singing tones:

"... *Quae nec reticere loquenti,*
Nec prior ipsa loqui didicit resonabilis Echo."

This time the Echo answered him, with most faithful repetition, even
the *s*'s returning audibly. We all expressed our admiration, and old
Hob from the coach cried out: "S'neaks, Echo mocks at honest English, but to Paris French she answers pat! A pox on the stale creature!"

Zara asked the gentleman: "Sir, what did you tell the Echo?"

He replied that, translated a little freely, it was to this effect: that
the nymph, being a woman, had the good manners neither to be the
first to begin a conversation, nor to refrain from a reply when decently
addressed.

Zara chafed, believing that he snibbed her. Then, without being a
second time invited, he called out again, and would not tell us what he
cried, but I think that it was some very peevish verse that the Echo
returned.

The old lady said: "Sir, you seem to be a man of learning. They
spoke at my house the other night of tautological echoes—now tell me,
what may they be?"

He explained that these are echoes which repeat the same words
twice or more often; and he drew little lines in the turf with the point
of his sword to explain the mathematics of it. He said: "Such a tautological echo is found at Rome, at the foot of the hill upon which is
erected the white marble tomb of the Lady Caecilia Metella, and
there are many ancient walls thereabouts, of which one, called the
Capo di Buoi, has near 200 bull's-heads carved in marble on it. These
walls, being smooth, bandy the echo between them, so that if one
throw his voice along this line"—marking the line with a little sweep
of his sword—"he may hear the first verse of Virgil's *Aeneid* repeated
eight times distinctly, and then again broken and confusedly."

The old lady and the she-cousin thanked him for his lecture. He
bowed to them without smiling, and replied that it had cost him nothing. Then she asked whether she might, unceremoniously, enquire his
name.

At this he looked about him, in an odd manner, before he answered:

"Madam, to-day I have no name. But you may speak of me, if you will, as Tiresias; for by profession I am a poet."

With another stiff bow, he clapped his sombrero on his head, threw his leg over his bay mare, and galloped off across the park to the right hand, where soon he was out of sight in the hollow.

"Ay," says the old lady, "all poets are mad, I am told; mad and very forward, without doubt. Into the coach, all! Drive on, Hob, and here's your shilling for beer, and two half-pennies for the ale you bespoke, you maggoty-brained wretch!"

We were back upon the Enstone road a little before Their Majesties' outriders came through the town. We drove on at a smart trot, lest we be overtaken, and came into Enstone a hour or two later; where Sir Thomas awaited us and said that he had good seats for us from which to watch the spectacle. What this spectacle was, I shall now relate. That ingenious gentleman, Esquire Bushell, who farmed the royal mines in the Dominion of Wales, had some years before this cleansed a spring, then called Gold-well, having a mind to place a cistern there for his own drinking. When the ground, which he found quite overcome with briars and bushes, was cleansed of these and other encumbrances, he met with a great head of water and a rock so wonderfully contrived by Nature herself that he deemed it, as he said, worthy of all imaginable advancement by the arts of the engineer. Whereupon, he made cisterns and set pipes cunningly between the rocks; and built a summerhouse over them, containing a banqueting hall, with several small closets opening from it, and more rooms above. He also planted groves of various bushy trees such as would soon grow up tall and make a great show; with paved walks between, and little foot-bridges, and cascades and surprises of various sorts. Now that this pleasance was ready, he wished to give the King and Queen the first sight of it, and an entertainment proportionable to his loyalty and his large fortune.

We sat on benches, on a stage hung with green frieze, having flowers of coloured silk sewn upon it. It was on a knoll overlooking the water, where we had fine company on either side of us. Soon our gentleman from Woodstock climbed upon the stage, and another gentleman with him, very finely dressed, of whom Sir Thomas said in an undertone to his mother, "See, Madam, the gentleman in scarlet is Mr. Henry Lawes, of the King's Private Music, whose songs you know well. He is the same who together with Mr. Simon Ivy provided all the

music, two or three years back, for the famous Candlemas Masque at
Whitehall Palace."

"Then the other sleek-haired, hogen-mogen gentleman now speaking with Mr. Lawes is, I suppose, Mr. Ivy?" she asked.

"No, Madam!" said he, "I cannot tell you who he may be, but this at
least I know, he is not Mr. Ivy, whom presently you will see rise from
the urn beneath yonder arch, when the Masque begins, in disguise of
a hermit."

I overheard our gentleman, who now sat exactly behind us, how he
told Mr. Lawes that he had ridden out the day previous from Horton
in Buckinghamshire, and lain that night in Oxford. Mr. Lawes asked
him, in what work was he now busied? which he would not answer for
awhile, beyond that he was pluming his wings and meditating a
stronger flight; yet at last it came out that he was resolved to write a
play in verse, of King Macbeth, intending to outgo William Shakespeare who had written another play on this very subject, some thirty
years since. For Shakespeare (so he said) though a poet of strong
fancy had not treated the matter so tragically as he ought: he had
mixed noble sentiment with lewd in an insensate manner, greatly to
be condemned, and had so far neglected the unities enjoined by Aristotle as at times to tumble into absurdity. Our gentleman spoke in a
very sharp, clear voice, and it must have vexed Sir Thomas that, for
good manners, he could not break in upon it; for afterwards on our
homeward way, he told us most passionately that no playwright living could touch Shakespeare, not one, either in comedy or in tragedy;
and that he was either fool or knave who would attempt to outgo him.

Mr. Lawes presently began to speak of "our Michaelmas Masque at
Ludlow" and to complain that so many judges of literature (persons of
quality whom he could not well deny) had asked him for copies of the
poem, with the songs, that he was weary of the task of copying. Then
coming to the point, he asked: "Now, friend John, can we not have the
Masque printed in a pamphlet? For, say what you will, it is a lovely
thing and worthy of the greatest poet that ever breathed."

Our gentleman continued to make pettish remarks and raise difficulties, such as that there were many lines that he would fain amend.
"Why then, man, in Heaven's name what prevents that you should
amend 'em?" Mr. Lawes demanded; and he was so importunate that
Mr. Tiresias at last consented, but with ill grace and the condition that

his name must not appear anywhere between the covers of the pamphlet.

Presently came a sound of trumpets and an answering stir among the guests. All the lords and gentlemen uncovered themselves and rose to their feet—as we ladies did likewise—though as yet the trumpets sounded but distantly. Mr. Lawes thereupon made his excuses to our gentleman, saying that his place was with the musicians, and, thanking him heartily, hastened away. Some three minutes later the outriders and heralds and whifflers came into the garden, trumpeting and drumming the alarm, above which we could hear the hoarse cry of the country people at the gate acclaiming Their Majesties as they turned in from the public road. A gentleman of the Bedchamber observed two young men of fashion drinking tobacco under the trees, the reek of whose pipes was wafted towards him; he spurred his horse forward and snatched the pipes from their mouths very roughly, telling them that His Majesty's soul loathed the smell of the weed; and he asked, had they been reared among the painted savages of America? They were exceedingly abashed.

Soon the main body of the progress appeared at the foot of the water, both Their Majesties on horseback, the King on a tall Flanders mare—he was reputed to be the most graceful manager of a horse in his three Kingdoms—and the Queen on a little Arab gelding that ambled as sweetly as if his legs were greased with train-oil. With them rode some extraordinary handsome proper noblemen of the Court, the chiefest among them being three resplendent Scots, the Earls of Carlisle and Kellie and the Marquis of Hamilton, all members of the Privy Council, who were together of the greatest expense in their persons of any in that age, His Majesty himself not vying with them; and some very lovely ladies, well mounted and glittering with cloth of gold and jewels almost as spendidly as the noblemen aforesaid; and in coaches behind came bishops and grave heads of Oxford Houses dressed in their robes, and members of the King's Privy Council, of whom I remember only the Lord High Treasurer, the Earl of Portland, whose wife and daughter waited upon the Queen, being, like herself, of the old religion. The King at this time ruled wholly by means of his Privy Council, having a detestation of Parliaments; but the grand disadvantage was that, without a Parliament, money was hard to get.

When we made our reverences to Their Majesties, the King graciously permitted us to be seated; yet the lords and gentlemen, except those about his person, continued uncovered, though the sun was more than usual hot.

Being silly children, Zara and I wondered that the King wore no crown, and also that he was so low a man, being almost the lowest grown man in the garden, except for his dwarf. The Queen and he were led to rustic thrones, hung with the royal arms, and cool drinks and jellies were provided for them, and a negro boy, the first negro that ever I saw, fanned the Queen with a fan of ostrich-feathers. The King settled back into his throne with a smile and signified that the entertainment should begin.

At this a sound of gentle rippling music rises from concealed instruments. The cover of the stone urn lifts up, and out peeps a reverend old man who asks: "Whence comes this music sweet? O, what doth it portend? Etc." Presently he climbs out with a slow labouring motion and proclaims himself to be a hermit, whose diet is acorns and beech-mast and fresh water only, on which he thrives well—(here Sir Thomas gently snuffs and giggles to himself, remembering Mr. Ivy's notorious greed for delicate French confections)—and explains that he sleeps in this urn as a perpetual reminder to himself of our common mortality. He denies that he knows anything of what passes in the great world without, yet declares himself confident that all is well with England; for he has learned in a dream that a Gracious Prince, King Charles, now reigns and has a Queen that is worthy of his honour and love. Then he turns about and almost faints with amaze, and asks the trees and waters whether this can again be the glorious vision of his dream, etc., etc.—for there sit Their Effulgent Majesties themselves. He prostrates himself on the grass, but rising up again stumbles forward and invites them in a voice, warbling with feigned awe, to step forward a few paces, if they would see the wonders of his enchanted rock, the like of which there is "Not to be found in all Your glorious realms, From chalky Dover to chill Newfoundland, And the Barbadoes rich in sugar." Then, receiving no positive answer, he points plainly to the house over the rock, makes another deep obeisance and goes backward until he comes again to his urn, into which he clambers, and clap! pulls down the cover again.

The King was wearied, for that morning he had played two or three sets of tennis before breakfast and the day was languid. He looked surly, and would have tarried longer on his throne; but the Queen, as we understood, chid him good-humouredly for missing his cue and told him that she would be a visitant of the rock in any event, and he might follow if he pleased. Thus she shamed him into motion, and forward they went. There was a choir of singing boys from the cathedral school of Oxford, dressed as wild birds; these piped a little song consisting of questions, to which a hidden voice, playing Echo, made apt answers. This was a short Echo, of twenty-four geometrical paces (according to what we had learned that same morning), for only single syllables were returned; yet the song was so ingeniously contrived that each syllable spoken by the Echo came as a reasonable answer to the question asked. For example, as I recall it:

Question: Where is't that nightingales at noon we hear?
Answer: Here!
Question: And doth the drum sound, without drumstick-play?
Answer: Ay!

As the Royal pair passed by our seats we rose again. Then the Queen, who was black-eyed and swarthy and likewise of very small size, remarked to one of her Maids of Honour upon the colour of my hair, who replied that she conceived me to be of the household of Sir Thomas Gardiner, who stood next to me, and whose sister Mary had lately been recommended for Her Majesty's service. So I was beckoned, and climbed down over the benches and stage-side, and made my curtsey before the Queen; who stroked my hair and took me lovingly by the shoulders and called me a *belle mignonne* and praised me to the King. He, however, nodded absently and paid very slight heed. But at least I was among the first, after Their Majesties' selves, to enter into the famous grotto of the rock.

I was not abashed to be so handled by the Queen, for many other great ladies coming to our house had made much of me, in rank from marchioness downwards; and I had been taught a little French, so that I held my own with *"Oui, Madame la Reine"* and *"Je ne le sçais pas, Madame le Reine,"* and pleased her mightily when I told her I was called Marie after her. She cried that she would willingly have stood godmother to me, had I been of the true religion; but I told her in halting French that my father, like a loyal Englishman, owed his allegiance in religion not to the Pope, but to her husband. She pouted at me and shook her finger, and laughed merrily and whispered loudly in my ear that the King was a greater tyrant, and more obstinate, than any Pope; after which she grimaced at the King and laughed again.

The King observed nóthing of this raillery, though she plainly intended that he should, for he was speaking gravely with the Earl of Kellie about some obscure sickness that his falcons had taken in the Royal mews at Windsor Castle.

The Queen was delighted with the pleasant coolness of the grotto, but said that, looking about her, she saw nothing better to rest her eye upon than only a tall, wet rock. This rock was made up of large, craggy, moss-covered stones with great cavities between them, out of which water flowed with a brisk motion, dashing against the rocks below. Suddenly a music sounded from beneath our feet, which was a signal for the keeper of the waterworks, in one of the closets overhead, to turn on the brass cocks, one by one. Then, in the front of the rock, first rose up a chequer-hedge of water, from little pipes set at a slant, and next two stout side-columns of water, making an arch over the face of the rock, and then a third, round, upright column which rose to the ceiling above us and returned not again, but was received there into a hidden pipe. Then up sprang two little dancing jets of rose-coloured water, each tossing up a golden ball and holding it suspended at the height of about three feet.

The Queen reached forward and caught one of the balls, which was of hollow gold, and opened it and discovered a little French compliment inside and a marchpane sweetmeat, which she smelt of, and then popped into my mouth, where it tasted very good. She prompted the King to take his ball too, and when it was opened he found in it a little portrait, painted on ivory, of the Queen standing before these very artificial waters, with another written compliment. The discovery gave him joy, and he pressed the portrait to his lips. After this act, a water-pipe was made to warble like a nightingale, as the Echo had promised, and another rumbled dub-a-dub like a drum; and then, with due warning given, a whole canopy of water, like a great sheet of glass, was let down before the rock, and behind this canopy many other jets of water crossed and arched and seemed to interlace, so that the Queen clapped her hand for delight. There were lighted candles set on a mossy ledge of the rock, which continued burning all the while, not overwhelmed by the water, nor even guttering.

Next, Esquire Bushell, waiting upon the King, whispered into the Marquis of Hamilton's ear, who grinned and went to His Majesty and conferred merrily with him; and presently a gentleman was sent out to fetch the King's Fool, by name Archie Armstrong.

This Archie had been a Border rogue and a sheep-thief before he became licensed jester at King James's Scottish court: he was of a sly and peevish humour, but his cap and bells protected him from harm. He spoke a very thick English, little of which I could understand. He came running down to the grotto, tripping over his shoes constantly and falling flat along the ground, which simple jest brought each time a new roar of laughter from the company. Archie had a roasted chicken in his hand at which he nibbled greedily, and he astonished the company by snapping off the drumsticks and munching them as if they were sugar-sticks—which indeed they were, painted over with burned sugar.

Now he sits on the step outside the grotto and bawls some old corky jest at the company, at which all the Scots laugh lustily, and then the King asks: "Archie, thou girt thief, wast ever baptized?"

"Och, aye, Cousin," says he. "Aince and thrice, as I ken verra weel. Aince by the minister, aince by ane auld Devil, and aince by a plooky-faced wife of Gallow-gate—she cried 'Gardy-loo' from her window, but she cried tardily, having voided the full nicht-pot upon my hied."

"Come in, then, Archie, for a fourth baptism," says my Lord of Hamilton.

"Nae nearer than the doorway," answers wary Archie; but that was near enough, for at a signal given by the Marquis down came a great curtain of water from the lintel, and, when Archie turned to run out into the grove, down came a second and worse fall of water, which cut his retreat. Then the whole company made merry at his expense, for he was drenched to the very skin, the Scottish lords holding their sides for laughter and coming forward to mock at him.

Then Archie goes down on all fours and barks like a water-dog and shakes his ears, the bells of his cap jangling, and comes barking through the doorway and springs clean through the fall of water, as I have seen dogs at St. Giles's Fair at Oxford leap through paper-hoops, and then barks again and shakes his sides. Then he leaps upon the Earl of Kellie (standing a little in advance of the others) and wets my lord's fine crimson doublet with his paws, and makes to lick his face, and then again shakes himself, and barks, and would leap upon the Marquis of Hamilton, who avoids him and flees upstairs, Archie scampering at his heels.

Then the King says, with a half-smile, stammering a little, but very aptly: "I read but yesterday in Gervase Markham's excellent work on

the art of fowling, which he titles *Hunger's Prevention:* 'Not any
among us is so simple that he cannot say, when he seeth him, "This is
a Water-Dog, or a dog bred for the water." ' "

The name *Hunger's Prevention* was straightway taken up by Esquire Bushell, who informed Their Majesties with a deep obeisance
that they might ascend the stairs at their pleasure, for a banquet was
spread for them in the room above. The Queen then kissed me good-
bye and packed me off to Sir Thomas; and the great company, in exact
precedence of rank, ascended the stairs to the banquet; upon which
the lesser company entered the grotto and marvelled at the water, and
now and then a visitant of the humbler sort would be cruelly soused
in the doorway as Archie had been.

We were well entertained with meat and drink in the hall of the
great house, with two hundred other guests, where it was announced
to us that the Queen had graciously given her name to the rock and
fountain.* We watched for the King to come out from the banqueting-
room, for there were waiting for him, under guard of a beadle, some
half-score of people of the parish suffering from scrofula; whom, when
he learned that they were tenants of his host, the King consented to
touch upon their rough places, with each time "Be thou clean, for
Christ's sake!" They raised eyes of thankfulness, crying, "Heaven bless
and reward Your Majesty!" which made me weep for the poor creatures and my own skin itched for sympathy.

A little while after we rode homeward in the coach, and the dust on
the road rose in clouds from the many horses and coaches passing, so
that I was nearly choked; then we turned off the road until the rout
had quite passed and the dust was somewhat laid. We did not see the
gentleman again whom Mr. Lawes called "John," but who called himself "Tiresias."

I was asked by all my kindred, and by every one who came to our
house for weeks after, how had the King looked, how had the Queen
looked, what words had she spoken to me, how had I answered, and
many more questions, and Sir Thomas praised me to my father and
mother, saying that I had quitted myself like a true Powell.

When I looked back upon that day from a distance of near five
years, and wrote of it at leisure in my vellum book, I used less than
two pages to tell of the water-works and of Their Majesties, with a

---

* Esquire Bushell was also rewarded for this day's entertainment by being appointed warden and master-worker at a silver mint at Aberystwyth in Wales.

few lines only for the King, but three whole pages to tell of the strange gentleman, for even after so long a lapse of time his words beat in my ears still. I wrote how angry a man he was, and how like an avenging angel's his face—I meant the painted angel in the window at our church of St. Nicholas, who carried a sword in his hand—and I resolved when I saw my brother James again to ask him what he knew of this name "Tiresias," hoping perhaps to unriddle the gentleman's story. As I wrote, I bethought myself of what our curate, the Rev. John Fulker, had told us in a sermon: how a woman's hair should be covered, and why? For fear of the angels.

"That jumps well with what I remember," said I to myself, "for at Woodstock Town End this angel-faced Tiresias eyed my hair (which I wore naked of any hat or kerchief) with a certain hard fury as though it were of offence to him, and sleeked his own with one hand."

CHAPTER FOUR

Life at Forest Hill

O MITTING many childish things, of slight account—how I had the measles, very bad, at four years old, and how I was in my father's coach when it was caught in a snowdrift in the great snow of 1634 and remained in it all night and part of the next day—I will here briefly recount the manner of our life at Forest Hill before the storm of war broke upon our heads.

First, as to sport. We kept always a brace of strong Irish greyhounds, and a leash of hawks, and four or five good horses for riding. Hares there were in plenty on the Manor Land, especially in the fields this side of Minchin Court and across the pastures to Red Hill; together with partridges and other game birds. The Tyrrells, our neighbours, who had the great house at Shotover, gave us leave to hunt buck in the Royal Forest; yet this leave was for ourselves only, not for any guests of ours, and an under-ranger must needs always accompany us, which was a tedious condition. When Sir Timothy Tyrrell was Master of Buckhounds to Prince Henry (the well-beloved brother of King Charles, who would have been King had he not died untimely), one day in the Forest they ran down a fine stag. Sir Timothy held the beast's head for the Prince to dispatch it with his hunting dagger, but it struggled and tossed its antlers, and the Prince, using his dagger carelessly, cut a nerve in Sir Timothy's arm so that he never afterwards had the use of it. In reparation Sir Timothy was granted by Letters Patent the rangership of the Forest, besides the bailiwick which was hereditary to him. The rangership was an office that called for vigilance beyond the ordinary, because many young gentlemen from the University, wearying of a constant diet of river fish, stockfish and lean mutton, dared make free with the Forest and would carry venison out of it, though it went very ill with them if the rangers catched them.

At Forest Hill we had no common right of pasture in the Forest, yet we drove our herds of pigs to fatten on mast of oak and beech, and paid to the Tyrrells twenty or thirty shillings per annum for the right. Every pig must be ringed to forbid his rooting in the ground, and a pig found unringed was forfeited to the Ranger, because of the danger to a huntsman whose horse set its foot in a hole rooted by a pig. Beside the buck in Shotover there were badgers and foxes and wild cats: only the wild cats were not chased, because they preyed upon rabbits.

I went hunting, but seldom in the Forest, and never but once in company with the Tyrrells, who were not pleased with women at the hunt. They said that women and priests brought no luck with them; and their spite was confirmed one day when they heard that the Queen had unluckily transfixed, with an arrow from her cross-bow, the King's favourite hound. As for the priests, if ever my brother James held his bow a little awkwardly, one of the young Tyrrells would mock at him and cry, "An Archbishop of Canterbury! A proper Archbishop!" A sad tale hangs on that. In Hampshire, a year or two before I was born, Archbishop Abbot of Canterbury, being invited to shoot buck with the Lord Zouch in his forest, excused himself with a plea that he had little skill with the cross-bow; yet he was over-persuaded, and the first arrow that he let fly struck into the body of a keeper, who died of the wound. Here was a knotty problem for the professors of Canon Law, whether a homicide could continue to enjoy his archbishopric; and though King James acquitted him under the Broad Seal, and restored him to the full exercise of his office (from which he had been suspended until the case should be judged) the misfortune hung so heavy upon his mind that he was seldom seen at Court thereafter, and on the first Tuesday of every month he kept a solemn day of fast and humiliation.

This Archbishop's disgrace was the cause that the Arminians, or near-Papists, whose leader was Bishop Laud, swam up so easily into power when King James died. The Arminians held that the King ruled by Divine right and that if he commanded anything which his subjects might not perform because it was against the Law of God, yet they must obey without resisting or railing. Archbishop Abbot held a contrary view, and declared that Almighty God must not be made a lackey to any King or prince whatsoever; yet because of his unlucky day's hunting he could not maintain his point, and I think his heart was broken, though he lived a great while longer. Thus the more moderate, or orthodox, clergy were left without their natural leader, which was the reason that they contended so weakly against the Arminians.

Then, the Arminians pressing on with their plans for the entire subjection of the three Kingdoms to the King's religious authority, presently war was provoked in each of the three in turn; and all because (as the Tyrrells said) a priest had gone hunting that should have continued at his devotions.

Coursing of the hare did not please me, this being such a shy, gentle beast; and at home I reared one that my brother James had taken as a leveret from a place called Pole Cat End. I kept its fur sprinkled with a powder to make the house-dogs retch if they came too close, so my hare had a long life. Hawking I loved, and the fiercest of the gerfalcons that we kept was mild with me. My brother Richard had a hobbyhawk, with which he used to catch larks, but larks are petty game, and I liked better to ride across the stubble-fields in autumn and hilloo when partridge was sprung. At the first whir of wings my gerfalcon would stir strongly on my fist, though the hood kept him from fluttering his wings; and then I would whip off his hood and cast him into the air, and gallop after. How I cried with delight as my falcon soared and stooped and struck at the tumbling partridge; and I would praise him in very fanciful language when the quarry was safely in my falconer-bag, and he back again on my glove. I abhorred the sport of killing birds with shot blasted from a fowling-piece. Though falcons cost so dear and are marvellous troublesome to keep, yet hawking is a gentle and natural sport; and the use of gunpowder against wildfowl I find both unnatural and nasty.

How much I loved dancing is already sufficiently told, and I taught dancing to my little sisters and brothers, for that is the most healthy exercise known, and makes children grow up strong and graceful. I taught them the customary dances of the parish and new foreign dances as I learned them. On church holidays, whenever there was merry-making and sport beyond the usual, as at Hocktide and Michaelmas, we children of the Manor would be found on the Green dancing with the sons and daughters of our tenants, to show them our good affections.

When I was seven years old the Book of Sports had been read in our church, by order of King Charles, enjoining certain innocent recreations upon the people. In some godly parts of England this order was ill received by the Puritans, or precisians, who held it to be a profanation of the Lord's Day; but with us there was no outcry raised nor low muttering heard, except that on a Sunday (some time later) a young man named Messenger, who had gone to London some years before this to learn the trade of his uncle, a boot-maker, came back again a journeyman, and behaved very uncivilly at the morning service. It was not that he uttered any indecent railing, for he knew that the least word spoken in interruption of the curate, while he conducted the service, was common brawling and a breach of the peace. Yet he came in late, wearing rusty black, and stood in the aisle, under the round arch that leads to the chancel, with his face towards the pulpit, and lounged about there with his hat upon his head, during the singing of a psalm. Then when the curate began to preach upon the text "Why hop you so, you high hills?" and drew from it an encouragement for our country jigs and morrices, he fidgeted with his feet, coughed loudly as if to drown the curate's voice and at last turned upon his heel and with a rude clatter went out into the porch. Then when the sermon was done and the blessing given, and all the people came out of church, he lay in wait for the curate at the vestry door, where he asked him in a boorish tone: "Is not Dancing a Jezebel? Is not your striped Maypole an Idol? Come, come, Sirrah, answer me! Would you have these poor souls dance the Devil's morrice into Hell and be lost eternally? How did John the Baptist lose his head but that a whore danced a jig? For what purpose did King Hezekiah hew down the groves, but that they were filthy clusters of heathenish Maypoles?"

The curate, for all his faults, knew his rights as a servant of the Church, and he also knew the Bible better than this poor leather-aproned, black-thumbed rogue who had, I suppose, got by heart some book of Anabaptistical or Antinomian sermons, mumbling and tumbling the pages over between his tasks as he sat in the back room of his uncle's shop in Ludgate. The curate answered him that, as King David had danced before the Ark, which was God's former habitation, so should we all dance before his present habitation, the Church, and serve Him with timbrels and dancing; and none should hinder us.

Up then came my father, who having dozed through the service, as was his custom, had not noted the man's insolence until too late. He asked the curate whether the sexton and he had any charge to make against the fellow; being in the mood to listen to it.

The curate answered: "This man, your Worship, has asked me questions which, though they were phrased unceremoniously, cannot be construed as a breach of the peace. Yet, as I believe, he thinks that our striped Maypole is an Idol."

My father shook his head at this and, going out again to the Green, he called to all the people there: "Hey, good folk, here is one who having come into your Church with his hive upon his head, now alleges your Maypole to be an Idol. I pray you not to make an Idol of him instead." With that he winked plainly at them and went away and left them to their sport, taking the curate with him to absolve him of blame should any riot ensue, and also calling for the constable.

Tom Messenger had already vexed our people with his sneers and groans and godly vapourings, but they had not dared to do their do against him. Now that they were licenced, as they judged, to make sport of him, they clapped their hands for joy. Some held him fast while the others prepared themselves for dancing. It was the day that they called Robin Hood Ale, and the custom was for the young men to shoot with their cross-bows at a mark, and the one who shot closest, he was Robin Hood. His merry men led him to an arbour built in the churchyard, where sat Maid Marion, who bestowed a prize upon him and one or two kisses; and then all got drunk together and feasted in common upon pies and pasties and cold meats fetched from every house. But first, after sitting so long in the cold Church, they would all warm themselves with dancing at the Maypole. The Maypole they crowned with a garland of flowers and tied ribbons to the head of it, thereafter dancing around and in and out, weaving and unweaving the ribbons.

Since now their old Maypole was accounted a mere idol, they tied Tom Messenger's arms to his sides, garlanded his tall hat, put a stopper of rags in his mouth, and made a new Maypole of him: for they set him at his own height from the ground on the stump of a stone pillar standing at the corner of the Green, and tied his feet with ropes to the pillar in such manner that he could not leap off. Then they danced around him for a full half-hour to the sound of tabor and pipe. My father, watching from an upper window of the house, presently came out with the constable and clapped his hands for silence, at which the music ceased. Then he sighed and said: "O good people, what is this I see? Does this pragmatical fellow seek to bring contempt upon the Sports ordained by His Majesty, setting himself up as a Maypole in a public place and exhorting you to make an idol of him, to the great danger of the peace?" Then he cried to Tom Messenger: "O Tom, Tom, up so high above me, are these the ill fruits of your seven years' apprenticeship in London? Is this a fit return of gratitude to me who gave you five shillings and a great piece of cheese for your journey thither? Must you now come back to the place of your birth and corrupt old customs, setting yourself up above other men better than yourself and exalting your horn?"

But Tom could answer nothing, for his mouth was stoppered.

Then said my father: "Well, Tom, were it not for the kindness that I have towards Goodwife Messenger, your widowed mother, and towards your uncle Dick who is an honest man and a good maker of boots, I would see that you were this afternoon committed to the jail at Oxford to be tried at the Assizes. However, I have bowels of compassion and would not bring disgrace upon the town. Tom, you are free."

Tom Messenger was taken down from the pillar, and given a can of ale for his refreshment, and thereafter kept his mouth shut, though he would not consent to shoot at the mark with the other men, nor join in the dances or the vaulting with the pole.

So much for sport, of which I had no stint in those days, for my mother gave me certain set tasks in the house, and when these were done, I was free to use my leisure time in what manner soever I pleased, though I must always tell her where she might find me, and in whose company. I rose early even in winter and being a quick worker finished my tasks soon, and my mother did not take advantage of my quickness to lay more upon me that I could readily perform.

Now, as to other matters. My father had the Manor first from the Bromes, who had it from King Henry VIII, by whom it was taken from the monks of Osney when their Abbey was dissolved. He leased it for a term of fifty-one years, paying the Bromes the better part of the £3,000 that my mother had brought him at her marriage, and thereafter a chief-rent of £5 a year. The estate and the house were of an annual value of near £300, which was a comfortable sum, and he also held freehold and leasehold property at Wheatley, together worth at least £100 more. He made divers improvements to the Manor-house, which was somewhat ruinous when he took possession, and beautified the gardens; and he loved field sports and company, so that his expenses always overran his income by a fifth or a tenth part.

However, he had come to Forest Hill with a good sum of money in his hand and was confident that what was spent would return with usury. The old walls of the house, where they were not of dressed stone, he pargetted with good plaster of lime mixed with cow-dung;

and a skilled man from Norwich drew interlinked scrolls and ribbons
upon it while it was wet, and filled the intervals with painted pictures
of roses, thistles and fleur-de-lis; and vine-leaves with large grapes
hanging from beneath them; also an anchor, and (filling the gable-
ends) winged cherubim; and our first ancestors, decently clad, disputing together beside the Tree of Knowledge where the Serpent straggled among the boughs.

The garden he filled with all manner of fruits trees and with yew
and box fantastically cut, and dug fish-pools, and made arbours with
tiled roofs facing the south. He also laid out a walk with juniper
bushes on either side; which walk, if one stood in the middle of it
(where there were steps down to the fish-pool) and if one looked to
the right and left hand along it, appeared perfectly straight; yet this
was a deception, since from neither end could a person be seen approaching from the other. We had twelve bee-houses, among them
one with sides of talc, like a lantern, so that one might stare in and
watch the bees at their labour. We had two great hedges of lavender;
and of damask-roses a great many bushes, the leaves of which we used
to conserve with sugar; and a bed of clove-pinks, which we used for
making cordial liquor of sack and for flavouring hydromel. There was
an orchard next the garden, and a herb-garden, also a hop-ground
with the hop-kiln built beside it.

In the backside of the house were the stables, the sheep-pens, the
pig-styes, the hen-houses, the cattle-sheds, and the sheds for the carts
and wains; and also great stacks of firewood, and of timber, and heaps
of stripped oak-bark for tanning; and great piles of hurdles, of which
two men with frammers wove a dozen a-piece every day, working at
nothing else. These hurdles were chiefly made for sale to sheep farmers of the Downs, where hurdling is scarce. My father employed about
the house and garden, on the land and in the woods, some twenty
grown persons. Our bakehouse and brewhouse were always in a bustle, for there we baked and brewed for all the poor people of the town,
in return for a small payment.

My father and mother were well loved, for it never could be said of
them that they ate the bread of idleness or that they refused charity
to the needy and naked. Nor could they be accused of neglecting the
Church or failing to support it; for my father at his own charge set up
two great buttresses below the bell-gable; and he oversaw the curate
that he did his duty by the parish. This bell-gable is pierced for three

bells, yet there were never hanging in it, within living memory, more than two bells only. There is a song made of these bells of St. Nicholas, how they challenge and overbear those of all the other churches near by, of which Holton has three, Stanton St. John five, and Wheatley six:

> Holton sends her challenge still:
> *"Who rings best?*
> *Who rings best?"*
> Forest Hill, high on the Hill,
> Proclaims abroad "We two,"
> Stanton answers with a will,
> *"Nay, 'tis we who do."*
> Wheatley now takes up the tale,
> Ringing valiant down the vale,
> *"Who doubts that we ring best?"*
> Forest Hill will yet prevail:
> "We two; we two; we two."

In religion my father was for swimming with the tide. He desired no innovation, yet what the King ordained, on the advice of his bishops, why, let it pass, he cared not. His family was native to the Dominion of Wales, where the old religion was professed for a great many years longer than in England; and I guessed that he was brought up in it as a child. But he would tell us little of his life and circumstance before he married my mother, no more than that he was descended in a true line from certain Welsh princes; from which I judged that his family, though gentle, was exceeding poor. From his handiness with the axe when he gave instructions to his woodmen I judged also that he had done much labour in his youth that was below the dignity of a gentleman. My Aunt Jones would tell us nothing of her childhood, neither.

The Manor land was red land, very fat, and well watered by the stream that rises near Red Hill. About two-thirds of it was pasture or coppice, and the rest tillage. We tilled as early in the year as possibly could be, and dressed the fields—of which the great field at Lusher's would in a good year bring forth wheat worth £50 as it stood—with half-rotted manure from the mixen in the yard, twelve loads upon each statute acre. We also strewed on wood-ashes from the bakehouse and refuse from the brewhouse; and sometimes old woollen rags, got for very little from the Oxford halls and colleges, for these woollens were so sated with a well-rectified salt, left behind by the steam of the boys' bodies, that they made an acceptable manure for the land.

In Forest Hill the order of crops is this: first the barley, next the peas or beans, and last the wheat or mislan, after which we let the field lie fallow a year. The wheat comes last, for this very good reason that wheat, when it follows the dung-cart on rich land, is more liable to turn smutty; though against the smut my father would wash the seed in brine. He never stinted the land of seed, sowing four bushels of wheat or mislan or peas to each acre, with proportionably more of beans. And he would say:

> One for the pigeon,
> One for the crow,
> One to rot,
> And one to grow.

He would not let his seedsmen use their customary single cast, sowing the land at one bout, but would have them sow it twice, at two different bouts, casting the seed from furrow to ridge and afterwards from ridge to furrow.

We use the foot plough with a broad-fin share, the horses going in a string and keeping the furrow, to avoid poaching the land; and we cover the seed over with a bull-harrow armed with five-and-twenty iron tines. Our reaping is done with a smooth-edged hook, not with the sickle as in most counties; and we lay the corn in small handfuls all over the field that it may dry the sooner. After two days we bind it in very loose, small sheaves, and shock it rafter-wise, ten sheaves to a shock, in a manner that will marvellously bear out the rain.

Barley, which we sow always when the elm leaf is big as a mouse's ear, we count as ripe when it hangs the head, and has yellowed; we mow it with a scythe that has no cradle, and we never bind it, but only rake it together and let it lie so for a day or two to ripen the grain and wither the weeds. We cock it with a fork of three prongs, the cocks being well topped and of middling size; for great cocks take in more rain and often do not dry without breaking, and then must needs be pulled all to pieces, which cannot be done without loss. Beans and peas we also cut with the scythe, and gather them in wads, and cock them: only with this difference between them that we use no rake for gathering together the loose stalks, but take them up with the hand, the rake being apt to beat the beans out of the pods. We bring the harvest home in a two-wheeled long cart, having the shafts and hoops over the wheels, and this will take a heavy and broad load, as well as

LIFE AT FOREST HILL   57

a waggon almost. These methods and customs are far different from
what I have since observed in the country places near London.

To preserve our ricks of corn against rats and mice, we set them on
platforms resting upon stones about two foot high, called standers,
with rounded cap-stones upon them, past which vermin cannot climb.
We thresh with the flail, unless the wheat be very smutty, when we
whip it first, striking the corn (by a handful at a time) against a door
set on its edge, and binding up each sheaf again; which way is troublesome and tedious, but the smut-balls are by this means not broken,
as when they are struck with a flail, and by the strength of a good
wind the wheat will be left clean. We winnow the chaff from the seed
either in the field by casting it up into the wind with shovels: or else
in the barn with a leaved fan that artificially causes wind.

My father would often take me with him to watch these operations,
for he said that if I married a country gentleman (as he hoped I
would) and if he died or fell sick, I must learn to oversee the labourers, to prevent them from spoiling the estate. He also showed me the
different soils in the countryside about, and told me how each was
best dressed and planted, and how to keep the fields clean of weed,
and how to scare off the crows, and how to prevent stacks from burning by their own heat when the crops were harvested too moist or too
green. He taught me also the proper care of cattle, of which we had
always a herd of twenty cows, with a bull, which yielded abundance
of milk.

Our most leisurely times were in the month of May, when all our
seed was in the ground and no hay or corn ready to cut, and the latter
end of September, when the harvest was for the most part over, and
the wheat seed not fully come.

With the needle I had skill enough: I could sew an even seam and
stitch a neat button-hole. But lace-making and fine embroidery were
beyond my scope. I loved to spend the whole morning between the
kitchen and the pantry-closet, preparing some new dish. I would undertake faithfully to keep to the recipe given me, but always the Devil
overcame me and I would add something new, hoping to better it;
which was a great risk, for if the dish turned out well, I was excused
with grudging praise, but if I spoilt it my mother would take me up
to my chamber and whip me well for my presumption. I remember
her crying at me: "Too much nutmeg; unnecessary cinnamon; a want
of salt; too long in the baking; and again, a plentiful want of salt. O,

will you never learn obedience?" At each accusation there came a blow of the whip about my shoulders, which made me wince; but I did not weep or cry out.

When she had done I said faintly: "Madam, I thank you at least for excusing me the sweet-marjoram."

She raised her whip at that but then laid it down again and said smiling: "Nay, my dear, the marjoram would have been a wise addition, but for your other errors."

The work in the coppices of Shotover occupied a great part of my father's time. These coppices, as I have already written, had been much spoiled and decayed, with fallen trees rotting on the ground, and many of the stems and stocks dead and worn out: so that in truth they were, for the most part, undeserving of the name of coppices. Rather, they were thin sherwood, or underwood, overspread with thorns and brambles; and in the summer great bowers of the purple loosestrife grew there. However, my father owed the Bishop no rent for the first ten years. He put the coppices to rights piece by piece, and had sufficient gain for his labour in firewood and the wood that served for his hurdle-making and in such fallen timber as was yet sound. After ten years he would owe the chief-rent of £100 annually to the King and a further £100 to the Bishop; but by that time the coppice would be worth this rent and more, for Oxford City can never be satisfied with firewood. My father did not fell the coppices a whole stretch together, but "drew them out," as he called it: every year felling some, as the wood came to be of a sufficient height and bigness for cutting. According to the Statutes, each billet ought to be three foot four inches long, but the number of inches about it varied as it was named and marked.

My brothers were taught Latin by the curate, and the bailiff taught them to reckon and cast accounts. I learned a little Latin with my brothers, enough to read Cæsar's *Commentaries;* and my mother taught me French; and from my father I learned to sing and play upon a little guitar which he gave me, wrought with ivory and ebony on the back. The guitar is the most cheerful instrument of the lute kind, and I would brush the strings carelessly with my fingers or drum upon the sound-board; but trusted more to my voice, which is true enough in pitch, than to the instrument. From Trunco I had the arts of the stilling-room, and of simple physic. In short, I knew a little of most things useful for a woman of quality; and my mother, who was severe in her

judgments, agreed that I was marriageable and might soon make a
good match, even without a large dowry; but would rather have me
wait two or three years.

As a Justice of the Peace, my father knew more of the Law, I believe, than many of the learned gentlemen who sat with him at the
Quarter Sessions; but at Forest Hill, in those days before the war,
offences were few, and seldom were fastened upon any of our own
people, except for such small matters as broken fences or dogs that
preyed upon sheep. However, the Worcester road, in the summer especially, was travelled by numbers of sturdy rogues and vagabonds,
who stole sheets and handkerchiefs from the hedge, robbed henroots
and orchards and committed numerous other felonies. My father was
stern with these wretches, many of whom were old soldiers who had
served in the Dutch armies or under the Swedish King and cared little
for the blows that they received at our whipping-post, being accustomed to far more severe beatings from their serjeants; but knowing
that they hated cold water, he would have them soused in the stinking water of the yard, and thus give them a lesson to avoid Forest Hill.

There were often charges made against poor old women who were
accused of blasting pastures, of overlooking cattle to make them miscarry, of turning milk sour, and of afflicting little children with spots
and rashes; but these charges, when he closely examined them, were
always groundless and the aged trots guilty only of a miserable poverty. Old Mother Catcher, who lived in a wretched cottage of sticks
and turves down by Bayardswater Mill, was one day found with frogs
and snails and other small hopping or creeping things in a bag, and
also with some roots of curious shape. It was deposed by the wife of
Tomlins the Miller that she evidently intended some mischief against
the mill, for being suddenly surprised she let fall the bag and ran off,
and out hopped the frogs. Yet my father would not believe any malice
against the old woman and, by his kind demeanour, drew the true
story from her. She had a son, a labouring man, who would not cheerfully support her; and not wishing to suffer the disgrace of making
application for relief to the parish officers, or perhaps fearing to lose
her liberty, she sustained herself for awhile with roasted acorns and
cresses. Then finding this diet mean and tedious, and longing for some
flesh food, she had bethought herself that Frenchmen eat frogs' legs
and make a thin broth of snails, and why should not she? But she had
been ashamed when Tomlins' wife surprised her at her hunting, and

so ran off. The roots were orris, for drying and powdering, which had been commanded by the curate's wife for the perfuming of the Church linen.

So my father gave old Mother Catcher a few shillings, and a loaf or two of bread, and a lump of brawn, and recommended the miller's wife, if she hoped for reward in Heaven, to spare the old woman sometimes a parcel of spoiled flour to make griddle-cakes; which she undertook to do.

Afterwards, Mother Catcher showed her gratitude to my father by simpling for us; and one day she brought him a silver-gilt button, of a set that he prized, which he had lost from his coat when he went hunting.

CHAPTER FIVE

Mun Becomes a Soldier

Now to Mun again. Generally, all that happened to Mun that was of consequence to me grew out of the great events of these times; of which I must keep a running account if I would have my tale understandable. For so much water has now flowed under the bridges of Severn, Thames and Tweed, mingled with blood, and so many allies have turned enemies, and enemies allies, that most men have clean forgotten how affairs stood at the beginning of our troubles.

I had first become acquainted with Mun in the March of 1637. He rode out again from Oxford twice in that same month, and once in April; but was ashamed that any should know that his principal object in coming was to see a little girl, such as I was, and therefore behaved himself circumspectly. The first time, by good fortune, I had the happiness of sitting alone with him for a few minutes in the arbour by the bowling-green, while my father and my brothers finished their rubber. We said little to each other but I basked in his company, and he seemed cheered by mine. The second time, though, all went amiss: for I was kept working in the upper dairy-house all afternoon, and saw no more of him than his plume bobbing along the road as he rode away. The third time, when he came to take his leave of the household, because his angry father was come to remove him from the University, I contrived that he should see me go into the primrose coppice, where I waited for him half an hour or longer; and at last he came and lifted me up in his arms and kissed me, calling me his pretty fairy, and confessed himself utterly ruined by his follies. He assured me that of all the faces that he had seen throughout the time he had been at Oxford, mine was almost the only one he would miss when he was gone. Mun asked leave to write letters to me; but I denied him that, for my mother would never let me hear the last of it, if he did. Then he proposed to write often to my brother Richard, instead, with a loving message to me each time.

61

"O, no, Mun," said I, "that will be no better, not the least thing, for Dick will make sport of me and call you my Conquest. Dick is not to be trusted with any such message. Write to Dick, by all means, and tell him how you do, but append no particular message for me."

"You desire no message from me?" he asked. "You despise me for the manner in which I have wasted my terms at Oxford, and hoodwinked my father?"

"No, sweet Mun," I replied, "for I believe that there is no malice in you, only a love of great company (which I confess I share) and not sufficient fortune to bear it up. I have no doubt but that you will make amends."

"It would be easy to avoid falling into despair," he began in a very urgent, sad voice, "if only I could think——" but there he left the sentence hanging. After a while he continued: "None of my friends or kindred have any good opinion left of me, and if I could think that one person at least in this whole land——" Here he could say no more.

"Oh, poor soul," said I, weeping. I stroked his face and told him that he was dearer to me than any of my brothers, or my parents even, and that there was nothing in the whole world that I would love better than a letter from him, if it could be contrived without vexing my parents, but so it could not; and that I knew well that he would never fall into the same course of folly again; and that I wished him heartily well, and thought of him fifty times a day, and would so continue, I hoped, to the end of my life.

These childish words of mine put him into a better conceit with himself, and he told me that he was commanded to go to a Mr. Crowther, late of Hart Hall, for whom his father had procured a country living in Buckinghamshire, and repair his wasted learning under his guidance. However, I guessed that Mun had already outgrown his pupillage, and that it would be hard indeed for him at present to return to the rudiments of school-learning, even when roughly drawn away from his fine new friends. Then he declared solemnly that he hoped to be worthy of my esteem, but that he was cursed by a very facile nature: being easily drawn into mischief, unless there was a nail driven through the skirt of his coat to hold him back to his bench.

I was too young to speak rationally to him, but I looked affection and confidence at him, which gave him satisfaction; and he told me, half in earnest, half in jest, that as yet he loved no woman, but that one day, if I made haste to grow, he would ask my father leave to marry me. Meanwhile, I would be his little she-friend, and he my devoted servant.

At this I heard Trunco calling me from the yard, and I grasped his hand hastily and cried, "Farewell, Servant!" and ran towards the kitchen, while he went slowly off towards the stables to his nag; and that was all our good-bye for nearly half a year.

Within a month, Mun's tutor was taken ill and died, and he went to live with his uncle, Sir Alexander Denton, at a place called Hillesden in Buckinghamshire, and continued there for some time, helping his uncle with the management of his estate. Then, at the end of the summer, he rode over to see us, making it his excuse that he had a debt to pay at Oxford; and since he had meanwhile written three or four letters to my brother Richard, and always presented his dutiful respects to my parents, he was well received at our house. While he and I were together with the rest he teased me and talked big to me; but I took no offence, for as soon as we were alone his voice altered and grew tender. He was then in mind to go on a voyage to the Barbadoes with the Earl of Warwick, who had bought a plantation situate in the best and healthfullest of all those western islands. Many fine fruits were plentiful there, such as oranges, lemons, limes, plantains, pine-apples and guavas, with pepper, cinnamon and ginger, and cabbages that grew upon trees. The chief bread was potatoes, boiled and pressed, which were very nourishing and pleasant and did not weary the palate —not though one ate them at every meal. The greatest inconvenience of which Mun had heard was the land-crabs, which were thick upon the ground and would bite through a man's boot or nip off his thumb if he lay sleeping upon the ground; but there was also a great want of skilled labour, and of household stuff, both metal and linen, and the island lay at so great a distance from England that going there one might almost fancy oneself in the Moon.

In the end he did not sail, and for this reason only, I believe, that when he told me of it I wept and would not be easily comforted. I cried that I feared not on his account in the matter of the land-crabs, but that I hated the Ocean: he would surely be cast away and eaten by the sharks, either on his voyage there or as he returned. I do not know what excuses he made to his family, but he let them know that he had altered his mind. His elder brother Tom went in his place, but did not prosper and soon sailed home to England.

Meanwhile the Arminian clergy, led by Archbishop Laud (who had lately succeeded Archbishop Abbot, the unfortunate homicide) persuaded the King to lay such a uniformity of worship upon the Churches throughout his dominions as neither his father King James nor Queen Elizabeth had ventured upon. Ever since King Henry VIII quarrelled with the Pope of Rome, the Church had stood like a rickety table upon legs of uneven length, propped underneath with paper wads of tolerance and, whenever tolerance could not be granted to plain heresy, with wooden wedges of subterfuge; but now the Archbishop would saw the legs off even, and put the table level, and cast away the wads and wedges. Nevertheless, knowing the temper of the English people, he did not dare to foist his new Liturgy at once upon our nation, but thought it wiser "to try it upon the hound," as the phrase is, by administering it to the Scots, who were but a poor, small nation.

This proved a grand error, for the Scots had queasy stomachs and vomited out the Liturgy and ran and swore a Covenant together and, though the King was of the Royal House that they had themselves given to England, and though he had been born at Dunfermline in Scotland, yet they defied him. They challenged him to use force against them and called up their levies, which they officered with men who had seen service in the Swedish wars; and declared that, so far from accepting the Liturgy, they would not even acknowledge the rule of their own bishops who had recommended it to them, but would set church elders, or presbyters, in their place and govern the Church by assemblies.

When the first news of the uproar in the North came to the Court in London, Archie Armstrong, the King's Fool, meeting with Archbishop Laud on his way to the Council, forgot that the Bauble may not insult against the Mitre: he called him by a lewd name, and asked him, who was now the Fool? This jest was not taken kindly either by the Archbishop or by the King; and Archie, being hauled before the Council, was sentenced to have his Fool's coat pulled over his ears, to be kicked out of doors and never show his face at Court again; which was done, and his office given to another Scottish fool named Muckle John, who was a dull slouch, with a heavy eye and a hanging lip. It was a bold man who durst speak or write against the Archbishop, as our friend the learned Mr. Lambert Osbaldiston found about this time; who, for styling him a "little vermin and hocus-pocus" in a private letter written to the Bishop of Lincoln, was fined £5,000, deprived of his Mastership of Westminster School and sentenced to be tacked to the pillory by his ears in the presence of all his scholars. Yet Archie the Fool had the last laugh, for the Council that sentenced him is now abolished; and he has kept his head upon his shoulders longer than either the Archbishop or the King.

There was no remedy but that the King must take up arms against the Scots; and Mun was caught up into this war, such as it was. He was fitted out as a volunteer by Sir Edmund Verney, his father, who, being Knight-Marshal and Standard-Bearer to the King, marched to Scotland with the army that had been collected. The King had not summoned a Parliament, to ask money of them for the payment of his troops: for he knew that before they voted him any sufficient subsidy they would call upon him to redress the country's grievances, which had mounted pretty high in these many years of his governing without a Parliament. Besides, there was little love for our own bishops in many parts of England. Among the tradesmen and mechanics of London, and in the Eastern counties generally, it was openly said that the Scots were brave boys and did well to vindicate their rights. The King had written a letter to all the nobility, in January of the year 1639, calling upon them to bring their armed retainers to a rendezvous in Yorkshire. In answer, some nobles promised twenty horsemen and £1,000 of money; some £500 and five horsemen; some were wary and undertook to attend with as good an equipage as their fortune and the shortness of the time would permit; some pleaded poverty, reminding His Majesty of great debts owing them from his Treasury, and feared that they could send but little. In all, they did not offer much, and two noblemen, the Lord Brooke and the Lord Saye and Sele, refused together, unless Parliament should first give them the order—for which disobedience they were committed to custody. The Commons of every county and city were also called upon for free contributions; but the King's expectations were disappointed in the amount, the whole City of London offering no more than £5,200, about sixpence a head, which His Majesty considered paltry and refused with scorn. However, the clergy gave generously; for Archbishop Laud could draw money out of them by the screw of discipline, and told them plainly that His Majesty looked for a greater sum than in the ordinary way. Even our curate was expected to contribute £5, which was one-quarter of his annual stipend.

Early in March the Bishop of Oxford sent my father a letter for the curate to read out from the pulpit in Church: it was written by the

King himself, and in it those Scots who had taken the Covenant were accused of being enemies to monarchy, and of a design to invade England. This letter roused some of the congregation, especially the women, to groaning and calling down the vengeance upon these treacherous foreign dogs. But the men of substance heard it with composure, and afterwards in the porch Goodman Flight said that he hoped His Majesty might be mistaken, because the Scots, in a paper which he had read, gave a contrary account of their intentions; nor did anyone present take up Goodman Flight, who was reputed to be a man of sound judgment, but many said that they hoped the same thing, and that by God's will the two Kingdoms would not come to blows. Tom Messenger, who was now again settled in the village, held that the Scots, being so small a nation, would be bold indeed to try conclusions with the might of England; and that if they came out against us it would not be without assurance that the Lord was on their side. He would have spoken further, but my father told him to have a care what he said, for many a man had been laid upon a hurdle for less matters; so Tom broke off and begged the company's pardon. In April we were instructed to pray publicly for the King's success, repeating the words after the curate; but there was no fervency in the congregation, though three men were already gone from Forest Hill to the war. These men, however, had been chosen by my father as the three most easily spared. Two of them were incorrigible drunkards and idlers and the third had strange notions that nearly fitted him for the lofts of Bedlam. For my father was loath that any honest men should, through his procuring, hazard themselves among the dangers of war.

The King delayed a long time at York before he moved up to Newcastle and there remained another long time, with his army of near 50,000 men, hoping to over-awe the Scots. But the Scots had bought good arms from Sweden, and now began to put themselves into a proper posture of defence, and called fervently upon God, the ministers beating upon their pulpits as upon drums and bidding their congregation "fear nothing, for the Lord is with His people." Drill-masters also went up and down the country, instructing men in the use of arms and in obedience to the commands of their officers.

While he was on the road to York, Mun sent my brother Richard a letter by the sixpenny post, which he read out to us at dinner as soon as he received it. In it Mun expected that the journey would prove but an ordinary progress, and that the King would receive the dutiful submission of the Scots at the end, and that then he should have the happiness to renew our acquaintance in the autumn season. But if it came to blows, he wrote, he had as good hopes of coming back safe as any other, though he would not be backward in the use of his lance and pistols; and promised that he would send us a faithful inventory of any Scots he killed. I was very unhappy for Mun's sake throughout that spring and early summer. In June he wrote again from Berwick-upon-Tweed, to tell us that the Scottish Army was strongly posted on a hill that commanded the road to Edinburgh, well exercised and served with abundance of provisions; whereas with the King's army, he confessed, things were very ill. The soldiers were so unhandy in the use of arms they handled pikes as if they were hay-rakes; and a shot from one of their muskets had already gone through the King's tent. It appears that my father was by no means the only magistrate who, when called upon by the Lord-Lieutenant of his county to send men, had sent those whom he could best spare and, indeed, thought himself well rid of. But many a man had cut off his great toe that he might not be able to march, or done himself other injury. Moreover, the officers were discomposed and unready and there was continual grumbling, outcry and swearing for the common lack of bread and good drink. Mun feared that if the Scots came against such an army they would shear through it like a sharp hook through ripe barley; and he thanked God he had a good horse under him which would carry him out of the ruck if there were a general flight.

The King, seeing how he was placed, was persuaded by his Scottish lords to agree to a reconciliation; and their fellow-countrymen, being privately assured of his change of heart, made a supplication to him. Mun's father was sent to their camp requiring certain submissions before the King would treat, which were not so severe as to prevent a treaty from being concluded, known as the Pacification of Birks. In this treaty the Scots asked the King's pardon for angering him, but the King indulged them in all that they asked, namely, free parliaments and free annual Assemblies of the Church, by which Scotland should be governed in all civil and ecclesiastical matters whatever, without interference. Then both armies were disbanded, and it was like the break-up of a school for the summer holidays, with shouting and yelling and horseplay.

This, then, was a war without bloodshed, except among the dogs of Aberdeen: for Aberdeen alone would not swear the Covenant, and the

ladies there in contempt of it tied the blue colour of the Covenant in
ribbons about the necks of their dogs, and the Covenanters caught the
poor beasts and killed them. My father was soon afterwards shown a
letter from a Groom of the King's Chamber, in which he wrote that he
and his fellows had found the time long and tedious, the weather continuing wet and cold for weeks on end. And he added: "Yet we kept
our soldiers warm with the hopes of rubbing, fubbing and scrubbing
those scurvy, filthy, dirty, nasty, lousy, itchy, scabby, slovenly, snotty-
nosed, logger-headed, foolish, insolent, proud, beggarly, barbarous,
bestial, absurd, false, lying, roguish, devilish, long-eared, short-haired,
damnable, atheistical, Puritanical crew of the Scottish Covenant. But
now there is peace in Israel." There was more to the same effect, which
my father said was not convenient or decent to read out to us.

The troops were disbanded and made their way back, and it was a
long trudge, and of the three men from our town, the mad one died
on the way from a fever he caught from lying in wet clothes, and the
two rogues arrived hungry and barefooted, almost naked, having had
to part with their clothes in order to buy bread by the way. They reported that they had not been altogether sorry to part with their clothes,
for they were full of those creeping things, called "Covenanters," which
had swarmed into the seams while they starved in the Scottish camp.
But Mun came home without inconvenience.

One fine day, dressed in his buff coat of leather, he presented himself at our house. He was on his way to Oxford, where he purposed to
see the Act for the creating of Doctors of Arts. This time he was an
altogether different Mun from the poor humbled ignoramus of Hart
Hall whom, a little more than a year before, I had befriended and comforted. He was a hearty, gallant soldier who held his head erect and
stood in no need of consolation. Nor was I the child I had been; and
yet not a grown woman, but something between; so that he found it
not easy to speak with me and, as I thought, he avoided to be left alone
with me lest I should mistake his friendship for courtship. This grieved
me wonderfully, though he gave me no cause for offence, not teasing
me in company, but addressing me kindly and soberly.

He was now an ensign in the company of Sir Thomas Culpepper,
which would soon sail to Flanders to join the army of the States-General;
and told us that though he had a few creditors still at Oxford he had
sufficient money to settle with them all, and that then he should be free
with all the world and (here at least he stole a quick glance at me) he

would endeavour so to keep himself while he yet breathed. He brought us a tale that made us laugh, how a London merchant of his acquaintance wrote to his factor in Surat Castle, which is in India, and desired him by the next ship to send a parcel of conserved lemons, two great jars of oil of cinnamon and two or three apes; but this merchant forgot the *r* in *or*, and then it seemed to be 203 apes he desired. The factor sent him four score apes, and wrote on the bill that the 123 remaining should sail by the next ship. Mun said how great a pity it was that the four score had arrived too late to be sent against the Scots, for they were beasts with strong arms and great teeth.

Before he rode off he kissed the little children good-bye, and then turning to me he said with a smile: "Mistress Marie, you're too great a child for a kiss, I expect." And like a fool I answered: "Yes, I am no child now, Ensign Verney!" So he did not give me what I longed for with all my soul, but rode off smiling, and I knew that now he would write no more to Richard or to any member of our household. I went upstairs to my chamber to weep on my bed, but found Zara there, combing her hair with my comb. So I took it from her and thumped her and then went out again, very wretched, to tell my troubles to the geese in the orchard.

Mun was in no battles or sieges in Flanders; and in such a case an officer without interest has little hope of preferment; for there are no dead men's boots to draw upon his feet. Moreover, no captain cared to have so honourable an offer as Mun as his lieutenant, for it went against his conscience to make a fraudulent muster, by which the captain might draw pay in the name of soldiers who were dead or who had deserted the service. False musters were customary in the Army and the cheat was seldom found out; for the Colonel was given his share of the money earned thereby, and if ever a captain were desired by the General to show his company in full strength, soldiers could always be borrowed for the day from another. In the winter of that first year Mun was quartered at Utrecht, where there is a University; and here for many months together he studied seven or eight hours a day to amend his knowledge of Latin and French, and learn the art of fortification and other matters profitable to a soldier. But of this I knew nothing at the time.

Meanwhile, the King took his defeat at the hands of the Scots very ill, and prepared for revenge and consulted constantly with a junto of Ministers from his Council. In the end he was so hard pressed, not

knowing where to turn for money, that he resolved to call an English
Parliament (which he had not done since the beginning of his reign),
hoping to manage it with fair words and a pretence that the Scots intended a dangerous rebellion—though what need they had to rebel
when, at the Pacification, they had won all that they needed, did not
appear. In April, 1640, two days before Parliament met, the King made
play with a letter addressed by the Scottish leaders to the French King
in which they asked for his interest in the affairs of their nation. It was
true that they did not ask for his armed help, and perhaps sought only
his mediation; and it was also true that the letter had been written
before the late troubles; and, again, that it had never been sent, but
was a mere draft. Nevertheless, it read like treason, so he commanded
those Scots to come to London; and when they prudently stayed where
they were, this was disobedience and justified the war that he had in
mind.

The Parliament assembled; but few of its members glowed with
loyal anger against the Scots, and by a majority it was decided not to
discuss the twelve subsidies that the King required immediately, to
pay for his war, until he should have given answers to other questions
that Members might desire to ask him. They then compiled a long roll
of abuses with which they charged him and his Ministers, and demanded amendment; so in anger he dissolved the Parliament when it
had sat but three weeks. Yet money he must have, and he milked the
clergy again, and sold patents and monopolies, and increased the rates
of the Excise, and called upon the City of London for a great loan of
£200,000, first demanding from the aldermen of each ward a list of
citizens able to subscribe—yet for all his urgency they found him no
more than one-fifth of the sum he required. He also levied ship-money,
coat-and-conduct money, and I know not what other taxes and imposts
besides: by which my father felt himself hard pressed, and went about
as though he had a whitlow on his thumb. Few dared to oppose the
King openly; but things done in ill-humour or without stomach are
never done either speedily or well, and the three men whom this time
my father sent to the war—the two former men and another who had
become a charge on the parish, because he was a tailor and his sight
was failing him—these were commiserated and pitied as though they
were going to the block to lose their heads; and they held back from
going until a sergeant came up from Oxford to take them by force.

In May, Mun, together with other officers, had been called from The

Hague, where he then was, and given a lieutenancy in a disorderly company of foot that were to march against the Scots. Many of his soldiers had been sent to the war as a punishment for their Puritanical fervour, which was an ill reason; for on their way to the North they were a shame and trouble to him. They would break into churches, and if they found anything there not to their liking, they would set all to rights: wrenching up the altar rails, dragging back into the middle of the church the Communion tables, of which Archbishop Laud had made altars at the east end, carrying away candles that they found burning to no purpose, and tearing up surplices to make them handkerchiefs.

The Scots had early intelligence of something being prepared against them, and called their army together again, and prostrated themselves humbly before their God, and encamped in the same place as before. All their preparations were made by the middle of August, by which time the King's levies were still in a straggle towards the Border—ill-armed, ill-fed and most unwelcome to the inhabitants of Yorkshire and the other northern counties, where the year before they had eaten up much good pasture and carried off corn and pigs and poultry with no "by-your-leave" nor any payment but curses.

The Scots' orderly army would not wait for the King to marshal his men for an attack upon Edinburgh; but they boldly forded the Tweed at Coldstream, with their snapsacks of oatmeal upon their backs, and marched into England. They were well provided with artillery, and there was a sufficiency of muskets, except among the naked Highlanders who carried bows and arrows instead; but they wore no body armour, which was rightly judged a greater burden in marching than it was a protection in battle.

This was a strange invasion indeed: for no rapine nor plunder was permitted, but the Scots behaved as sedately as choristers in a solemn procession, protesting that they came only as friends to comfort their fellow-sufferers of England who stood under the same dangers to their religion and liberties as they themselves did, and undertaking to take nothing from them, not so much as a chicken or a pot of ale, without paying for it in lawful money. They hoped that the English would concur with them in this most just and noble way of obtaining the just and noble desires of both nations.

A few thousand men of the King's army were posted about four miles above Newcastle on the southern bank of the Tyne, to deny the

passage; but when the Scots came up, neither army was disposed to
pick a quarrel, for there had been no enmity between the two nations,
I believe, since the time when the King's great-grandfather, a Scottish
King, had been slain at Flodden Field. The horsemen of both armies
watered their horses at the same stream, though from opposite banks.
At last a drunken English musketeer discharged his firelock at a Scottish officer across the water, and so the truce was broken. Other muskets popped, and the Scottish ordnance roared off, each piece being
recharged as often as once every three minutes, and the English fled
from one of the two trenches that they had been digging; whereupon,
the tide being low, the Scots forded the stream and the English fled
from the other trench also. Some squadrons of our English horse stood
their ground, but finding themselves alone and almost surrounded,
went off after they had lost two or three score men. The Scots had a
huge advantage in their ordnance, which disastrously outnumbered
and outshot our own, the cannoneers who served them being as skilful
as bell-ringers in touching them off. Besides these great pieces they
also brought up many of those portable and dangerous iron guns, no
more than four foot long and of their own invention, that carried a
bullet of two or three pound weight and were deadly at 300 paces.

The Scots swarmed along the road to Newcastle, whither Mun's
regiment had come from Yorkshire, by forced marches, two nights
before. He found horrible confusion in the streets of Newcastle, where
nothing was prepared, and his soldiers were hastily set to improve the
fortifications where they were ruinous; who worked almost without
ceasing, both day and night. Yet then Mun's company had orders to
abandon the works and march out again, for the case was hopeless;
and for want of horses nearly all their baggage was left to the enemy.
Back they straggled to York, as quick as they had come, or quicker.
The Scots did not, for pity, press upon the rout, as they might have
done; but considered it prudent to occupy peaceably the counties of
Northumberland and Durham, and there possess themselves of all the
coal mines and stocks of coal, which was ill news at first for the coal
merchants of London and for housewives and bakers who depended
upon coal to heat their ovens. However, the Scots kindly refrained
from any interruption of this trade, so that they won great praise for
their forbearance. As for Mun, he lost all the possessions that he
brought with him, but except only the clothes that he wore, which

were the very worst he had, and he got nothing back but, some months later, one trunk out of his three.

The Forest Hill men deserted their ranks and each in turn made his way back, so that they were all home by Christmas to eat their plum-porridge. Our constable charged them with being deserters, but when my father examined them they deposed that their officers had fled, who had never given them a penny of the pay due to them, and very little meat or drink for their bellies; so my father discharged them. The two rogues returned to their tippling and idleness; but the tailor found his eyes strengthened by long absence from the needle and my father made a woodman of him, and he proved of good use to us.

Of the nobility and gentry, our neighbours, most were very hot against the Scots, but hotter still against the English traitors who had been in league with them: for it was common knowledge that those in England who hated Bishops and did not love the King had encouraged the Scots to march.

The King, being then petitioned by the Scots to call an English Parliament, was in no posture to deny them, and Parliament was called; which is the same Parliament of which I wrote in mv first chapter that Sir Robert Pye the Elder was a member. Indeed, it is the same Parliament whereof a poor remnant still rules at Westminster, after twelve years, having since done great and terrible things. In those days Parliament was generally well disposed to the Scots, and liked that they should remain in England until a treaty could be signed agreeable to both nations; and most members did not grudge that they should be paid at the rate of £850 a day while they remained, if so the King might be over-awed into obedience to the will of Parliament. Yet there was this inconveniency, that a residue of the English army remained at York which for shame's sake they could not disband, and must pay likewise; this army they were not careful to pay so regularly as the Scots. Then they busied themselves with providing for the security and perpetuation of the Parliament; with abolishing the Courts that had been the instruments of the King's arbitrary power; with asserting again the ancient right of the People not to be taxed without the common consent of Parliament; with abolishing monopolies and patents; and finally with restraining and limiting the power of the Bishops.

Mun continued with the broken army in York, ill at ease and out of pocket; and he was there in that Christmas season of 1641–1642 when, as related in my first chapter, my godmother, Aunt Moulton, gave me my vellum book. Here at last I have caught up with the beginning of my story, where I made too hasty a start, and will undertake never to go backward in it again.

CHAPTER SIX

I Fall into Piety and Out Again

I N THE spring of that year, 1641, when I was recovered of my supposed plague and went about the house again, I fell in a dump of melancholy, for I had loved my warm pampered life in bed, and could find little gust or appetite for my customary tasks.

My mother said that I had fared too sumptuously during my sickness, and resolved that I must be cupped of half a pint of blood each day for ten days to restore me; and now that I was no longer under Trunco's care there was no denial, but I must submit patiently. Which loss of blood weakened me much and made me more melancholic yet. My father called in Dr. Bates, an Oxford physician, who was confident that I had a scurvy and prescribed me acrimonious medicaments: boiled scurvy grass, wormwood beer and mustard at every meal, which my stomach loathed.

Moreover, I had the spring as an enemy to contend with. Our poets pretend that spring is a jocund season, but doubtless they borrow this conceit thoughtlessly from the Italians and Spanish, in whose gardens almond trees are in firm fruit, while ours are scarcely in flower. At Forest Hill in that year the east wind blew very bitter throughout Lent, a wind which, according to the proverb, is good neither for man nor beast; and our house, being an old one, was not tight against the blast. The primroses were backward in blooming and gave me little pleasure, with no Mun at my side to gather them; yet in recollection of him I still ordered and tied my nosegays as he had showed me.

The season was further overcast by the coming trial, in Parliament, of the Earl of Strafford, the King's principal adviser and most skilful commander, on the charge of illegal and treasonable acts done by him in Ireland. It was evident to all who considered his case that he had been a most faithful servant to His Majesty, and that if he were a traitor to England, why, then, so was his Master who approved his acts —unless it were that a King could do no wrong. Yet those in Parliament were bent upon condemning the Earl to death, as an exemplary warn-

ing, and not any lesser penalty would satisfy them, for "stone-dead hath
no fellow", as they said. Nobody could think so ill of His Majesty as
to believe that he would suffer a faithful servant to die; on the other
hand it was said that if he offered the least interference with the course
of Parliamentary justice the Kingdom would hardly escape a tumble
into civil war. There was a saying quoted by the Parliamentarians—for
already the parties were thus ranged, Parliamentarians against King's
men or Royalists: "No man can well say how many hair's-breadths
make a tall man, and how many a short man; yet we all know a tall
man, when we see him, from a short man; and how many illegal acts
make a traitor is not to be said, yet we all know a traitor, when we see
him, from a man who is true and loyal."

My father was discreet, and offered no opinion, but would say to
the contenders of either party: "I cannot dispute the truth of what you
say, yet I hold this to be a very ill business, and dangerous." And to
one who sought to inflame matters by violent speech he would say:
"Softly, sir, softly! Remember that he who will blow the coals with his
mouth must not wonder if some sparks fly into his face!" But my
mother, being born a Moulton of Worcestershire, which is a very loyal
county, was all for the King and ranted against "the currish dogs and
traitors led by that rogue Pym."

In Passion Week my Aunt Jones came again to our house with my
Uncle Jones, a very austere man, who took advantage of my continuing
dark mood to converse very earnestly with me about my immortal soul;
asking shrewdly, did my conscience prick me, had I fallen into carnal
faults, did I hope to be numbered among the elect of God? etc., etc.
In our house we were as light-hearted in religious performance as my
father was in his execution of justice: we did as others did, and as the
Law required us to do, in the matter of church observance—no less and
no more—making no dismal burden of our mortality. I hardly knew,
indeed, that I possessed an immortal soul of my very own; for the
curate in his sermons touched little upon questions of individual salvation. He treated rather of the large bounty of God and of the generous
love that is found between good neighbours, crying in the words of
the Psalmist: "Brethren, what a joyful thing it is to dwell together in
unity!" and he often promised us that, if we walked in meekness and
good cheer and charity together, and avoided any offence against the
Law, our whole congregation of St. Nicholas parish would march together at last into the bliss of Paradise, in due order of rank and sub-

stance, and there all become blessed angels together, to sing Hosannas for everlasting ages.

My Uncle Jones now told me that I must remember my Creator in the days of my youth, that the evil days might not come (as they had come to him and to my aunt) when I should say "I have no pleasure in them." This was something new, which I heeded because of its strangeness and sharpness, and when my Uncle went away again he left two books with me, Dr. Sibbes' *Bruised Reed* and Mr. Robert Bolton's *Four Best Things, and Instruction for the Right Comforting of Afflicted Consciences,* which last was a new edition imprinted in that same year.

The *Bruised Reed* I could not stomach; but Mr. Bolton wrote very comfortably, and convinced me that I had a quick, tender conscience; and searching this new-found, quick, tender conscience well, I found it afflicted by an innumerable of sins that I had not known before by so black a name; and I instantly resolved to repent and to amend all and to walk before God with a perfect heart. Then a watery light of holiness seemed to shine about me, and I was licked, as I thought, by the tongues of that hopeful fire whereof the books made promise.

This was a short-lived mood, for soon the light of holiness dimmed, and the flames languished, and before night came I had returned into the old mire of my errors—the dog to his vomit, as the Scripture says —and called myself a miserable, hard-hearted sinner, a wretched back-slideress, a filthy beast. I turned my vellum book upside down and began to write at the other end, keeping a very precise inventory of blessings and crosses for every day; and another of temptations that had beset me, with an addition sign or a subtraction sign to signify whether I had overcome or fallen; and another of resolutions taken and whether performed. The signs that I most noted were: of gluttony, for I had a passion for sweetmeats of every sort and for the tender breast of chicken; of vanity, which was cockered up by my new dress made of red and green flowered chintz, bought in London at thirty shillings a yard; of sloth, for I would never be the first, of Zara and myself, to rise from our bed, but would wait until she was fully attired and had her hand on the door to go out; of lying and glozing, with which I covered myself when my mother asked me questions that I would not answer; of anger, how I fumed and chafed when I was ruled by an elder person; of cruelty, to Trunco, when I was out of patience but dared not vent my evil humour upon anyone else, for I let fly at her, knowing that in her great love for me she would not long resent it.

This keeping of accounts I found a great inconveniency, for either I had to hold the items constantly in my head, saying them over to myself for dread of forgetting them before night when I should write them down; or else, many times a day, to fly up to my chamber and unlock the book, and get out my pen and ink-pot and write the tale down, and then sprinkle the ink with the sand-caster, and wait until it was dried and then lock the book again. This, with the watchful guard that I kept upon my tongue and hands, put a constraint upon me wherein I might have gloried, but that it was so irksome and unnatural. I could, thus far, regard myself as merely in the condition of Preparatory Grace, and not yet having that Special Grace which is vouchsafed to saints; and my awakened soul, the more I searched it, appeared in a very dreadful and passionate plight. To check my vanity, I cultivated a negligence of my hair and apparel which ill became me; and when my mother observed that I ate and drank more sparingly than usual and that I went about softly and answered her submissively, she concluded that I had done something mightily amiss, which I wished to hide from her. She called me to her chamber on the morning of the second day of my new life and tried to draw a confession from me, but I had nothing to confess beyond small things which to her were not worth the confessing; so that she thought that I deceived her, and railed at me. I humbly cast down my eyes to the floor, but said no word to her of my Preparatory Grace—if Grace at all it was, and no illusion—lest she should rail the louder.

My mother often taunted at my Uncle Jones, though never to his face or in the presence of my father, for his canting, puritanical, hypocritical ways. She called him a fox who had lost his tail in a trap, and who would persuade all other foxes (and vixens, too) to lose theirs, so that he might not feel abominable in his tailless condition. I felt myself strong enough in the faith, but was not of the stuff that martyrs are made of, and would do nothing that would provoke my mother to mock me as a she-disciple of my Uncle Jones with his plain collared bands and absurd hat. However, one day after dinner, my mother watched how I crept up to my chamber, thinking myself unobserved; and came softly after me and broke in upon me just as I was unlocking my book to write. She did not give me the lie when, trembling at the alarm, I told her faintly that I was keeping a private account of my sins, which I intended only for my own eye and that of my Maker.

Instead, she burst out laughing in my face. She said that it had been just so with her when she was of an equal age with me and had fallen in love with my father—she had eased her afflicted heart by writing her longings in a book like mine, some of them in plain prose, but some turned into indifferent good verse. Then she kissed me, and laughed again, and told me to love whom I would, but to be as discreet as she had been, and to guard my maidenhead well, which was a valuable commodity, a pearl of price, not to be thrown away on any handsome rogue, but to be preserved for a good match. And she said that she hoped I would not marry a poor man, as she herself had done; for though the fortune that she had brought my father had caused him to treat her with unusual kindness, yet because of the leanness of his purse she must constantly deny herself of pleasures that she had thought never to be without.

I had a mind to cut the lecture short by assuring her that my only love was for the Lord Jesus; but I refrained. For, in the first place, she would have thought that I added the fault of blasphemy to that of deception and would have pulled my ears for me; and, in the second, I could not conceal the truth from myself, which was that in the perversity of my heart I loved Mun, a sinful man, as dearly as anything else whatsoever.

My mother thereafter, if I chanced to be remiss or behind-hand with my household tasks, would twit me light-heartedly, and before my brothers and sisters, with being love-sick, and would propose the most improbable persons as the objects of my love with "Confess, daughter —surely it cannot be he?"

I was discomposed and abashed, and knew not how I should answer if she named Mun. To avoid this peril, I strove to forget him and to give my heart wholly to God; but I could not pluck him out from the chief seat. Then my sins mounted, for I could not show myself meek, try as I might. Zara twitted and taunted me to distraction, playing my mother's game, yet in a silly, spiteful manner.

At last, five or six days after Easter, as we sat together in the hall at our needlework, she cried suddenly: "I have it, I have it—it is Mr. Tiresias, him whom we met that day at Woodstock! I overheard you when you asked our brother James to tell you all that he knew about the other Tiresias." Then I dropped the band that I was stitching and flew at Zara and scratched her cheek with my nails and thumped her in the belly.

Yet even in her shrieks and tears she exulted, crying: "So it is he! it is he! I have guessed it. Marie languishes for love of Mr. Tiresias."

Oh, I mauled her so savagely with my teeth that my brother Richard had to pluck me from her, wrenching me back by the hair with both his hands.

Then ensued a great repentance, with a heinous sin to mark down in my book, for (as I wrote) had not my brother Richard by the Grace of God passed by the hall and heard the hubbub, I should have murdered my own sister, who truly meant no great harm. Yet I comforted myself a little by writing that though temptation at that time had prevailed against the spirit and the love of God, yet it was not to the setting up in me of the contrary habit in predominancy. I had been tripped up by the Devil, yet by God's grace would rise again refreshed.

When I had written this, I heard my brother James calling my name, and went out to him and he kissed me and said: "Sister, you have not gone riding for ten days or more. It may be that what has put you into such an ill-humour is this: that you have not jogged and jolted yourself sufficiently, so that your blood stands still in your veins and poison scums up. Come out with me now on Roarer and we'll ride towards Red Hill."

I was grateful to him, and made ready, and forth we went. My spirits soared again, so soon as ever I was back in the saddle. The greyhound with us started a fox and, as we coursed after him, half a field behind, he turned his muzzle towards Beckley and ran stoutly. My Roarer was a great unruly sorrel, and because I had not lately exercised him he was mad for the chase and took the bit between his teeth, so that I could no longer manage him. I clung to the pommel of my saddle, and prayed wildly to God to preserve me, for the fox was running to hide in a deep, old pit, called Shepherd's Pit, which has gorse bushes at the lip. My Roarer swerved aside, avoiding the danger, and leaped over a bank instead, into a narrow lane that led into the pit. He tumbled me over his head, where I lighted up to my elbows in mire, and took no hurt; and he lighted with two feet on one side of me, and two on the other, in a marvellous manner, not hurting me, though he trod the shoe off my foot.

This was a great mercy, worthy to be recorded in my book; but when we returned home, having killed the fox in the pit, I found that a spark from the hearth had leaped into my sewing-basket, where I had left it in the hall. The fire had scorched a hole in the lace-band that I was stitching, and had spread and burned the brocaded lining of the basket, with a pair of fine lace gloves wrapped in paper, and other small things that I prized, as ribbons and silk thread, and the basket was smouldering with a sour smoke.

Was this not too much to bear? I knew well that Zara had seen my things burning and purposely let them burn, though she protested that she had not set foot in the hall again after my cruelty to her. That night, though I made up my inventory, I ran two lines beneath it with my pen, to show that it was now at an end, and that I had struck sail. For Special Grace was long in coming, and too much thought upon sin breeds sin; and I trusted that God would not be severe with me when I owned my incapacity at present to serve Him as faithfully as Mr. Bolton or Dr. Sibbes or my Uncle Jones would have me do.

The next day I lay in bed ten minutes longer than I needed to lie, and took pleasure in it, and was myself again, and have never since wilfully taken up any book of sermons or other pious writings which might remind me of that most precious but horribly uncomfortable possession, my soul. My family made no more sport of me, and Zara feared my rage; nevertheless, it stuck in the memory of the household how wrathful I had been when Mr. Tiresias was named as the man for whose love I languished. What James could tell me of the other ancient Tiresias, whose name our gentleman had borrowed, was only this, that he was a Theban poet or prophet in ancient days and that he was blind; but when he went to London, as he passed through St. Paul's Churchyard, he thought to enquire of the booksellers there for a Masque published under the name of Mr. Henry Lawes (whereof Mr. Tiresias had written the poem) and was directed to where the book might be bought, and brought it back as a gift to me.

I had read poems before, especially the long, pleasant verse-tales by Samuel Daniel and Edmund Spenser, which my mother had, but more for the matter rather than for the art. Now, however, that I had put by my godliness as unseasonable, I turned for the refreshment of my mind to the reading of poems. I was of an age to fancy myself a judge of the art, and read as many of the newer books as James could borrow of his friends at Oxford; and this Masque I judged to be exceeding fine poetry. There were two brothers in the poem, with a sister, who was lost in a wild wood by their negligence. A sorcerer named Comus, with a rabble of tipsy monsters, finds her out and tempts her to wantonness; but she protests that she is chaste and that no sorcerer has any power over chastity. He argues that chastity is no jewel, but a bauble—she still protesting the contrary—and offers her a magic cup to drink, which shall overcome her scruples. At this the brothers rush in with swords drawn, and scatter him and his rabble. The rest of the action is concerned with the difficulty that the brothers meet of over-setting a charm which has fixed the lady fast in her chair, and they call in a Nymph who sings a lovely song and so looses her.

The verses fascinated my mind with their serpentine mazes of sound, and the argument bit in deep. I asked my brother James to give me his true opinion of the poem, but to weigh it well first, for I thought the verses extraordinary good and would not be pleased with a con-trary judgment.

James answered judiciously, when he had read it, that this was an extraordinary poem indeed, and presented two notable paradoxes. The first, that it appeared a compost or mosaic of many other poems that he had read, set in a frame borrowed from the *Comus* of Henri du Puy—a Latin poem which had been published in Oxford a few years since and a part of which, James said, he had been instructed to turn into Greek hexameter verses as a college exercise. Yet, said he, none could deny that this new *Comus* outwent them all for smoothness and beauty, or that the poet was a discoverer of new things by means of the old. The second paradox was that, after the arguments *pro* and *contra* upon the true worth of chastity had been bandied between the Lady and Comus, Comus was defeated, yet that this defeat was only by the sword, not by force of reason; moreover, the lines that had the greater compulsion in them and which would linger longest in his memory were those that the Sorcerer spoke against the ungrateful folly of abstinence, and against the puritanical manner of living "like Na-ture's bastards, not her sons."

James also said: "The man who wrote this, though I dare call him a very skilful poet, yet seems uncomfortable in the imaginations of his heart and unhappy in the acuteness of his mind. One thing I will wager: he is not a nurseling of our own University. This smacks to me of Cambridge, where they tune their viol strings always a little sharp. It is a poem to admire rather than to love; and here is another paradox, for how can any man truly admire what he does not love? Almost, I prefer the silly, homely verses of Taylor the Water-poet to these: for with Sculler Taylor there is nothing hid, but all bubblingly well ex-pressed, though the matter be trifling. Nay, I mean not that, for there is no comparison between poet and rhymester. Indeed, I know not well what I mean. 'Tis the case with me: *Non amo te, Licini, nec possum dicere quare*—I do not love thee, Liciny, but cannot tell the reason why."

James could not let the argument rest there, but came back to it often in his discourse and carried it further. "Dear heart, this fellow Tiresias troubles me much. You say that in the garden at Enstone he spoke of pluming his wings. This word 'pluming' might be understood in two senses: either as smoothing and dressing his wing-feathers, or as furnishing his naked wings with borrowed plumage. For he has plucked out the feathers from other poets' wings to make of himself a great immortal Phœnix; yet has gone about it so cunningly and with such admirable judgment that these plumes glow with richer colour upon his wings and tail, as he preens them, than in their former places. Or, I might say, he has stolen the laborious honey from the hives of his fellow poets, to spread it thick upon his own white roll, and now says to them scornfully: '*Sic vos non vobis mellificatis, apes*'—Thus, bees, you gather honey, yet not for your own maws.' And I think that I can read his secret: he is more passionately set on literate fame than in love with poetry itself. Yet, by God, I have no flaw to find in a single line, search as I may. There's a turbulent devil in him, which devil shows his cloven foot, as I say, in the speeches of the wizard Comus."

I would not agree with James, and held it fitting that the *pro* and *contra* of chastity should be exactly counterpoised, and that only the sword, or compulsion, should decide the cause in Virtue's favour. If it were not for the Law's compulsion, what woman born would not follow the inclination of her heart and prostitute herself to the first handsome young man for whom she took a liking? I said, also, that what he said about the University of Cambridge showed the spiteful bias of his judgment. And I pressed him for instances that would prove this poet a plagiary or copyist; some dozen of which he then gave me, but in every case the resemblances between the old and the new seemed slight and accidental. James, though he was a patient and affectionate brother, almost lost his patience with me in the end and cried out: "O Child, Child, cannot you see, cannot you hear? It is not the single words or phrases so much as the cadence or very soul of the verse that he has borrowed: here from William Browne's *Pastorals,* and there from John Fletcher's *Shepherdess,* and there from George Peele's *Old Wives' Tale,* and here again. . . ."

"I neither see it," I said, "nor hear it. This Masque is a lovely poem. Then, as for literate fame, how can a poet not desire it? Fame assures him readers and patrons; without readers and patrons a poet is undone, his poems are locked up in the prison of his cupboard drawer and serve no purpose."

"The more that a poet regards Fame, so much the less will he regard Truth," said James.

To this I objected: "I had not thought that it was for poets to speak truth, which is rather left to the divines and philosophers to expound."

He answered: "Sister, you are fallen into a vulgar error. Poetry without truth is mere honey-cake and sugar-works."

"I am a glutton for both," I confessed.

"Then it will be your ruin," said he, a little too soberly for my liking. He begged me not to be offended, but asked me whether it were not true what Zara had said, that I had conceived a sort of love for the author of this masque. I answered him, that he could think what he pleased, yet I could not help but be mightily offended by his question. He begged my pardon, which I grudgingly granted. Yet I thought it perhaps a useful thing for my purpose that the hounds were running on a false scent. Let them bay after my supposed love for this Cambridge scholar and poet; I would be secretly happy in my love for an Oxford dunce and soldier.

Then the East wind abated, and a mild wind blew from the South, and soon the little lambs in the fields were grown half as big as the ewes; and though the Earl of Strafford was convicted of treason and beheaded, yet the King, who had undertaken that not an hair of his head should be touched, let him die, for fear of worse things; and the country breathed again, because the threat of war had passed. The Parliament pressed on with its legislation, wresting from the King a great part of his powers, though leaving him the name and honours of sovereignty, and none expected that where he had once yielded—very basely, as many considered—he would dare to stand again. The Scots were still kept under arms in the North, as a caution to him that he must mind well what he said and did.

We had good crops that summer, of hay, wheat and barley, though other farmers were not so well advantaged, whose lands were fried up by the unusual fierce sun. Nothing remarkable happened in our house or village except that upon a complaint of two householders to Bishop Skinner (who succeeded Dr. Bancroft, recently dead) the curate was

examined by my father in private; who judged his familiarity with
Molly Wilmot to have become scandalous, though there might be no
adultery proved against him. My father liked the Rev. John Fulker
well, who was a good-hearted man, though a loose liver; and did not
bring him before the Ecclesiastical Court, but sent him off quietly and
I do not know what has become of him. My father was careful in his
choice of a successor, and therefore consulted with my Uncle Jones
and asked him to recommend a priest fit for the times: that is to say,
one who would be content to obey Parliament, yet without railing indecently at the bishops.

Thus the Rev. Luke Proctor came to us, who was a tall, grave, budge
man, with a leaning towards the Presbyterial discipline, and no fond-
ness for Whitsun-ales and leet-ales and clerk-ales and our other regular holidays. He did not rail against bishops, but neither did he mag-
nify the bounty of God; preaching instead of the terrors that lay in
store for the whole land, unless we repented. Once at evensong, when
the sun set as he was preaching to us, he said: "My brethren, I doubt
not but that you see this broad red glow as a jolly sunset, and as 'the
shepherd's delight'; but to me it shines as the distant glow of that Hell
which is prepared for the ungodly, the hard-hearted, the scoffers, the
liars, the adulterers and the fornicators."

Whereat John Mathadee's young child, in a seat behind us, set up
a wail, and the curate pointed at him and said: "Yea, wail, child, you
do well to wail! For in that day shall women rejoice who are barren,
because of the curse that has come upon their sisters whose wombs
were fruitful." By this he offended my mother, who led all her younger
children out of the church; and so did Goodwife Mathadee.

The poet whom the Reverend Proctor loved best and from whose
facile, flat verse he quoted oftenest, as "very apples of gold with pictures of silver," was Mr. George Wither, a Puritan—he to whom old
Ben Jonson had denied the title of poet, naming him "a mountebank
of wit and scorn of all the Muses," because he wrote merely to suit
the capacity of the rabble. Mr. Wither (who has since become a high
officer in General Cromwell's army) had prophesied to England after
this manner, which sounded lovely in our curate's ears:

> Upon thy fleets, thine havens, and thy ports,
> Upon thine armies and thy strong-walled forts,
> Upon thy pleasures and commodities,
> Upon thine handicrafts and merchandize,

Upon the fruits and cattle in thy fields,
On what the air, the earth, or water yields,
On Prince and People, on both weak and strong,
On priest and prophet, on both old and young,
YEA, ON EACH PERSON, PLACE AND EVERYTHING
His just, deservèd judgments God will bring.

"Yea, Amen, Amen, Amen and even so," cried our curate—"unless ye repent!"

When at Michaelmas, by order of Parliament, my father was obliged to blot out or break all deceitful idols that were to be found in the Church, whether images, pictures or painted glass, this curate was ready enough to comply and was for breaking the glass with a stick; but my father would not have it, because, as he said, by such awkwardness some child might run a splinter into his foot or hand. He conveyed the glass away himself that night, and gave out that he had thrown it into a pit in the woods, together with the dark old pictures painted on boards, and the little decayed statue of St. Nicholas holding a child on either arm, and the ancient pulpit-cloth of purple velvet handsomely broidered with plumed angels, and the ancient cope broidered with six-winged seraphim and other devices. However, I believe that he hid them somewhere in the cellar of our house, in the hope that one day a milder Parliament would reverse this harsh and foolish judgment. The people grieved heartily when these ancient ornaments were ordered to be removed, and when they saw how the curate himself with a spud, or scurvy knife, had scraped from the plastered wall of the chancel the pictures that we had known and loved from childhood: of Saint Nicholas, who wore a tall mitre, distributing cakes and apples to little children, and of St. Nicholas dealing the heretic Arius a great whirret on the ear with his fist. They muttered that good luck had left the town for ever; but they could do nothing, for it was too late and Parliament not to be gainsaid. Then the Church officers came to view the Church and presently certified that the thing was done according to order and all relics of superstition removed.

The Reverend Proctor always climbed up into the pulpit holding a long roll of paper in his fist, the other end resting upon his right shoulder, as it might be an axe. He gave out his text in a resolute voice, twice over, sawing it off like a log from the massy trunk of Scripture and, after he had glowered awhile at the pews and benches, addressed himself to the task of splitting it with his axe. Sometimes the wood proved soft or of a straight grain, so that with one or two little taps he would soon reduce it to billet-wood; but sometimes it was knotted and twisted and he must scheme and writhe and struggle and sweat, using a beetle and twenty wedges to rive it apart into consumable pieces.

I remember how once he told us: "My brethren, here is a fine sweet discovery, that I have found in the three-and-twentieth chapter of the Gospel according to Saint Luke, the eight-and-twentieth verse: *Weep not for me, but weep for yourselves.* See now how easily these eight words may be divided: our text falls apart, it falls apart, I say, as easily as a Valencia orange, into eight several divisions, or little pigs as the children call 'em.

1. Weep not.
2. But weep.
3. Weep not, but weep.
4. Weep for me.
5. For yourselves.
6. For me, for yourselves.
7. Weep not for me.
8. But weep for yourselves.

These eight headings are like the points upon the mariner's compass, the four cardinal points and the four intermediate points. Now to begin from *Due North,* that is to say from 'Weep not.' Here the Lord plainly commands us not to weep. Who are we to gainsay or disobey Him? Yet may we humbly inquire whether His injunction is conveyed to our inward spiritual eye or to our outward carnal eye, or whether to both? My brethren, when I come to *North by East* I shall have somewhat to tell you upon this score. But in the meantime, listen how the Lord commands you to weep not, to restrain the fountains of grief (if only for an instant of time) that, weeping not, as children startled in the midst of their grief, ye may the better give ear to His words of terror and judgment. . . ." And so he would continue, splitting his fine ash log into slivers which he gathered up at the end, winding them together with a cord and heaving them upon his shoulder. The people called him Woodman Luke.

He had that horrible habit, when he prayed, of rolling his eyes inward so that the pupils vanished, which is called "hoisting the white"; and he pronounced words strangely in the new Presbyterial manner,

with "Aymen" for "Amen" and "glaurious" for "glorious" and "the
Laud's murcy" for "the Lord's mercy". He always preached with an
hour-glass on the pulpit ledge beside him until all the sand was
through. One day, being the feast of All Hallows, he would have
turned the glass about again and preached a second hour, but my
father cried out from his seat: "Sir, I smell a stink of burning. I pray
you, excuse me!" All the congregation ran out after him in fear, leaving
the preacher in the pulpit, preaching still.

Then Goodman Mathadee asked my father: "Your Worship, did you
indeed smell burning?"

"Ay, neighbour," said my father. "I smelt the little veal pasties burning in the oven of our bakehouse. Ten minutes more of the sermon and
they would have been cinders."

CHAPTER SEVEN

A Strange Tale of Sympathy

ABOUT this same time, the Scottish and English armies being again disbanded, Mun, who had been a captain of the garrison at York, went home to his father's house at Claydon; and late in the afternoon on the second day of November, he rode over in the company of our neighbour Sir Thomas Gardiner the Younger. Sir Thomas came upon some business which concerned lands, lying near to ours at Wheatley, which had been bought by his father, the Recorder of London; as also to desire our good wishes upon his betrothal to Mun's little sister Cary. I expected that it would again be otherwise between Mun and me than at our former meeting, for between-whiles I was grown into a woman, being equal in age with Cary, who was already counted marriageable; besides, I had greatly improved my person and manners and address, and sharpened my wit. Yet how marvellously far otherwise our meeting would be, I could never have imagined.

We sat down that day to a good supper, fifteen or sixteen of us at one board, with two green-geese-pies before us and three excellent hare-pies (prepared with butter that had been clarified, and strong red claret sauce, and onions quartered and thick lardons of lard) and, besides, for those who were of good appetite, a well-dressed Spanish salad of cold roasted turkey, sliced thin, with lettuce, rocket and tender ciboules.

The discourse turned upon some experiments of our friend Sir Kenelm Digby, in the matter of curing of wounds by sympathy. Sir Kenelm held that if a powder of his own invention, which was compounded of Roman vitriol and other elements, were applied, not to the wound itself—being too igneous—but to a handkerchief or garment dipped in the blood of the wound, or to the weapon that had caused it, then the wound would presently heal by sympathy, though the man were thirty miles distant. Sir Thomas Gardiner drolled jocularly at the

notion, but Mun, who had become learned enough from his reading in
Utrecht University, asked why such a cure should be held impossible?
Pliny the Roman philosopher, said he, had used this word "sympathy"
to stand for the fellow-feeling or amity that is natural not only between the body and the soul (so that, if one suffers above the ordinary, the other will suffer likewise), but between inanimate things, for
example between the magnet and iron, or between amber when it is
rubbed and wood ash.

James then said his say, how that there can be sympathy also between animate and inanimate things, as between crabs and the moon;
which point was much debated by Sir Thomas and my father.

Mun was thereby encouraged, though shy of airing his knowledge
in company, to touch upon a sort of echo called a bombus. I found a
world of difference between his hesitant, modest explication of the nature of echoes and the stern lecture upon the same subject that I had
once heard from the lips of Mr. Tiresias at Woodstock Town End.
Mun's theme was of the perception that resides in otherwise senseless
and inanimate bodies; thus, some seats in churches and chapels are
thrillingly affected with certain notes of the organ and some by others;
there are arches (as that in the gate-house of Brazen Nose College)
which answer to particular notes—this echo is called a "bombus." He
also spoke of the blue turquoise that turns pale if the wearer fall sick,
and of the pearl that loses its lustre if the woman grow melancholic
who wears it.

Here my mother who, in common with all the Moultons, cared not a
fico what she said, nor in what company, cried: "Why, damn my soul,
Captain Verney, the power of sympathy is known to every housewife.
How does she protect her poultry against the fox, but by giving 'em
the lungs or lights of a fox to eat? For thus they cry cousins with the
fox, who sympathizes with them and will not eat them, be he never so
hungry. And if a naughty serving-man dare to let down his breeches
outside the kitchen door, as unwilling to run out to the house of ease-
ment, because of the dark or the rain, why then in the morning—if
none confess the fault—we touch the nuisance with a red-hot spit and,
by God, you would laugh to see with what a sudden shriek the guilty
man claps his hand behind him!"

When the laughter had a little subsided, my father told of a strange
experiment made by Taliacotius, professor of physic and surgery at
Bologna University in Italy, to the truth of which Sir Kenelm had sol-

emnly vouched. When a certain gentleman had lost a piece of his nose in a duel, and the piece could not be recovered to be clapped on again, this Doctor built him a new one, cutting a piece of flesh from the brawny part of a coachman's buttocks, and grafting it to the stump of the nose, but leaving two holes for nostrils. This supplemental nose lasted the gentleman very well and seemed firmly grafted. But one day he felt the tip of his nose quiver and then suffer a convulsion, and finally it grew numb and decayed; for the coachman had met with an accident from which he died, and the nose suffered sympathetically and died too.

However, Mun was not to be drawn off from the theme by these lewd instances, but warmed to it and in a simple and eloquent manner reasoned that husband and wife, when by the blessing given them in holy matrimony they are made one flesh, often become so united in spirit as well that (as in a case he had known) the wife sitting in an upper chamber thinks to herself: "Now, alack, I am come here without my thimble! I left it upon the shelf in the parlour, I believe"; and the husband drinking wine in the parlour starts up from the company. "By your leave, gentlemen," says he, "my wife has need of her thimble, but does not wish to break in upon our discourse—I will take it to her." And so he does.

My mother said, sneering a little, that this was indeed a good and complaisant husband and that she regretted that she was not married to one who could read her thoughts so well.

"O Nan," cried my father, "how did you know that I cannot so? Indeed, I can, but often it is not convenient to come running with your thimble, your fan, or your little gilt-leaved prayer book. Why, my dear, I was down in Oxford City, these four or five days past, and as I sauntered along the High Street, there I saw a mercer standing in the door of his shop displaying to a lady some very wonderful French velvet of cream colour with fine gold flowers upon it, at two guineas the yard only. And I heard your voice, as clear as I hear you now, saying in a coaxing voice: 'Dick, Dick, pray buy me five yards of that fine velvet: it is a great bargain at the price.' And I answered you aloud: 'Willingly, my love, had I but the money!' which astonished the mercer, and gave the lady great offence, for she thought that I addressed those words to herself."

My mother made my father pay dearly for this drollery, for she swore that she would not lie on the same bolster with him until she had the velvet in her hands, for she longed for it as a breeding woman longs for cherries, and would not be denied.

This new interruption did not stagger Mun, who ingenuously told us a tale of love at first sight. He told us how in a garden at Paris a young Catalan gentleman, who had never loved in all his life before, meeting for the first time with a young French woman who was in the same case as he, the two looked fixedly upon each other and found themselves, like the magnet and iron, drawn together so violently that, though the young woman's aunt was present in the garden, and the young man's elder brother, the two lovers immediately clipped and kissed as in a swoon and knew of nothing else but that they loved.

My mother put in her spoke again. "Fie, the wantons," she bawled out, with that huge laugh of hers. "I wager then that the young woman's aunt and the young man's brother caught the infection by sympathy (as yawns are caught at the hour of bedtime) and went off to *make the beast with two backs* among the rose-bushes. Nay, Captain Verney, if I may call you Captain, when you have no Fortune to command—this is a dangerous medicine for young girls. Come, will somebody tell us instead a true tale of natural antipathy, which would be of equal interest with its opposite."

Then James gave us an account of what he called an "antipathetical bombus": how a newly elected fellow of King's College, at Cambridge, being one day required to read the second lesson in the Chapel, began to read from St. Paul's Epistle to the Corinthians, the chapter upon Charity, but his voice was of so peculiar a sonorousness that no sooner had he begun than the stalls shrieked, the arches rumbled, the rafters groaned, the floor quaked, which put him into great fear and astonishment. He hastily tumbled the pages back, thinking doubtless that the uproar was in objection to St. Paul rather than to himself, and read instead from the parable of the vineyard; but again the same commotion was stirred, and the Master of the College comes running from his seat and cries: "In God's name, Sirrah, leave off, or the roof will leap up and fall on us again, and beat us into a hash!"

This tale Sir Thomas capped with another: about a cousin of his father's, now dead, a fine-looking man, living at Bristol, who there upon the Quay met with an Irish woman of conspicuous beauty; who, upon their first sight of each other, fell into such a sudden causeless and single hatred that nothing would serve them but they should marry, and thus each be in a condition to provoke and torment the other perpetually; and married they were within the month.

My brother Richard asked, what came of the match? Were they long in one house together?

"For three-and-sixty-years," says Sir Thomas, "and neither was he ever faithless to her, nor did she ever wrong his bed—she, because she wished to give him no occasion for a separation, lest, with herself away, he might be merry with other women; and he because he knew well that every night spent under the same coverlet with him she accounted perfect misery. The greatest trouble for this antipathetical couple was that they had many tastes in common, and opinions too: indeed, they could find no grand point of disagreement, either in fashion or in religion or in the management of the estate, upon which either might take a stand; and neither would ever appear before the other but smiling and self-possessed; they were like practised duellists, or great sovereigns at enmity. He died the first and she wept inconsolably, to think that he was escaped out of her hands, and survived but for two days more. They were buried at the one time and their numerous progeny mourned them as the honestest couple in Bristol."

"To be sure, love and hate may often be confounded, the one with the other," says my brother James, "especially by persons of a sensual nature. I mean this: that just as it would be hard to declare certainly whether that bombus of King's College Chapel were a sympathetic or antipathetic one—whether the fabric of the building groaned for joy or for loathing when the Fellow read—so it is sometimes a case of *odi atque amo* between two persons caught in a mutual flame of passion."

"Well said, James," cried my mother, who had taken a cup or two of mead beyond what was ordinary with her, "for despite our immortal souls, what are we corporeally but beasts? Look out into the farmyard: when Goodman Chantecler seeks out Goodwife Partlet and treads her, does he slobber her with kisses first, or does he tear at her head with his beak? And my Lord Tom Cat, when he comes wooing my Lady Tib Cat, what a song of hatred, what scratches, what bites and scuffles! Look not abashed, daughters! As Eve was my grandam, so also was she your great-grandam; and as men have four legs by nature, so also have women. It matters not greatly whom any of you may take for your husband, since all flesh is but flesh, and since sympathy and antipathy have, by Sir Thomas's logic, been proved equals;

only be sure that the gentleman can show you a good estate and is clear of debts and of the pox, and has honour enough to prefer a stroke with the sword to a buffet with the fist. And if he comes drunk to bed, why, so much the better! Especially avoid deboshed third sons and cashiered captains, I speak to *you*, Zara"—for my sister Zara was making great eyes at Mun, so that I glowered with rage—"for when you have married such a one you will lie sick one day in a Westminster garret, with a pack of lousy brats tugging at your skirts and crying 'bread, bread,' while mounseer your husband ruffles it at the tavern around the corner, and dices away your silver pap-spoon and your lace apron."

Mun laughed pleasantly at my mother's raillery, but said: "Madam, surely you will not deny me whatever sympathy may flow to me from any one of your household? Cashiered captain I may be, but I am promised a company in the troops that are sailing to Ireland in a little while. Who knows but what I may one day be preferred to high rank and find myself indifferent rich?"

"Put this sympathy to the trial, then, my bold warrior," cried my father. "Come, now—think steadfastly upon some single object, and let us see whether there be a woman here will sympathize and hit upon the same thing."

"Allow me half a minute only," said Mun, "and I will be ready. . . . Now, gentlewomen, do your best by me, for I have thought upon something. Tell me, each in turn, what is in my mind."

My mother guessed a string of Bologna sausages; my she-cousin Archdale guessed an Irish wolf-hound, my sister Zara guessed a weeping willow, my sister Ann a white cloud; and when my turn came the words leaped into my mouth almost against my will: "It is the bolt on the Church door."

Mun startled when I said this, but told us with an affectation of sorrow that we were all antipathetical to him, for none of us had guessed aright: he was thinking, he said, upon a pious book which his brother Ralph had sent out to him to his leaguer in Flanders, and which he had studied at York a few months since—it was called *The Four Best Things*, but the author's name, he said, was no matter.

I had the prudence to keep silence, but my heart leaped within me. As I knew well, Mr. Bolton was the author of this book and clearly the name "Bolton" had been thrown from his mind into my own, and there displayed in a rebus, or riddling picture, as a *bolt on* the church door; and that this was so Mun himself evidently knew, for he had glozed over the author's name.

The conversation continued for a while longer as it had begun, my mother very ribald, Sir Thomas facetious, Mun courteous, my father light-hearted, James grave, Richard dull; and so we came to our dessert, which in autumn was often the best course of the meal, with Royal Windsor pears, medlars, Green-hastings apples, Kentish pippins, walnuts, filberts, marchpane comfits, conserves of quince and damson (moulded into little figures of men and beasts) and sweet wines of Greece and Portugal.

Suddenly there blew a bitter cold draught from the West. For the Clerk of the Peace came running in, with a hasty reverence to the company and, upon my father sharply asking him his business, he cried out: "Oh, your Worship, there are come from London with the post very woeful and heavy tidings from Ireland!"

"Ireland!" cried my father. "What in the Devil's name is Ireland to me? I have no moneys there, nor land, nor any kindred but some cousins of my mother whom I never saw. What care I for Ireland? No, Sirrah, had you told me that the least thing was amiss in the Dominion of Wales . . ."

But my mother bade the Clerk to speak up and not heed his Worship's raillery. Then he told us what he knew, that the Irish papists, upon the instigation of one Rory O'More, having sworn a solemn covenant and protested both their faithful allegiance to King Charles and their abhorrence of his Parliament, had suddenly risen to the number of 30,000 armed men at once, and made a horrid massacre of the Scottish and English settlers among them. They were going about in great divisions, and had already possessed themselves of the whole of the Province of Ulster, and it was thought likely that by this time Dublin Castle and the Pale were also in their hands; that in short, all Ireland was lost, for there were not above two thousand foot and one thousand horse to defend Dundalk and Drogheda and the other few places that remained untaken. The Irish, to revenge themselves for past injuries, when their ancestral lands were wrested from them by the Scots and the English in the several plantations, had behaved, it was reported, in a manner almost incredibly barbarous.

The Clerk told of thousands of men, women and children in County Tyrone stripped naked and murdered—either burned alive in their plundered dwellings or forced into bogs and rivers to be drowned; in particular, of eighteen Scotch infants hanged on clothes' tenter-hooks; and one young fat Scot butchered, and candles for the altar made of his grease; and of another who had collops cut off him while he was alive and fire-coals forced into his mouth on a tongs—with equal horrors from each of the other counties of Ulster, as also from Connaught and Leinster. He went on, spewing up these black gobbets of report, until my father told him that we had heard enough for our dessert, and so dismissed him.

For about the time that one might say the Lord's Prayer there was silence at the board; and then Sir Thomas said in a tone of great resentment: "If they had not taken off the noble Earl of Strafford's head, this evil thing would never have come upon us. My Lord of Essex who was appointed in his room has never yet set foot in Ireland, and his lieutenants are men of straw."

My mother spoke tartly. "Well, Captain Verney," said she, "if you are sent into Ireland, I doubt not you will find brisker work to do there than you could undertake against the Scots. . . . However, if I make no mistake, Parliament will send those same Blue Bonnets into Ireland now, to snatch the chestnuts out of the fire for us, as Æsop's ape used the cat's paw."

My father said: "It is very ill news, which will serve to divide this country further and heap yet greater taxes upon us all."

Mun said nothing at all, save that he must return in the early morning to his father's house at Claydon, and so proceed to London for his orders and commission; and heartily wished it were not so, for he would have rejoiced to come coursing with us instead, as my father had invited him.

Not many minutes later, Mun and Sir Thomas took their leave of us. I had no occasion to speak with Mun alone, for Sir Thomas continued in his company; and yet I knew that he was drawn to me in no common manner, and knew it by all the answering signs that woman ever felt in herself when a man is fallen in love with her. I chafed within myself against my mother that she had used Mun so discourteously, and would have told him how sorry I was that he must go off to the wars again before we had spoken together apart; but I could do nothing, and therefore purposely avoided the ceremonious leave-taking at the gate, when all the household gathered to wish him good fortune and begged him to take a bloody revenge on those savage wolves of Irishmen. I hoped that Mun, when he missed me from among the rest, would know that I could not bear to be one of the general rout who waved their hands and kerchiefs to him for farewell, and that I could not trust myself to withhold my tears.

Now, this was a marvellous thing that, though he and I had exchanged no single word directly during the whole time of his visit— except when he first greeted me; and at another time when he asked me a civil question, how went the guitar music, to which I made some slight answer; and then, again, in the matter of guessing what was in his thoughts—yet, I say, it was a marvellous thing how well I knew that all his discourse upon the sympathy of souls, though addressed to my father and mother and to the company in general, was intended for me alone, because of the strange drawing together of our souls across the table.

I excused myself and went early to bed, but could not sleep, and wrote out in my book a general curse upon Papists, Presbyterians, Arminians and all other religious people, orthodox or schismatic, who these many years throughout the Continent of Europe, and now at last in our own islands, had plunged the Sword of Christ into one another's bowels. It was because of them that Mun must go off and leave me in the very instant that we had discovered our mutual love. After a while I fell into an uneasy sleep, with inexplicable dreams, and when I woke it was to hear, bim-bam! the twelve swingeing strokes of midnight borne up on a breeze from Great Tom, the bell of Christ Church, and to find Zara lying asleep at my side. I know not whether I was fully awake, but I arose quietly and put on my clothes in the half-light, and the words continually ringing in my head were "The bolt on the Church door." I felt a strong and irrational compulsion to go out into the cold air, though it froze me to the marrow, and see whether the Church door were bolted or no.

The old hound by the fire growled at me as I came down the stairs, keeping close to the wall; but I quieted him with " 'Tis I, Jowler—'tis Marie, your friend," and he came up and licked my hand in the dark. I avoided the kitchen, where the cook slept rolled in a blanket by the warm embers, and went out by the pantry door, whereof the bolts slid easily back, and so into the yard, where nobody was stirring. I walked slowly, keeping in the shadow, and out at the gate and was going towards the Church in the dim light when suddenly a screech-owl let out his terrible voice from where he roosted on the faggot-stack a few paces away. At this I leaped into the air and ran back, as though the charm were broken, and when I came to myself I was again at the pantry door.

I turned the knob quietly and pushed at the door, but it was fast; and then I pushed harder, so that it rattled again, but I could not open it, though it was an easy door even in wet weather; and presently it came to me that, while I was outdoors, someone had come after me down the stairs and drawn the bolts again. I went around to the other side of the house, and into the garden, and threw pebbles at the window of my chamber to wake Zara; but though I struck the glass fairly three or four times she did not thrust out her head.

I grew angry, and said to myself: "What do I fear? Must I run off because an owl shrieks in my ears? Nay, since I am barred out from my bed and cannot come in again, I will at least finish the business for which I came out. To the Church again, Marie, and be not afraid of owls or bats, nor of evil spirits, nor of Raw-Head-and-Bloody-Bones nor of long-legged beasts nor of any other horrible bugbear that may lurk in the churchyard at this hour among the holly bushes and the yews."

With that I fell back under the former spell, and feared nothing, and walked boldly across the yard and down the road, and there was St. Nicholas's Church, a dark shadow rising up against me. As I came nearer I could distinguish the bell-gable and the two bells hanging side by side against the sky, and I began to sing softly to myself the tag-end from the rhyme of bells, "We two, we two!"

I unlatched the wicket gate and went up the path between the hollies to the church door; and there on a bench outside sat Mun wrapped in his cloak, waiting for me patiently. He said nothing, but took me up at once into his arms; and how long we embraced I know not. When I began to shiver, so that I thought my limbs would be racked apart by the shivering, despite his close holding of me, he said: "The bolt on the church door is drawn, I find; let us come in together out of the wind," and he led me in. We went into the bell-ringers' place and I began to sing again in a sort of ecstasy, "We two, we two!"

Mun took out his tinder-box, and with it lighted a lantern that he had with him. We went into the pews and gathered some hassocks and footstools and brought them into the bell-ringers' place and made us a couch there; and Mun spread his cloak over me and we began to speak together in whispers.

This was no ordinary love-prattle, as may be imagined, because of the strangeness of our meeting, and the holiness of the place, and the brevity of the night-time yet remaining to us. Indeed, we spoke, as I remember, in a language that seemed not to be that English tongue which is shared between every John and Jane Doe in the land, but was compounded of phrases that were curious and fanciful and peculiarly our own; so that, as I believe, any eavesdropper would have mistaken us for Chinaman and Chinawoman.

We kissed and caressed often, but though my body was wholly his own he did not lie with me, as might be supposed, nor did I care whether he did so or whether he refrained, it was all one to me, being caught up in an excess of love for him that seemed to soar us beyond carnality and into perfect bliss—that bliss which perhaps is prefigured in the Scripture which says that in Heaven there is neither marriage nor giving in marriage. What was more to be wondered at, we did not speak of his going to Ireland; nor of my remaining there widowed, as it were, in Forest Hill; nor of our next meeting; nor of the sending of letters between us and how this should be contrived; nor of any such temporal matters. We spoke only of how it was between us, and how it had been these months past, and of love, and of the bells. When I asked Mun: "Mun, Mun, tell me, which are the Four Best Things?" he answered: "Why, they are Marie and Mun and Alpha and Omega! Or, to put them in their due order of time, Alpha and Mun and Marie and Omega." By this I knew that Alpha and Omega were the proper names of two bells above us, being emblems of the beginning and end of Time that enfolded my Mun and his Marie.

When the light that comes a little before dawn shone down to us from the bell-windows, and we could now see along the whole length of the ropes, we knew that it was time to be stirring. Mun sat up and said soberly in his every-day voice: "My dear, it is nearly day. If we delay longer, it may go ill with us."

"You must go out and leave me," said I, "since I cannot at present return to the house. I shall remain here until a little before breakfast-time, and then return boldly. I shall tell my mother, if she should ask me, that I rose early while Zara slept, and went to the Church; which is the truth."

He kissed me again, but neither could bear to utter a good-bye, having a double presentiment: first, that one day we should meet again, and second, that before our next meeting we must each suffer a world of sorrow. He lighted his lantern again for a minute or two (which was an error and proved our undoing) while we restored the mats and hassocks to their several places and then I went to the door and looked out. The town slept fast, and I came back and for awhile we spoke together of indifferent matters—of my sister Zara, and of his horse which he had left hoppled in a coppice a mile away, and of the cold.

Mun took a ring off his finger and looked at it awhile, but put it back again, and "Marie," said he, "we have no need to exchange keepsakes. Fail nothing by any means and there shall be no neglect in me. You know well that you have my whole heart, as I have yours."

"For a thousand years," I answered him.

"Nay, for twice so many," he said. "Setting Mun and Marie together, we have 'MM,' and this is the Latin manner of writing two thousand years. And even two millenniums are not the whole span between Alpha and Omega."

"They will serve for a short beginning of our acquaintance," I answered, laughing, and held out my hand to him, which he did not kiss, but clasped in his own, and looked steadfastly at me for a small space. Then he turned about and strode out of the church, clapping his longplumed hat upon his head.

I sat down in our pew and began to pray, if prayer it may be called, since I asked God for nothing, but only gave thanks, from the fullness of my heart. Presently I was interrupted by the sound of a horse trotting down the road in the contrary direction to that which Mun had taken; but it went past the Church and died away in the distance, so I knew that it was not Mun returning. I rose up and went into the bellringers' place again and my heart sang, "We two, we two"; and I knew that Mun's heart echoed the same on his road to Cuddesdon.

CHAPTER EIGHT

I Fall into Disgrace

Mun had ridden perhaps so far as Wheatley when I heard trudging footsteps on the path that led to the porch. I slipped out from behind the screen and knelt down in the aisle, where I determined to continue as in prayer, whoever it might be, to avoid disturbance or questioning. It was Ned, the sexton, who came past me without pausing, and went in and began pulling at a bell-rope. These were single slow strokes, and only upon the second bell, that Mun and I called Omega; by which I knew that he tolled for a death that had been reported to him in the night. I arose from my knees, and asked him who was dead, that he tolled the bell. He answered, pulling at his forelock, that it was Old Mother Catcher, down by Bayardswater, who was found drowned in the mill-pool. The bell struck so ominously upon my heart, being only a single bell, which cried "Death! Death! Death!" with a great pause between each stroke, that I ran out from the Church in a horrible agitation of heart. I had come to the wicket-gate and was opening it, to hurry homeward down the road, when a man slipped out from behind the holly bushes, where he had been lurking, and clapped his hand on my shoulder.

I cried aloud for terror, but turning about saw that it was the new curate, the Rev. Luke Proctor, clad in a torn cassock and an old woollen nightcap, and that he grasped a bill-hook in his hand.

"So it is you, Mistress Marie Powell!" said he.

"Good morning, Sir Reverence," said I, recovering my wits. "I suppose you are come here with your hook and nightcap to trim the holly bushes. Continue with your unseasonable work, and remove your hand from my shoulder, you fuddled wretch!"

But he held me the faster and asked me: "Where have you been, woman?"

I answered: "Sir, I confess I am a woman, but if you were sober you would remember your manners and not address me ungenteelly by

101

the name of woman only, as though I were a trull. But to leave that, and come to your question. I have been in the church, praying. I felt a great compunction to go thither and pray, and I found the door open and went in."

"Where is your lantern?" he asked.

"I have none," I answered. "I came without any lantern or candle."

"I saw a light shining out from the north windows not half an hour ago," he said, "as I rose up to let in the cat. I put on my apparel in haste, to see what thieves were at large in my church, and snatched up this hook, and came to the porch and listened. I heard voices within, and stood perdue in the bushes. Presently a young gallant came striding out, but when I saw his sword I durst not apprehend him, but waited until his companion should come out also. Then the sexton entered in at the gate and did not espy me in the bushes where I was. I called to him in a low, hissing voice to warn him of his danger, but being deaf he heard not. He went on into the Church and by God's grace took no harm, but began to toll the bell. Unless there be another person still within doors I shall conclude that you and the young gallant were alone together in the Church at the time when I saw the light shining."

"You may conclude what you please, Sirrah, and if you find anything disordered in the Church, or anything spoilt or stolen you will not blame me, pray: you will blame your own boozy self, who left the bolts drawn on the porch door when you let yourself out last night at the vestry door. As I have acquainted you already, if you were not too drunken to hear, I arose early from my bed and came in here to pray. The sexton found me upon my knees in the aisle, as he will tell you; and that is all that I know to your purpose."

Yet he compelled me to come back with him into the Church, threatening me with his weapon; and there he found the lantern, which Mun had forgotten, standing on a mat in the corner. He handled it and found the metal part to be still a little warm.

Then he called me a harlot and rolled his eyes, like the Turkish knight in the mumming play. He said that I had defiled the Church by using it as a stew; and that for this sin I should fry in everlasting Hell.

I was beside myself with wrath, when he spoke in this fashion. I caught up the lantern and swung it against his head; but he avoided the blow and the lantern struck against the bill-hook and was broken. He named me a frantic termagant and a Babylonian witch. The sexton was not so deaf but that he heard these horrid words: he stood still in amaze, and missed his time for tolling, but said nothing.

I ran off and came to our house and found all the doors open, and went in, and heard the bustle and clatter of breakfast coming from the hall. I met with a servant or two, who looked curiously at me, as I thought, and saluted me, but I had no speech with them and went up to my chamber again, the hour being not yet eight o'clock, to order my dress and hair. I found Zara lying awake in bed, munching biscuit.

She said to me: "Marie, your hair is in lamentable disorder! Whence do you come?"

"From the Church," I answered shortly.

"Have you been long away?" she asked in a cooing voice.

"The bell is tolling for Old Mother Catcher," I said, hoping to divert her questioning. "She was found drowned in the mill-pool. Do you think it possible that she flung herself in?"

"Why should it not be possible?" Zara answered, giggling softly. "Even it is possible that you pushed her in yourself, you nasty schemer. You have been away from this bed long enough to have drowned a dozen such old hags."

I ran to the bed, with my long-handled bone hair-brush in my hand, and would have caught her a crack on the skull with it. When she took refuge under the quilted coverlet, I thumped at her knees and elbows as well as I might through the quilting, and warned her that if she spoke another scurrilous word I should drag her out by the ears and twist her wrists till she wept for mercy. I could never manage Zara, but only by the use of threats and blows. My sister Ann, on the contrary, was a sweet child and could be ruled by kind words and kisses; Ann was two years younger than Zara.

When I had dressed myself to my satisfaction, and washed the night from my face, and put my hair into better order, I went downstairs again and came into the hall and made my curtsy, to my parents, who, to my relief, greeted me without any alteration of countenance. They were entertaining my Uncle Jones of Sandford, who had come in half a minute before me. He was telling them that he had risen very early to go on a matter of business to Beckley, hoping to catch a gentleman before he went off for the day; which business he had concluded and ridden homeward without breaking his fast, but, fainting for hunger, he had dismounted here to try his pot-luck.

After my uncle had spoken volubly upon indifferent matters, my parents answering him shortly (for at breakfast the rule with us was taciturnity and grunting), he said: "As I came riding by your house very early this morning, a little worse than a mile before I came to it, in the half-light, I almost rode down a gentleman who was walking towards me. He threw a short curse at me as I trotted on, by which I instantly knew the very man, and yet could not put a proper name to him. Now suddenly it has come to me: he was the undergraduate from Magdalen Hall whom I met here at this very table four years ago or more: the young man who was so backward in his studies, a younger son of the King's Knight-Marshal. He has grown into a hearty fine rascal since that time."

My mother pricked up her ears at this, like a hound, and "You mean young Edmund Verney?" she asked.

"Aye, that was his name," cried my Uncle Jones. "He had long dark tresses, a great nose and a melancholic look."

"Now, here's a pretty riddle!" cried my mother, giving her tongue full rein at last. "He was here yesterday in the afternoon, in young Sir Thomas Gardiner's company; but an hour after supper was ended, I mean about eight o'clock, he gave us his lugubrious farewells (for he is destined for this new war in Ireland) and rode away again to Cuddesdon with Sir Thomas."

My Uncle Jones coughed in a pensive manner and said: "Being a dissolute young spark, it may be that, after leaving you, he dismounted at the ale-house and drank and played at dice, and at last diced away all his money and his horse, too; so that when dawn came, perforce he went off on foot."

My brother James objected against this, saying: "For Captain Verney to have alighted at an ale-house, and that not of the better quality, after having supped well at our house, and to have left Sir Thomas to continue his journey alone, while he diced and drank ale with our village sots—that I find inconceivable. I dare swear that you have mistaken your man, Uncle. For I have noticed that often, when a man has been in a place, he leaves behind him a sort of phantasma, which does not walk disembodied, but fastens itself upon another man of equal size and height; so that, as I remember once, three times I thought I saw my Uncle Cyprian Archdale in a street in Westminster, and each time I was deceived, yet the fourth time it was himself in person— though I had no intelligence or belief but that he was in his house at Wheatley, whence he rarely stirs."

I had felt my face flush and my ears burn at the mention of Mun, and pushed aside my trencher of cold boiled venison and sweet pickled pears, to bury my nose in my ale-cup. But James's interpretation of what my Uncle Jones had seen passing as reasonable, I breathed freely again, for soon my Uncle Jones went crying after another fox, namely, the sad massacres in Ireland.

I muttered a silent prayer that the curate might stand sufficiently in dread of my father, who paid him his fee, not to come to him with an account of the passage between us, and that he would enjoin silence upon the sexton too: for to have called me a whore upon no evidence but his own dirty imagination was nothing for which he could expect praise or gratitude at the Manor-house. Besides, it had been by his own carelessness that the door was left unlocked and unbolted; which was a grave fault in a curate. In a word, he was as deep in the mud as I was in the mire. As for Zara, I could, I hoped, manage her. But what puzzled my wits was to know by whose hand the pantry door had been made fast after me. Likely enough, I thought, it was the cook's, who had heard the door bang in the wind and rising up from beside the fire had bolted it and returned to his slumbers. If that were so, I could heartily thank him: since but for his officious act, I should have returned again to my bed, and Mun would have waited for me in the Church porch until morning, and gone away again without a sight of me.

I asked leave to retire from the table, which was granted, and ran upstairs again, just as Zara came down. In a low voice I threatened her that if she told anyone, whomsoever, that I had been out betimes praying in Church, I would strangle her that night as she slept; for I wished nobody to know that I was inclined to thoughts of salvation and godliness.

Zara gazed impudently back at me and, says she: "I shall tell whom I please, for if you are indeed regenerate in spirit you will be bold in the Lord and openly confess your new faith, and you will also forgive me, whatever I may do against you; and, as for strangling me, how can you hope for salvation if you become the murderess of your own sister?"

"That is nobody's business but my own," I answered. "Mind your tongue to-day, Zara, or it will sentence your throat to be squeezed to death to-night."

With that we parted, and I went out to my accustomed tasks in the fowl-house and the upper dairy-house.

At eleven o'clock Trunco sought me out in the dairy-house. I could see that she had been weeping and the skin about one eye was bruised; and in a great affright she cried, gasping: "Oh, my darling child, Madam your mother commands you instantly to the little parlour."

"Why, what is amiss, dear Trunco?" I asked.

She answered me: "His Reverence, Sir Luke the Woodman, has come to your father in the little parlour with a complaint against you —I know not what, but he carried a broken lantern in his hand, and Ned the Sexton lagged behind him, brought along in evidence, I suppose. I dared not listen at the keyhole, for the bailiff was waiting outside to speak to his Worship your father; but I saw to it that he did not listen, neither, and presently he went off. And then his Worship called for your mother, who came out from the kitchen, and I heard a great sound of altercation within doors, with your mother's voice prevailing; and then Madam your mother bursts out and bawls for your sister Zara, who comes running; and then I heard a greater sound of altercation, with the sound of blows and Zara setting up a screech, and then the Curate's voice roaring out rhetorications and prevailing. After this, Madam your mother comes out once more, distracted and passionate, and spies me lurking in a doorway and runs at me with her fists, and strikes me in the eye, accusing me of eavesdropping; and sends me to seek out 'that brazen little bitch-fox, my daughter Marie.'"

I wiped my arms and hands clean of the whey and took off my apron and folded it neatly, as I meditated what I should say. Then I went out, in no haste, with Trunco blubbering at my heels. Well, I had no sin on my conscience and feared no person living, not even my mother, though I might expect so great a drubbing from her with a holly-stick as I had never before felt. As I went across the hall and came towards the door of the little parlour, I seemed to hear Mun's voice speaking low in my ear, and saying: "We two, my love, we two! Alpha and Mun and Marie and Omega. There is nothing can hurt or harm us while we are conjoined in spirit and commune, we two together."

This voice refreshed me wonderfully. I drew a deep, sighing breath, pushed open the door and went in.

My mother was the first to speak. It was a wonderful surprise to me, after what Trunco had told me and what I had feared, that she addressed me so sweetly and lovingly. I soon understood that, however

wroth against me she might be, it was her evident duty as a mother
to defend me against all accusers as a spotless innocent, even had I
been caught in the very act. For, however it may be in other countries
—I know not—a spoilt virgin is not accepted in marriage by any gentleman of Oxfordshire; no, not though a great fortune be offered for
dowry, will he accept her.

My mother laughed a little, though it were a forced laugh, and says
she: "Marie, my she-darling, here's our new man of God has come to
your father with an absurd, far-fetched tale and dares stand and call
you whore!"

This emboldened me to answer, pat: "The two elders in the scripture
accused Susanna of the same fault and, as it proved, with as little
truth. I am not much astonished that this rogue is bare-faced enough
to come to you with the tale after the passionate manner in which he
used me this morning early. Madam, I was charitable enough to bring
no complaint against him, but since he seeks to shield himself by
making false accusations, then I must tell you how it was. Waking beyond my custom early this morning, I felt strangely drawn to go towards the Church. I pulled on my clothes and went downstairs and
out into the yard; and coming to the Church I found the porch door
unlocked and unbolted, and went in to pray. In what manner I prayed
is between my Maker and myself, and I know not how long I was
there; but presently one comes in, who was Ned the Sexton here, and
began tolling his bell for a death. I continued praying the more fervently, but then a rider went down the road and passed with a clatter,
who I suppose was my Uncle Jones; and this broke the spell of my
devotion. I rose up and asked Ned for whom he tolled, and he answered, 'For Mother Catcher who was found drowned in Bayardswater.' This cut me to the heart and I went running from the church
and came to the gate. There his reverence your curate, lurking in the
bushes like a cut-purse and clad in a very unseemly fashion, caught
me by the shoulder and threatened me with his bill-hook, mouthed a
few drunken words at me, called me harlot and dragged me by my
arm into the Church. Then he took up his lantern and thrust it at me—
I know not why—and grimaced and said that it was yet warm. Then
he called me Babylonian witch, as honest Ned here will agree; and I
was so affrighted, judging him to be stark mad, that I swung at him
with the lantern and ran off."

"Aye, Dick," says my mother, "your St. Luke is a very sorry rascal,

I believe. I counselled you against sending away our good John Fulker, who served you well and faithfully for fourteen years and was beloved of the whole parish."

Then the curate broke out with: " 'John Fulker, John Fulker,' says she! An acknowledged adulterer, an ale-house haunter, a wolf in shepherd's smock, a prelatical poison, a touch-me-and-die fungus, a Pope's lap-dog, a stink! He who in one of his sermons publicly wished that every knee which would not bow at the name of Jesus might ache sciatically! Your Worship, this daughter of yours vaunts herself as a chaste Susanna; but Susanna was proved innocent of the accusation made against her by the elders because they contradicted each other in their testimony. Here the matter is altogether another-gates. For I, with these two eyes of mine, just before dawn, saw a lantern shining through the north windows of our Church; and rose hastily and waited in the bushes, and heard voices within. Presently out comes a young gallant with a drawn sword in his hand, swearing horribly; whom I let go by, being myself armed only with a hook, and he takes the road to Wheatley. Then Ned comes by and goes up into the Church and begins tolling the bell, and I wait behind the bushes, and then out comes your daughter, running with her dress disordered, and I catch at her civilly, and she gives me filthy abuse. What is this, Madam, but plain chambering and wantonness? And has not your second daughter, Mistress Zara, declared without any prompting from me that she awoke at the noise of stones thrown at the chamber window, a little after midnight, and that she heard a man say something in a low pleading voice, and that then she slept again, but woke once more about dawn and found her sister gone from the bed?"

This was good news to me. I understood at once at what door the wind blew. It was evident that my deceitful sister had feigned to be sleeping when I went out, and had come downstairs softly after me; and that it was she who, for a prank, had bolted me out; and that now she had lied to save herself from a drubbing.

"Zara often has strange fancies in the night," said I, "and I can swear before Almighty God that no gallant threw stones or pebbles at my window last night, unless when I was sleeping. Now then, in despite of these accusations, to prove myself a very Susanna—though indeed she had a handsome young lawyer to plead for her and confound the Elders in cross-examination, whereas I must undertake my own cause —now, tell me this! If I am accused to have arisen shortly after midnight because, forsooth, someone threw stones at my window, then how is it that the door by which I went out bolted itself behind me, or that the shutters locked themselves again? For I believe that if you question the servants you will not find any of them hardy enough to swear that they found the house so ill-guarded with bolts and shutters as our Church now is, since this man became our curate."

Here my father nodded his head to mark his approval, and said: "Mark that, Mr. Proctor, mark that well!"

This encouraged me to greater boldness. Hitherto, I had told no lies, though I had omitted a great deal of the truth; but now that the two witnesses had lied—Zara in the matter of the man's voice, and the curate when he covered up and excused his cowardice with a ridiculous tale of Mun's coming out of the Church with a drawn sword and horrible oaths, and when he pretended that my dress was disordered —well, now I felt myself absolved from tedious truthfulness. I said to my father: "Yes, indeed, sir, I rose up very early and heard from the kitchen the noise of the fire being blown up, and I found the yard door open by which the cook, so soon as he rises, lets the hounds run out to ease themselves; else, how could I have gone undiscovered, unless I leaped head foremost from my window in the dark?"

This defence was too strong for the Reverend Proctor to pierce, yet he asked me how the lantern came to be in the Church.

I pressed my advantage with: "That, Sirrah, is for you to answer, not me. If you keep the Church door unlocked all night, you may expect to find the chalice and vestments stolen, with old iron and rags left in their place. As for the disorder of my dress, why, you churl, you rumpled and tore at it yourself in your rude struggles with me! The Rev. Fulker may have been an ale-house haunter, but that was a sociable fault in him and a world better than drinking solitary, as you do, at your villainous brandy wine and other strong waters."

Then my father very judiciously dismissed me, lest I spoilt my case by saying a word more. I know not what phrases he used to the curate, but certain it is that he reproved him in a grave manner for his negligence in the matter of the Church door, and for his drunken and violent behaviour towards me; and hoped that he would walk more warily in future, for otherwise he would find himself without a cure of souls.

My mother then began railing violently at the curate, but my father rebuked her and desired her to be no less charitable than I, though he had wickedly slandered innocence itself. However, she threatened

him the more violently, and would not cease until my father had
screwed a promise out of him to say nothing at all upon the matter to
any living soul, except to deny what he might already have said; and
Ned, who had stood blinking all this while, and turning his hat round
in his hands, gave the same undertaking.

My mother and my father understood each other very well, and
played their parts in this comedy off-hand without either prompting
the other. Both knew that there was no smoke without fire, and that
they would be unwise to dismiss the curate, for if they did he would
take his complaint to my Uncle Jones of Sandford, who had recommended him to my father, and who was the very man who had met
Mun in the road. Were his tale and the curate's put together they
would meet in a dovetail joint; and then it would go very ill with us all.

I knew that when my mother spoke privately to me again she would
not smile and call me her she-darling, nor presume with such confidence upon my chastity; and so it was. After dinner she took me up
into her own chamber and locked the door after her, and said to me:
"Marie, you are a shrewd lawyer and, I confess, I did not give you
credit for such slippery tricks as you showed the curate: ay, you took
him down handsomely, my bold girl! Nevertheless, you are a plain
whore, as you well know, and as I well know, and as your father well
knows. My meaning is, that however subtly you may have contrived
your exit from this house last night, yet you lay all night in fornication
with young Verney on the floor of the Church. You have spoilt your
maidenhead, I say, and unless God be kinder to you than you deserve,
you will in nine months' time breed us a bastard, to your utter ruin.
In the meanwhile, I intend to give you the fiercest beating that ever I
gave you, or gave anyone else, in all my life!"

When she waited for me to speak, I looked her between the eyes and
answered her: "Madam, you are my mother, and for that reason only
I do not scratch out your eyes for this idle accusation. I did not for-
nicate with Captain Verney last night, nor with any other man, nor
have I lost my maidenhead, thank God; but I am as chaste as our little
Betty—and this I will swear to you by the most sacred oath you please
to put into my mouth. As for the castigation you have promised me, go
about it, if you please, madam; but remember that when I come
weeping and bleeding from this chamber, and when the household
sees what a rage and resentment possesses you against me, it will be

thought I am indeed the whore you name me; and if I am everywhere called whore, why, you will be called bawd, conformably."

That struck home, and she said: "Upon my soul, King Harry did very ill when he dissolved the nunneries hereabouts! If there were yet nuns at Minchin Court, my daughter, we should soon find a close cell that would hold you, and a scourge for your mortification, I dare undertake. But, alas, what may a mother do now who has a spoilt virgin on her hands?—pray tell me that! No gentleman will marry such an one, and she gives the house and her sisters an ill reputation. Marie, you have undone us all!"

"I am no spoilt virgin, I tell you," cried I in sincere indignation. "And, lest you should ask me any further unnecessary questions, I am ready to take my oath upon the Scriptures, first, that no gentleman with a drawn sword in his hand came out of the Church while I was yet in it; second, that Zara lies if she says that any man threw stones at our chamber window; third, that I had no letter nor other message from Captain Verney before he came to our house yesterday, nor exchanged any words with him while he was in our house, but what you yourself heard; fourth, that I rose up early and went to the Church upon a spiritual compunction only, not by any agreement with Captain Verney or with any other man—and so I could go on, splitting my text (from the *Book of Susanna*) into one hundred, forty and four slivers, as confidently as ever Woodman Luke splits his."

At this I burst into tears like an infant and cried: "Indeed, Mammy, 'tis true, 'tis true; believe me, I do not lie to you."

My mother took pity on me, and though she guessed that there was something that I yet hid from her, she knew at least that the Curate had been mistaken in calling me whore. She kissed me and stroked my head and at last told me to go about my business as though nothing untoward had happened; and she undertook to treat me as cheerfully and lovingly as before, and said we must then hope that tongues would soon cease wagging.

So I dried my tears and wiped my nose and thanked her dutifully, and curtseyed, and left her.

However, though my mother was true to her promise and showed, in public at least, a greater love and affection towards me than ever before, I was soon made aware by the looks that the servants cast my way in the house, and that the townsmen gave me when I walked down the street, that the slander against me had gone the rounds. I believe that the Curate had emboldened himself for his complaint to my father by a dram or two of strong drink and a consultation with two or three parishioners of his confidence; and afterwards there was no recalling the tale he told them, for it spread like fire through a barley field. For my part, I cared not what was spoken of me, for I felt sufficiently rich in Mun's love to laugh at sour looks and whispered slanders; but I was grieved for my mother and father that they had suffered by my imprudence.

The village came to Church in a great expectancy on the Sunday following, believing that the curate would withhold the Communion cup from me when it came to my turn; but they were disappointed in this, for the curate offered it to me in a gracious manner, and I could see that he was in anxiety.

One day, in the week before Christmas, James met with young Mr. Ropier (the same who had ill-treated the fiddler) as he rode out from the gates of Sir Timothy Tyrrell's house, where he was a guest. James saluted him civilly; but young Ropier, hardly slackening his pace, said to him with a sneer, "I hear that your mother now chains your hot sister Marie to the bedpost every night with a padlock!"

He was riding on, but James turned his mare about and spurred her sides and coming after young Ropier, caught him by the collar and hauled him out of the saddle upon the hard road. Then, dismounting, he picked him up and set him upon his feet and gave him a buffet on the ear and cried: "Now draw your sword, you rogue, and I'll draw mine."

Yet nothing came of that, neither, for when young Ropier looked about him and saw that nobody had observed the quarrel, he declared that he scorned to fight with a little boy; upon which James kicked him for an abject knave and struck him another buffet (which broke a tooth for him) and remounted and rode off. James was honest enough to tell nobody of the encounter, but me only; and young Ropier held his tongue for shame.

That was not a gay Christmas for England generally. The weather was tempestuous, with much snow and severe frosts. The plague that had raged in London throughout the year now slew two or three hundred persons each week. The quarrel between King Charles and the Parliament had grown so bitter that on St. Stephen's Day there was bloodshed in the streets of Westminster, the King's officers running out with their naked swords against the riotous rabble of citizens and blue-aproned apprentices.

For me particularly, Christmas was a very sorry, mirthless time. I did what I might, in the way of forced gaiety, to show that I cared not for whispers and glances and petty slights and insinuations; but I could not have missed them except I had been both deaf and blind. I shall make no detailed account of these trifling pricks and pinches, for my soul loathes to dwell upon such mean things. Yet because of them I began to wish that Mun and I had exchanged keepsakes, after all, or that I had some evidence which I could touch and handle in proof to myself that our loving discourse together, under the bells, had not been a fantasy of my sick brain.

What galled me was that I could not know for certain where Mun might be, whether still in England, or crossed over to Ireland; yet I felt a suspense in my thoughts of him, which argued him still on this side of the water. This afterwards I found to be true: for he was wind-bound at Westchester until Christmas, when he sailed thence with his company, and in the New Year of 1642 came safe to Dublin.

CHAPTER NINE

An Account of Mr. John Milton

T HE New Year opened in a manner no less ominous than that wherein the Old Year had closed. The King was beside himself with vexation against Parliament, which had proceeded against twelve bishops on a charge of high treason and had packed them off to prison as companions in misery to Archbishop Laud, who was already fast by the heels; so that only six bishops were now left at large, and our own Bishop Skinner not among them. His Majesty would yield in almost anything, except in this one matter of suffering his bishops to be shorn of their temporal power; and two days before my sixteenth birthday, that is to say on January 4th, 1642, he could not restrain his passion, but came striding into the House of Commons, which was in session in the Chapel of St. Stephen's, with a band of about four hundred armed men behind him; and these attempted to seize five members, among them Mr. John Pym, leader of the Country Party, and Esquire John Hampden, a relative of Sir John Pye and the richest gentleman in all England, whom he roundly called traitors. This entry was a grave abuse of ancient privilege, and besides it was ill managed, for the members had timely warning of his project. His Majesty, looking around the House, saw, as he said, that his birds had flown, and withdrew after making a poor, slight apology.

These were busy days in the printing-houses, pamphlet-warfare being very hot on the battle-ground of "Bishop or No Bishop"; which since the King had taken his stand firmly upon the side of the Bishops, opened upon a second and wider ground, which was "Court or Country," "King or Parliament." But as yet the fight was openly fought upon the narrower ground only. My brother Richard one day brought up from Oxford a budget of pamphlets written upon the King's side of the prelatical question—seven of them sewn up in a single cover and entitled: "Certain Brief Treatises, written by Diverse Learned Men Concerning the Ancient and Modern Government of the Church." I confess I did not read the book then, nor have I read it since, but it occasioned a deal of sharp disputation in our house, my father and my brother Richard holding that the pamphlets, which were written with greater moderation than most, were conclusive and not to be gain-said; my Uncle Jones and the curate finding fault with them, as tending to idolatry; my mother holding them to be (as she said) not idolatrous enough to content her. My mother was a common Protestant, which she held to be a virtuous medium between Papist and Puritan. The Moultons and Archdales had left popery only because it grew out of fashion (like balloon hats and great starch ruffs) and in their hearts still inclined that way.

At last, one day in January, my Uncle Jones rode over to see us and threw down a thin pamphlet upon the table in the hall. He was old-gamester enough to cry: "Here's a plain trump will take all your best coat-cards." My father happened to be away on business at Thame, and besides Richard there was no other man present but only a little chuckling, plump-cheeked, slow-moving clergyman, named the Reverend Robert Pory, whom Richard had brought to the house. My Uncle declared this pamphlet to be angelically written, and read out extracts from it to us in his rolling voice. It was titled *The Reason of Church Government Urged against Prelaty*.

The author argued in favour of a Presbyterial discipline for the Church, like that in use among the Scots, and rejected the contention that Bishops alone kept the Church free of schism—that, forsooth, if they were put down, an innumerable of heretical and independent sects would follow. He wrote that if they did indeed keep away schism, it was by bringing a chill and numbing stupidity of soul upon the people, and that with as good a plea might the Dead Palsy boast to a man that it kept him from cramps, pains and wounds and from the troublesome feeling of cold and heat. He charged also that the Irish rebellion lay at the Bishops' door, inasmuch as they had spiritually starved the native Irish, who had revenged upon English bodies the Bishops' negligence of their souls.

"This style," said Richard, when my Uncle had read out a page or two, "is choice and poetical, greatly above that used by other pamphleteers; so that the author seems like one who, though his proper art is that of a goldsmith or lapidary, has set himself to the task of forging brass field-pieces and cannot refrain from unnecessary chasing and embossing of the breech."

"Nevertheless," said my Uncle Jones, "the bullets fired from this or-

namental brass piece strike to kill. Read and see what great holes he
knocks in the arguments of Bishop Andrewes and Archbishop Usher
of Armagh. Whosoever dares to bandy argument with this young man
—for a young man he here acknowledges himself—will find his proposition racquetted back into his face."

Richard took up the book, read a little in it, and nodded sagely
once or twice. Then he thanked my Uncle and undertook to peruse
it that very night. But the Reverend Pory, catching with the tail of
his eye the name upon the title-page, cried out: "Why, upon my soul,
here's a name that I know as well almost as my own. He and I were
schoolfellows together at St. Paul's School, and went thence together
to Cambridge University, to Christ's College, where we were chamber-
fellows, and we passed in the Schools at one and the same time, and
afterwards we came to Oxford University together to be incorporated
and take our degrees there also. Since that time, our roads have di-
varicated. Ay, that will be the man, on a wager of twenty pounds to a
cracked farthing—Mr. John Milton."

My Uncle Jones was eager to learn all that the Reverend Pory could
teach him concerning this Mr. Milton; but Mr. Pory was reluctant,
declaring that he knew him too well. He said that to have been thrown
for fifteen years into close companionship with another, from childhood upwards to young manhood, and never to have quarrelled with
him and never to have conferred intimately or lovingly with him, and
(when there was a parting of their ways) not to have grieved, nor to
have written him a letter nor expected one from him, nor to have
sought him out in his house in London (though it lay but four or five
streets off from his own) and on meeting him in the street once by
chance to have gone by with no better than a civil "good day"—all this,
Mr. Pory said, argued such neutrality of affection, that he did not think
it befitted him to speak at large upon the subject of Mr. Milton, though,
for courtesy's sake, he would answer any question that were put to
him.

"Tell me first," said my Uncle Jones, is he a man of the extraordinary erudition that he here professes, or does he use the bookish
labours of another?"

Mr. Pory answered: "His nose was never out of a book, hardly, during the whole time of our acquaintance, unless he were at his music,
or fencing, or disputing in the Schools. Even at seven years old he
would always rather book it than whip a top or bowl or hoop along.

At College he would lap up a whole library with as little ado as a cat laps up a great bowlful of milk—sip, sip, sip, sip, sip, sip—rustling the pages over regularly and without pause. Greek, Dutch, Spanish, Hebrew, French—it was all sweet milk to him."

My Uncle Jones then asked: "Have you read any of his verses? He writes in the preface to the second part of this pamphlet that his mind has been hitherto wholly set upon solemn and wholesome poetry, and that he has long meditated a noble poem in the English tongue in celebration of this Island's glory: intending perhaps to leave something so well written to aftertimes that they should not willingly let die. But he considers that in the present tribulation of our Church it would be cowardly and ungrateful not to rise up and plead the cause of God and the Church against insulting enemies. And that he will now leave the calm and pleasant solitariness in which he has versified, to embark in a troubled sea of noises and hoarse disputes; and he undertakes that, when the voyage is over and our land freed again from 'this impertinent yoke of Prelaty, under whose tyrannical duncery no free and splendid wit can flourish,' he will return again to converse with his Muse."

"That is John Milton to a tittle," said the Reverend Pory. "Nay, I have read but few of his verses. There were one or two Latin poems, I remember, which he published while he was at the University—a devout elegy miserably lamenting the death of Dr. Andrewes, Bishop of Winchester, the same man indeed whose work he now disrespectfully confutes, and the other the death of Dr. Felton, Bishop of Ely, in which see lies Cambridge—for John was a valiant Prelatist in those days. Unless my memory deceives me, he wrote of them both as walking through the fields of Heaven in snow-white rochets and gilt sandals. Ay, also I remember another pretty set of verses upon the Gunpowder Plot, how Guy Fawkes and his fellow-conspirators were seduced by Satan himself to the abhorred condition of would-be regicides. It was enough to set a man's bowels quaking to read John's geographical report of the infernal regions where the plot was hatched. It had in it something of Guillaume du Bartas, I remember. Of his poems in English, I never saw but two, if I except some trifling pieces."

"What were those?" asked my Uncle.

"The first, which he showed me himself," said Mr. Pory, who spoke very slowly, "was an 'Ode upon the Morning of Christ's Nativity,' and I believe that he looked that I should fall down upon my face with admiration at his condescension in letting me be the first to read it:

for the ink was hardly dry upon the last verse. It was indeed very
smoothly and ingeniously written: a variation, as I thought, upon a
merry conceit of the Frenchman François Rabelais, who makes his
heroic lumbering ogre weep tears as large as tennis-balls when he
hears of the birth of Our Saviour. John had foraged through all the
legends of antiquity, and the Hebrew Scriptures, to pull out great,
gloomy gods to weep in a like manner; but their tears were no laughing matter to John as they had been to mad Rabelais. When I told him
cheerfully and openly: 'Why, John, you have made a very pretty and
ingenious improvement upon Rabelais' conceit of the tennis-balls,' he
was so wroth I feared he would make a tennis ball of me. Yet we were
habituated not to quarrel, and I begged his pardon, saying that I had
intended no offence and that I was no great judge of poems; he forgave me, but observed that 'If Rabelais has sharked from me my own
natural theme, using the advantage of his priority of birth, and sullied
it with his filthy French additions, savouring of the jakes or bagnio,
what is that to me? Rabelais is less than nothing and I detest him. Let
me never hear more from you of Rabelais.' "

"And after that?" asked my Uncle Jones.

"Why, after that," said the Reverend Pory, between a chuckle and a
yawn: "after that, he huddled his verses away from me in his pocket
or in drawers and could cast down his pen if ever I came into the room
while he wrote them. However, there was another piece I saw, which
was published about three years ago, in a book of *Obsequies* printed
at the University Press. At Christ's College in our time there was one
Ned King, whose father was a person of great consequence, being Secretary of State for Ireland during three reigns; and to Ned, by the
King's own mandate, was awarded a College Fellowship which fell
vacant and which John had marked down as his own. It was a sore
trial to John to see a youth five years younger than himself and his
inferior in all studies and in all accomplishments but only tennis and
horsemanship, seated above him at the Fellows' table. I should not
dare to allege that John Milton felt envy: one who considers himself,
as he did, at least the equal of any man in the world (whether actually
or potentially) cannot be stung with so ignoble a passion as envy. Yet
it is soon espied where the thorn pricks. A College Fellowship to one
of John's spirit was but a trifle, a toy, a bauble: but that this toy was
denied him which he had, in prospect, stretched out his proud hand to
accept, was not to be tolerated. There was a very scurrilous lampoon,

or *Pasquinata,* in Latin verse, written against Ned King, which was
found pinned to the buttery door; it was so sharp and well-turned that
its authorship was evident, and John won secret compliment upon it
from some of the Fellows of the Country Party who loathed that Ned,
though an affable and gracious lad, was foisted upon them by a Royal
mandate."

Richard asked: "How was this .ampoon an obsequy?"

"Nay," said Mr. Pory, "you must hear me out. The obsequy was written in English. For though Ned was a nimble tennis-player and a gallant huntsman, yet he had never learned to swim; and in a voyage to
Dublin as he sailed upon a calm sea, not above a bowshot from the
Welsh coast, his ship struck against a rock and for want of a boat
down he went with her, calmly kneeling in prayer upon the deck. Then
because he had been esteemed an ornament to our University, there
was a book made of verses composed in his memory, in the Latin,
Greek and English tongues, by a dozen or twenty poets of Cambridge.
John Milton contributed an elegy in English, which brought up the
rear of the obsequious procession. That I thought a very smooth and
elegant piece, likewise, and John had so far forgiven poor Ned King
for the crime of climbing into his chair before him and drinking off
his claret, that he lamented him in verse no less gravely and sorrowfully than if he had been his brother—or one of the aforesaid two
bishops—and strewed his laureate hearse with all manner of sweet
flowers bound in mellifluous posies. Nevertheless, unless I misjudge
him, he had not yet forgiven King Charles for that unlucky mandate
—nay, I mean not to charge John with disloyalty or treason, but that
a King should have the power to interfere with the College's choice
of Fellows and intrude his own candidate, this he resented strangely."

"I confess I am with Mr. Milton in this resentment," cried my Uncle
Jones.

So encouraged, the Reverend Pory continued in his leisurely manner: "John's animosity towards the Bishops I think I understand well
enough. Our tutor, when we first came to the College, was Mr. William
Chappell: he fell out with John, whom he called a proud rebel because John justified, by quotation, a false quantity that Mr. Chappell
thought to have found in a Latin verse of his. To this name of 'proud
rebel' John returned no answer but 'ha, ha!' spoken very mirthlessly
and sarcastically. Then Mr. Chappell caught up a ferrule, with which
he used to beat the younger scholars; and he would have thrashed

John soundly (though this was against the laws of the College, John being adult, past breeching) but that John wrested it from him after a stroke or two——"

Here he broke off, a little abashed, having let his tongue run on further than he had intended, yet chuckling still to himself. My brother Richard encouraged him to proceed with: "Nay, Sir, you tell your tale impartially, and make all as plain as the hand of a clock. Come, what happened next?"

"Well," said Mr. Pory, "John was sent away from the College for awhile, for Mr. Chappell refused to continue as his tutor, and without one John could not remain within the gates. However, he did not lose a term; another tutor was presently found for him, one Mr. Tovey, with whom he agreed better. Then Archbishop Laud chose Mr. Chappell to be Provost of Trinity College in Dublin, and made him Bishop of Ross—who became, as you know, the Archbishop's chief instrument in enforcing uniformity upon the Irish Church. This appointment, I believe, snatched from John all the former respect and awe in which he had held Prelaty; and into the same verses upon Ned King, whom he celebrated as 'Lycidas,' there sneaked, somewhat unseasonably, a few well-disguised scorns against the Bishops who mishandled their pastoral staffs and were unfaithful to their flocks. For he suspected that the Bishop of Ross had been instrumental in procuring the aforesaid Fellowship for poor Ned."

My Uncle Jones durst reprove Mr. Pory for uncharitably representing this John Milton as swayed by mean motives; but he protested that he had meant nothing amiss and that the story was forced from him by my brother Richard. Richard laughed at them both, and said he hoped that the pamphlet which my Uncle had confidently recommended as angelical were not in truth penned by a spiteful imp thirsting for revenge against a tutor who had taken a stick to his shoulders.

I had myself kept silence during this narration, being busied with my needle by the fire. Now I laid it down and, begging pardon for my interruption, took up the cudgels on Mr. Milton's behalf, for I misliked Richard's derisions and laughter. I said that I could not regard the alleged motive as mean: for if a man has experience of a particular injustice, he naturally and rightly moralizes upon it, not confusing the instrument of injustice with the authority that wields it. Let a great number of men be abused or robbed by twenty or thirty several bishops, and the moral conclusion that each man fastens upon, namely that

Prelaty is an ill form of government, is in a fair way to substantiation when their complaints are compared and added together; and if the abuses of Prelaty had been few or none, the general complaint against Bishops would never have been framed so blackly as now on all sides. "I have nothing against Bishops myself," said I, "nor against His Majesty; yet if a bishop came into this hall and began finding fault with my needlework and testily pricking and cutting me with my scissors; or if by Royal mandate my little sister Betty were preferred to me at the dinner table and given the chair nearest to the fire, which is mine—why, then, I should doubtless incline to Mr. Milton's opinion. Nobody can judge a case but from his own experience."

The Reverend Pory thanked me for my speech and presently began praising to my Uncle Jones Mr. Milton's lively humour in disputation. "I heard him at his best," he said, "in a gaudy, or festival, which was held in the Hall of the College, when he was in his twentieth year, and they elected him 'Father' or President of the day. He led the philosophical dispute, speaking on the theme 'That sportive exercises on occasion consort well with the study of Philosophy.' I must first tell you this: he was so fair and pale of countenance and delicate of hand; and so curious in his apparel, wearing new-fashioned gowns of primrose colour or sky-blue, albeit with hanging sleeves, and silk stockings of rose or crimson (against the laws of the College); and he loved his own long tresses so well—which (while he studied) he was for ever slowly combing with an ivory comb, using first the right hand and then the left—that they nicknamed him 'The Lady of Christ's.' This jest he now caught up and threw back again in their faces, asking how a Lady could become a Father? For, said he, the sage Greeks held that a woman remained always true to her sex, unless a god violated her, when the touch of his divinity made a man of her; and a man likewise remained true to his sex, unless he had the misfortune to kill a snake which (according to the Greeks again) is a spell that changes a man into a woman for a space of years, as once happened to the poet Tiresias. . . ."

When he had uttered the word "Tiresias" I did not allow him to proceed, but begged him to tell me the colour of this John Milton's hair—was it a light auburn?—were his eyes a dark grey?—were his nose and chin long?—did he pronounce his r's very hard?

"Why, that is Mr. Milton! How are you acquainted with him?"

"I am not acquainted with him," said I, smiling at him. "You may believe, if you wish, that I deduced the corporeal man from your account of his actions." At this I took my leave, allowing them to make what they could of the mystery.

The next that I heard of Mr. Milton was that there was published a confutation of a former pamphlet by him. This confutation was written by Bishop Hall of Exeter, then a prisoner in the Tower, with the help of his son. The two struck lustily together in unison, like smiths who beat upon the same piece of iron lying on their anvil; and they gave Mr. Milton the name of a "scurrilous, grim, lowering, bitter Fool" and "carping poetaster" and alleged that he had been "vomited out from Cambridge University into a suburb-sink of London which, since his coming up, had groaned under two evils—him and the Plague"; and asserted that he spent his days between the playhouse and the brothel. The authors also charged (but immediately after withdrew the charge as uncharitable) that it was from disappointed ambition, from knowing that his own head would never fit a mitre, that Mr. Milton assailed the Bishops; and that he wrote his profane and beggarly pamphlets in the hope of winning the heart of a rich anti-prelatic widow.

My brother Richard said that this warfare of words pleased him as well as any play; but that if either party thought to heal the wounds of the Church by plasters of this sort, it was a most unskilful surgery. He told me: "Yet, I warrant, your Mr. Milton will rise again from the rushes where this buffet has laid him and at the next bout cast both the Bishop and his son out at the window."

My sister Zara, who was there, asked him: "Why do you call him Marie's Mr. Milton, Brother?"

Between Richard and Zara there was the same amity as prevailed between my brother James and myself; and he answered that I, being a girl, had warmly defended a pamphlet of Mr. Milton's against the ill opinions of three gentlemen, and this was the reason. As yet Zara did not know that Mr. Tiresias and Mr. Milton were one and the same person; but now I told her, I know not why.

She opened her eyes at that and, "Aha, Marie," she said, "so you are back again worshipping at the old shrine! In truth, I never believed that your heart was set on any other than him, despite the talk in the town." Then putting herself behind Richard, for protection, she said: "No, no, that you went out like a cat to company with Captain Verney, that night when pebbles were cast at our window, I have always believed incredible. He is far too gentlemanly and nice a man ever to cast his eye upon such a fliperous coquette as yourself."

I mastered my anger very well, and answered her in an off-hand manner. "Why, my dear, I never claimed to be so fortunate. I suppose, forsooth, that observing the great eyes and lewd writhings that you offered him at supper that night, he was overtaken by an amorous itch, and that it was for you that he cast his pebbles, not for me. As for my devotion to Mr. Tiresias, or Mr. Milton, you may make of it what you will, you pert, snotty, snivelly, snaggle-toothed, unkempt little jade." With that I went out and left them standing.

Now, some believe that coincidence of thought or event comes about by blind chance, that if (for example) two persons seated at ends of the same long table both begin speaking at once (they know not why) of Cousin Tom, of whom perhaps they have not spoken nor even thought for a twelvemonth, there is no more to say than "So it chanced!" Yet I believe that there is design in this coincidence, that invariably it presages news, within a week or two at least, of this same Cousin Tom. I felt the like superstition presage in the case of John Milton, who because of the singleness of his heart and mind and because of his evident jealousy to be John Milton and no other, though he died for it, was a man who threw a long shadow before him. I concluded that since now I knew him by his own name and not by his alias, "Tiresias", I should soon meet and become acquainted with him.

In the meantime I had Mun perpetually in my thoughts, and every morning between sleeping and waking I ran over our discourse together in my mind; yet one day, when I took my vellum book and began to write down in it our words as I remembered them, they faded altogether from my mind. It was as when the features of a corpse found in an ancient leaden coffin suddenly crumble into dust, so that nothing is left to behold but a grinning death's head. Only a phrase or two I could catch and record; and thereafter, even in half-sleep, all clear sound and vision of Mun was denied me, and when I tried to conjure up his image by resolute thought, I could contrive but a blotched and partial image of him. Sometimes as I went about my work, or rode with my brothers, I had sweats and confused visions of horror, which I knew were from across the sea from Ireland, and oftentimes felt hungry and thirsty even when I had dined well. Once, when we had a Friday's dish of herrings, I could not eat of them and cried: "In God's name, herrings again! Is there no meat to be had but herrings?" Now this was the first time for a fortnight that we had eaten herrings, and my mother gazed at me as though I were mad. As I afterwards learned, it was Mun whose mouth was cloyed with the taste of herrings, which, with salt beef, was all the provision procurable in his camp. Who will deny this to be marvellous?

Sir Thomas Gardiner knew nothing of the scandalous tale that had been put about concerning Mun and me, for he was at his house in Covent Garden when the tale was new; but one day he came to Forest Hall upon some matter of business, and told us in passing that he had news of Mun in Ireland. Mun had written to him that the rebels, though outnumbering the English by ten to one, dared not give them battle, but fled to the protection of strong castles, of which they had many fit to withstand a long siege, and came out again to do mischief when our people retired. Mun asked in this letter, why did not Parliament send soldiers to Ireland? If ten thousand had been sent in the New Year, the rebels would be already vanquished; but the longer the delay, the more head they would get. Moreover, Parliament, Mun said, was the worst paymaster in the world. The soldiers were murmuring very loudly for want of pay and necessaries, for they were not bred to live upon air alone, like chameleons; and the message was passing from mouth to mouth, "No longer pipe, no longer dance." Which notwithstanding, the common soldier fought with great resolution against an enemy who showed a degree of barbarousness hardly known even among heathen.

Sir Thomas appeared grieved by this letter, for, said he, it was by no fault of his father's faction in Parliament that the troops in Ireland were so scurvily treated: it was John Pym and his damnable confederacy who would not pay the King's officers in Ireland, nor vote money for the levying of more troops to send over, unless the King yielded to Parliament his ancient power over the Militia of England. For it was pretended by Pym and his junto that if a Militia were raised to be sent to Ireland, it would first be employed by the King against the liberties of the English people; and Sir Thomas said that there were not wanting members who charged that the horrible rebellion and massacre had been plotted by the Queen with a view to this very thing. To the Earl of Pembroke, who was sent to the King, where he lay at Newmarket, to persuade him if possible to yield the power of Militia to Parliament, His Majesty had very properly replied: "No, by God, not for an hour!"

Sir Thomas, having made this recital, told us in a light manner: "I warrant there are many pretty ladies in England who grieve for Captain Mun in his present plight, to a multiplicity of whom, I believe, he writes by every packet; and I heard from my dearest Cary that her cousin Doll Leke, to whom he writes the most lovingly, looks to marry him upon his return, whether he be a beggar or no. Cary told me somewhat of a ring of Mun's hair that he had given as a keepsake, which Doll said made her heart quail a little (though it were a fault to be superstitious), for it seemed a legacy rather than a keepsake."

It can be imagined in what a sadness of heart this cast me. I knew not what to think. I could not doubt but that Mun loved me, as he had said, above every woman living; and I knew that he was speaking to the point when he declared that he and I had no need of keepsakes. I reassured myself that he and I, lying side by side together in the Church that night, had been bound by the highest of love of all, which is called Platonical, that is a communion of two souls in a love of beauty without thought of carnal fruition; yet (I asked) were we not also man and woman? Could we not expect in fairness to our mortal natures to love, one day, in a more homely and ordinary manner than the highest? Or must we admit between us only a love so ethereal and transcendent that it set Mun free to write letters to numerous young gentlewomen, yet not to me, and (if Sir Thomas were to be believed, who evidently spoke not in guile) even to give rings of his hair to a she-cousin?

This was a very troublesome and knotty point which I could not resolve, nor yet ask Mun to resolve, since I had no safe means of sending him a letter; nor would I have known how to compose one in suitable words. For the singularity of our case was that the more absolutely I prized his love for me, and he mine for him, the more abstracted it seemed from all practical and natural consequences. "To be married to Mun by the Reverend Luke Proctor," I thought, "or by any priest of the Church would be perfectly absurd—it is a paradox that I should feel that the holiness of our love was smutched by his blessing of our union. Yet can I live a maiden all my life because forsooth a man loves me too well to marry me?"

I wept all night, secretly, in a peck of puzzling doubts; yet the morning brought me neither comfort nor intelligence.

CHAPTER TEN

I Agree to Marriage

M Y PRESAGE, or presentiment (of which I wrote in the last chapter), that since the long shadow of Mr. Milton had fallen across my path he would soon appear himself in person, was justified, and in a startling manner. One morning in the first week of May, as I was going up the stairs to my chamber after breakfast, my father came up behind me, two steps at a time, and putting his arm through mine, drew me towards his study; there he put on a merry countenance and shut the door behind him and said to me: "Dear child, I believe that I have agreeable news for you."

"That would be a novelty, sir," I said, "for since some weeks past I have heard little news from yourself or from anyone else but what is extreme bad."

"That is very true," said he, sighing. "Now that His Majesty is removed to York and there defies Parliament, and draws his leading Lords and Councillors away to him from all the country over, and the Queen is sailed, as it is said, to purchase arms abroad—why, the set-to cannot be long delayed. Alas! for our poor country! Soon blood-brothers will be charging pikes and lunging with naked swords at one another so heartily that one might mistake them for Germans. Moreover, the contending parties being so evenly matched and resolute, I cannot conclude but that the war will be long and remorselessly fought. In Oxford they promise the King victory in three weeks' time, once he takes the field, but I say no! The South and the East, which are the richest and strongest parts of this Kingdom, are united against His Majesty, who cannot there command the loyalty even of the nobility; and the Scots, though they profess themselves satisfied with the accommodation lately given them by His Majesty, are treacherous dogs and study no interest but their own. I foresee that which side soever gains the mastery will govern a ruined country: as the wars of religion in Europe have made deserts of prosperous duchies and ruined whole kingdoms."

"Come, sir," said I, "now that you have given me this sad prolusion to your agreeable news, pray let me have the news itself."

He appeared uneasy when I made this request and rambled a little in his discourse, complaining again of the uncertainties of the times. Said he: "My dear, though your mother and I hold up our heads very well here among the gentry of the neighbourhood, it is hard indeed to make ends meet with so large a family, such heavy taxes, so chargeable an estate, and so little money in hand. Let me open the case to you, now that you are of a ripe age to understand and pity my vexations. The truth is, I know not to-day where to turn for money. This Manor-house and all its appurtenances, which I took from the Bromes upon a long lease, I mortgaged soon after to Mr. George Fursman (whom you know) for a loan of £1,000, to be repaid by the midsummer of two years ago; which sum I could not rake together in good time, and, Mr. Fursman growing importunate—as one would expect from a man of his quality—in my distress I turned to good Sir Robert Pye, the Elder, to whom I already owed £300, and he comforted me. He paid Mr. Fursman on my behalf in full; and thus I owe Sir Robert £1,300, with £100 more which he asked as a consideration; and he became the mortgagee instead of Mr. Fursman. I would rather, by far, owe £10 to a knight or a gentleman than £5 to a boor."

"So would I the same," I told him, "if I had no prospect of paying either of them."

My father continued: "Some years ago, also, I borrowed £400 from Mr. Edward Ashworth of Wheatley and, for his security, made over to him our freehold land there; but I fell in arrear with the interest, and just before Christmas, to prevent his entering into possession of the land and cottages, as was his right, I sold a little parcel of poor land in Wales, which was left me as a legacy and which brought me £100; and I borrowed another £300 from my cousin, Sir Edward Powell, to whom in return I assigned an under-lease of my leased land in Wheatley, for twenty-one years. So I paid Mr. Ashworth this last January, and defeated the demise; but the arrears, alas, are still unpaid."

"All this is news indeed, sir," said I, "but news that has a far from agreeable sound."

"Hear me with patience, Child," he said. "With good luck and diligence your mother and I hope to keep swimming yet, and your brothers are good boys and run me into less expense than many sons do their poor fathers, who have pinched and scraped to send them to the University and equip them for the world. However, I have not yet told you the whole tale; and while you listen to the rest of it, here is a rose-peppermint comfit to suck. Well, there was an old, old under-ranger of Shotover Forest, living in Stanton St. John, about thirty years ago; he was a Papist and a man too proud (as he said) to bow his knee in the House of Rimmon. He dared to tell the parson in his church that it was a merrier world when ministers might not marry, and that the parson's children were bastards before God; and, having said his say, he did his do. For he absented himself from the Church for three months and was fined in a sum of £60 for his recusancy; but would not make submission even then and was fined in a sum of like amount a few months later, which was a heavy loss for a yeoman worth not more than £20 a year. This man, whose name was Dick Melton, had a son whom he sent to study at Christ Church, but who was there inclined to the new religion—which was the very cause of disagreement between my own father and myself—and whom he there-upon disinherited. The son went to London and became at first, as I have heard, a clerk to a goldsmith, and then a broker and scrivener, and grew rich and lived carefully. He was something of a musician, and composed a madrigal that was sung before Queen Elizabeth, in the same year that his recusant father paid his second fine."

"Well, sir," said I, "what has this fine or this madrigal to do with you or with me?"

"Nothing," he answered. "Yet hear me out. This scrivener-musician, John Melton, lives yet, and is a harmless, sober dust-box, who has not yet lost his ears for fraudulent dealing. His old father, the recusant, claimed to be of gentle birth, alleging the worn plea that his family was undone by the wars of York and Lancaster; and the son therefore made application for a coat-of-arms to the Garter King-at-Arms, who carelessly granted it—namely, *argent*, a double-headed eagle displayed *gules*. Now, these are the arms of Mitton, a family well known in Shropshire and elsewhere; and certain it is, for the last six generations at least, that the Meltons were never Mittons, though they wrote them-selves Mylton as often as not. However, the Company of Scriveners, in London, have a double-headed eagle as the chief device in their arms, which this John Melton had long displayed as a sign over his shop in Bread Street; and therefore, I suppose, he considered that he had a lien upon it. This I tell you in all fairness, for I would not connive at

an heraldic fraud; but the fact is that the Garter King-at-Arms duly
granted, or confirmed, the Mitton arms to the son of Old Dick Melton;
and the grandson (of whom I intend to speak to you to-day) is therefore a gentleman of one descent at least, and of honest stock. There
are Meltons at Stanton and Beckley, all sturdy men, though mere
abecedarians in learning; and of good repute, though of lean purse."

I asked my father a question which startled him into confessing
what I believe he had intended to hide from me: "Sir, are you under
any great obligations to the Melton, or Mylton, or Mitton family, that
you recommend it to me so heartily? Do you owe one of them money,
perhaps?"

He sighed very heavily and, said he: "Dear Child, you draw it from
me—I do indeed. When old Dick Melton died he bequeathed certain
cottages at Wheatley to his grandson, passing the scrivener son by, to
show his continued displeasure at his religious change of coat. The grandson, another John, who had been sent to Cambridge University, but
otherwise dwelt at Horton in Buckinghamshire, sold these cottages to me
together with a parcel of land that marched with mine; which com-
binded estate I afterwards mortgaged to Mr. Ashworth as I have told
you, but he rented it to me again. The price that this grandson asked
for his cottages and land was £312, which I told him plainly I could
not pay him at once. Well, Child, since I see you have swallowed down
your comfit, I will not weary you with a more particular account of
the transaction; but the plain black and white of it is that, since I
never paid this grandson his £312, I now owe him £500, which is a
great sum, and upon statute-staple, too; this is to say, his claim over-
rides all other claims upon my lands and goods, so that he can at any
time enter into possession of my houses or lands until the payment be
made to him in coin of the realm. This dormant bond has long lain
asleep in his pocket, but at any time it may awake and begin to yawl."

"That was an extremely awkward bargain," said I with a gasp, "especially as it seems that all your other lands are already mortgaged
to other gentlemen."

He bowed his head and mumbled: "What is more, I confess that I
did not think to acquaint Sir Robert Pye with this transaction when
I went to him for help; for, if I had, I think he would not have been
so willing to grant it."

"I hope, sir," I said somewhat tartly, "that the agreeable and acceptable news will presently come hopping out, like Hope from the

box of Pandora in the tale, when all the winged Spites had already buzzed out and bitten and stung her to distraction."

I was sorry for him when I had said this, because I perceived how near to weeping he was. I took his hand and stroked it and "Come, my dear father," said I, "out with it—tell me the worst! I presume that you have a desperate notion to marry me to Mr. John Melton the Younger, as in Muscovy a father will toss his child out of the sledge to delay the pack of wolves pursuing him. Is the agreeable news merely that my mother will not oppose the match if Mr. Milton can be lured into it?"

"He is a very proper gentleman," said my poor father, speaking quickly in a low voice, as though he were a schoolboy saying his lesson by rote, "of a small but sufficient estate, and he was an ornament to his University for his eloquence; and now he is well spoken of in London as an author. I have myself read a masque which he wrote for my Lord the Earl of Bridgewater, the President of Wales, which was enacted at Ludlow Castle and commended by all the nobility of Shropshire as a wonderful fine performance. As for his prose-writings, which are four or five pamphlets upon the question of Prelaty—I confess I am not of his way of thinking, but they are shrewd pieces and well Englished. Your Uncle Jones thinks the world of them. By the by, never address him or speak of him in his hearing as Mr. Melton, for in that point he is very tender and touchy."

"Tell me, sir," I broke in. "Am I, though a woman, expected to go a-wooing this Mr. Milton, of whom I have (as it happens) heard some account from his chamber-fellow at Cambridge, the Reverend Robert Pory, or will he come to me?"

"Hearken to me, my dainty girl," he answered, smiling now: "you must not suspect me of any fraud or unkindness. John Milton sincerely loves you and came to me, as honestly as Jacob in the Scripture came to Laban, Rachel's father, to demand your hand in marriage."

I expostulated: "How should this man love me when he knows not even my name?"

"That is easily told," said he. "Your Uncle Jones went to London, a week or two ago, to present his compliments to Mr. Milton upon a little book which you will confess to have yourself seen, and found him in his commodious house in Aldersgate Street, and liked him well. It came into his mind to tell Mr. Milton how at the house of his wife's brother, Esquire Powell, there had been some disputation between his niece Marie and his nephew Richard—Richard railing against the said book, but she defending it. Mr. Milton, who had been a little unceremonious and off-hand with your Uncle Jones, then asked him sharply: 'Do you speak of Marie Powell, of Forest Hill, a young girl remarkable for the glory of her hair?' Your uncle confessed that you were the very she; and upon Mr. Milton's eagerly desiring it he spoke of you at length, and praised you. He knew from your sister Zara that you had read an English poem of Mr. Milton's and spoken of it admiringly to your brother James, though he had slighted it. What poem was that?"

"It was the Ludlow masque," I answered. "I misliked James's judgment upon it, which was a raw one."

"I think it a fine piece, mighty fine," said my father. "But to come to the matter: when Mr. Milton heard that you had admired his poem he nodded his head once or twice and cried aloud: 'Now, is this not marvellous? Is this not marvellous?' Forthwith he told your Uncle Jones that he had heard enough, and asked whether you were promised in marriage to another. Your Uncle Jones answered that he believed not, but that your mother and I were exceeding grieved at a lying, heedless report put about against you (doubtless by a certain rich young gentleman whom you had flouted when he addressed his love to you), and added that he would wager his head that you were certainly a virgin. Mr. Milton then laughed shortly with: 'Bishop Hall and that losel Bachelor of Art, his son, have made a similar scandalous report of me and put it about in print. But that to me is so much birdshot discharged against a strong tower; for my honest manner of life is known to all, and being a man I can defend my honour with a sword, if need be, or with a pen if that cut the deeper; however, for a maid to be so bespattered with filth is very hard, and I commiserate her.' "

I asked: "Did Mr. Milton, then, remember me from the day, long ago, when he saw me with the old Lady Gardiner at Woodstock Town End, and again conversing with the Queen at Enstone, where the waterworks were?"

My father answered: "Exactly, so he told me yesterday when, by appointment, we met at your Uncle Jones's house at Sandford. He said that he had heard your name from your own lips when you told it boldly to the Queen and presently, leaving French and returning to your mother tongue, you announced your descent from the ancient Prince of Wales."

"I had forgotten that particular!" said I.

"Yet he has not," said my father. "Nor has he forgotten the respectful yet easy way in which you conducted yourself with Royalty. His heart was so warmed, as he tells me, that he determined, when you were of a ripe age for marriage, to seek you out for his wife. To that end he had ridden after your coach from Enstone and observed at what house you were set off, and then inquired from the inn-keeper whose house it might be."

"Here is a strange working together of accidents," said I, "and I know not what to answer. I confess myself flattered that a gentleman of his nice discrimination should have fixed his heart and mind upon me for a wife: and I have no fault to find with his person, as I remember it. But, sir, do you not think me too young to marry? Is it well that a woman should breed children while her own bones are yet green?"

"Why, you are already past your sixteenth birthday, Marie!" said he. "My mother had borne and buried two children by the time she reached your years."

"Aye, poor soul!" I cried, "and I understand that she died in child-birth of her fifth before ever she was twenty. Hers was no fortunate life, I dare say."

"Your grandfather doted upon her," he said.

"Aye, sir, so it seems," I answered, "if filling her with untimely babes be any proof. However, Mr. Milton would perhaps treat me with civility if I pleaded with him to withhold the consummation of the marriage for a short term."

"But otherwise you will agree to it?" he asked, his face shining with joy.

"How could I otherwise, sir?" I replied. "I see that your affairs are in a difficult and almost desperate condition; and if I could save from ruin those whom I love it would be my duty to give my life, even, as a ransom; for I am no ungrateful child. In the matter of the lying report put out against me by your curate, you used me very well and have never once reproached me for my imprudence which occasioned this report; nor did you alter your countenance towards me, though the malice of my enemies made my name a by-word. Well, well, I will do what you wish, and cheerfully. I cannot undertake to love Mr. Milton, for love requires an equality of feeling which cannot be commanded; yet if he treats me well, I shall treat him well again. I have

read enough of his writings, I think, to judge what manner of man
he is, and I believe that we can fadge well together, being both proud
spirits who love liberty above all false submissiveness. Make the best
marriage bargain with him that you may (as Laban did with Jacob)
but do not tell me what you have settled. I care not for money and
will confide my affairs wholly to you. The one condition that I dare
to impose upon you is that our maid Trunco goes with me; and I cannot think that you will deny me this."

He thanked me heartily and exclaimed that he was indeed fortunate
in his children; and undertook that Trunco should continue at my side
through thick and thin. Then I asked him: "When am I to meet my
husband?"

"This very afternoon, if you wish," he answered.

"That will content me, sir," said I, "for this afternoon my mother was
to have bled me of a pint of blood and given me a strong purge to
cure my ill-humour, as she said. Perhaps that may now be excused
me."

"I undertake that it will," he said. "And see, here is a gift from your
Uncle Jones—another pamphlet, very fine (so he says), from the pen
of Mr. Milton."

As I went out of my father's study, I was overtaken by a sort of
giddiness and sat down upon a chest that stood against the wall. As
I sat, I wondered suddenly what foreign spirit had entered into me to
make me answer my father as I had done. I seemed as one who had
been bewitched into signing away her body and soul, and with no
merry compensations, neither. I cast down the book I held in my hands
and arose from the chest, and began walking back to the study. I
would tell my father that I had spoken too soon, and thoughtlessly and
foolishly; that I loved another man and that I could never love any but
him; that I had been drawn into a defence of Mr. Milton's books not
by any affectionate admiration of him but by a disputatious desire to
take the contrary side to my brothers; that, in short, I felt rather anti-
pathetically than sympathetically inclined towards the husband who
was offered to me; and that some newer means must be found to pay
old debts than yielding me to the creditor after the Turkish or Tan-
gerine manner with women.

Yet, after all, I found I had not the heart to rob my father, a poor
shipwrecked mariner, of the one plank with which he hoped to bear
up his head and keep his mouth from sea-water. Moreover, I thought

again of Doll Leke and of the ring of hair which Mun had given her;
so I shrugged up and returned again to the chest, while outside the
church bells began tolling for some holy day or other.

Then along came Trunco, and cried that Madam my mother was
seeking for me everywhere. "Why, dear Trunco," said I, "here I am
and will go to her now; but I shall not be here to be commanded for
many weeks longer."

Trunco held up her hands and cried: "Oh, Mistress Marie, you fright
me! Are you sick? 'Not for many weeks longer,' you say. That is a sorrowful way for my dear mistress to speak in the time of Spring flowers."

"Ah, Spring flowers, the Spring flowers!" I cried. "The Lord deliver
me from the deceitful primroses and violets and cowslips and cuckoo-
flowers! And I wish that those two church bells were stilled for ever,
they ring so foolishly with their 'We two, we two.'"

"Tell your Trunco what ails you," she pleaded.

"Why, nothing, Mother Smutty-Face," I answered. "Only that I am
to be married soon to Mr. John Milton of Cambridge University and
London, Esquire, a poet. Yet the affair is a secret as yet: keep it close
for my sake."

Trunco cried: "I do not know the gentleman. You have not told me
that you ever exchanged a word with any Mr. Milton."

"Nor have I," I said. "Nevertheless marry him I must."

She saw that I was in no mood to be questioned further, but began
to weep and lament loudly at the thought of my departure; but I told
her that she would come with me when I was married, for so I had
bargained with my father. Then she dried her tears and blessed the
day and wished me the greatest happiness imaginable and began cracking her fingers with joy, which was a trick of hers that always vexed
me; and I said that, one crack more and I would not take her. Then
I rose and went to seek my mother, who drew me into her private
chamber and began to enlarge in a serious manner upon the great
shame and inconveniency to her of the slanders put about against me
by our enemies. She asked me whether I was prepared to be ruled by
her and redeem my fault?

I laughed softly and said that I hoped it would not inconvenience
her yet more to know that my father, though he had clothed the matter
in another dress, had spoken to me in the same strain a few minutes
before and had urged me to marry one Mr. John Milton.

This took her aback, for it seems my father had engaged himself not to speak with me in the matter before she did, and she flew into a rage. But I calmed her very soon by saying that my father had put the case very plainly and discreetly and that I was ready to be ruled by him.

"Why, Daughter," she said. "I never credited your father with a tongue glib enough to talk you over so speedily. What arguments did he use? A child owes perfect obedience to a parent, yet had I been in your shoes I swear I would not have yielded so speedily—unless perhaps he cozened you? Did he cry up Mr. Milton to you as a man of huge wealth and noble family, and of right opinions in ecclesiastics and politics? Did he so? Did he perhaps promise you a rich jointure?"

"No, Madam," I answered. "He gave me Mr. Milton's short but sufficient pedigree; promised me the modest comfort of a house in Aldersgate Street, in London; disavowed any good opinion of Mr. Milton's writings; but told me in a nutshell that marry him I must to keep the duns away from this door. He appeared so sorrowful that rather than he should weep, I promised him to be a dutiful daughter. One condition only I made: that Trunco should go with me. For I shall be lonely without her, and if things go ill she will stand by me."

My mother clapped my shoulders: "You are a wise girl and can see what is to our common advantage. I do not know the man any better than does the Pope; but your absurd Uncle Jones gives a good report of him, and he will beget healthy children on you, I dare say, and love you well; and he seems a shrewder man with money than your poor father, at least. I will not deny that I am miserably disappointed in the match, but since you have spoilt your cake in the baking by leaving open the oven door, why now you must eat bread; and not the best white bread at that."

"And Trunco, Madam?" I asked.

"Oh, by God, yes, you may take the baggage with you!" said she.

Nothing of the projected marriage was said to my little brothers and sisters, but that afternoon my mother and I rode in the coach to Sandford, my father and my brother James going ahead on their horses. My Aunt Jones entertained us there in a little house, meagrely furnished, and without any fire on the hearth. She said that my uncle and Mr. Milton were not yet back from the quarries at Headington, where they had ridden to inspect some great bones that had been found there by the stone-hewers. While I waited I read again to myself from Mr. Milton's new book, over which I had spent an hour or two that morning. I found a passage in praise of male chastity, where it was written that "if unchastity in a woman be such a scandal and dishonour, then certainly in a man it must be much more deflowering and dishonourable." From which I could not but conclude him to be that strange thing, a he-virgin of thirty-four years old! And another passage I found, answering the taunt by Bishop Hall and his son that he was aiming to win a rich widow with his pen. He answered that whoever had written this was more ignorant in the art of divining than any gipsy: "for I care not if I tell him this much, though it be to the losing of my 'rich hopes,' as he calls them—that I think with them who, both in prudence and elegance of spirit, would choose a virgin of mean fortunes, honestly bred, before the wealthiest widow."

There was a deal more written in modest self-esteem, besides the main matter of the pamphlet, which was to abuse his adversaries, extol Parliament, rail against the dry, barren and impertinent English Liturgy then in use, and condemn the clergy in general as illiterate bunglers. I stumbled also upon this passage: "Where my morning haunts are, he wisses not. These morning haunts are where they should be, at home: not sleeping, or concocting the surfeits of an irregular feast, but up and stirring: in winter often ere the sound of any bell awake men to labour or to devotion, in summer as oft with the bird that first rouses, or not much tardier——"

"Good," said I to myself, "I hate to be the first to rise from a bed. I wonder whether he will be a kind enough husband to warm me a cup of milk in winter time, with sugar and cinnamon, to give me resolution to rise up after him?"

". . . to read good authors, or cause them to be read, till the attention be weary——"

Spelling the passage out to the company, I asked my father: "Sir, what does this mean? What monkish habits has this would-be husband of mine? Will he expect me to arise at cock-crow to read him out from a lectern the Legend of the day?"

My mother interrupted: "Nay, Child, did not your father warn you that this suitor of yours is a whip-arse or, if you will, a schoolmaster in a small way? He has two nephews and I think one or two more urchins whom he teaches. It is these, doubtless, who do the reading for him as a part of their studies."

"You have set my mind at rest, Madam," I said. "I cannot abear good authors before I have breakfasted, nor bad ones, neither." I read on aloud to the company:

"'. . . then with useful and generous labours preserving the body's health and hardiness, to render obedience to the cause of Religion and our Country's liberty, when it shall require firm hearts in sound bodies to stand and cover their stations——'

"Mr. Milton writes here as though he were perfecting himself in martial exercises," I said.

"I should not marvel at that," said my father. "The City Artillery Garden lies not far from his house, where the officers of the Trained Bands daily instruct citizens in the postures of the pike and in the several exercises of the company."

"The damned rogues," cried my mother. "They would sooner discharge their pistols against His Majesty's officers than they would against the heathen Irish!"

My Aunt Jones was about to make some warm reply, when there came the noise of horses down the street and my father, looking out at the window, told me: "My dear, here comes your husband-to-be. Be advised by me, speak little and listen well."

CHAPTER ELEVEN

Mr. Milton's Courtship

MY UNCLE JONES came into the house and saluted the company and presented Mr. Milton to us; whose apparel was again well cut though of a darker hue than that he had affected when I saw him before; and he was the same vigorous, proper man but that his hair was a little less lustrous, and the whites of his eyes not of so clear a colour. He greeted the company with an affable bow and kissed my mother's hand, but did not kiss mine when my father presented me to him; only, he looked very hard at me. Though I thought at first to return his stare boldly, yet for the sake of good manners I cast my eyes upon the floor. His words to me were: "Mistress Marie Powell, I am pleased to behold you again, and hope that presently we may become well acquainted."

The saucy answer that leaped to my lips I swallowed back and was content silently to return him a curtsey; to which he did not, however, reply with a bow, but turned briskly to my father, as it were dismissing me from a mind that was already fully taken up with other business. Said he: "Mr. Jones and I have been disputing a point upon which, I hope, sir, you will consent to give us a decision as arbiter. It concerns this scallop-shaped stone hewn from the quarry at Headington, where we have been this afternoon, and where the workmen say that *fossilia* similar to it are very often found. Mr. Jones is of opinion that it is a true shell which, having been conveyed here by the Flood in the days of the Patriarch Noah, was filled by the petrifying juices of the Earth and became in tract of time a stone. *Per contra* I hold that this stone, with others similar to it, which I have seen in the form of oyster-shells, cockles, sea-urchins and the like, are not and were never shells (as he pretends), but are *lapides sui generis,* naturally moulded by an extraordinary plastic virtue latent in the Earth of those quarries wherein they are discovered, in conscious imitation of the living creatures directly created by the hand of God."

My Uncle Jones put in his oar: "I believe, sir, that you will find nothing in the Scripture to support your ingenious but fantastical theory, which is something so remarkable that, were it true, a nook or cranny might have been found for it by Moses in his account of the Creation, or at least by some minor prophet in his inspired writings. That God created the World, and that He created the formed gems in the bowels of the Earth: and that He created all living and creeping and growing things and gave them liberty to increase and multiply and procreate after their own kind—this we certainly know. We know also that God rested upon the seventh day, when all was duly created and set in motion by His hand. But that He should have bequeathed to the insensate Earth the power to give secret birth to a second or mock Creation—that notion, sir, I find incredible and well-nigh blasphemous."

Mr. Milton blew air downwards from his fine nostrils and, said he: "That there is no precise mention made in the Scriptures of the virtue that I have already sufficiently adumbrated, need not disquiet you as a Christian. The Patriarchs and Prophets, whose genius was spiritual rather than encyclopedical, stood mum and mute upon many notable questions, especially those latterly propounded in Physics and Mathematics and Music: and whether God had distinctly vouchsafed the answers to them I think we need not now closely enquire. For is it not said generally by our Lord Jesus Christ that 'All things are possible with God?' And when that which is possible can, by shrewd and lively reasoning, be demonstrated to be not only probable, but the single inescapable *Sol* of diverse difficult *Obs*, how shall we deny it to be very truth?"

"Yet I confess, sir, I do not find your *Sol* altogether a necessary one," my Uncle Jones said, "when Noah's Flood would settle the matter for us out of hand."

Mr. Milton waved his hand with an impatient good-bye to Noah's flood. "Sir," said he, "I am not one of those carping lynxes who deny the Deluge to have been universal, and contend (forsooth) that at most it overwhelmed only the single Continent of Asia, sparing Africa and Egypt—for if Ararat were for a while submerged, how was Egypt spared, which lies low beside the Middle Sea? Nor do I presume that other notorious floods, such as the Ogygian or Deucalionian, in Greece, and that which Plato declares to have overwhelmed the Continent of Atlantis, were distinct and national deluges: nay, in faith, there was but one Flood only (whereof the tale survived imperfectly among the

Gentile authors, but was perfectly revealed to the Hebrews), in proof
of which God set that glorious and reassuring arc, the rainbow, in the
heavens. But this Universal deluge proceeded from a forty-day flood
of rain, the rushing torrents of which would have carried shells down
further into the sea, rather than drawn them up into the high places."

"You forget, sir," put in my Uncle Jones, "that the fountains of the
great deep were broken, and that the Deluge, though it began with
copious rain, proceeded partly from the over-flowing of the sea, which
naturally would cast up shells upon its uppermost strand."

"Nay, I believe I have a pretty good memory of that chapter," said
Mr. Milton with a short laugh. "I do not forget that God 'caused not
any wind to pass over the Earth till the waters began to assuage';
wherefore (as must be plain to the veriest clod) the rain raised the
height of the sea gently and commodiously; which being so, why
should I believe that such shellfish of the testaceous kind as cockles,
oysters and the like, which commonly cling to rocks and have no loco-
motion but what is afforded them by the furious movement of great
waters when they are driven by a tempest—that these (I say) being
wrenched from their customary beds and carried indiscriminately aloft
to higher ground should now—and as near to here as at Charlton-upon-
Otmoor—be found lying in beds as orderly as if these had been their
native breeding-places?"

Though Mr. Milton paused for breath after this ponderous and well-
articulated sentence, my Uncle had nothing to answer, or else he did
not wish to rouse Mr. Milton's anger and so disincline him from his
present intention towards marriage with me.

However, my brother James spoke. Said he: "Sirs, if I may be so
bold as to break in upon your disputation, I undertake to answer the
objection to the cockles. Otmoor lies not many feet above the level of
the sea, and the waters of the Deluge, subsiding in Armenian Ararat,
must have driven outwards towards the outer rim of the Earth to
whirl at last over into the great gulf; which motion must have caused
a current sufficient to roll along with it all manner of shells, stones and
fishes. Then Otmoor, which was ever a marsh, would have become for
a while a salt marsh, or lagoon, and the dissettled shellfish would have
found a home and thriven there."

Mr. Milton gazed at him, as at a schoolboy who interrupts his master's grave discourse with an impertinence, and replied disdainfully:
"Ay, boy, I warrant they were fine oysters, every whit as good as your

juicy, grass-green Colchesters! Had we fortuned to have been born in those ancient days we should have sat down on the strand where the church now is and passed a crooked oyster-knife from hand to hand, banqueting like London aldermen. Here, Sirrah, take this poor scallop as a gift, for I have no tasty Otmoor oyster by me to-day! Eat, eat! Break your teeth upon the sweet meat under the shell!"

My father laughed and applauded Mr. Milton's retort, saying: "That was indeed a choking oyster for my son, whose contentiousness I pray you will pardon. His heart is in the Oxford Schools, where every day of term he wrestles with his fellow-students of the College. This Whitsuntide vacation irks him, he would be back there again, disputing and confuting."

Mr. Milton's anger was assuaged by his triumph, and he confessed James's fault a forgivable one, saying that he himself as a youth had ever desired to break into disputes of men elder and more learned than himself; and sometimes in the Hall at Christ's College his impetuosity had overborne his modesty, and he had interjected a word or two even at the risk of being cast out of doors by the beadle. Then, pausing awhile as a victor upon the field, and raising a trophy, he advanced his colours and pressed upon the rout. "Now, Mr. Jones," said he, "I was prepared to hear you oppose an objection to what I have laid down concerning the plastic virtue of the Earth, to wit, that you find it contrary to the infinite prudence of Nature (which is observable in all natural works and productions—namely to design everything to a determinate end, and by no way or means that contradicts or runs counter to human ratiocination)—you might perhaps, I say, have fribbingly advanced it as imprudent in Nature to have elaborated these *fossilia* (which were never shells, but only stones), with all those curious figures, adornments and contrivances for which they are remarkable—as witness, for example, this pretended hinge to the stone scallop-shell—and to have elaborated them with no more reasonable end than to make a vain exhibition of pattern and form——"

"I should never have dared," cried my Uncle Jones, "to cast such a slur upon the wisdom of God, Who, as is generally confessed, enhances His marvels by inscrutability."

". . . why then," continued Mr. Milton, "if you had, I should have ground you to powder by this observation, that the wisdom and goodness of the Supreme Nature, or *Naturans,* which orders the *Natura Naturata* here below, commands not only the production of commodious and useful things, to maintain man's health, but also that of beautiful and curious things to instruct his eye and cheer his soul. What other use have lovely flowers which lack any proved medicinal virtue, as daffodils, anemones, Turk's caps and asphodels, or such strange and coloured fish as are not fit meat for man to eat; or the innumerable distinct kinds of campestrian grasses upon which the dull ox promiscuously grazes—but to beautify the earth and raise man's soul to admiration of the infinite kindness of God?"

"Ay, what use indeed!" my Uncle Jones echoed devoutly.

"So, this matter is settled," said Mr. Milton, "but there remains the other matter of the great bone which we saw to-day at the house of the master of the quarries. You maintained, sir, did you not, that it was not bone but a mere stone, which had not more than an accidental and deceitful likeness to the lowermost part of a man's thigh bone? For, when I measured it, you objected that, so great it was, being in compass (near the *capita femoris*) just two foot, that no animal was ever bred in England proportionable to it?"

"Aye, sir, that was my contention," said my uncle; "but now that you have convinced me of the plastic virtue of the Earth, a property with which before I never credited Nature, I beg leave to withdraw it; and am the more strongly convinced that it is no bone, nor ever was, but one of those *lapides sui generis* whereof you spoke. For in the quarries of rubble stone near Shotover Hill are found stones in the likeness of some parts of the abdomen; and some near the Windmill at Nettlebed so perfectly resembling the secret parts of a man's body that, for modesty, I will not make any description of them in this company; and on Stokenchurch Hill are flint stones strangely like to human paps, having not only the *mamma* but the *papilla*, too, surrounded by an *areola* and studded with small protuberances—"

Here my Aunt Jones excused herself and drew my mother out with her into the garden, but I sat on, to hear what Mr. Milton would say in reply. Well, he would not let my uncle go to ground easily, but ran in after him like a terrier dog that pursues a fox or badger into his hole and unkennels him with furious barking and snarling.

"So, Mr. Jones," he cried, "if you are not man enough to stand by your first opinion, let me tell you this, that until I have seen the other stones whereof you speak, I cannot pronounce an opinion upon them. But of this great bone we know that it was found embedded in stony earth in such a manner that no other bone can formerly have been joined to it there, and that even the lower shank of the same bone was wanting; and therefore we must accuse Nature of forming a broken and partial object, as the spooner's unskilful apprentice spoils many a horn before he cuts a good horn spoon; which would plainly be to blaspheme."

My father courteously inquired of what living animal Mr. Milton concluded that this gigantic bone (which he had himself seen) had formed a part before it became petrified in the quarry. He asked: "Was it perhaps an elephant? For I read once in Dio Cassius's history that Claudius Cæsar, when he was called from Rome to the assistance of his Prætor, sorely pressed by the Britons, brought his elephants over into this island——"

"Pray give me leave to contradict you in that, Worshipful Sir," answered he, "for Dio Cassius alleges no more than that the Emperor *gathered together* his elephants, not that he ever disbarked them in this island; and Suetonius in his *Twelve Cæsars*, who also makes particular mention of this expedition, speaks no word about the use in battle of any elephant; nor in the time of Nennius did any memory survive of this unwieldy beast having ever pounded English earth with his great feet. Wherefore I conclude that no elephant came to this land until about four hundred years ago, when one was sent as a present by the Ninth Louis of France, to our Third Henry, which Matthew Paris accounts to have been the first seen this side of the Alps since Hannibal's crossing of them; and four hundred years hardly yield time for a thigh-bone to petrify in like manner to this one, even had King Henry been to the pains of disjointing the beast when it died and parcelling out its bones to several obscure sepulchres—for bones of similar bigness are reported to have been found at Chatham and at Farley in Kent, and at two small places in the County of Essex. Then, since no horse ever had bones of this bigness (even the great horse, which was not known here until the Norman knights showed it to us) and no ox neither, reason is it to suppose that this bone is a relic of those giants whom Brutus the Trojan is related to have encountered and subdued when, from a fleet of three hundred, four and twenty sail, he and his fellow Trojans came ashore at Totnes in Devon; and among them was one Goegmagog, who was full twelve cubits high and exceeding strong. Such a bone as that we saw, which was perfect bone, though petrified, and showed both the posterior and anterior sinus, and the marrow within of a shining spar-like substance, would

be proportionable to a person of Goegmagog's height; and it embol-
dens me to give credit to a history, so glorious to our nation, which
otherwise might be exploded for fiction. Now, as you know, Goliath
the Philistine is reputed to have been a little above half the height of
Goegmagog; and we have the testimony of Josephus in his *Antiquities
of the Jews* that among the presents sent to the Emperor Tiberius by
the King of Persia was a Jew named Eleazar, who was taller than Goliath by a span or two; and, to come closer to the business, in the Town
Hall at Lucerne—though I confess that in my late passage from Italy
I did not turn aside to examine so great a curiosity—is exhibited the
complete skeleton of a man, found under an old oak near the village of
Reyden, which falls short of the reputed height of Goegmagog by a
bare ten and a half inches. . . ."

Mr. Milton continued to speak of giants, comparing their heights,
and the trustworthiness of the authors who measured them, for near
an hour longer, until my father, taking advantage of a pause, suggested that since the time was at hand when we must ride home to our
supper, Mr. Milton and he should break the ice of their business
together.

My Uncle Jones lamented that the feast of wit was cut short, for
never had he heard such bold opinions, such apt language, or authori-
ties so carefully cited; and gratulated my brother James that he had
come in upon it. "I warrant," he said, "you never receive such lively
instruction from your College tutors at Christ Church."

James, wishing to avoid a comparison between the sister Universities, was content to let this go by; but when Mr. Milton and my father
had gone into another room and my Uncle Jones down to the cellar
for wine, he complained that the husband who had been found for me
was a marvellous monologian. When I did not know the word, he interpreted it as one who loved to hear himself talk and could not abear
that another should be the protagonist in any drama of words.

I laughed at him and, "Don't be peevish," said I, "just because you
spoke out of your turn and were rapped on the knuckles for't. Every
man is by inclination a monologian, I believe, though not every one
has the skill to gather an audience together and hold it. You cannot
deny that to-day Mr. Milton spoke both learnedly and to the purpose;
nor would you, I believe, conjecture him to be a man who utters the
same argument or anecdote in the same words to every new acquaintance. To me, he seems a man with a very copious store of knowledge,

keen judgment and so ready a tongue that I cannot believe him to be ever overcome in argument; for wherever his knowledge proved insufficient he would patch it out with sharp railing and splendid eloquence and bear away the board. Nor does his voice drone mournfully in the common style of University doctors or the clergy; for he varies each sentence with lively inflections of his voice."

"I am content if he contents you," said James, "forasmuch as you are my sister and I greatly desire your happiness. Nevertheless, I could have wished you married to a man nearer to you in age, and one who wanted that cold, dry peremptory air usual in a capable schoolmaster."

I answered: "Since I am not to be his pupil, but his wife, and will have the management of his household, I trust I shall not be inconvenienced by the air whereof you complain. You are still a pupil at the University, and naturally you chafe against any speaker whose voice and bearing remind you of the whippings you earned when you were a naughty school-child tussling with your *Propria quae maribus*."

Then my mother and my aunt came in again, and my uncle with a bottle of Cyprus wine, mantled over with spiders' web and dust, which had been long lying in his cellar and which he held dotingly in a napkin. My aunt set out a few saffron biscuits upon a plate, and we sat waiting until my father and Mr. Milton should have agreed upon the articles of the marriage settlement. My aunt discoursed to me upon the honourableness of marriage in a way that did little to recommend that condition to me.

"Remember," said she, "that Eve was formed from Adam's rib, not from the bones in his head, and that therefore woman cannot presume to argue with man. Man was created the perfect creature, and not the woman with him at the same time, as happened with both sexes of other creatures; nor was she made to be his equal, but for his use and benefit, as his servant. You must look to your husband evermore to reverence him and obey him, and please him, and sail by no other compass than that of his direction. If he be angered with you, rest not until you have pacified him; and if he blame you without a cause, bear it patiently without an unkind word, and rather take the fault upon yourself than seem to be displeased. Oh, may the Lord give you a patient command of yourself to do nothing that will discontent him! Avoid idleness, avoid vain babbling and a proud carriage, preserve a decent sadness in your behaviour and apparel, give yourself to honest exercises—to spinning, sewing, washing, wringing, sweeping, scouring and the like. If your husband praise you, let your heart sing. Put off the tom-boy, put on the grave matron. Go not from the house except as he give you leave: for the cock flies abroad to bring in, and the hen sits upon the nest to keep all at home. Marriage is a grievous condition for a woman, but honourable; for though she be by nature weaker than a man, both in mind and in body, yet she is an excellent instrument for him if she yield herself wholly."

My brother James brooded to himself by the window; my uncle clasped his fingers together, keeping his two thumbs free to roll slowly round and round like a water-mill. But my mother began to grow uneasy, wondering what sort of a bargain my father would drive. She said to my uncle: "I hope, brother, that Dick will not try to play Laban with this Jacob, for despite your declaration that Mr. Milton has a soul above lucre, yet a scrivener's son is scarce likely to be a fool in these matters, and Dick may catch hold of the worse end of the staff. Moreover, if I recall the scripture, Jacob, being of honest Hebrew stock, over-reached that scheming old Welshman, or Midianite, before he had done." She began to fidget in her chair, and at last could sit there no longer, but must go out and along the passage. Presently we could hear her high, gay voice breaking in upon the earnest interlocutory mumble of my father and Mr. Milton that came from the room next to us.

How my mother settled the business I did not then know, nor for some weeks after; but soon all three returned together, Mr. Milton complacent, my father a little downcast, my mother roguish and merry. My mother spoke first and said to me: "Daughter, this troublesome matter is now safely behind us. Your father and I have agreed together very harmoniously with Mr. Milton, and the wedding will be celebrated so soon as ever the banns can be asked in our church; which will give you three Sundays more of your virginity. Here, my girl, come over here and kiss your husband, and if you have the wit that you were born with, you will hereafter render him a careful obedience; for he is a very choleric man, I believe, if ever he is crossed, but cherishes well all that is his own."

She winked boldly at me with the eye that was turned from Mr. Milton, which I answered with half a smile; and I rose up and went over to Mr. Milton, who did not take me in his arms and give me the hearty kiss that any other man in his place would have given me, but stepped a pace back. He said: "Mistress Marie, before ever I set my lips to yours in token of spiritual union, or set my seal beneath a civil contract of marriage, I must insist upon hearing from your own lips that you are verily what you pretend to be."

I feigned not to understand his drift. I answered: "Sir, I cannot think that I have ever made any pretension to you of accomplishments worthy of your esteem. I am not good with the needle; I thrum the guitar indifferent well, though my voice be true; of my household management my mother is better able to speak than I——"

He broke out impatiently: "Nay, nay, my meaning is, are you the maid I take you for?"

I resented his question and answered it thwartly: "If you mean to ask whether I am my father's daughter, that is a matter upon which I cannot positively enlighten you; but I have ever believed my mother to be an honest woman."

My mother laughed aloud at this, and "Alas, Daughter, it is true," she said. "No great lord lay with me before your birth, and though your hair is Moulton hair, I fear that your nose and chin are sadly Powell. Your suitor, I think, wishes to hear from your own lips whether we are selling you with a cracked maidenhead or no. I tell him that it is a case of *caveat emptor*—for there is no sending of you back again to us (once you have bedded with him) on the ground that you are not what we warranted you to be. However, if such an advertisement content him, you need have no shame in assuring him that no man has been admitted there before him where he would fain go. Come, say the words after me: 'I, Marie Powell, do swear by Almighty God——'"

Mr. Milton hastily interposed that he required no such vain oath from me, but only a simple declaration before witnesses that I came to him as an unspoilt virgin.

"Why, sir," I answered, smiling, "if it please you, I am an unspoilt virgin; but I will not swear to it, since you excuse me the oath."

"This is no smiling matter, Mistress," he said, ruffling up again.

"Is it not, sir?" I answered. "Cry pardon! My easy conscience smiled, not I."

He had to rest content with the ambiguous phrase I gave him, but I could see that he was ill-content with it, for he said: "Since you have made this solemn declaration, in the company of five of your kindred, that you have never yet loved a man or known him carnally, I will kiss you and take you for my wife." Then he drew me to him by the shoulders and kissed me, and though I did not protest, yet I did not return the kiss: for the words that he had put into my mouth, namely, that I had never loved a man, were untrue in fact.

After this there followed gratulations and compliments, and my Uncle Jones drew the cork of his bottle of Cyprus wine and poured out. We all drank, but Mr. Milton excused himself, saying that he never took wine except a little at meals, for his stomach's sake; where-at my mother made a face, for she held that a man, however severe in his diet he may be, must not stand upon a crotchet when civility demands that he waive it. The others pledged our healths, and my Aunt Jones pressed a biscuit into Mr. Milton's hand, which he took and ate absently; but then thrust his finger into his mouth and hooked out the piece he had bitten off and tossed it through the open window to the birds.

My mother opened her eyes very wide at this and reached for a biscuit, saying to my aunt: "These seem to be excellent good biscuits!" Yet when she had put a piece of one into her own mouth she began to choke and, going to the window, spat the biscuit out again. She clapped Mr. Milton on the shoulder and said: "Son John, I am glad to see that you put good sense before civility. Only a fool or a knight-errant would have swallowed that biscuit. I dare swear it had lain so long in my Sister Jones's cupboard as the wine in my Brother Jones's cellar. Come, Mary, confess, when was it baked? In the year that you first wore your preposterous old balloon hat, or two years before that?"

My poor Aunt Jones began to weep. "Why, had I known in good time that you were coming to-day, I should have baked fresh. I trusted that they were still good, for I had kept them close in a wooden box. I baked them for you a week before Lent, when you undertook to ride over to see us, but you did not come."

Then we were all very merry together over my Aunt Jones's February biscuit, which was our first and only point of common agreement, Mr. Milton nicknaming her Dame Joan of Cappadocia, for it seems that one John of Cappadocia, a Chief Quartermaster, provided ill biscuit for the Roman soldiers when they sailed against the Vandals of Carthage, so that five hundred of them perished of the colic. But the time for our return journey had come and we took our leave of Mr. Milton, who informed us that he was to be found at Oxford at the house of his friend Mr. Rous, the librarian to the University; and that he would ride out to see us in two or three days' time, if the weather and his studies permitted.

Thus ended John Milton's courtship of me, and it pleased me that he had not made love to me in the sugary and adulatory manner that I might have expected of a Cambridge poet, for I could not have remained patient; and it argued well for his honesty that he had scanned me with a sharp, unloving and yet covetous eye, as a husbandman scans a fair-seeming plot of ground that is offered to him in quittance of a debt.

CHAPTER TWELVE

My Marriage

A s we made ready for supper this same evening, I said, off-hand, in a railing speech to my sister Zara upon her unkindness to me: "By the bye, I shall require you for my bridemaid in about a month's time. I hope you will not disgrace me in the church, nor put stale crumbs between the sheets when you deck my bridal bed."

She laughed at me, for as yet she knew nothing of the match, nor of the purpose of my ride to Sandford. "Oh, yes, indeed," she drolled. "I suppose you are to marry your sweetheart, Mr. Tiresias Milton."

"Whom else?" I asked tartly. "You have so persistently linked us together with your idle quips these twelve months or more, and made such a coil of the matter that you have brought it at last to sober earnest. The man dotes on me."

"Pooh," she said, "I hate your jests; they have no bottom to them. You could never gull even little Betty with such extravagant nonsense as that."

"Nay, Sister," said I, "there you are at fault. It is no nonsense, I assure you upon my word."

"I do not accept your word," she said; "you have forsworn yourself too often for that. However, I will accept a fair wager upon the point."

"What will you wager?" I asked her. "Come, you doubting she-Thomas, I am ready for you."

"My jasper locket against your pearl locket that I have long coveted," she cried at once. "Now strike hands upon it, if you dare!"

"I am not loath," said I.

We struck hands and at once she caught me by the arm and lugged me downstairs to my brother James and, said she: "Here's Marie has accepted a wager of her pearl locket against my jasper; she declaring that she is to marry Mr. Milton this coming month, and I that it is a nonsensical lie."

For answer James reached over and unhooked the locket from Zara's chain and then, putting it into my hand, clasped my fingers over it.

Zara screamed at him for a base, cowardly confederate and tried to snatch the locket from me again, but I kept it. When she saw that she could do nothing by main force she ran off to make a complaint against me to my father, who laughed in her face; and she concluded that the whole household had entered into conspiracy to rob her. I presented the locket to my sister Ann, who had no trinket of her own at all, not even a ring; but she pitied Zara and after a time restored it to her.

On the third day we saw Mr. Milton again, which was the Sunday that the banns were asked in Church for the first time; and he sat beside my father to hear them. There was a great stir when my name was read out in accouplement with Mr. Milton's, and a buzz of talking, and everyone craned his neck for a closer sight of the gentleman seated in our pew. At sermon-time the Reverend Proctor was kind enough to make amends to my parents and myself, for his injuries to us, by enlarging on the Scripture of the woman taken in adultery: "Where are now they that condemn thee? Neither do I condemn thee. Go and sin no more."

My mother drew a sharp breath, clamped her teeth and bristled up her crest when she heard him read out the text; but he continued very prudently with his discourse and no scandal ensued. For now that this fine gentleman had dropped out of the sky (as the people whispered) to make an honest woman of me, the Reverend Proctor would do nothing in hindrance of his project. Indeed, he split his text very easily and charitably, his conclusions being that since God can condone neither fornication nor adultery, which are deadly sins, worthy of hell-fire everlasting; and since also our Lord, being God, had more perfect knowledge of the woman's case than the Jews, her accusers—then, either we must believe that she had lain with a man who was, in truth, her husband, though this was not commonly known; or else that she had not lain with him, but that these Jews mistook culpable but silly frivolity for filthy copulative intercourse. The moral with which he bound up this edifying faggot was that careless women, using familiar words and gestures to men who are neither their husbands nor their kinsfolk; or timorous women who marry in hugger-mugger (for fear of their kinsfolk) and continue to pass for virgins—that all such foolish hussies must expect to be reproached for whores when they are catched.

As we came out of Church Mr. Milton complained to my father, who inquired of him, why did he not seek Church preferment, that though he had from childhood been intended for Holy Orders by his father, he was prevented in this by his conscience from taking them, because of the Bishops and the Liturgy; he also said that he who would take Orders must subscribe "slave" and take an oath withal, which would be, for himself, rank perjury. Yet if this were true (as my brother James said, after Mr. Milton had departed the house), how came it that his conscience had not kecked at the customary oath, when he became a Master of Arts at Cambridge University, and later when he was admitted to a degree at Oxford? For there he willingly and *ex animo* confessed that the King's Majesty, under God, was the sole spiritual authority in his Dominions; that the Book of Common Prayer and of Ordering of Bishops contained nothing in it contrary to the Word of God; and that the whole Thirty-Nine Articles (with their ratification) made in the year 1562 were agreeable to the Word of God.

On that afternoon Mr. Milton proposed to my mother that he and I should go out riding together and become better acquainted, but asked that for decency's sake my brother James should ride with us. My mother pleasantly agreed to this and the horses were fetched. When we were already mounted and come to the gate by the road my brother James inquired whither we were bound. Mr. Milton answered: "To Wheatley, to see the lands of my inheritance, which I sold to your father, but which are mortgaged to me since two years ago."

I said nothing, though this matter was new to me; my father, I suppose, not having wished to confess to me that he had mortgaged to Mr. Milton an estate already mortgaged to Mr. Ashworth. This mortgage to Mr. Milton was doubtless made in confirmation of his old debt under statute-staple; but doubtless also Mr. Ashworth still had a claim upon the land until the interest due to him by his mortgage should be paid; which interest, reckoned at 8 *per centum*, must be now risen to near £300, which was the amount of the original loan.

For awhile we three walked or trotted our horses side by side; and it was a cold, dull day with more of November in it than May. At first Mr. Milton discoursed to James upon the Latin and Greek poets, commending this one and condemning that, until James said: "I confess, sir, that though, for my studies, I must needs acquaint myself with these old Greeks and Romans, yet I love better by far the poets of our own tongue and century. I regret often that I am not of an age to have assisted at the gatherings held at the Devil Tavern by Temple Bar in the days when old Ben Jonson held court there. Since, sir, I learn that you dwelt in a house not far from The Devil and that you wrote verses precociously, I expect to hear from you that you were 'sealed of the tribe of Ben'; and that you were familiarly acquainted with many of those whom I hold in reverence, as, among dramatic poets, John Ford and John Webster and, among satirists——"

Mr. Milton interrupted him: "Nay, Boy James, you have mightily mistaken your brother-to-be, who was never sealed of any man's tribe, but is as truly his own priest and ancestor as Adam was. I deny not that once or twice I was a visitant at the Apollo Room at The Devil, drawn there by the hope of meeting with some particular person with whom I desired discourse; but there were many several things that I disliked in the management of the society that gathered there. First, the idolatrous adulation paid to that rugged-faced canary-swilling monster Ben Jonson, who, though learned enough and a skilful contriver of plays, was neither omniscient nor civil, and could not bear to come off second-best in any amicable trial of wit; did any young man dare to contradict this Polyphemus in a point of learning, there rose up minions ready to huff and hustle him out of the room as though he were a vulgar church-brawler. Second, the familiar manner of address in use in the Apollo Room, with every Thomas a Tom, and every Robert a Robin; since I have never answered to any name but my baptismal name of John, I would not be a Jack to please them. Third, that by the rules of the society learned women were admitted; I hold learning not to be a requisite in a woman and dangerous when it cocks her up to argue rationally with men upon such questions of art and science as were there debated. Fourth, that of old Ben's favorite sons, the most were drunkards and many were raddled with the pox (as his now-laureate successor, William Davenant, one of your Oxford she-men, yet perhaps inheriting something of the wit of his godfather, William Shakespeare, whose bastard he is commonly said to be); or else they stank of the claps so that I could not relish their company. Indeed, 'The greater part, beasts were in life and women were in heart.' Fifth, that they bandied across the tables, where they sat, boorish and fescennine jests, mingled with vain interjections of God's name. Sixth, that old Simon Wadloe, the host, charged for wine above the legitimate price and every night called for a collection of

money that palsied old Ben might fuddle himself into insensibility at
the common cost. Seventh—let me roundly conclude with a seventh—
that on the few occasions when I was present I heard nothing, either
spoken or recited or sung, that was worth a wise man's crossing the
street to hear; why, at my last visit all the praise was for the swinish
rough rhymes of one John Skelton, a scandalous buffoon, by our
Eighth Henry in merriment styled his Vicar of Hell, and for the amatory poems of evil John Donne, sometimes Dean of St. Paul's, whom,
most crack-patedly, Ben cried up as 'the first poet of the Age in some
things, above Edmund Spenser even'—which put me into so great a
choler that I went out."

James tried Mr. Milton with another question, saying: "Yet, sir, since
I believe that poets are wont to seek out the company of poets,
doubtless you made one of the select company that met often, a few
years since at my Lord Falkland's house of Great Tew, which lies
beyond Woodstock, where no man presided magisterially over his
fellows, not even my Lord himself——"

"Nay, for how could he have so presumed upon the accident of his
birth?" cried Mr. Milton. "A little black-eyed, flaggy-haired, scurvy-
visaged poetaster with an ill-attuned voice in which he smatters of
many sciences, having mastery of none. He did at one time indeed
make a handsome show of throwing open his house to men of eminent
parts and faculties who might study there in his well-stocked library;
but either he had poor judgment in his choice of whom he called
thither, or else they abused his hospitality; for upon my word, scarce
one came to Tew whose parts or faculties I could admire. I remember
that there was a great session, or *convivium* of London Wits once held
there (an overflow from the Devil Tavern). Old Ben himself was
somehow conveyed to the house, drunk as a wheelbarrow, dressed in
his old slit coat, like a coachman's, and all untrussed, with a rabble
of Carews and Wallers and Sucklings and Montagues and such trash
following after. I myself was not bidden to come; the which I accepted
for a compliment rather than resented as a slight; for Ben's way was
ever to engross the whole stage, vapouring only of himself. Lately, I
hear, the Lord Falkland has thrown over these pretended poets and
dabbles with philosophy instead, putting himself under the discipline
of one Chillingworth, a saturnine Oxford man, who preens himself as
a theologian (having, forsooth, been godson to that little red-faced
crop-head, Archbishop Laud) and who was, for a while, a Papist, and

is now, on account of a foolish book he has written, cried up as a second Richard Hooker—as though one *Ecclesiastical Polity* were not idol enough for the time! This is the same man who turned spy and informer to the Archbishop when my former schoolmaster, Mr. Gill, spoke some sharp words against the King in your College buttery of Christ Church."

"I am well acquainted with Mr. William Chillingworth," said James, "who is my godfather, as the Archbishop was his, and shows an extraordinary kindness towards me."

Yet Mr. Milton paid no heed, and ran on: "Besides this Chillingworth, the Lord Falkland called in Dr. Sheldon of All Souls College, a shrewd man of business, who jests at religion except as it be used as an instrument of State, and pretty Jack Hales who is so tenderhearted that he has avouched that he would renounce the Church to-morrow if he were obliged by it to believe that any other Christian should be damned for holding a contrary view to his own! Like his master the Lord Falkland, he is suspected to be a Socinian, after the detestable school of Racow in Poland, now happily broken up. Out upon the little short-arsed ninny-hammer!"

"Nevertheless, sir," said James, "I understand that the learned antiquary John Selden, before he was elected to this Parliament, was so long a guest at Great Tew that almost it became his domicile."

"Ay, true," Mr. Milton answered. "Mr. Selden is a most indefatigable plodder and searcher of obscure records, from whose discourse I have profited; but I argue from the strange company which he customarily keeps, dwelling so much in the imagined society of outlandish and long-deceased barbarians, that he has grown callous and indurated to the faults of living men. Or it may be that, being born in a nasty hovel, of mean parents, he was never choice in company from childhood forward."

My brother James continued: "And what of Mr. George Sandys, who has translated a work of Grotius——"

"For Grotius I confess a profound reverence," interrupted Mr. Milton. "I had the honour of his acquaintance when I went travelling abroad three years ago, and deplore that any work of his pen should be barbarously Englished by Georgie Sandys! Have you perhaps read his inept translation of the *Metamorphoses* of Ovid? Ovid, though a paltry, whining wretch, was tunable at least; and Sandys unkindly denies him even his tunableness and leaves plain beastly what was beastliness disguised. And his versifying of the Scripture—it is indeed nothing decent! I believe that your Lord Falkland has complimented him in verse upon his rendering of the Psalms, writing that 'he shakes the dust from David's solemn lyre.' 'Shakes the dust' quotha! The dust on David's lyre lies golden like the pollen in the lily; but Sandys, with no more knowledge of Hebrew than an ass has of brewing beer, and not the least awe or respect for David's immortal verse, puffs off this golden dust with his insensate bellows, and shakes on, instead, the dust of coal and fallen soot from a smooty hearth-basket."

Since he found that he could make no headway in this conversation, my brother James excused himself and asked leave to gallop across a wide, rough field on our right hand; to weary his horse, he said, which dragged at the bridle too freshly.

Thus Mr. Milton was left alone with me, for the first time in our acquaintance; but said nothing for a long while, and neither did I. I had decided to reserve my thoughts and opinions from him, so far as that were possible, until he chose to enquire for them. At last he said: "Your hair delights my eye, pretty Child. Without doubt, Eve had tresses like yours."

I answered ingenuously: "Indeed, sir, your delight contents me. Every morning I quicken my hair with my brush."

Then he said: "After I had seen you for the first time, your hair became an obsession of my mind: for it wreathed itself between my eye and what book soever I studied, though it might be the Holy Bible itself, coming with a gadding or serpentine motion until it choked the sense of my reading."

"I am sure that I am heartily sorry if I inconvenienced you," said I, playing the simpleton.

"Yours was neither the first nor the only hair that ensnared my eye," he said, "but certainly, it drew its snare the tightest; however, when I found experimentally that by no act of ratiocination, nor any ascetic exercise, could I circumvent or remove this strange affection of the eye, and also that only the hair of virgins had the same grand compulsion for me, I was no longer dismayed. I concluded it to be God's will that I should render humble submission to Him, and so enter into wedlock, wherefrom for certain choice reasons I had conscientially refrained: for thus I should be able to gloat upon your hair legitimately, and soon (because of its daily and nightly familiarity) I would be no more plagued with it, in my visionary sense, than I am now by my own ears."

"I am but ill instructed in the ways of the world," said I, "but confess that this sounds as a queer reason for a man to come courting. Now perhaps you will answer me fairly: what were your consciential reasons for avoiding marriage?"

Then speaking to me in simple language, without his customary convolutions of oratory, he answered: "Since you are to be the wife of my bosom, I will now disclose to you what I have never broken to any other person living. I made a private vow of chastity when I became a poet, as other men have made this vow upon their entry into a monastic order. To be a complete poet, a man needs a pleasant and secure life, without the cares attendant on commerce or the Law of husbandry—and in such a life my wise and generous father has ever indulged me. Also he must seek out and gather up for his use a huge store of various learnings, with all the arts and sciences linked together philosophically in a commodious and comprehensive system; and music he must have in sufficiency; and foreign travel. Yet all this, I said, is nothing without perfect chastity, for in chastity resides a magical power of compelling words to subservience; without which no poet may hope for immortal fame, 'lively to flit from mouth to mouth of men,' as Lucretius wrote.

"Now, as you may know, there are two main branches of the Tree of Poesy, namely the lyric and the epic (but with the lyric goes the pastoral poem, the ode and the hymn; and with the epic goes the grand dramatic poem); and a complete poet, as Homer, Virgil and Dante, is found excellent in both branches. Lately, when I considered that I had attained to a certain perfection in the lyrical art, I resolved (though tempted to write a few odes and hymns before passing on) at last to undertake the epical. However, I bethought me that as there are two kinds of poetry, so also there are two kinds of chastity, namely the chastity of the unmarried, which is perfect abstinence; and the chastity of the married, which is neither to commit adultery, nor to be greedy of the sensual pleasures by Nature permitted to a married man. I concluded that as lyrical perfection is conformable with the chastity of the unmarried, so is epical perfection with that of the married; and that, before he may write a noble and immortal epic, or grand dramatic poem, a man must first achieve the satisfaction of his natural flesh. That I have never known a woman carnally is, I believe, the cause why I am now so greatly delayed in the task which I have set myself—for no sooner did I set my lips to those new pipes, than they burst their bands and flew in sunder. My conscience tells me: 'Marry.' And in that opinion I was confirmed when, having offered up a prayer to God, I opened the Bible at a venture and looked, and read the text where my eye rested, which was this, from the one-and-twentieth chapter of Leviticus:

" 'And he shall take a wife in her virginity.'

" 'A widow, or a divorced woman, or profane, or an harlot, these shall he not take; but he shall take a virgin of his own people to wife.'

"My own people, as you know, Mistress, have resided upon this same ridge of hill that we now ride upon, for generations out of mind."

"You have answered my question so freely," said I, "that I am emboldened to ask you yet another. Why was it that, when I first saw you, at Woodstock Town End, you gave your *alias* as 'Tiresias'?"

"This question too," said he, "is pertinent to my discourse, and I will answer it. As a child, I was at first bold and vigorous, but one day, when I was about eight years old, a playfellow of mine died very suddenly as we tumbled together in Lincoln's Inn Fields. He was suspected to be dead of the plague and when I came home they stripped all my apparel off me and burned it in the bakehouse oven, and shaved off my hair close to the poll, and enclosed me in a room where sulphur burned like Fogo so that I was nearly choked. I did not take the plague, and I believe now that my playfellow died from some other cause; yet from that time forward for many years, until my hair had grown again to its full natural length, I was feeble and womanish, with headaches, megrims, and ill vapours ascending from the stomach to the brain, and also I conceived strange amatory fancies for persons of my own sex. Indeed to one friend, who was of Italian blood and died not long ago, I was in my affections more like a solicitous wife than a trusty comrade. I can yet remember how a woman's heart longs for a man, but because of a sense of decency, common to us both, I was never catamite to this friend, and therefore my remembrance is void of shame.

"Doubtless, the poet Tiresias who, as the Greeks allege, killed a sacred serpent, and so became for a while a woman in body was, when at last he was restored to masculinity, the better poet for his

long unmanning; for the power to put apt speeches in the mouths of
women is necessary for the complete poet. I am assured that the
Greeks in this legend made reference not to serpents slain, but to
serpentine locks unluckily shorn off. For in the man's hair resides the
holy masculine virtue of man: as the Lord said unto Moses, speaking
of the priestly sons of Aaron: 'They shall not make baldness upon
their heads.' This same mystery was understood of Samson and the
Hebrew Nazarites; and may also be apprehended from the history of
the Romans, who (by a foolish glabrification of their heads) sheared
away the original Republican virtue which was their glory and became, first effeminate factionists, then slavish worshippers of an Emperor, and at last a prey to the lusty, long-haired barbarian. Remark,
also, the effect of the priestly and monastic tonsure upon wisdom and
learning: how the glorious locks of ancient Greece are cropped and
depilated, and true religion debauched! Moreover, as we read in
ancient histories, the powerful bards of our own island would not
suffer their locks to be shorn, and thereby kept their prophetic power
unimpaired."

Mr. Milton paused, in the expectation that I would say something.
I said, to soothe him (for he had told his tale in a very passionate and
pathetic manner), that this single clipping of his young hair had perhaps served to make it shoot the stronger; as had happened with
Samson's love-locks while he was in the prison-house at Gaza.

My observation evidently pleased him. He told me that whenever
he was busy with a poem he, like a Nazarite, or like Tiresias and
Homer, drank nothing but pure spring water the while. Then boldly
he asked me, did I not consider that he had a fine head of hair?

I replied merely: "Yes, sir. I have no fault to find with it." Whereat
he appeared more than a little dashed in his pride, yet said nothing.
I could not lie: for Mun's hair was the longer, the silkier, the more
thick-set, the more curling, the nobler beyond comparison. However,
I covered what was in my mind, by saying: "I have been accorded so
much undeserved praise on account of my own hair, and so little on
account of the rest of my person and whatever deserts I may have,
that I cannot readily admire fine hair in another."

He replied: "Yet you must learn to admire mine, for I am to be your
husband. Now to tell you another thing. Between women and men
almost all things go by contraries; and when a woman cuts off all her
hair, which is her crowning glory, she becomes unwomanly, a lusty,

swearing virago of a muscular strength equal to a man's, and falls
into unnatural inclinations. Therefore since a man requires docility
and humility of heart in his wife, I have in my prudence marked you
down as mine, being assured that your copious hair bespeaks perfect
femininity."

"I trust you are right, sir," said I, giving him a grave look. "For
though I may be simple and unlearned, yet I hope you will not find
me saucy."

James had been coursing a hare, which he lost when his hound
started another; and presently giving up the chase for weariness he
rejoined our company. He persuaded Mr. Milton to speak about the
poems which he was writing or had in mind; who spoke so largely
and eloquently that the discourse took us to Wheatley (where he
viewed the estate very attentively) and halfway back again. He told
us of his grand and solemn drama, divided into five Acts, to be titled
Adam Unparadised.

"Before the First Act," said he, "Moses prologizes, recounting how
he assumed his true body after his disappearance from common sight
upon Mount Pisgah—how this body corrupts not, because of certain
pure winds, dew and clouds that preserve it, since it was once made
wholesome by his being with God upon the Mount. Then, because it is
not convenient to present a naked man (much less a naked woman)
upon a public stage, he acquaints the audience that Adam and his
newly created wife, Eve, are with him upon the stage, yet cannot be
seen, because they are yet in their state of innocence, and no gross
eyes may look upon them."

"That is a very sly and circumspect avoidance of a difficulty," said
James. "Pray tell me, sir, how does the First Act go?"

"Why in the First Act," he answered, "the Archangel Gabriel appears and gives some account of Paradise, and explains that since this
Earth was created he is as frequent here as in Heaven. A chorus of
Angels inquires why he is so often seen, and he replies that since Lucifer rebelled he must keep his watch upon this excellent new creature
Man, lest Lucifer seduce him. Then enter Justice, Mercy, Wisdom (resplendent figures) and debate what will become of Man if he fall. The
Chorus then sing a tremendous Hymn of Creation with strophe and
antistrophe; but of this Act as yet only scattered lines have been communicated to me and none at all of the Second. However, I know that
in the Second Act Lucifer appears, after his overthrow by the Arch-

angel Michael, and bemoans himself and seeks revenge on man; when the Chorus, who prepare resistance at his first approach, inform him that since a woman has been found to keep man from loneliness, and a beautiful one, Lucifer can hope for no success. Yet this he denies and tells them that his task is now, contrary to their opinion, made easier. Then, after discourse of enmity on either side, he departs and the Chorus sing another great hymn of the battle and victory in Heaven against Lucifer and his accomplices."

"Have you written anything of the Third Act?" asked James.

He answered: "I have indeed, and though this is not above five-and-twenty lines it would be ungrateful in me to God to pretend that it is not sublime work. First Lucifer appears and insults. Then Adam and Eve, having by this time been seduced by the Serpent, appear confusedly, dressed in garments of leaves. Conscience, in a shape, follows after Adam and accuses him, and Justice cites Man to appear for God's examination; in the meantime the Chorus entertains the stage and is informed by some Angel of the manner of his Fall."

I asked: "Does not Conscience also follow after Eve? Is she not also cited to appear?"

Mr. Milton did not answer me, but raised his voice a little as if in warning against needless interruption, as he proceeded: "This Act closes, as I said, with the Angel's account of Adam's fall. The Fourth Act, which is not yet ripened and come to any degree of digestion, will show Adam and Eve again, who accuse one another; but especially Adam casts the blame upon his wife, is stubborn in his offence. Then Justice appears again, reasons with him, convinces him, and the Chorus admonishes Adam, offering Lucifer's impenitence as an ill example. In the Fifth and last Act comes an Angel with a sword to banish the guilty pair from Paradise; but, before, presents Adam with a masque of all the evils of this life and world, which he horrifically names (as he also named the brute creation) with the new names of Labour, Grief, Hatred, Envy, War, Famine, Pestilence, Sickness, Fear—as being shapes not before known. He is humbled, relents, despairs. At last appears Mercy, comforts him, promises the Messiah, then calls in Faith, Hope and Charity, who instruct him. He repents, glorifies God, submits to his penalty. The Chorus briefly concludes."

"Pray tell me more of our mother Eve," said I. "Was she indeed untroubled by Conscience, and thereafter unrepentant, as seems from this account?"

"The title of my drama," said Mr. Milton sternly, "is not *The Famous History of Adam and Eve*, as you would make it, but *Adam Unparadised*. Adam, being of the perfecter sex, is the protagonist, and Eve is but the incidental instrument, or accessory, of his crime against God. She suffers with him, since she originally was his rib taken from him while he slept; and being his wife she is, on this account also, one flesh with him; she has not dividual standing before God, but is included in her husband's penalty, and not more particularly itemized in the indictment than those other guilty ribs which were still joined to his breastbone. Nay, indeed, it was Adam's foolishness, when he pleaded that Eve sinned and not he, which exasperated God. He was as a froward child who cries when he has broken a cup or platter: 'It was not I who broke it, Mammy, it was my hand!' "

"Does this mean," I asked, "that a woman can do no wrong, except as her husband does wrong too?"

"That is an ill-considered question," he answered. "A woman's whole duty and knowledge should be attentive obedience to her husband, and this, if he does not enforce, so much the worse for both of them. Certain is it that a woman cannot be any better conditioned, as to her soul, than the man with whom she is united in flesh—if he sink to hell, necessarily he will drag her with him—whereas a man who is bound to an evil woman may yet save his soul by separating himself from her, in like manner as the Scripture requires him to pluck out an eye that offends him, or hew off an offensive hand."

"That is a hard conclusion," I said, "and a rough warning to fathers to marry their daughters to men of good principle."

To give the conversation a shove in another direction, James then asked for what stage Mr. Milton had designed the play; for the managers of the common playhouses would look down their noses at a play in which they found no modernity of incest, murder or bawdry: for those were the only get-penny themes of the day. Besides, as was well known, the new Parliament—in vengeance of Presbyterial Mr. William Prynne, M.P., who by the King's order had been close-cropped of his ears and long imprisoned for his book *Histriomastix*, written against players and play-goers—Parliament was resolved to close the theatres altogether, as being beyond hope of reformation. This play which Mr. Milton had described, said James, being in five Acts, was drawn out in time beyond the customary length of a masque or interlude, even were a nobleman found both devout enough to approve the theme and rich enough to bear the expense of staging it.

Mr. Milton rode on pensively for a while and then he said: "I have hopes that, with the alteration of the times, Parliament will be persuaded to act upon a design which I have in mind: which is to borrow from the Attic Greeks their custom of solemn dramatic panagories upon holy days—such as indeed were once presented in this country under the title of 'mysteries,' but then indiscriminately and lewdly by companies of tradesmen, not with noble and considered magnificence by command of a sovereign parliament. What I have in mind is, that tragedies of stateliest and most regal ornament should be performed in such places as Westminster Hall or the Great Hall of Christ Church at Oxford, and that stale comic hodgepodges or villainous ranting exhibitions of blood and brutishness should be everywhere by Law forbidden. To a theatre thus renewed and reformed, a millenniary phœnix, I design to bequeath my play."

This sentiment closed our conversation, and being now arrived again at Shotover, by common consent we spurred our horses forward and were soon riding in at the Manor-house gate.

Mr. Milton came up from Oxford to our house twice or thrice before the wedding and discoursed a great deal. We were all mighty busy in the house with the making of wedding clothes and fitting me out with necessaries. I was promised two black silk gowns, but received only one, and a pink-coloured gown to be married in. The expense of the clothes alone cost my father above £60. I loved Mr. Milton neither better nor worse as I came to know him. I had already deduced his character and stature from my first sight of him—*ex pede Herculem,** as the saying is. Mr. Milton's stature (to write figuratively) was not above the middling; yet he hoped, by taking religious thought, to add four or five cubits to it and straddle across any hall or court like a Colossus of Rhodes. In agreeing to marry him, I had reasoned that he would hold himself in such haughty superiority that I could live, in a manner, apart from him; as I could not hope to do with any man of lesser pretensions or earthier inclinations. Only thus could I preserve

---

* Once a clever Greek, knowing that a certain racecourse had in ancient times been stepped out, for a thousand paces, by the demi-god Hercules, calculated the length of a single pace and, from that, the stature of Hercules: which, by the way, was less than that either of Goegmagog or of Goliath.

unhurt that true and enduring love that bound me to Mun. How nicely or how mistakenly I thus reasoned, my consequent story will show.

Meanwhile, to tell of our marriage, which was performed on a morning so wet that I had to be carried by my brothers all the way from our coach to the church porch, because the path between the hollies was a rushing torrent. The old wives prognosticated from this flood that the marriage would be a fruitful one.

However, the rain abated as soon as ever the jangling bells ceased —they jangled so in my ears that morning that they drove me nearly out of my wits. Not a great many of our kinsfolk and acquaintances were gathered in Church, for the notice given them had been but a short one. It was also on this very day, as it happened, that Mun's little sister Cary, who had been wedded to Sir Thomas Gardiner the Younger, came with him from London to his house at Cuddesdon; and much company was drawn thither to congratulate not only his marriage, but also the enlargement from prison of his father, the elder Sir Thomas.*

Mr. Milton had at first made difficulties about the use of a ring in our marriage, holding it no less idle and superstitious than the cross in baptism. My mother declared that he might please himself about the baptismal cross when he had begotten children on me, but "no ring, no wedding," said she, for without a ring she would not consider me truly wedded—neither would I myself; and I must not have my conscience forced in this. Let him say what he might say, she would not tolerate the omission of the ring. So he yielded to her, for though the curate seemed willing enough to let him have his way, my father was the rector and had the last word.

In acknowledgment of Mr. Milton's suppleness in so "bowing his knee in the House of Rimmon" (as he expressed it), my father at his request forbade the customary tilting at the quintain. For this old sport was still in use among us in Oxfordshire, and the man who, riding at the board with a stave for a lance, could first break it, wore the gay

* Sir Thomas Gardiner, the Elder, who had been the King's candidate for the office of Speaker in the House of Commons, was complained against to the House that he had put obstructions in the way of persons signing a petition, which was for the removal from Parliament of Bishops and Popish Lords; he was committed to the Tower by the Lords and thereafter impeached for opposing Parliament in the matter of the Militia, and for saying that it was "a dangerous thing to anger a King." Yet now he was a free man again and a perfect martyr in the eyes of all the countryside.

garland and was accounted the Best Man at the wedding. He had for his reward the privilege of carrying home the bride with her legs about his neck, and when she was fairly over the threshold, of pulling off her garters to wear in his hat. This Mr. Milton held a rude and nasty custom; but that children should strew flowers as we walked from the Church door to our house, he accepted as jolly; as also that there should be rustic gitterning and horn-blowing before us and a scrambling for halfpence by the boys, and comfits of honey and almond bestowed upon the girls.

In the Church porch, where my brother Richard was brideman at the spousals, I played my ceremonial part in a sort of trance; and when the ring was drawn upon my finger and I solemnly plighted my troth, I heard my voice proceed as it were from another mouth than mine, and concluded from the strangely-worded undertaking, to which I engaged myself, that it was not myself who spoke.

All the country sent us in presents—a brace of bucks from the Tyrrells, and from others wine, fish, wild fowl, fruit and all good things; and in return my father gave or sent out a score and a half of bride-laces, and three-score pairs of coloured trimmed gloves for wedding tokens, of Oxford make. It had been agreed that the celebration of our marriage should be in several parts: a breakfast at the Manor-house, whither all the tenants should come and drink ale and eat tarts and pies—which they had already done, very voraciously; next the spousals at the Church door and the blessing given in the Church; next, a banquet in our hall, for the nobility and gentry, with bumpers and speeches. After this, our whole family would take horse or coach to London, to conclude the merry-making there at Mr. Milton's house: for my husband held it indecent for a woman, on the first night of her marriage, to be under her father's roof. He railed against the vicious and frantic fashion of dancing in use at country weddings. He said there was such running and leaping and capering, against all tune and measure, such obscene, naughty language, such rude tumbling of the women's apparel by the young men and shameless lifting up of their skirts, as he would never suffer in his own house; and he detested that his bride should be required to keep foot with all dancers and refuse none, however drunken, scabbed, bepoxed, rude, awkward or stinking-breathed one might be. Moreover, he intended on his bridal night to be where he could set a guard at the door of the chamber, that no

mannerless louts and hussies might stand outside, to sing smooty bal-
lads and take turns at the keyhole, as the base custom was.

Of the banquet in our hall I remember little, for I was in such a
confusion of mind, which I increased by drinking a great deal of
cherry cordial, that I scarce knew who was who, confounding my Godmother Moulton with my Aunt Archdale (to the disgust of both) and
returning distracted answers to simple questions. Only, I know that
Mr. Milton, in his plain black suit with very fine lace and crystal buttons set in silver, was called upon for a speech; which he delivered
not in the halting, grinning, stumbling manner that seems hereditary
with bridegrooms, but, being stark sober, stood for three-quarters of
an hour or more, with modulated voice and graceful gesture tracing
the honourable history of matrimony from the most ancient times to
the present; and for conclusion recited a stanza or two of his own composition—which I think were intended for his play, to be sung by the
Chorus of Angels in honour of Adam and Eve. My Uncle Jones and
one or two others afterwards declared that he had spoken seraphi-
cally and raised them to a sort of ecstasy; but upon the light spirits of
the company almost a gloom descended, as though they said to themselves: "We hoped that we had done with Church for to-day, yet
here we must sit through a second thunderous sermon." However, they
buried their faces in their tankards and drank themselves merry again.

CHAPTER THIRTEEN

I Am Taken to London

S O SOON as ever the bridal banquet was done we said our farewells
and started for London: Mr. Milton, my whole family and myself. The gentlemen rode on horses, my mother and I and the
children in our two coaches. There was no place for Trunco, but she
was found a seat in the wagon of the common carrier and was packed
off the next morning. At the first hill where the horses slackened their
pace, my husband said to me through the coach window: "Now, Wife,
since you have changed your father's name for mine, I intend to make
a reformation of your Christian name, too; for I hate all cringing
Frenchery. Understand that from henceforth your affected 'Marie', that
has a whine in it, will be honest English 'Mary'."

"Husband," said I, "you may call me what you will, but I dare say
it will be a great labour to persuade my kinsfolk and acquaintance to
follow your example."

"That daunts me not," he replied. "Those of your kinsfolk and acquaintance who are too stubborn to conform civilly to my wishes shall
not be admitted into my house."

My mother, who sat beside me in the coach, but with her face turned
away to hide her tears, now blew her nose like a trumpet and cried in
a challenging voice: "My child was named in honour of Her Majesty
the Queen. How can you dare to change her name?"

My husband answered respectfully: "Dear Madam, since the Queen
has put in pawn, or sold, the best of the Crown jewels to purchase arms
for the King's use against his People, think you that any honour ought
still to be paid to her?"

My mother replied: "The answer, Son, is according as you are a
loyal subject or a damned Roundhead"—for this appellation was lately
come into general use—"and to prove that myself am no Roundhead's
wife I shall continue to *Marie* my daughter; and I expect not that you
will be so hardy as to forbid her a sight of me."

167

"Why, Madam," said he, "mothers are by common custom allowed to babble to their daughters whatever fond gibberish talk may please 'em; and while I am resolute in what I have laid down as touching my wife's kinsfolk and their use of the name *Mary*, I am not so careless of language as to include her father or her mother among her kin."

"*Ton discours est parfaitement gentil, mon beau petit beau-fils,*" cried my mother derisively.

So the quarrel was smothered, and we rode forward in silence. When I wondered that we took the Abingdon road, I was informed that we went not by the direct way to London, but would lie that night at the house of my husband's brother Christopher, a young lawyer who had established himself at Reading, and had been prevented by an accident from seeing us married.

As we drew near to the town bridge of Abingdon, we heard from across the river a great roaring and a hooting noise; and over the bridge came ragged outriders of that country procession called with us "the ride to rough music," but here and elsewhere "a skimmington," whereby a woman who has wronged her husband's bed and turned shrew is given a mock triumph by her neighbours. When these outriders came past, blowing beef-horns and banging upon kettles and pots, with "Make way there, cuckolds all, make way!" my husband refused to oblige them, and clapped his hand to his sword in warning, but my mother bawled to the coachman: "Ned, Ned, pull us off the road at once—there, to the right hand, in at that gentleman's gate!"

The other coach drew in after us, only just in time to avoid halting the procession; and my husband, when he saw what followed behind the outriders, bethought himself and spurred after us. First came striding a mad old man with long white hair flying, dressed in a leathern suit and burst boots, who blew upon a flageolet of the sort that sow-gelders use to announce their presence in a village or hamlet. Next, upon an ass, rode a standard-bearer with a woman's petticoat nailed to a pole as his standard, and tattered bagpipers marched alongside, playing "My Lady Greensleeves" in a villainous snuffling manner. These wretches were followed by an old hag, a true Mother Grime by her look, seated upon a bony carthorse, with a pannier on either side of her filled with stinking night-soil which, with a skimming ladle, she tossed indiscriminately among the mocking crowd of bystanders, and over her shoulders at the retinue; her horse had spreading paper antlers tied to his head. Then came the main persons of the progress: a little, pale, sharp-faced woman riding astride a horse, without her petticoat, but with a great wooden spoon in her hand; and, tied with his back to her, so that he faced the horse's rump, was a great burly red-faced man, her husband, holding a spindle and distaff in his hand; and the louts and slouches pacing beside him, in the guise of whifflers, threatened them with clubs unless the wife constantly beat her husband with the spoon, and unless he plied the distaff and spindle laboriously. Then followed a general dirty rabble of the Abingdon popular, every man and woman armed with a musical instrument snatched at random from the kitchen or shop or cowshed when they heard the summons to the ride—such a clashing of saucepans and pails, such a twanging of Jews' harps, such a drumming with marrow-bones upon salt boxes, such music of keys and tongs, I never heard in all my life.

My parents, my sisters and my little brothers laughed at this spectacle till their sides ached. My husband looked grim and chuckled, my brother James in disgust turned away to watch the swans on the river; and, as for me, a sort of amazed disgust overtook me at the barbarity of these townsfolk, for though I had often heard railing threats of a ride to rough music, I had never before witnessed the act.

My husband, when the rout had gone by, began to discourse learnedly upon it to my father, observing that a flouting sort of anti-masque of a sordid nature had customarily followed Roman generals when they rode through their city in god-like triumph, which was a reminder to them of their mortality; and he supposed that, similarly, this skimmington had in ancient times followed at the heels of all grand nuptial processions, as a horrid reminder to husband and wife of the immutable relation of man and woman—he the absolute ruler, she the willing and obsequious servant.

"Nevertheless," said my father, "though in England a wife is *de jure,* as you say, but a servant or chattel, yet I have heard it said that were there a bridge built across from Calais to Dover all the women of Europe would make haste to run over: for *de facto* the Englishman is so respectful and tender towards his wife that he gives her the uppermost place at table, and the right hand everywhere, and puts upon her no drudgery or hardship that he can without shame take upon himself."

To which my husband answered with a dry mock: "I believe you are right, sir. Some Englishmen there are, and some Welshmen too, who are so indulgent to their wives, that the Dame has the best cham-

ber in the house for her sulking ground, while the Master must cast his
accounts in a little dark closet that serves also as her linen-room."

My father replied merrily: "You prick me there, sir; yet my wife
brought me in a full £3,000 when we married, and it is well known
that 'he who pays the piper may call the tune.'"

My husband then said, off-hand, with a smile to me: "Wife, I read
lately in the *Papers* of Mr. Richard Hakluyt how it is among the Rus-
sians when there is love between two. The man, among other trifling
gifts, sends to the woman a whip to signify what she must expect if
she offend. And it is a rule among them that if the wife be not beaten
once a week, she thinks herself unbeloved, and is the worse. These
wives are very obedient and stir not forth but at set seasons. Upon
utter dislike of his wife the husband divorces, which liberty no doubt
they received from the Greek Church upon their first conversion."

I answered nothing to this, not even an "Oh," or a "Lord have
mercy!"

We reached Reading after nightfall and ate a supper at Mr. Christopher Milton's house, with fatted chickens, though not near so good
as our own, a fine dish of salmon, fresh-boiled peas with butter, a salad
of the hearts of artichokes, and plentiful strawberries and cherries. Mr.
Christopher was a pleasant gentleman, with the keenness of mind to
be expected in a lawyer, but with nothing of my husband's austerity.
He came closer to the Powell way of thinking, in the matter of religion
and politics, than my husband; and his wife Thomasine was a sweet
woman and considerate.

In a controversy at supper my husband began to speak of the rights
of Parliament, declaiming that it was the highest court in the land and
that the King had no shred of power to diminish its liberties and
privileges. Yet his brother Christopher held otherwise: he quoted Dr.
Cowell, Reader in Civil Law at Cambridge University, who had pronounced the King to be lifted above the Law by his absolute power
and declared that though His Majesty, for the convenience of making
laws, admitted the Bishops, the Nobility and the Commons into council with him, that was not of constraint, but of his own benignity. Of
what use, Mr. Christopher asked, was the empty title of King, if His
Majesty could by Parliament be bound to laws repugnant to his spirit?

Then my husband began to roll his voice thunderously across the
board and to maintain that this new-fangled doctrine, lately foisted
upon England, namely, that the King's pleasure is the People's law,

was a foreign whim-wham, a poisonous goblet which Parliament would not be slow to vomit out.

"Aye, Parliament!" cried my mother. "Parliament may vote a turd to be a rose; but a turd it still remains!"

This observation my husband disregarded and cried: "For four hundred years and more, ever since old Bracton published his treatise upon the Law and Constitution of this Kingdom, there has risen, each in his turn, an unbroken succession of honest witnesses to maintain that the King of England cannot at his pleasure make any slightest alteration in our well-contrived laws; so that this free people, governed by laws enacted by our own consent and approbation, is not to be deprived of goods, lives or liberties by any puny, stammering Scottish——"

"Have a care, brother," broke in Mr. Christopher, "for my Reading and Mr. Justice Powell's Oxford are more loyal places than your City of London."

My husband continued, unabashed: "—stammering Scottish pretender. Here, then, Brother, is the case at issue. And when it is asserted, as lately by Dr. Roger Mainwaring, that 'the King's Royal will and command doth oblige the subject's conscience upon pain of eternal damnation,' such blasphemous and hypocritical fucus upon the face of monarchy cannot long be tolerated by our noble people, who will strip it off before long, with a rough hand, and fetch some of the skin with it. Be assured that before this summer is out (unless I have greatly mistaken the times) it will come to open warfare, in which I for one, weapon in hand, will maintain the cause of the People."

Mr. Christopher answered very smoothly: "Well, Brother, you may be right both in your politics and in your prognostication. But I, for one, cannot believe either that there will be found in England sufficient persons furious enough to take up arms against their King, on pretence of some ancient principle of liberty now overgrown with rank weeds and moss; or that you and I—for I am loyal to my King as the head of our Church and as our sovereign militant—shall ever find ourselves fratricidally opposed in battle, however warmly we may dispute in argument. Look out of your window, John, to-morrow when you arise, and watch the jolly people going to the market; and listen to the cheerful neighbourly greetings that pass between them, and then tell me whether a nation that looks so wholesome in the face can in any part be sick enough to run into civil war. Go to, John, you may rail

and roar, but there is no more sign of war in England to-day than
there is frost in my strawberry beds."

The rolling and jauncing of the coach over so many miles of hard
road would have wearied me, even had the earlier part of my day been
spent in an easy and careless manner; but now I was so worn out that,
over-passing the stage of drowsiness, I was again wakeful, somewhat
hysterical and with a headache that seemed like a sword thrust in behind my eyes.

The bridal chamber was hung with garlands, and scented heavily
with vervain and southernwood and with bowls of flowers—the damask-
rose, the carnation, and the double-clove gillyflower—and there was a
silver tray set beside the bed with a flagon of wine and glasses and a
dish of little caraway cakes upon it, and the first nectarines and John
apples of the year. The white satin coverlet was sprinkled with gold-
dust, that glinted and winked in the light of seven fat wax candles set
in a glassen candelabrum over the foot of the bed. Zara and Ann, who
had slept in the coach, now performed their part of bridemaids, un-
lacing me and taking off my shoes and stockings and under-linen and
leaving me naked at last between the fine linen sheets; after which
they sang a little song and told my brother Richard, a brideman, to go
call my husband in to me. Then they kissed me good night. There was
nothing in Zara's manner of which I could complain, for she stood in
awe of my husband; and Ann was her own sweet, childish self.

Then my husband came in, who locked the door; and, the shutters
being already bolted, there we were alone together.

When he had taken off his clothes he climbed into the bed with a
Bible in his hand. He kissed me tenderly, and began to read me out a
portion from the Canticles, where Solomon praises his mistress for her
beauty, likening her belly to an heap of wheat, and her breasts to two
young roes which are twins. Then he closed the book, after he had put
a petal or two of the rose between the leaves, as a remembrance; and
spoke very lover-like and sweetly to me, but in some foreign language,
which sounded so uncouth that I believe it to have been the Syriac or
the Aramaic. Then I must get out of bed again and kneel down beside
him, and give thanks to God for his Infinite Bounty that he had created us male and female, with a deal more which I repeated after him.
When our Amen was said he lifted me back again between the sheets
and caught me in his arms and trembled with a strong passion. When
I said nothing, but lay numb and stark, he raised my head, saying,

"Ah, modest reluctancy—I admire you!" and presented a cup of wine to my lips. I sipped a little, but though I had resolved to please him, I could not catch the infection of his passion. He wooed me next with a pretty tale of his going to Italy in search of a bride: how one day while he was at Cambridge University he had walked out into the country beyond Grantchester, and being weary of much study had slept beneath a tree by the roadside. Passed two handsome young ladies in a coach, of whom one (the handsomer, as he learned afterwards from one who saw what was done) had fallen in love with him as he lay there. She wrote with a pencil on a little piece of paper, which she then thrust into his sleeping hand, a verse in the Italian language to the effect that if his closed eyes had slain her with their beauty, what would they not do when open? He could not by diligent inquiry discover who this lady was and had gone into Italy to seek her blindly. However, he had not found her there, and now being wed to me he regretted her not.

How could I answer him but with "Oh" and "Ah" and "Hum"? As he spoke he toyed delicately with the ringlets of my hair.

A great lassitude from the heavy fragrance of the herbs and flowers overcame me; and the wine sickened my stomach, and "Oh, Husband," I cried, "my head splits! Will you not fetch me a little cool water on a handkerchief, from the bowl of flowers standing in the window, and tie it about my brow?"

When a dog greyhound and a spaniel bitch once began coupling in the backside of our house at Forest Hill, Trunco caught them in the act and souse! she flung a pailful of cold water over them, which cooled the bitch's rut in a trice; as for Jack the greyhound, he stood shivering in a foolish manner which made us all laugh, and then began to howl dolefully. It would be exceeding indecent to compare that event with this, yet my inopportune request for the moistened handkerchief was no less rude a shock to my husband's nature than Trunco's dousing had been to Jack and Blanche. He looked chapfallen and incredulous and knew not what to say. Presently, disengaging his arms from about my shoulders, he blurted out: "A headache! By the body of Bacchus and the sweet milk of Venus, only hearken now to this phlegmatic and ungrateful wretch! Where any other would almost have swooned with the luxury of being wooed with poetry and wine and prayer and the scent of roses and holy verbenas, and not in wanton disport but in the holy and legitimate bond of marriage—instead this miserable clod newls out that she has a headache and would have me lay a wetted rag upon her brow!"

"I meant not to offend you, Husband," said I faintly, "but if you had a headache to match mine I dare undertake that you would not be so poetical as this nor so impassionate. If you truly love me, as you say, you will give me what I ask."

He replied: "Nay, Child, I love you too well to indulge or yield to you even in so pelting a caprice as this. I am your husband, not your simpering gallant for whom disdainfully you drop a glove and expect that he will stoop to recover it; nay, nor any slobbering water-spaniel to whom you cry 'go fetch, Sirrah!' If you must have a moistened handkerchief for your brow, I give you leave to fetch it yourself!"

I wept a little, but for pain and resentment, not for self-pity; then rising from the bed, and holding my head that throbbed like a drum, I went tottering to the window and dipped my fingers in the bowl of water, and dabbled my brow with it. Then I took up a silk neckerchief lying upon a table and was for using that as a bandage, when he roared at me not to handle his clothes; so I stumbled naked around the room, seeking a kerchief of my own. Yet since Trunco had not been suffered to come with me (who would have laid my necessaries neatly in a drawer for the night), I could find nothing, and came miserably back to bed.

"I am not in general subject to the headache," I said, wishing to placate my husband as he sat upright in the bed, glowering at me, "except when there is a storm brewing, or because of the flowers. To-night——"

"The flowers!" he interrupted. "What a froward, drivelling flibbergib have I taken to my bosom? The night air is cool and mild, so that she dare not accuse the weather of causing her pretended headache; then must she complain of these perfect roses—blooms surpassing those of Rhodes and Sharon, and archaically consecrate to nuptial rites?"

"Nay, Husband," said I, holding my temples tight in my hands, "you misunderstand me. I spoke then of *the flowers,* meaning that the time of the month with me——"

He leaped out of bed and cried: "Oh, heavens! Is it possible? Can she be so ignorant and sluttish or unthinking as to play this trick upon me? Wife, did your mother never tell you that these *flowers* defile a man, and that a husband must, by the Law of God, separate himself from his wife while they are upon her?"

I protested: "Nay, they are not yet upon me; for all that I said was——"

"I heard all what you said, you moon-heifer," he answered roughly. "You know as well as I, or better, that the headache is the warning herald of your monthly sickness, and that therefore before morning, while I slept, I might have been defiled."

He was so petulant, impatient and thwart and my head ached so sorely that I could not venture upon a further explication; yet I meant to say no more than that the weather and the time of the month, were, in general, the causes of my headaches, but that to-night it was the rumbling and joggling of the coach that had caused it. Well, it was easier to let him believe for the present that he could not enjoy me because of the time of the month; and in the morning, I hoped, the headache would be gone and perhaps he would laugh with me at our cross-purposes when I told him my meaning. Meanwhile, he rolled out the truckle-bed from under the great bed and tossed a blanket or two upon it and bade me lie down there, which I did, while he lay propped on an elbow with his back turned to me and read a Greek book which he had with him. I complained that the candle-light hurt my eyes, but he paid no heed to my complaint and continued reading; so I drew a tress of my hair over, and presently fell asleep.

Very early in the morning I was awakened by a sound which affrighted me, as of a man weeping. The candles were out and I could not recollect at first where I was. When it came back to me that this was my bridal night and that I was at Reading, between blankets on a truckle bed, with my husband above me, on my right hand, lying in a great bed under a coverlet sprinkled with gold-dust, and that it was he who wept, I knew not what to do. I was a little better of the headache, and that I had caused him such disappointment of his longings that he wept for frustration was painful to me; being tender-hearted, I would have done anything, almost, to assuage his misery.

I asked in a low, whispering voice: "Husband, what ails you? Why do you weep? My head aches hardly at all now. May I come up to comfort you?"

His sobbing ceased, but he returned me no answer. I repeated my question, a little louder, adding that I was sorry if I had vexed him by my stupidity.

Again he did not answer, but I could hear him reach for a glass of

wine and sip it slowly; by which I knew that he was wide awake, yet
desired no conversation with me.

I shrugged and, turning over, fell asleep again. I had a wild dream
of the storming of a castle in Ireland, and especially I saw the lean,
frightful faces of young Irish labourers as they fought upon a turret,
armed with turfing spades, and were presently caught by the English
pikemen and tumbled over the battlements. Mun's face shone and vanished and shone again between clouds of smoke as the castle gate-
house burned.

When I awoke a few hours later my husband was gone from the
chamber and Mrs. Thomasine Milton very kindly brought breakfast to
me in bed, to spare me the shame of appearing before my family at
the common board—a maid no longer, as she supposed. I observed
that my husband had removed all his clothes and baggage from the
room. I hoped to make my explications when he came back to the
chamber to bid me good morning, and so spare him a gloomy day.
But he did not come, though I lingered in the expectation that he
would. Presently Zara ran in to tell me, with a giggling face, that the
coach was ready; and when I came down my husband was already
mounted. The explications must wait until nightfall.

I climbed into the coach and drowsed in my seat for the greater part
of the journey, but once or twice was called upon to thrust out my
head to gaze at notable sights: such as Windsor Castle, with its round
whitish towers, of which my husband told us he had written a couplet:

> Towers and battlements it sees
> Bosomed high in tufted trees,

and amended it several times before it was perfect to his mind
and ear.

We passed through the thriving town of Brentford, where was one
of the King's richest manors, and the village of Turnham Green; and
after we were come to Hammersmith there was a continuance of
houses all the way on either side of the road, until our journey's end.
Here was Kensington, and leaving on our right hand St. James's Palace
with its broad acres of gardens, we drove down past Whitehall Palace
and Charing Cross and along the Strand—all names famous to me,
but the things themselves now seen for the first time—and so continued
into the heart of London itself.

Here there was such a hurly-burly, such cries, yells, screams, jostlings on the pavement, that I asked whether this were a market-day, or whether the people rioted. My mother laughed and told me that, the month being June, the Town was emptier than usual, for many persons of quality who had no business there had already gone out into the country with their servants to their summer houses. I had been often in Oxford and Thame, and once so far as Worcester to visit my mother's kinsfolk at Honeybourne; but none of these places even on a market-day was ever so crowded as this, nor stank so ill. The profuse dung of horses on the cobbles, enough in a fifty yards' stretch of street to have dressed a twenty-acre field, with cabbage stalks and peasecods and old rags and other filth of the gutters, smoking together all day under a hot sun, were enough to set my head whirling round again. Above all, a sort of sulphurous odour and a thick greasy, evil smoke spouted from the chimneys and puffed along the street; for in London, I found, they burned no wood hardly, but only sea-coal. To one who has not been born with that villainous smell in his nostrils it is a suffocation.

"I wonder," said I, "how anyone can live in this place without either going mad with the hubbub, or fainting with the stink from these gutters."

"You will soon grow habituated to the bustle of London," said my mother, "and find country life stale and wearisome by comparison. To a true Bow-bell cockney, it is said, all is Barbary beyond Brentford, and Christendom ends at Greenwich. And, indeed, London is become the grand centre of this Universe, I believe, since Rome decayed—than which it is now double so numerous in citizens."

At this my husband acknowledged himself to have been born so close to Bow Church (at a house called the Spread Eagle in Bread Street) that had the belfry been struck by lightning the bells might well have dashed out his brains as he lay in his cradle.

There was now a flashing of lanterns and torches, for the evening was cloudy, and the tall houses shut out what little light remained. The crowds were of such denseness that our horses could only advance at a walking pace; and once we were forced, by an obstruction to the train of vehicles of which our coaches formed a part, to halt for fully half an hour. As we waited, a band of about four hundred apprentices marched back from the ground where they had been at drill, carrying pikes with edges chalked against the rust; and then another band of about two hundred musketeers, whose song was *The Bishops' Last Good Night,* with the refrain:

> *"You are too saucy, Prelates! Come down, Prelates!"*

"The atheistical fly-blown dogs!" cried my mother, shaking her fist at them.

I know not by which streets we rode, not then being so well acquainted with them as I now am, but I remember my first sight of St. Paul's, rising up monstrous above us as we rode by. The steeple that had once reached no less than five hundred feet into the sky was now cropped by a good deal, the upper part having been broken by a great storm of wind and taken down for fear of worse things. At last, passing by the Church of St. Martin-le-Grand, we came to a great gate called Alder's Gate, one of London's seven, which has two square towers of four storeys in height, joined by a curtain of masonry set across the street.

"It was by this gate that King Trouble first entered into London," Mr. Milton cried in at the coach window. "See, there he glowers in judgment upon you!"

We looked up and saw above us the shadowy form of a King seated on his throne. It was King James, who had ridden in by this gate when he came to take possession of the City, bringing with him the "Caledonian maggot of Divine Right," as my husband called it.

"He is bold enough, your husband," said my mother to me, aside, "now that he is back home among his fellow Cockneys and eaters of buttered toast."

Then my husband asked her: "Madam, have you not heard what the learned Mr. Selden has said? How a King is a thing that men have made for their own sakes; just as in a family one man is appointed to buy the meat?"

We passed through the gate, and a few turns of the coach's wheels brought us to an entry on the right-hand side of Aldersgate Street, which was long and straight and lined with spacious houses, uniformly built. At the entry we alighted from the coach and walked in, down an alley, and presently came to a pretty thatched house of ten rooms, plastered rose-white, having before it a garden with a lawn and an arbour of rose-bushes and a broad bed of white gilliflowers, and a young mulberry tree, and the leaden statue of a boy with a goose.

"This is now your home, Mary," cried my husband in a voice that showed he had come far towards forgiving me. "Here we may be at peace at last among my own possessions and people." He added, whispering in my ear, "And now you may at last love me without strangeness or terror, submitting to me humbly, according to your vows before God."

For a moment I expected that he would catch me up in his arms, as was customary, and lift me across the threshold; but he refrained.

The first to greet us was his father, John Milton the scrivener, a mild, sweet-natured, careful old man, who came out from the parlour having the bow of a viol in his hand. He had passed his eightieth year, yet was as brisk as many a man of fifty and could read small print without spectacles. He made much of me and called me a sweet child, and brought Ned and Johnny Phillips, his two grandchildren, to salute me. These were the children of his daughter Anne, who had married one Phillips, secretary to the Clerk of the Crown (an office of importance under the Lord Keeper), but, being left a widow, she had married Mr. Thomas Agar, her husband's successor in this same office. My husband had now for two years been tutor to his two nephews, of whom Ned, the elder, was eleven years old and Johnny ten. They were grave, slender-limbed, timorous boys, as unlike those three sturdy boisterous comradoes, my brothers, John, William and Archdale, as herons are to hawks. They seemed to be in great awe of my husband. The only other person dwelling in the house was Jane Yates, my husband's servant, a fiddle-faced, sour-looking virgin, very primly apparelled and five-and-forty years of age or thereabouts. Since there was not room in the house for all of us, it had been arranged that seven of my brothers and sisters, namely, all but little George and Bess and Betty,* the three youngest, would lodge at the house of Mr. Abraham Blackborough, in the Lane of St. Martin's-le-Grand near by. Mr. Blackborough was a collector of books and pamphlets, and related to my husband, though distantly.

That evening after supper we had music—Mr. Milton and his brother Christopher, who had ridden with us from Reading, and the two nephews, singing plaintive madrigals together; my husband took the

---

* I have two little sisters of the same name, Elizabeth. The second was so christened when the first, the elder by four years, was on that very day pronounced by the physician to be stone dead; nevertheless, she awoke from her trance and lived.

tenor part, his brother the bass, the boys the treble and the old gentleman accompanied them very truly on his viol. After they had done,
my mother called upon me to play my guitar, which I did, happy-go-
lucky; and though all the Powells gave me their plaudits, for I had
sung my best and the tune was a lively one, the Miltons were behind-
hand with their approbation. I could see that music with them was a
more serious and religious study than it was with us. Their last choice
had been a sad, grave piece composed by the old gentleman himself,
of which one verse ran:

> O had I wings like to a dove,
>   Then should I from these troubles fly;
> To wilderness I would remove,
>   To spend my life and there to die.

But I had chosen a boisterous ballad by Humphry Crouch, to the tune
of *Cuckolds All in a Row,* of which I remember these two verses:

> A countryman did sell his nag,
>   Three heifers and a bull,
> And brought to town a canvas bag
>   With writings fillèd full,
> But a Scrivener took the gold he had,
>   The canvas bag also—
> "Alas! poor man, thy cause is bad,
>   *We are beggars all in a row.*"

> I have a Mistress of mine own
>   That bears a lofty spirit;
> Though gold and silver she has none
>   Nor any goodly merit,
> Yet will she brave it with the best
>   Wherever she may go,
> And shine at every gossips' feast
>   *With beggars all in a row.*

I was encouraged by my father to sing another merry piece; but my
husband interposed hastily with, "No, no, sir, your daughter's voice
already flags; if she sing again she may strain it and do her throat an
injury." Afterwards he took me aside and, said he: "Never sing that
ballad again in my house, not at all: it is offensive to my father, and
a mean, silly piece besides."

I asked his pardon, saying: "Truly, Husband, I sang but for the music's sake, not thinking any hurt at all."

To this he answered: "The music is nothing, and your voice, though not an ill voice, grated upon me with its bagpipe artlessness. When it began to drone, truly I thought the bears were coming!"

The Miltons then went to it again, very exactly and tunefully, this time to music of the organ which my husband played; but my little brothers began to yawn and fidget, so we pushed back the table and chairs and played a game or two for their amusement—"Rise, pig, and go!" and "Fire," and "I pray you, my Lord, give me a course in your park," which contented them. Presently it was the hour for them to depart to Mr. Blackborough's—where the old gentleman also lodged for the nonce—and for my husband and myself to go to bed.

Throughout the day I had rehearsed to myself what I should say to my husband, and by the time we went into our chamber, which was very handsomely furnished, as indeed the whole house was, I had it pat. I watched him while he combed and braided his hair, in silence, and took off his clothes, and pulled on his nightcap. Then he signified that I should roll out the truckle-bed and sleep on it again; yet addressed me affably enough. I plucked up courage, and said I: "John, dear Husband, I am exceeding sorry that last night, when I touched upon my headache——"

I paused, for he had glanced away and was busying himself with his finger-nails. Then he cast at me over his shoulder: "Enough, Wife, speak no more of it. It was indeed a grave fault in your mother never to have warned you——"

I interrupted, and said very quickly: "Nay, nay, let me speak, it was no fault but my own. It was a laughable error what I said about my headache: I meant not what you understood me to say. And in the early morning I could not abear to hear your sobs and I was for climbing up into your bed——"

He thundered at me: "Did you not hear me when I said that I desired no single word more upon this matter? What is past is past; and that a reverend rite was thus grossly profaned, whether because of the stupidity of your mother, or wilfully by yourself, is a sorrow now beyond mending."

"But hear me, husband——" I pleaded.

He paled with rage. "Open your rude slot again to-night," said he, "so much as to pip at me like a chicken, or dare to lay your hand upon my coverlet, and I warrant it will go very ill with you. Catamenia makes unclean for seven days and nights; and it is a loving indulgence that I permit you to sleep here in the same chamber with me."

Well, I had done my utmost, and could do no more. I laid my head down on my pillow and was soon asleep; and how my husband passed his night—whether sleeping, reading or weeping—I neither knew nor, I confess, very much cared, so utterly weary was I.

CHAPTER FOURTEEN

I Say Farewell to My Family

TRUNCO came to Aldersgate on the second night, and mighty glad I was to see her. She complimented me upon the decent furnishings of the house, and if she had misgivings upon how my husband and I would fadge together, she was good enough to conceal them from me. She shared a mattress in the garret with Jane Yates, whom she helped with the house-work. I asked my husband, should I not now take over the charge of the household? But he answered that there was no necessity, for it was yet but honey moon. This he said a little sourly, for the honey moon is a Londoner's term for such as are newly married and who will not fall out because of the exceeding strength of their love; it is honey now, but it will change as the moon when their mutual desire begins to assuage and the taste of honey to cloy. "When your parents and your swarming brothers and sisters depart," said he, "that will be time enough to look into the matter."

Jane Yates had declared it to be beyond her power, even with the aid of Trunco and a young cook-wench (who came every day to us, in her father's market-cart from Highgate), to prepare dinner and supper for so crowding a multitude of people. Then though Trunco offered, if my husband gave her leave, to undertake this impossible task under my direction, he would have her know her place, and discouraged her. He reckoned to put himself to less expense by sending daily over the street into Little Britain where there was a cook-shop for the sale of indifferent pies and dressed meats; and also a confectioner who made tarts, jellies and the like, though Trunco could have made far better at half the cost. He did not allow the presence of my parents to interrupt what he termed the *curriculum* of his little University; except that he devoted that part of the time after supper, which came between the religious instruction of his nephews and his own Hebrew studies, to music, dancing and general conversation.

The Powells were content to spend the whole day out of doors, for such soberness and regularity irked them; and the weather continuing fine, they found great pleasure in visiting friends and kinsfolk, some of whom they brought back with them to supper; as also in watching the sport at the bear-garden and the cockpits; in hiring boats to row up the river with the tide as far as Richmond and Twickenham, and then down again with the ebb; and seeing the principal sights of London and Westminster; and going to the play-houses, whereof there were five or six at this time on one side the river or the other. Trunco cheerfully minded the little children the while, and strove to subdue their wild spirits, for my husband would come roaring at her if Bess or Georgie raised their voices at each other or if they tormented Betty. He forbade me to attend any place of public amusement even in the company of my parents, declaring that he would not suffer my mind to be vitiated; and my mother was constrained to humour him. "But, Son," said she, "I would have you remember that for fifteen years I have had the sole charge of my daughter and if her mind be not as yet vitiated, as you call it, one hour or two in the bear-garden or at the Phœnix play-house in Drury Lane will make little odds. Besides, I think it mighty hard that my daughters Zara and Ann should watch the sport, and Marie be prevented."

To keep the peace I protested that indeed I had no great appetite for seeing poor Bruin's ears torn, or how he took revenge upon the dogs by cracking their ribs against his breast or gutting them with his paw; and that, as for the play-house, I was content to wait until I could attend a play of Will Shakespeare's or Ben Jonson's in my husband's company; for in a poem of his that he had shown me he had praised these two play-makers. This speech of mine my husband approved, nodding his head and saying: "In good time, all in good time!"

I shall not easily forget my first walk, in my mother's company, down Cheapside, the first street in the world, that runs splendidly along its whole course from Paternoster Row to the Poultry. The first thing that I saw was Goldsmith's Row, the most beautiful frame of houses imaginable, of ten dwelling-houses and fourteen shops, all stuffed with treasure of gold and silver. These houses are four storeys high, and above each principal door is a statue, richly painted and gilt, of a woodman riding upon a monstrous beast. Then I saw the Standard in Cheap, a shaft of stone, carved with pictures and a trumpeter at top, a monument which the rebels Jack Cade and Wat Tyler made infamous; and a plenitude of noble inns; and the Conduit, a building like to a castle, with a huge leaden cistern into which flows sweet water, fetched from the little town of Paddington; and the ancient gilt Cross in Cheap (which same, being regarded as a Popish idol, was pulled down twelve months later by command of Parliament, with frantic shouts of joy); and a grand array of mercers' shops with velvets of deep pile and rich silks (as striped soosies; figured culgees; fair, smooth atlasses; transparent, shining taffetas that made my mouth to water), displayed in diverse hues of scarlet, crimson, violet-colour, orange-colour, French green, purple, gingerline, snow-white, cream-colour, frost, sky-blue, tawny and crocus-yellow—with marvellous embroidery, and cloth of gold, and gold cuttanee, and silver tissue.

There are all manner of other shops in Cheapside and the streets leading off it, with men in aprons standing before the open doors, crying "What do you lack, what do you lack?" who sometimes hustle prosperous-seeming passers-by into their shops and press goods upon them in a blustering tone. My head grew giddy from watching the passers-by, of whom I remarked a great many foreigners; and I was glad to be back in my husband's house, where all was quiet, the distance at which it lay from Aldersgate Street being a great protection against the crying and shouting and noise.

One early morning I went out with my husband, Trunco following behind, to the Artillery Garden where he performed his military exercises in a company of volunteers from his Ward banded together by their common religious interest. He told me, as we went, that he was a pikeman, not a musketeer, and that pikes are more honourable arms than muskets, in respect not only of their antiquity, but also of the colours flying upon their heads; and because with them is the Captain's proper station, the musketeers being posted at the flanks. He himself, he said, stood in the most honourable post of any Gentlemen of the Pike, namely in the hindmost rank, of bringers-up or Tergiductores, upon the right hand; which also had the advantage of security. Then with his sixteen-foot pike, which he carried with him, he showed me, as he went, the several postures of the pike—the trail, the port, the shoulder, the advance, the cheek—and discoursed upon the use of each posture, heedless of the jests of the citizens and the winks of their wives whom we passed in the street.

In the Artillery Garden, Trunco and I watched the exercises, which were very exactly performed; Serjeant-Major Robert Skippon, Captain of the Artillery Society, himself being present. The companies, which

were drawn up abreast, with the files six deep, were all distinguished
by the colour of their scarves—black, or grey, or russet; my husband's
being the grey. Serjeant-Major Skippon wore a blue coat and white
breeches. He was of middle age, swarthy, sedate, with a little beard
and a stout nose and a scar, upon his right cheek, earned in the Dutch
Wars in which he had begun as a simple waggoner; no scholar, but a
devout Christian; a simpleton in affairs, but reputedly a lion upon the
field of battle; and beloved of his soldiers.

The command from the Captain of my husband's company, after a
few simple movements had been performed, was: "Files, double your
depth to the right, every man placing himself behind his bringer-up."
The Captain, made uneasy by Serjeant-Major Skippon's presence, gave
this order to "double the depth to the right," yet pointed with his
sword in the contrary direction; which brought a great confusion upon
the ranks and one or two men were pricked by the pikes of the men
behind them.

Trunco laughed aloud at the sight, and Major Skippon cried out:
"As you were, As you were!" and then addressed the company thus:
"Shame on you, Gentlemen of the Grey Company! Are you children
that you cannot distinguish your right hand from your left? What think
you will come to pass on the Day of Judgement when the word goes
out: 'Sheep to the right, double! Goats to the left, double!' and when
the Angels are your bright sergeants? Will not some of you by a re-
peatal of this morning's error, find yourselves trailing your pikes like
slovens down the slippery slope of Hell?"

He spoke in no dry, mocking manner, but heartily and earnestly;
and the gentlemen with the grey scarves appeared abashed, but mur-
mured among themselves at their Captain. This was the last time
that they fell into any disorder, and we watched the musketeers fire
off their pieces; but these were false-fires only, each man putting a
pinch of powder in the pan of his musket and popping it off, thus in-
uring his eyes to the flash, and learning not to shut them when he
fired. After all the companies together had been made to exercise in
a single body, with "Battle, wheel to the left," "Battle, wheel to the
right about," and the like, the muster was dismissed.

We saw my husband coming towards us, expostulating very sternly
to his Captain that he was unfit for his rank and should yield up his
office to some better man. The Captain excused himself, holding that
his words were clear enough, and that his pointing with his sword in

the contrary direction had merely been a sign to the men posted upon the left flank (who were those worst trained in their exercises) to mark his command well. Yet my husband would have none of this and said sternly: "Have a good care, Worshipful Sir, or one day we shall choose ourselves another Captain."

Having thus set the saddle squarely upon the right horse, as he said, he came towards us again and asked us which of the companies had performed its exercises in the most martial manner; and we pleased him by extolling the Greys. He said: "We keep a sort of Presbyterial discipline among ourselves, with a synod called every Wednesday morning, and therefore we excel at our exercises, being united in a common religious spirit and agreed to tolerate no disobedience and no awkwardness." Then he turned to Trunco and said: "Woman, you laughed very ill-mannerly when our Captain made an error."

"Nay, sir, I did not laugh," said Trunco. "Or at least not at the company or their drill. I chanced to remember an old jest about a fish-porter and a goat."

"Out with your jest," says my husband in the stern manner of the practised pedagogue.

"If your Honour will give me leave, it would not have made fit hearing for my innocent Mistress," answers Trunco, "wherefore, I have forgotten it in haste."

"If you are saucy," he mutters with compressed lips, "you may expect a beating from me when we are home; and I warn you that I lay on hard."

"The Lord have mercy on us all!" cried Trunco.

That day before we sat down to dinner my brother William came creeping up to me and asked in a whisper: "Sister Milton, won't you give me the broken string from your guitar and lend me your little scissors?"

"Why, yes," I answered absently, "if you give me the scissors again."

He took the string and snipped it into a score or two of little pieces, which he caught carefully in a paper. Then he said to me: "Sister, I think Brother Milton is very unkind. I overheard him when he forbade you that song of *Beggars All in a Row*. You are better at singing songs than all the Miltons and Phillipses in London."

"That is no business of yours, William, I thank you," said I. Yet I could not find it in my heart to be angry with him, neither then nor when at dinner-time he played a scurvy and revengeful prank, privily casting the snippers from his paper upon my husband's mess of hot veal pie. But, Oh Lord, into what an affright he put me; for presently the warmth of the meat made the little pieces of gut to curl and wriggle, as though the mess were alive with maggots. Yet I could do nothing without making the matter worse.

Besides myself, only my mother saw him do what he did. She laughed silently until her shoulders shook up and down like coach wheels on a bad road. My husband, who was holding forth upon some learned topic, thrust his spoon into the meat on his plate and began eating and discoursing with his mouth full, but remarked not that anything was amiss. My mother near burst her midriff in restraining her laughter and at last feigned to be chôking and ran from the table; whereupon my father espied the maggots and began to laugh too, but aloud and without restraint, as if at a jest that my husband had chanced to make in the very nick; so that the whole table was soon in a roar. My husband continued to eat and at last wiped his trencher clean with a lump of bread. He smiled with satisfaction, saying: "Sportive fooleries I hate, but a smart salty jest, now and then, gives relish to the most learned conversation." Alas, for William's poor prank, that bounced off from my husband like a tennis-ball struck against a church wall!

On the morning of the Sunday following, my husband told my parents that they might worship where they pleased, but that, for his part, he would not attend the service at St. Botolph's Church, where the minister was a calumniator and rank Prelatist, namely the Rev. erend George Hall (a son of the Bishop of Exeter who had written against him). Instead, he would go to hear the Reverend John Goodwin, M.A., preach at St. Stephen's, in Coleman Street, and I should go with him.

My father asked: "Is that not the same Goodwin who made a public protest two years ago, against Archbishop Laud's canons?"

"That is the man," answered my husband, "who is also learned in Hebrew antiquities and esteemed the best preacher in the City. Alderman Pennington, Member of Parliament and Colonel of the White Regiment, is his parishioner and friend, and another is the mother of Mr. John Hampden, M.P."

"Why, then," my father replied, "I think that I shall take my family to St. Botolph's, for I confess that I am myself a rank Prelatist."

The service at St. Stephen's differed in many points from that to which I was wont; but what struck me with the most force was the demeanour of the congregation. At Forest Hill our people bustled into the Church with as little ceremony as into an inn, calling cheerful greetings across the nave and eating bread and butter; some women knitted stockings and some men had dogs at their feet, and bottles of beer went thick from mouth to mouth; and all this was done in the eye of my father and the curate. Once in poor Fulker's time there was a rat chased in sermon-time, which was done to death in the corner by the font; and even Woodman Luke had not altogether subdued the people's boisterous ways. But here the congregation entered the Church with fear and trembling and trod delicately down the alley between the pews and sat stock still until the preacher entered; yet I marvelled that the men kept their hats upon their heads during the singing of the psalms, and afterwards the sacrament was taken sitting, not kneeling.

The Reverend Goodwin was a vigorous yet calm person with a cannon-ball head bound in a tight skull cap, and a scornful nose. In his sermon he did not rant and rage or strive to excite his congregation by pounding and drumming on his pulpit-ledge, as (I believe) did most of his fellow preachers; nor did he split his text like Woodman Luke, but, as he himself confessed to us, he held that the care of a true orator should not be to cajole his listeners to believe him by any artifice or ornament, but simply to convey to them those arguments by which they would be persuaded.

He preached upon the text: "Oh, what a joyful thing it is, Brethren, to dwell together in unity!" and enlarged upon the word "unity." Unity, said he, could not be brought about unless the whole congregation took thought together as one man, rejecting from among them any who was of a heterodox or schismatic mind. He made a comparison between a congregation and a company of soldiers; showing how needful a thing it was for each soldier to observe his exact station in the ranks and to keep his due distance, and to be distinguished by the same badge or coat as his fellows and, when the Captain gave an order to move to the right, for none perversely to turn about to the left. He praised the behaviour of the Scots in the Bishops' War, whose discipline had proved what power the English soldiers too could achieve upon the field of battle if they wished, being (man against man) the equals of the Scots in any enterprise. Yet such a unity, he held, must be a willing and natural unity, not a uniformity forced upon his flock by fear of punishment. He would punish no man because he could not stretch his conscience to worship in this parish church or that; but, if reason and kindness failed to restore him, then the man should be given leave to depart and mend his conscience in another. And he would be so bold as to suggest that within the Church of England, toleration of small, though very-very small, differences of opinion might wisely be allowed between the several congregations; as in an Army some regiments wore blue favours, some white, some red, some purple, but all fought together as brothers under the same Captain-General and agreed in the same general Covenant.

This was a very daring speech for those Presbyterial days; and my husband was not altogether pleased with it, arguing that Toleration might become so great an evil as Tyranny, and give licence to the Devil to spawn an innumerable of sects, each presumptuously hugging to itself some trivial and absurd article of difference. However, he changed his mind a year or two later, as will appear, when the boot of uniformity had galled his heel.

Place had been found for us to sit close under the pulpit and, hearing a stir behind me so soon as the text was named, and glancing over my shoulder, I could not but think it ludicrous how the whole congregation leaned forward and, every man and woman, cupped their hands behind their ears under pretence of hearing the better; which, since most of the men wore their hair short and the women confined theirs under plain hats, gave them a ridiculous bat-like appearance, the ears showing so large that it put me in mind of the Island Arucetto (written of by Purchas in his *Pilgrim*) where there are men and women having ears of such extraordinary bigness that they lie upon one as upon a bed and cover themselves with the other as with a blanket.

That evening my father conversed with my husband, enquiring of him what course of instruction in Latin he gave Johnny and Ned, for he doubted whether the Reverend Proctor, under whose instruction his own boys were now, had chosen their authors well. My husband answered that, so soon as the boys had gone through Lilly's Grammar and could read a little Latin, they should be set to study the four great ancient writers upon Agriculture, namely Cato, Varro, Palladius and Columella; and then the use of globes and maps; and presently they might read Vitruvius upon Architecture, Mela upon Geography, Geminus (Latinized) upon Astrology, Celsus upon Medicine, Pliny upon Natural History——

"Hold hard, Son," cried my father. "Cato, Varro and Columella were well enough in their own time and place; but England is not Italy, being of a climate more chill and moist by far. If my sons were to follow such antique directions as these authors give, I could not expect that the annual yield of my Oxfordshire lands would be large. If they must read writers upon agriculture, I would have them read such modern English writers as Gervase Markham and Leonard Mascall, and then they would have the less to unlearn. As for Mela, the New World would have been news indeed to him; and were Geminus living he would call Galileo a mad paradoxist or pitiful jester; and Celsus would shudder to hear from our Dr. Harvey so monstrous a truth as that the blood circulates in the body against the fixed laws that the ancients assigned to it. Why should my sons not study Cicero and Sallust and Livy, even as I did?"

To which my husband replied only: "What you term Dr. Harvey's truth is but a wild speculation, unconfirmed as yet by experimental proof; and though I would not forbid enlightened modern comment upon Columella, where Columella nods, yet I would not call in such lewd drummers as Markham and Mascall to awaken him; and though the excellent Galileo, lately deceased, whose acquaintance I enjoyed in my visit to Italy, made notable discoveries with optic glasses of his own contrivance, yet he spoke wildly when, forgetting the scripture (how the foundations of the Earth are planted so sure that they cannot be moved), he asserted the Earth to be a mere satellite of the Sun. But enough: I cannot permit myself to argue a case with a disputant who knits together so wretched a tissue of error and half-truth; only, this I will say, that if you know better than either your curate or myself what Latin authors are proper for your boys to study, why then, go your own way about it, for it is no concern of mine!"

My father asked his pardon, and would have reargued the question; but my husband took a book from the shelf and studied it with so bold an ostentation of interest that he forbore. Then, to cast a bridge over an awkward piece of water, my father-in-law went to a cabinet and unlocked it with ceremony and pulled out a gold medal and chain which he asked us to admire, and which we passed from hand to hand. They were presented to him by a Polander, a Prince, at whose desire he had composed a great piece of sacred music, an *In Nomine,* in forty parts. "This is but an ostentatious trifle, though of fine gold," said he. "I am happier by far in the thought that when my frame corrupts, the music that I have made will sing on for a great while longer."

There were many other skirmishes between my husband and my family, yet neither side wished for open battle, and old Mr. Milton usually mediated with a laugh or a worn homely jest. Thus my father and mother were able to take their leave, when the week was over, with professions of gratitude and good-will. My mother called me to her before she went away, and "Dear Child," said she, "from the bottom of my heart I pity you that you have so ungracious a husband. But do not let him crush your spirit; stand up for yourself boldly, and give him nothing in return for nothing, and mighty little for his pennyworth. Certain it is that he dotes upon your beauty, which if you use prudently, I believe that you can make him almost your toad-eater. Doubtless in our company he is ashamed to show his fawning affection for you; but when we are gone I warrant you he will go on his belly along the ground to win the smallest favour from you that you choose to withhold."

However, I knew better than to believe this, and it was with a heavy heart that I said good-bye to her and to the rest of my family.

Now that the household could resume its customary course, with old Mr. Milton back in his own bed-chamber, of which my parents had dispossessed him, the diet altered. Bread, cheese, butter, honey and garden stuff, with small beer or water, and a flesh-meal but every second day, and neither pastries nor pies, neither jellies nor junkets, nor any tasty fricassees—such was the rule in Aldersgate Street. My husband was not a small eater, but he ate whatever was set before him, indiscriminately, without seeming to taste of it, and never stayed long at a table unless to dispute or discourse. Jane Yates, though she swept and scrubbed with almost a religious fury, was a wretched kitchen manager. She spoilt the peas and cabbages and cauliflowers by her cooking of them and brought home lean, stringy meat from the butcher's stall, which some days stank so ill that neither Trunco nor I could stomach her stew. However, my husband swallowed the mess down voraciously, having a book propped before him as he ate, which he annotated with a pencil of black lead; and the two boys and the old gentleman stood too deep in awe of him and of Jane Yates to question that it was not the choicest meat that Smithfield could provide.

When I told my husband, a few days after my parents' departure, that I was willing to take over the management of the household from Jane, and would try to please him by a variation of our diet, he told me that he was content with things as they were. He was no belly-slave, he said, and I must neither waste time unprofitably nor put him to unnecessary charges, nor yet pervert the taste of his pupils, by introducing into the house a greater luxuriousness of living than had hitherto sufficed to keep them in health and well-being. He told me at the same time that Jane Yates had complained to him of Trunco, that she was a loose-mouthed, ill-natured, idle, contentious, ignorant country woman, not worthy of her hire; and warned me to wean myself of Trunco's company, since he had the same opinion of her as Jane Yates, and to remember that Trunco was a servant and without breeding. He said that, because of the undertaking made to my parents, he would not turn her away yet, if she would accept the place and wage of the little cook-wench (whom he had that day dismissed) and lie at night on straw in the kitchen.

I grew indignant, declaring that Trunco was almost more a friend than a servant, that she wanted not breeding and was a skilled stilling-room maid, and that though, for the love she bore me, she would not herself make any complaint if she were degraded to be a cook-wench and lie upon straw, yet I felt in honour bound to speak up and demand more honourable treatment for her.

"We have no stilling-room here," he said, "in this modest suburban home of ours, and therefore your Trunco cannot be a stilling-room maid. You are neither so rich and curious in your dress nor (I hope) so idle in your ways as to need the services of a tire-woman; wherefore, since I abhor idle hands, either she must be cook-wench or else she must depart. I am master here."

I remembered my mother's advice and answered: "Aye, husband, you are Jane Yates's master, but I am Trunco's mistress and I am resolved on her honourable treatment."

He laughed at me with a show of pleasantness. "That would be a generous and laudable sentiment," he said, "were it you who found her in victuals and paid her wages."

"I would rather sell my few brooches and rings," said I, "than make Trunco subservient to your old woman, who must herself be of a nasty, contentious nature to go with tales to you against her."

"Jane Yates," said he composedly, "is a very faithful and devoted servant to me. When I was a schoolboy, going every day to St. Paul's School, and sat up with my books until past midnight, it was Jane who sat up for me and had a cup of warm milk ready against I went to bed, and a warming-pan for the cold sheets. I will not suffer her to be abused."

"Your faithful Jane has abused my dear Trunco, whom I love," said I stubbornly. "If one of the two must rule the other and sleep on a flock mattress in the garret, then Trunco is the more proper woman. At least she is not buffle-head enough to go to market and bring back a fore-rib of abominationly stinking beef; or to spoil a pair of good cauliflowers by leaving them too long in the water and stinting the salt. And she would have been at pains to pick out the fat, green caterpillars——"

He smiled at me, being resolved that day not to let me force him out of his good humour. "You take too much upon yourself, my dear," he said, "and so forget yourself."

"I must ask your pardon," said I, "if I have spoken hastily; but this I will say, without fear of contradiction, that at Forest Hill, if ever a meal had been served as to-day's was, my mother would have cast it at the cook's head."

"I do not doubt it," he said. "Your mother is a very conceited and passionate woman."

At this I burst out weeping, and ran up the dark stairs to our chamber. My husband did not follow, either to comfort or chide me, but sent for Trunco at once and told her of the choice before her; whereupon the good-natured woman vowed that it was all one to her whether she sewed cushions or beat hemp, so long as she might continue in the same house with me. She undertook to yield her fellow-servant perfect obedience. "And as for sleeping on straw," said she, "with a good conscience one woman sleeps as sweetly upon straw as another upon down; and as for the wages, Master, you may pay me what you please."

When I came downstairs again, having, in the dark, washed my eyes and composed my spirit, I found my husband reading a treatise on Divinity. I did not disturb him, but took up another book and began to read it; it was *Britannia's Pastorals,* by William Browne, which choice he noddingly approved. My husband had some time before written notes in the margins of this book, and I laughed to myself when I saw what verses of old Browne's had caught his fancy. He had

written in one place "A beautiful virgin undressing herself." This was
set against the verses:

> And as a lovely maiden, pure and chaste,
> With naked ivory neck and gown unlaced,
> Within her chamber, when the day is fled,
> Makes poor her garments to enrich her bed:
> First puts she off her lily-silken gown,
> That shrieks for sorrow as she lays it down, etc., etc.

("Heigh-ho!" I sighed). And against other verses stood such pithy
sentiments as these: "Poets live for ever," and "Good Poets are envied,
yet in spite of envy get immortal praise," and "Men strive to get fair
Mistresses," and "The Miseries of those that marry for beauty," and
"All are born for love." But the clearest mirror of his mind was his
"Very beautiful" written over against the lines concerning a shepherd
asleep:

> His arms a cross, his sheep-hook lay beside him;
> Had Venus passed this way and chanced to have spied him,
> With open breast, locks on his shoulders spread,
> She would have sworn (had she not seen him dead)
> It was Adonis. Or, if e'er there was
> Held transmigration, by Pythagoras,
> Of souls, that certain then her lost love's spirit,
> A fairer body never could inherit.

(Heigh-ho, again, for his fruitless journey to Italy! Had he thought
to meet there with Venus herself?)

When he had read to the end of a chapter in his book, he addressed
me, telling me that Trunco had consented to serve as his cook-wench
at a yearly wage of £1 5s., but hoped that she would not make trouble
in the house. "And," says he, "if she prove to be an honest and capable
woman I undertake, when your father shall have paid the marriage
portion promised me, to give her as much as £1 15s. per annum."

I cried: "Was there indeed a marriage portion promised? It was not
a large one, I hope, for my father is not of a great fortune and has
many charges upon his estate."

"Nay," said he, "not so handsome as I had expected; indeed, no more
than £1,000. Your father will pay me at Michaelmas, when a large
sum falls due to him on account of his lands in the Dominion of Wales;

and at the same time he will repay me certain other moneys long due
to me, but unaccountably overlooked."

I was amazed at this news: for I could have taken my oath that my
father owned not an inch of land in Wales. And if he had lands there,
why had he cozened me into this marriage by his plea of absolute
poverty? Could it be that he had also cozened my husband by a promise of money that he knew well was not to be found?

I thanked my husband for his undertaking in respect of Trunco, and
returned to my reading, but with my mind still puzzling over this
riddle of my portion.

Presently he closed his book and came behind my chair and ran his
fingers combingly through my hair and parting two tresses of it with
his hands (as one might draw apart a pair of curtains), he printed a
kiss upon the nape of my neck. I knew not what to say, and continued
my pretence of reading; but he sportively took the book from me and
clapped it shut, and having locked and bolted the doors of the house,
bade me come upstairs, where a surprise awaited me.

I faltered when I saw that the bed-chamber was draped with curious Indian silks and ribbons and the bed decorated with spangles of
silver and gold, and that a little love-feast had been prepared, with
wine in a silver beaker and choice fruits and little caraway cakes again.
"Oh, husband," said I, "why have you hit upon this night for such
bravery? For you cannot company with me now, as you might have
done on any of the twelve nights that I have been with you."

"And why may I not, pray?" he asked, going as wan as the gills of a
sick turkey-cock.

"Because," said I, "the flowers have come upon me to-night."

"The flowers!" he cried. "The flowers again!"

"Roll out that truckle-bed," said I, not knowing whether to laugh or
weep.

"But did you not tell me——?" he began.

"And did you not interruptingly command me to silence?" I asked.

CHAPTER FIFTEEN

I Come Back to Forest Hill

THE more pertinaciousıy I tried to make my husband understand how he hindered his own end by an impatience and severity towards me, the more impatient and severe he grew. He is a man who never graciously acknowledges himself at fault, fearing by any such admission to impugn his own authority and judgment. For though he has often changed his mind and turned cat in pan even upon matters of religious principle, yet (this I write without irony or reproach, but as a mere matter of fact) he is constant and loyal to one thing at least, which is a humble faith in his own infallibility: no man in the world was ever so sincere and modest in his self-devotion. Now, as a punishment for what he called my foolish glozing and deceit, he banished me from his chamber altogether for the space of three weeks, giving me a bed in a cramped back closet that opened from it; and by day kept me a close prisoner in the house and garden. I had no work to employ me, because my clothes and his were all in good repair, and at broidery I have no skill, and we kept no poultry nor brewed our own beer. Kitchen work I love, but my husband told me that Jane and Trunco needed no third pair of hands in the kitchen, and that I would but delay their necessary work by gossiping with them. Since also he would not suffer me to play and sing on my guitar, which he said distracted him from his studies, and since there was no one to play at cards with me, I could find little to do besides reading; yet every time I wished to take a book from his shelves I must first ask his leave, and if he considered the book to be improper for my reading he would forbid it me. When I asked whether I might sit and listen while he taught our nephews Latin, forasmuch as I had not yet forgotten the rudiments learned from our curate, the Reverend Fulker, he answered that my presence would distract the boys and be a great inconvenience to himself. "And besides," said he, humorously, "one tongue is enough for a woman."

Those days drew heavily, as it were a train of old broken carts with huge loads and axles ungreased, hauled uphill through the mire by weary oxen. The post brought me a letter from my mother, in which she wrote how sadly she missed me, and not only for my company, but for the great help I had afforded her in managing the younger children, and for my dairy-work and care of the geese and poultry; and "even I have learned to value that whoreson Trunco who was the cunningest woman in the stilling-room that ever I saw, and a good-tempered, willing rogue into the bargain." This brief, blotted letter ended with: "Oh, to have you back again in this house until Michaelmas at least; 'twould be a great blessing and lighten a thousand burdens. I confess, dear child, that though you have proved the most troublesome by far of all my eleven children, yet there is none lies closer to the heart of your harassed, real affectionate mother, Ann Powell. Your father sends his loving remembrances to Mr. Milton and yourself."

She had put into the envelope another little shred of paper, which she rightly expected that I would conceal from my husband, on which was written: "I sorely fear you will go through purgatory for a month or two, with that stiff-necked, canting, Judasly rogue, before at last you have him there where I would fain have him be. If you have any guts in your brains you will yield nothing, no, not a half-inch; else he will make a dull-eyed spiritless scape-trencher of my princely daughter, who deserves better of life than that, God help her!"

I had heard that my husband loved cheerful faces about him, and true it is that though he kept me confined still, yet, perhaps for shame's sake, he did not alter his countenance towards me in the presence of the household; and at meal-times would seek to engage me in pleasant conversation. However, I saw no cause why I should be bound by the rules of his game of make-peace. I answered with "Yes" or "No" or "I know not" but not a word more; and feigned no happiness which I could not feel. I moped, refused my meat, moved sluggishly, sighed often, yawned during his discourses, and put my kerchief frequently to my eyes. The more this irked him, the more melancholically I mumped; yet without open complaint or incivility.

Trunco fell foul of her fellow-servant Jane after a day or two. Jane did not like me, either at first or second sight, nor I her. But since she durst not show any direct spite against me, she showed it indirectly by her injurious treatment of Trunco, whom she abused up and down stairs, whenever my husband was within earshot, accusing her of idle-

ness, impudence, and pilfering. Trunco had resolved to be patient Gri-
zel, and never to answer Jane back; and Jane, who had the name of
God ever in her mouth but the Devil himself in her heart, grew still
more incensed against her, and made the kitchen a little hell for her
and contrived crooked plots to bring her into ill-favour. She would
herself come into the dining-chamber, where Trunco had neatly set
the table, and would lay the spoons and knives awry and, snatching
away a platter or a cup, put it back on a shelf; or would herself disorder my husband's papers after that Trunco had cleaned his study.
At last one day I caught her in the act of taking a pan of dust, which
Trunco had collected by hard sweeping, and emptying it upon the
stairs. I said nothing, but waited for her to accuse Trunco to my husband of leaving the stairs unswept; but he, coming upstairs soon after
began to rail at the litter and called Trunco himself and asked her,
how had she neglected to sweep the stairs?

Then I said: "Husband, this is no neglect of my Trunco's. Your Jane
Yates, whom I watched with mine own eyes, took a pan of dust and
sprinkled it upon the stairs, I suppose to the end that you would find
fault with my poor woman; for this lick-dish Jane, you know, who has
wrought herself so much into your favour is, for all that, a very spiteful, deceitful, greedy creature."

Then ensued a great commotion, Jane Yates solemnly declaring her
innocence and accusing me of bearing false witness against her in the
hope of covering up Trunco's ill-doings by a cruel injury; and asking
my husband: "Have I not served you faithfully, Master, since both of
us were children, with never a single error or transgression? Would
you accept the word of this pert girl, your wife, her word before mine,
when she charges me with a crime which, were I guilty of it, would
unfit me to keep house for you an hour longer?"

My husband soothed her, and appeared to be in a sad perplexity
whether to vindicate my honour or slight hers; but old Mr. Milton
coming along settled the matter very judiciously. He declared that
doubtless I had been mistaken, and pressed Jane until she admitted to
have taken a pan of dust downstairs in her hand, of which perhaps a
few grains had overspilt in her passage; but it was certainly agreed by
the three of them that Trunco was to blame for the unswept stairs.
Against them I argued that if the stairs had not been swept, as they
said, it was strange how the dust lay in little heaps, intermingled with
little shreds of green wool from the carpet in the old gentleman's study;

yet they would not heed nor hearken to me, and my husband said that
he had "raked long enough in that puddle" and ordered me to keep
silence, lest I make matters worse for my woman. Then he laid his
stick across Trunco's shoulders, three or four times, pretty roughly; but
for my sake she uttered no complaint.

My husband's frustration in the matter of our companying together
and the settled glumness with which I accepted my unjust punishment
altered him so strangely that I began to fear what would become of
us all; and whether it happened that Ned and Johnny Phillips were
afflicted at this time with a coincidental fit of dullness and sloth, or
whether it was that he vented his spleen upon these poor innocents,
I know not. But twice or three times every day I heard the heavy
whack of his stick upon their tender bodies or the sharp clap of his
flat, pear-shaped ferule upon their inky fingers, and they yelped and
howled most lamentably. Without his permission, they might never
speak to him except in Latin or Greek; yet when an ash-stick whistles
down, or the ferule blisters, how can a child remember case, gender
and conjugation in his pleas for mercy?

I asked my husband privily one day, when he had trounced Johnny
so hard that he could not eat his meal but standing upright and with
his pale face pitiably beblubbered, whether this severity were needful.

"Why, Wife," he answered, "do you think yourself wiser than Solomon, whose considered judgment it was that a rod spared is a child
spoilt? Besides, this morning the child added obstinacy to his stupidity,
and tried to justify his fault."

My ears still rang with Johnny's howls and his yells of "*Miserere,
Domine! Ignosce, Domine, ignosce!*" and I asked my husband impudently: "Did not your tutor at Cambridge ever ferule you for the same
fault?" Then I walked away, not waiting for his answer.

This was the tenth day of my captivity, just before supper, and going
to my coffer in the closet I took out my vellum book, and unlocked it
and began to write. I was trembling with rage and could hardly shape
the letters as I set down: "Marie Powell was married to John Melton,
alias Milton, Junior, and he altered her name to Mary Milton. Thus she
exchanged the honourable arms of Powell (which her father blazoned
for her on the title page of this book) for the arms of Mitton, which
were in error bestowed upon his father, a scrivener, by the Garter
King-at-Arms, who thereby endowed the said ungenteel John Melton
Junior, with the fraudulent titles of Armiger and Gentleman."

Then I left off writing and began to read and dream of Mun. My husband came to the door and pushed it open without knocking, as was his custom. He saw me with the book and asked me what I read.

"Nothing," I replied.

"Were an answer of that nature given me by a pupil of mine I should beat him severely," said he.

"I do not doubt it, Husband," I answered, my rage rising again. "You seem to be more generous with the ferule than with the fruit pastry."

"What book do you read without my permission?" he asked again, threateningly.

"My own book," I answered, and locking the clasp hastily, I put it underneath me where I sat upon the coffer.

"Give it to me," said he, "or I will pluck it out from under you."

"Not I!" was my answer. "It is my book, and was given to me by my Godmother Moulton, with advice never to show it to any person living."

"Wife," he said, "beware to remember your bridal vow: you have now no worldly chattels that are not mine."

"Very, very true," said I. "You also made the same endowment of your chattels to me; but since you have withheld several of your books from me, you cannot complain if I withhold this single one from you."

"You disobey my plain command to yield up this book?" he asked. "You dare to oppose me in a point of house-rule?"

"I do," said I, beside myself with wrath, "and if you lay a finger upon me you must beware, you leather-sided villain! I will not cry out for pity in the Latin tongue as your miserable pupils do, but defend myself, tooth and nail, as once you defended yourself against your tutor, Mr. Chappell; and, s'blood! I warrant I will leave my mark upon you."

"So!" he said, breathing heavily. "So it has come to this! My fire, my spirit, my blood!—your earth and phlegm, your cold, muddy, scolding nastiness! Well did Solomon write that a bad wife is to her husband as rottenness to his bones, as continual dropping!"

"Do not provoke me to bandy the rhetoric of Turnbull Street and Billingsgate with you, Stinkard, Base Slubberdegullion, Cheesy Plagiarist, Immortal Whip-Arse, Eater of Stinking Beef!" I cried; for, by God, when I was angered beyond endurance, I was my mother's eldest daughter. "Do you take me for Issachar's ass that I should bear all your scandalous revilements and submit to them in patience?"

He looked incredulous loathing, and with no more farewell than, "I shall speak with you again to-morrow morning," he went out again, locking the door after him. I laid me soberly down upon my bed, pulled off my gown, drew the quilted coverlet over me and with no more ado fell asleep. I slept sound, with very cheerful dreams at first, but meeting suddenly with Mun, in the last dream that I had, I found him rolling bowls by a river, with a ruinous castle behind him, and soldiers coming and going. I asked him: "How do you do, sweet Mun?" He answered "Do? How should I do, when you are married to another? I roll bowls, I smoke my pipe, I look forward to better days." He turned his back upon me and walked into the castle, where I could not follow him because a sentry stood guard upon the door. The sentry was armed with a pike, and began to show me the several postures, with "Mary, this is how the pike is trailed; see, Mary, this is how the pike is ordered." I looked more closely at his face and lo, it was my husband! "Oh, go off and leave me!" said I. "Where shall I go, Wife?" he asked plaintively. "Why," said I, "to whom else but to your evanishing mistress Micol, the Queen of the Fairies, whom once in a thicket at Babraham, near to Cambridge, you invocated with candle and wand and with whom you bargained immortality at a high price." (Why I said this, I know not.) Then I made to push past him, but his shoulders began to heave up and down with sobs. I was sorry for him, and said: "Nay, Husband, I did not mean to vex you!" Then he thrust his hand into his pocket and pulled out a piece of paper in which were wrapped several little caraway-cakes, and proffered them to me. "By now they are musty and stale," said he, weeping again.

I remember no more, but I awoke laughing and there was my husband in coat and hat and shoes standing over me. The dawn had come, but it was as yet too early for me to rise, so I wished him good-morning and asked him why he was already astir.

When he made no answer, I told him that I was heartily sorry for the quarrel between us, and was resolved to be a good wife to him; but that being confined strictly in his house all day, like a prisoner, with no employment nor any means of exercising my body, the gross humours were naturally pent up and worked upon my mind like a poison, so that I had said I knew not what.

He answered shortly: "Nay, Mary, we did not quarrel; for there can be no such thing as a quarrel between master and servant. You were rebellious and impudent and disobedient; and all this night I have watched and pondered upon my trial, and at last with the dawn I have been granted illumination. To correct you corporeally as you deserve I cannot, or not without scandal—and, as wise Virgil says, no man can win a memorable name by conquest of a woman; to prolong your confinement would be neither convenient nor healthy; I cannot mulct you of money, for you receive no wages; you are insensible to gentle chiding; to forgive you would be weakness. I am determined to put you to public shame, by sending you back to your father's house at Forest Hill; nor will I receive you to my bosom again until I be assured of your hearty repentance. Moreover, at Michaelmas-tide, when I expect your return, Esquire Powell must pay me your promised marriage portion of one thousand pounds, as also the other money owed me, five hundred pounds; without the money you will not be welcome, as he must understand plainly."

I began to laugh and when, being taken aback, he asked me why I was so unseasonably merry, I answered that by Michaelmas-tide the little cakes would be every whit as mouldy as my Aunt Jones's biscuit.

"What little cakes?" he asked.

"Cry pardon," said I, "they were but little dream-cakes which a sentry fetched out of his breeches-pocket in my dream. I am still between waking and dreaming."

I believe, by the manner of his eyeing my naked arms and shining hair, where it straggled over the pillow, that if I had then pleaded humbly, with a tragical show of tears, that he would mitigate his anger towards me, he would have relented speedily enough; indeed if, without a word said, I had made room for him to come into the bed to me, he would have there and then cast off his coat and breeches and made me passionate addresses; nor given a thought for the poor trembling little boys who waited downstairs in the cold study, ready to read him out the passage that he had set for them from Pomponius Mela or Julius Solinus Polyhistor. However, I had a proud spirit. I remembered his partiality for Jane Yates, and poor Trunco's sufferings, and how severely he had used me, and his rude demand to see my vellum book, and the unnecessary beatings he had administered to his nephews. Besides, had he not threatened to send me back to Paradise? Wherefore, all that I said was: "Why, do as you please, Whey-face, it is all one with me. Yet I confess that of two disproportionate evils I prefer public shame at Forest Hill to private misery in Aldersgate Street."

He glowered magisterially at me, griping at the air with his hands, until I drove him out of my chamber with these words: "Since I am your wife in name only, and since you are determined to pack me off home again, a virgin yet, it ill becomes you to stand there gaping at me, with offence to my modesty. Mercy guard me! Remember how the chaste Lady in your Ludlow Masque answered the lascivious wizard when he held her prisoner in his castle and lusted after her with his rolling eye."

When I was apparelled and had dressed my hair, I went downstairs to breakfast, with a calmness of spirit that I doubt not but that he remarked; and ate a good breakfast. At table I said to the old gentleman in the hearing of the boys: "Father, I am sorry to take leave of you, but the fault (if fault it be) lies with your son John, who has been a wonderful indulgent husband to me. For, seeing how little work there is for my employment in this neat house, whereas my mother has written beseeching me (if it be in any way possible) to come back and help her for a few weeks in the management of the Manor-house, John has consented to let me go, for he has perfect faith in my discretion; and he will send me off by the public coach this morning, with my woman Trunco to see that I come to no harm."

My husband was about to interpose some harsh and contradictory sentence, but thought better of it, and contented himself by answering drily: "Yes, sir, my wife leaves us this morning; and I hope that she returns to us with a greater love for Aldersgate than I have yet found in her."

The old gentleman cried in his chirping voice: "I applaud your good nature, John. And I warrant her mother will be sensible of your kindness to her. For you know how the case is: whereas in the city the labour of a house is light in the summer but heavy in the winter, in the country it is clean contrariwise." Then turning to me he said: "Dear Child, I hope that you do not hate our reserved and philosophical manner of life here, or sigh for your hawking and hunting and other country joys. John is a noble man, and if he proves no less honest a husband to you than he has been a son to me, you are the most fortunate of women."

I replied: "Father, I will think of you with great kindness and affection while I am away."

My coffer was already packed with my ends and awls and Trunco soon had her bundle ready. She was not loath to depart by any means;

and, my husband excusing himself that he expected learned company that morning, the old gentleman undertook to see us to the coach, and a man was found to fetch the coffer away on a barrow. My husband, just before we went off, called me into his study as if to kiss me farewell; but instead he set a paper before me which he required that I should sign before he would release me. In this paper it was written that "Whereas I, Marie Powell, alias Mary Milton, do this day, the fifth day of July of the year 1642, of my own free will and consent, depart the house and abode of John Milton Esquire, Junior, situated in the Second Precinct of St. Botolph's Parish in the Aldersgate Ward of the City of London, I, the same Marie Powell, do hereby solemnly declare that I now return under sufficient escort, to the house of my father, Richard Powell of Forest Hill in the County of Oxon, Esquire, Justice of the Peace, and acknowledge myself to be no less a virgin than the aforesaid John Milton Esquire, Junior, found me when I first came to his house, and furthermore I declare that the same John Milton has used me well and has not withheld or kept back from me any part or parcel of the goods and moneys that I brought with me when I first came of my own free will to the same house."

This paper I signed and sealed in the presence of Jane Yates, who put her mark to it in witness; but since she could not read, and since my husband did not communicate to her the matter of my declaration, the secret was well kept. I believe that I would have signed any declaration, almost, to be enlarged from that rose-white prison, and since the words written there were no more than the truth I thought no harm of them. I supposed that he doubted my truthfulness and that the purpose of the paper was to prevent me either from vilely complaining to my father that he had used me against kind or otherwise abused me, or from taking a casual lover on the way.

It was delightful for me to walk down the alley and out again to freedom in Aldersgate Street, and through the bustling streets to Bishopsgate. The old man walked beside me very briskly, and continually pointed and mourned how London was changed since he first came there in the middle years of Queen Elizabeth's reign.

I had the curiosity to ask him his opinion of my husband's poems; but he would say no more than that his John was an ingenious boy with a good control of words; and that, for himself, he held not the skill and art of poetry in base account, but only the abusers of it, and that poetry might well make a pleasant remission from the bent of graver affairs and studies.

"Why, Father, I understand you perfectly," said I. "You would that John had consented to be bred in some useful profession?"

"Tell him not so," he answered smiling, "but pity my lost ambition for him. Poetry will never butter his parsnips or his toasts."

There were no vacant seats for us on the public coach, but in the yard I espied a horse-racing gentleman whom I knew, Captain Windebank by name, son to Secretary Windebank, who had a great house at Bletchingdon, to the north of Oxford, and was returning thither within the hour with his aunt and a servant. He agreed to take Trunco and me for the usual coach-fare, which the old gentleman paid him.

So we said our good-byes, and presently the coach rolled out of the yard, which was a comfortable coach with well-fed cattle harnessed to it, and away we went with crack of whip and bawling coachmen. I told the gentleman's aunt that I was lately married and now returning home for a few weeks to my mother, who was sick and needed me at her side. The old lady was not inquisitive, and treated me kindly, but she said: "I wonder that in times like these your good old husband is content to let you go from his side for even a short space of days."

"Nay," I answered, laughing, "that is my father-in-law, not my husband."

"Well," said she, "no matter. Have you not heard the news? There is a ship sailed from Holland, sent by the Queen, with arms and ammunitions of war for the King at York. To-day his ship is expected in the Humber, and soon enough the ordnance will roar, the pikes chatter and the pistols pop; for yesterday Parliament appointed a Committee of Safety, which is as good as to levy war against His Majesty. Yea, though the flames of war have not yet broke out in the chimney-tops, yet the black smoke ascends everywhere. It is on this account that my nephew and I are returning at once to his house at Bletchingdon, though our business here in London is not yet concluded. I pray God will raise up some good hearts about the King to second the desires of his Parliament. For I know the temper of the Commons at Westminster, which is very stubborn."

Captain Windebank, who was a Cavalier, but civil to his Puritanical aunt, said: "Madam, for my part, I pray God will change the hearts of those mean-spirited worsted-stocking men in Parliament, that they may abate their desires."

"Amen," said I. "Let there be an accommodation found. A civil war is nonsensical policy."

"That I deny not," cried the old lady, "nor that God can turn it all in a moment, if we turn again to Him. It will be from want of our prayers if this judgment comes upon the nation. Let us women especially pray with great earnestness and fervour, forasmuch as war is an ill time for us, of all creatures, being exposed to so many villainies."

Captain Windebank said: "Madam, I agree that Papist, Puritan and Protestant will be brought to common ruin, if matters continue as they do; yet I believe that the cause of this ruin will not be a want of praying but rather over-much praying in perverse forms of prayer."

I marvelled to see how many soldiers there were upon the roads, both horse and foot, coming and going; and before we were well passed out of London into the country we heard a distant booming sound—then another and another; which startled the horses and ourselves alike. Captain Windebank said that the sound proceeded from iron cannons, which the Parliamentarians were shooting off to try them. "God grant they shiver in pieces!" said he.

"And that nobody be hurt!" cried his aunt hastily.

Then the Captain said that, because of these warlike preparations, almost every mechanical trade throughout the country but those of armourer, cannon-founder, saddlemaker and the like was already much neglected and interrupted; and that the coffer upon the roof of the coach was filled with gold and silver plate, which he was fetching from London for the King, to be coined into money for his wars. Yet when the Captain alighted for a moment to untruss by the roadside, the old lady whispered to me: "He is no fool, in truth, and though doubtless we shall eat off pewter in his house until these unnatural times be passed, I assure you that the silver, the greater part of which is mine, will be safely buried under the roots of an old oak, or under a stone in the cellar." I was surprised that no Parliament officer stopped our coach to search it.

We lay that night at Aylesbury in Buckinghamshire, and Captain Windebank was good enough to pay the landlord with the fare that old Mr. Milton had paid him, else Trunco and I must have remained in the coach and gone hungry; and the next day about supper time we passed through Thame and were back in a country that I knew well; and after a few miles more Trunco and I saw the bell-gable of St. Nicholas's Church and the smoking chimneys of the Manor-house.

"Why, Trunco," I cried, as she and I went in at the gate, after I had taken grateful leave of my friends, "it is good to be back in Christendom again out of Heathenness. But in God's name, say nothing to your fellow-servants against either my husband or his household. Remember that (as I told the old gentlewoman in the coach) my mother made earnest suit by letter that she might enjoy my company for the residue of this summer; which my husband has affectionately granted. If I come to hear that you have said one word more than this, I will tear out your tongue."

"You may trust poor Trunco," she answered, "who lives only to serve you."

A sealed letter which my husband had entrusted to me for my father's hand I sent into the house by Trunco, for perhaps he might refuse me entrance when he had read it; but my mother came running out from the little parlour to embrace me, so soon as ever she heard my voice. Then she held me at arm's length and cried out in a loud voice: "Why, alack, the girl has lost all her colour! Daughter, surely you cannot already be breeding?" She also remarked the thinness of my cheeks and asked me: "Has he abused you? Has he beaten you? How have you come back to the house like a sick cat, without warning?"

She drew me into the parlour and sent Trunco out for Spanish wine for me and a piece of cold roast breast of veal with sweet pickle and salads and bread and butter; and then in came my father. I could see at once from his looks that I was welcome, despite what might have been written about me by my husband. Then while I ate and drank as greedily as a militia-horse he read the letter out as follows:

"WORSHIPFUL SIR,

"Your daughter Mary, with my free permission (and in earnest of my continued kindness) is now coached back to your house, in like manner as Mrs. Powell in her letter desired, intending to continue with you until Michaelmas. I confide that before that same Feast has passed you will have duly paid me the marriage portion agreed upon in the paper lately signed by our two pens and that you will also have made your promised quittance of the elder debt of £500 contracted upon statute-staple while your daughter was yet in swaddling clothes. She (unless I am to believe the common buzz that she was debauched before ever she came to me) remains virgin; and I pray, now that she is returned under your governance, that, for my sake, you will keep her guarded and secure from all scandals and intem-

perate follies. With the blessing of Heaven I will beget you grandsons upon
her body when she is restored to me, and when the cheerful performance of
your undertaking shall have enabled me to bear the expenses naturally con-
tingent upon their generation and genteel rearing.

"That you will remember me most affectionately to your Lady beseeches
"Your Worship's most sincere and faithful servant and well-wisher,

"JOHN MILTON."

My mother cried out at the close, and railed against Mr. Milton,
calling him a whoreson Ibis and saying that if indeed he had failed
in his duty by me (unless he were impotent) he deserved to be
whipped with a bull's pizzle through the longest street in Saint
Botolph's parish. She bade me tell my tale in a plain manner, which I
did; and when at last I came to the paper that I had been instructed
to sign, my father was as wroth as she. "Though he has wedded you
by lawful ceremonies of the Church," said he, "and duly bedded with
you, for which fact there are witnesses enough, he is in hopes, I believe, to discard you and slide out of his bargain, as though he were a
barbarous Russian. He will doubtless seek a flaw in the marriage
contract, which for a shrewd canon-lawyer is never difficult. Marie,
you acted unwisely when you signed that paper, for a marriage that
has not been consummated by *copula carnalis* is easier to break than
one that has been so consummated. Yet I believe that in a court of law
your avowal of present virginity would carry little weight, if it were
pleaded on your behalf that you signed it under duress. Have no care,
my child: I will see you are not further abused. And I am mighty glad
that you are home with us again. Let nobody know but that you come
hither for your health, the foul London airs not agreeing with you—
the paleness of your cheeks will, so to say, give colour to this ex-
planation—and nobody will think much upon the matter, and at
Michaelmas-tide we shall see what we shall see."

"Indeed, sir," said I, "I do not altogether mislike my husband. I
believe that he doted upon me at first, but his impetuous virgin passion
unbalanced him so that he tripped over his own spurs, as it were, and
fell headlong. Nor would he then laugh against himself but, starting
up again to his feet, accused me of contriving his mischance."

"Ay," said my father. "Or you may call him the fabled bear with the
kettle. He burns his chops upon it, and in rage hugs it to his bosom
so that it burns him the more."

"Or like the Emperor's Indian ape," said my mother, "who was

splashed on the belly with a little gout of mud. He scratched and
scratched at it to cleanse himself, until with his sharp nails he had
scratched through the tender skin and was mauling his own guts."

"Well," said I, "similitudes enlighten, but do not mend. Moreover,
I heartily regret that you are obliged to sell your Welsh lands and pay
so great a portion to my husband, when in this letter, as also in the
paper that I signed, he has not even acknowledged me to be his wife.
I might well, as you know, have married a fortune and helped to repair yours, had it not been for the rank tattling tongue of your mad
curate. If my husband will not beget children upon me until he has
your golden Jacobuses jingling in his canvas bag, or piled up in little
heaps upon his study table, I cannot believe that what he wrote in his
book concerning the 'virgin of mean fortunes honestly bred,' was
meant sincerely. However, I have now the honourable name of wife
in this town, which he cannot easily take from me; and nothing will
please me better than to continue awhile with you in my old way of
life; and I warrant that you will have no complaint against me for
idleness. Come now, let me sing you a song upon my guitar, the playing of which was forbidden me in Aldersgate Street! I'll give you *The
Lament of the New Wedded Wife*—the one that goes:

> 'Of scouring and sweeping I'll never complain,
> Were I safe home at York with my mother again.'"

So they kissed me, and bade me good night and gave me the little
chamber over the kitchen, to have for my own; for Zara and Ann now
shared the bed in my former chamber. I had my vellum book with
me still, and in the morning I would mount my nag and take my
gerfalcon on my fist and clip away at full gallop over Red Hill.

CHAPTER SIXTEEN

The Beginning of the War

I N MORE peaceful times, I doubt not, this sudden return to my parents' house would have occasioned no end of cruel gossip in Forest Hill, where (as the rhyme says) "tongues are never still." But now it wanted a few weeks only before the ordnance boomed in earnest and the muskets were discharged without false fires. Already in July there was in our town little talk or thought of anything but civil war; and signs were observed that portended the country's ruin. That summer the white gilliflowers would not bloom, but there was unusual abundance of poppies in the fields, blood red, and in our cellar three hogsheads of good beer were turned to vinegar by a storm of thunder.

Our county of Oxfordshire was divided in its allegiance, three of the nine Members sent to Parliament inclining towards King Charles and six towards King Pym; in Oxford itself, the University was for King Charles, but the Town against him. On the King's side, Commissions of Array were granted to noblemen and knights, empowering them to raise troops "in protection of the Kingdom"; on the Parliamentary side, the Militia Ordinance was voted, by which Lords-Lieutenant were appointed to raise troops for the very same purpose. The Lord Saye and Sele, nicknamed Old Subtlety, was the Lord-Lieutenant appointed for Oxfordshire who, though of most ancient lineage, was a grave Puritan who hated Court manners and had been foremost of the nobility in his resistance to the King's arbitrary rule. Of the other noblemen, knights and gentlemen of good estate in our county the greater part favoured the King: as, for example, the Tyrrells and the Gardiners, Sir Timothy Tyrrell being granted a colonel's commission in the Royal service.

When at last the King's proclamation from his Court at York was read at Oxford by the public magistrate, many houses of our neighbours were found to be divided against themselves—sons against fathers, and brothers against brothers. In this proclamation, for the

211

suppressing of what was termed "a rebellion under the conduct and command of Robert, Earl of Essex" (who had accepted the supreme authority over the Army of Parliament), His Majesty inveighed against "the malice and pernicious designs of men, tending to the utter ruin of our Person, the true Protestant religion, the Laws established, the property and liberty of the subject and the very being of Parliaments." On the other side, the Parliamentary proclamation which made traitors of all who took up arms to oppose the Earl of Essex, was written in terms very loyal and tender towards His Majesty: he was represented by them as "led astray by Papists and other evil counsellors, who design by these means to bring about the utter ruin of the Crown." However, both sides equally called upon all good people to contribute their assistance, in their persons, servants and money, with all alacrity and cheerfulness, the King therewithal offering to protect Parliament against its enemies and Parliament offering to protect the King against his. All seemed inside out and arsy-varsy.

Mun's sister, the Lady Cary Gardiner, rode over to ask my father's help in some small matter of a warrant. She told us that her husband (whom she dearly loved) was already gone from her to the King's Court at York; that her brother Mun was fighting for his life against the rebellious Irish, with Parliament as his paymaster, though no man living was more loyal to the King; and that her brother Ralph was of Mr. John Pym's party in the Commons. Now her father was sent for by the King to play his part as hereditary Knight-Marshal, and to raise the Royal Standard with ancient ceremony—though where it should be raised was not yet settled, because of much envy and jealousy between the great Lords for this honour. The Lady Cary asked my father, very ingenuously, to which side he himself inclined; who replied with a laugh that he was a convert to *Kyhoysasism*. When she inquired what this strange new profession might be, he answered that the word was spelt out by the lines of the ballad "Keep Your Head On Your Shoulders, And So I Shall Mine." In short he was a Neuter. He would obey all orders that came to him lawfully, but would undertake nothing voluntarily; and if he fell between two stools he hoped he would fall soft. The Lady Cary was then emboldened to discover to us that her father, the Knight-Marshal, had no reverence for the Bishops for whom the whole quarrel subsisted. He had written to her that he heartily wished that His Majesty would yield to Parliament, but that he had eaten the Royal bread for thirty years and therefore

would not desert him in his need. Indeed, he had declared that he
would rather lose his life to preserve and defend things which were
against his conscience to preserve and defend, than renounce his
allegiance and his duty. To this my father replied that, as he heard,
the Lord Falkland also, though he had been an enemy of Ship-Money
and of prelatic rule, had taken up arms for His Majesty—secretly de-
testing the cause in which he was engaged, yet unable in honour to
abandon it.

Then we began to exchange reports and rumours of the ill-behaviour
of the Parliamentary soldiers as they went about the country to their
musters, how they plundered houses and cottages, and desecrated
churches, breaking the organs and dashing the pipes with their pole-
axes, crying scoffingly, "Hark how the organs go!" and how the King's
soldiers similarly plundered cottages and houses. And my father told
how a party of the King's men had led their horses into a church
(where the congregation was made up of godly precisians), and there
blasphemously baptized them at the font, though without use of the
cross, with such Puritanical names as "Day-of-Humiliation Esau" and
"Curse-God-and-Die Job"; and how their corporal had climbed up
into the pulpit and whined through his nose in a canting sermon to
"all devout Horses, Mares, Jennets, Hinnies, Jack-Asses, Milch-Asses,
Colts, Foals and Fillies here in faith and love assembled."

The Lady Cary and I walked together in the garden, it being good
handsome summer weather, and when we were private she stood still,
and "Mistress Milton," said she, "you will pardon my freedom, I hope;
only tell me, why have you used my dear brother Mun so ill? How
had you the heart to marry another so lightly? Before he went to
Ireland he confessed to me that you and he had a perfect understanding together, and charged me to love you like a sister; and when
I was married to Sir Thomas and settled at Cuddesdon I was to ride
over often to see you, and keep you ever in mind of him, and report
to him how you looked, and take from your lips any loving messages
that you might wish to send him. Well, Mistress, I was prevented in
that; for because of my husband's father being imprisoned it was not
until June that I came to Cuddesdon and upon the very day that you
were married to this Cambridge scribbler and nobody. From a letter
that came to my hand to-day I believe that my poor Mun's heart is
near broken and all the courage he can at present muster is little
enough to keep him alive."

I stood dumbfounded and asked her: "But my lady, is it not so that Captain Verney is betrothed to his cousin Doll Leke, and that lately he sent her a ring of his hair? For so your husband assured us."

"No, no," she cried, "the ring of hair was for his mother, and Doll Leke complained and was jealous of the gift, as I told my husband plainly. My brother Mun writes that when he was aware that you were married to Mr. Milton, he felt a faintness to seize his spirits in an extraordinary manner, so that he broke out in a cold sweat, and the distemper of his mind quite dispersed his spirit."

My eyes began to prick and I begged her, if she pleased, to acquaint Mun with the true course of events; how I was suspected by the curate and by the whole town of being debauched by Mun, and how my life was made miserable, and how when I heard that he was to marry his cousin Leke I had despaired; and how I had consented, upon an urgent motion from my parents, to wed Mr. Milton, to whom my father owed a great sum of money upon statute-staple. "And add this," I cried, "that I am the most miserable of women, but a maid yet—for I have come away from my husband upon a quarrel, and he has not known me."

The Lady Cary Gardiner had in her features much that recalled Mun, though she was by no means handsome, and when she wept and pitied me it was as though she were Mun himself. She took me by the hand and pressed it, and promised to come again to see and comfort me.

I pressed her for news of Mun. She told me that he had lately been sick of a violent fever and given over to the physicians for a dead man; which, I suppose, was about the same time that I had been so melancholic with my husband. But now, she said, he was in a way to recovery and had gained about £50 by pillage from the Irish. Then she undertook to act as a go-between for Mun and me, so long only as it was nothing dishonourable that I asked her to convey to Mun; for she held matrimony sacred, however inadvisedly entered into.

I said: "Tell him that it is 'we two' once more, but only so long as I am reprieved from my duty to my husband, and that meanwhile we may commune in spirit only; for to meet in the flesh would be madness, even were it possible. Tell him that I love him as I have never loved any other in my life."

She promised to write this to Mun, and kissed me and so departed.

In this same week two soldiers of the Lord Saye and Sele's regiment had carried off some geese from our field, for which, however, my father received full satisfaction upon his bringing information against them, and the felons were made to ride the wooden horse for an hour, with muskets tied to their feet, goose feathers in their hair, and their fault written large on a paper pinned to their breasts. He took the occasion to inform the Lord Saye that the Manor of Forest Hill, with all its appurtenances, was not his own, but was leased from the Bromes, and held in mortgage by Sir Robert Pye the Elder, a famous Parliamentarian; and he desired that his Lordship's regiment should be instructed to avoid trespass or plunder. At the same time he sent to the nearest commander of the King's troops to inform him that, though he was himself past the age of active service, his two elder sons were engaged for the King and his own loyalty was well known. When persons came to the house notorious for their affection toward the King, then my mother was the chief speaker; but my father conversed reasonably with persons suspected of a contrary opinion, and then she held her tongue.

My brother James was one of those scholars of Oxford who, together with the privileged men of the University, were called up by Dr. Pinke, the Deputy Vice-Chancellor, to be trained under his eye, for the defence of Oxford; for soldiers of the Parliament were continually passing through the county in two's and three's and in whole companies, and Dr. Pinke feared that an attempt would be made by them upon Banbury, by which Oxford would be endangered. There were a few old weapons in the colleges, with which the scholars were armed: and one day in the middle of August the whole muster, over three hundred men in all, marched from the Schools along the High Street until they came to Christ Church, where they were put into battle array and exercised in their postures, until it began to rain a little, when they marched back again. James was provided with a pike, the troops being divided into two companies of musketeers, one of halberdiers and one of pikemen. He marched shoulder to shoulder with a Doctor of Law on his right hand and a Divine on his left, and ahead of them went the Drums and Standard of the Company of Cooks to the University. There was another muster three days later and more than four hundred men came together at the Schools. After being instructed in the words of command and in their postures, they skir-

mished together for a few hours; but the muskets were all refuse stuff
and unserviceable except for false fires, some even having no touch-
holes.

On the next day, which was Sunday, came James to droll with us
upon the martial madness that had overcome the University. We asked
him how it was that the Town had not also trained that day, as had
been commanded. He answered that the burgesses had privily forbidden the citizens to muster, lest they should seem to do it for the King.
I asked him, drolling, too, did he not think it glorious to manage a
pike, this being the most honourable of weapons in common estima-
tion? and he laughed. He held that when serviceable muskets and carbines and pistols had been distributed to the armies, the pike was a
very ill weapon indeed, which he would think it no honour to wield.
Said he: "Pikes against pistols and carbines which can kill and sink at
a hundred and twenty yards off and more—that is a very unequal con-
test. I would desire to know whether there is any wisdom or glory to
stand with pikes only against leaden bullets? Nor is there one pikeman
in twenty who with his utmost skill and strength can wound a man
mortally who wears a steel corselet, or even a buff coat. In an uproar
in the Low Countries, as Mun Verney lately told me—the quarrel aris-
ing from a game of cards in which a Switzer accused an Englishman
of cheating him of a few halfpence—the true value of pikes was ap-
praised. For a division of Switzers stood with pikes charged, and there
came against them two buff-coated soldiers of Colonel Barclay's regiment, armed only with swords, who forced their way into the midst of
the body and lopped off a dozen pike-heads and came out again un-
scathed, with three or four pike-heads held in their hands, which they
threw among the Switzers with great derision, crying: "Oh, do us no
harm, good men!"

But it would have made an old pig laugh to see what ancient rusty
arms were distributed to the soldiers at this time—brown-bills and
lances that were relics of the Civil Wars of the Roses, with breast-
plates, gorgets and pots that seemed relics of the Crusades. My father,
in appointing a guard for our town against marauders, bade every man
use the weapon that was handiest to him: the labourers, their mattocks
and pitchforks and hedging-hooks; the woodmen, their axes; the coop-
ers, their hammers. For he said that there was no excellent virtue in a
halberd or pike unless a man were long habituated in its use. And sure
it was that, towards Shotover, one of our shepherds, being threatened

by a rude soldier with a brown-bill, ran at him with a pair of shears and would have clipped great pieces off him had the soldier not incontinently dropped his weapon and run off.

On August 24th came news that Sir Edmund Verney had raised the King's Standard at Nottingham, on the field behind the Castle. This Standard had a flag hung on top of it with the King's arms and a hand pointing to the Crown, and this motto, *Give Cæsar his due.* In accepting the charge, Sir Edmund had sworn that, by the Grace of God, they that would wrest that Standard from his hand must first wrest his soul from his body. However, as we heard, the weather was unseasonable and when the Standard had stood for awhile it was blown down by a strong and unruly wind and could not be raised again that day; which was taken as an evil presage by the King's friends. Nor had there been any great conflux of people to the ceremony: but few soldiers and fewer arms.

It was wonderful to me that though nine men of every ten throughout the country were opposed to the war, and would rather sit still than fight, yet that remaining one-tenth of vicious and heated harebrains could preach or curse or goad the rest into warlike action. To honest, quiet people it seemed a war directed by drunken and profane Publicans and Sinners on the one hand and by hypocritical Scribes and Pharisees on the other; and because of this general unwillingness to fight it was conducted irregularly, sluggishly and (until there were revenges to be exacted) in a humane and gentlemanly manner except by a few insensate, barbarous rogues of either party, or by old soldiers who had learned to be cruel and base in the German wars.

Now the talk at Forest Hill was all of stones taken up to the top of Magdalen tower at Oxford, to be cast down upon any who attempted an assault upon the College, and how the highway by the East bridge, not far off, over which we passed into Oxford, was blocked with great logs. This obstruction was a great inconvenience to the country people, for every time a cart passed over the bridge with victuals or anything else, a kind of timber gate must be lifted up by chain and pulley. There was a very strict guard kept here by night; as also at the crooked trench which they dug across the entrance to the city between Wadham College and St. John's College Walks; and at Penniless Bench at Carfax. However, my brother James told us that all this was but vain show and pretence, for the Town was on the contrary side to the Gown, and when the Gownsmen began, for the greater security of the city, to pull down the stone bridge over the stream at Osney, the Townsmen in great numbers marched out and made them leave off. Dr. Pinke feared that if the Lord Saye and Sele came against him in force, the city could not be held for more than half an hour—for besides his scholars and privileged men he had with him only 150 indifferent troops who had ridden in under the command of Sir John Byron—and that the halls and colleges would be sacked and set afire. He therefore rode off one day to deprecate for himself to his Lordship at Aylesbury, and report that the troopers were to be sent away, and the scholars disarmed, so that Oxford would lie wide open and in-offensive. Yet the Lord Saye was not there, and his lieutenants gave Dr. Pinke no welcome, but called him a perjured malignant and sent him off to prison in London.

A few days later, about nine o'clock in the morning, came the ru-mour to our Manor that a great body of Parliament horse was riding along the road from Thame towards Oxford; and our harvesters left the fields, though the carrying-in of the harvest was much behind-hand because of the tempestuous weather of August, and ran to watch the array. They did not return to the field that day—to my father's great loss, forasmuch as on the next day it rained, and again on the night following. It was generally feared that these men would do great harm to Oxford, plundering the colleges and showing no respect for the painted windows or the libraries; but since the scholars had laid down their arms and Sir John Byron's troopers were gone away, little trouble ensued. The Lord Saye coming into the city, in a carriage with six horses, gave order for the fortifications to be demolished. He sent men to search the colleges for hidden plate and arms, and found plate hidden behind the wainscote at Christ Church and seized it. No college plate was seized that was not hidden, but the heads of colleges were constrained to promise not to employ it against Parlia-ment. His Lordship lodged at the Star Inn, and there was a bonfire, heaped in the street before this inn of a few popish books and pic-tures taken out of churches and colleges. No harm was done to the fine painted windows at Christ Church and elsewhere, which the troopers wondered at as shamefully idolatrous; but a London trooper, a stark precisian, as he rode by St. Mary's Church in the High Street, discharged a bullet at the stone image of Our Lady over the porch, and at one shot struck off her head and that of the child held in her arms. Another tried his pistol against the image of our Saviour over the gate of All Souls College, but he missed his aim and an alderman came running up and entreated him to husband his powder and shot; so he refrained from a further essay.

Then a regiment of London blue-coats marched into Oxford, and another of russet-coats; they were all terrible inexpert in the handling of their arms and mutinous in demanding the pay promised them, which was five shillings by the month for every man, besides their bread and cheese; but the Lord Saye clapped the loudest-mouthed of them into prison and pacified the rest with promises.

This was a few days before Michaelmas, and all this time I had been so busy in my household tasks and so content to be at home again that the weeks had flown like days. Now I went to my father and asked him point blank what his intentions were, whether to send me back with the money, or without, or not at all. He answered that he had no money in hand, nor if he had would he be fool enough to send any great sum in coin to London, which assuredly would be seized by the soldiers on the way; nor would he have me go to London without it, lest my husband should refuse to accept me, and so cast me adrift. Said he: "My dear, be ruled by me. Sit you still and do nothing, and if your husband write us a letter, answer it not, for neither will I; it is common knowledge that all letters are now stopped and opened by the way and that many are kept back. Mr. Milton will have no proof that his letter has come to your hand. Then let us watch in what manner the war goes, and be guided in our actions. If the King gain an outright victory, as is promised him before Christmas, and march to London and over-awe it, then your husband is likely to be apprehended and lose his ears and be branded of both cheeks and rot in a jail, and it were better not to be married to such a one."

"But if the King be defeated, sir?" I asked.

"Why, that will be grievous," said he, "but at least you will have a good home ready to receive you; for your husband, with his gift for writing in the Parliamentary interest, is likely to become one of their chief men. Nay, he cannot deny that he is lawfully married to you, and when I plead that I have lost all my wealth in forced contributions to the losing cause, he will have no honourable course left but to take you back without the promised portion."

"It will be unkind not to answer his letters if they are honestly written," said I, "for I believe that he loves me too well rather than not well enough. Indeed, I judge him to be guilty of the sin against

which Dr. John Donne inveighed in a sermon, that of loving his wife
as hotly as if she were his mistress. His austerity towards me, which
some would call cruelty, is turned towards himself also; so that I
cannot bring myself to hate him. Moreover, if he be irrevocably bound
to me by the vows he made in our Church porch, why, so am I to him
by the vows that I made him in that very place."

"This sentiment bespeaks a good spirit in you, dear heart," my father
said. "Yet for the present nothing can be done, I swear it cannot. I am
now poorer by a great deal than before you were married; my Welsh
estate is but a figure of speech naughtily intruded by your mother into
my bargaining with Mr. Milton, when he was obdurate and stuck
upon his demand for a great sum of money; and, as you know, this
year's harvest is so miserable that I cannot expect my tenants to pay
me their agreed rents, nor will I fill my own barns above one-third
full."

What could I say? I stayed on. Many more companies and troops
of soldiers now passed into Oxford; but the trained bands of the city
marched out in a contrary direction to Thame, where all the militia
of Oxford were mustered by the Lord Saye and received arms from
him. On the day following Michaelmas there was a riot at Carfax in
Oxford between blue-coats and russet-coats: for the blue-coats continued mutinous and were bold enough to raise a cry that the King
was a better paymaster than Parliament, and that if they were sent
to fight him they would go over with their arms in their hands. At
this the russet-coats, who were of a more disciplined and religious
sort and scandalized by the blasphemies with which the blue-coats
interlarded their drunken invectives, drew upon them. There was
brisk play with naked swords for awhile, and some soldiers on either
side had fingers sliced off, or thumbs; but none was killed. This riot
put our country people into such an affright that for some days they
dared not bring provisions into the city.

Then first the blue-coats and then the russet-coats were marched
out of the city against the King, who was with an army at Shrewsbury;
but many of them were missing at the muster and their captains and
sergeants came scouring the countryside for them and gathering up
the arms that they had cast away. A dozen or two of these cowards
took refuge in Shotover Forest, and would creep out at night and steal
our geese and poultry; but they were at last apprehended and sent
back to be whipped through their companies. At a time when three

thousand soldiers were billeted at Oxford in one night, there was an overflow into all the towns and villages around, and a hundred fierce-looking troopers came to Forest Hill; but when my father showed their captain his contract with Sir Robert Pye, M.P., they behaved in a docile and peaceable manner, and paid for anything that they required. Our curate also preached in a manner familiar to them, whereby they believed themselves among friends, though indeed Forest Hill stood resolutely for the King, if it stood for anything at all. What pleased them most was that every day he would rise before dawn and preach to them by candlelight, so that they would be singing their psalms before ever the cock crew: for they held an hour of candlelight worship to be worth three of sunlight in the Lord's eyes. These troopers rode away on the fourth day, and soon the country was empty of all soldiers but a few late stragglers.

Towards the end of the month of October came confused rumours of a great battle fought on a Sunday at a place some forty miles northward from us, but how it had been decided, none could say. This was the fight of Edgehill. The King, with 14,000 men, had marched from Shrewsbury towards London and the tidings were brought to Worcester, where the Earl of Essex was leaguered; who thereupon made haste with his 10,000 men to intercept the King and bodily bar his progress. Yet the Parliament scout-master had no certain information of His Majesty's whereabouts, and the two armies marched along roads that ran in the same direction, but twenty miles asunder; and both were alike ignorant of this circumstance during a ten days' march. But at last in the south of Warwickshire there was a chance encounter of troopers at forage, and the Earl hastily interposed his army between the King's army and the town of Banbury; but half his ordnance, being drawn by oxen, was a day's march behind him which loss was much felt.

Battle was joined at Edgehill, in country which belonged partly to the Lord Brooke and partly to the Lord Saye and Sele, who both commanded regiments for Parliament. The King's nephew, Prince Rupert of the Rhine, General of the Royal Horse at the age of twenty-three, disbanded a part of the Parliament army with a charge; but his men turned to plundering the baggage carts, and meanwhile the Parliament army rallied a little and pressed forward against the King's foot, the most of whom had gone hungry for two days because of bad management and were without much spirit. There ensued fierce fight-

ing for the possession of the Royal Standard, which was carried in a
troop of the King's Life Guards, composed of young noblemen and
knights of such quality that their estates were reckoned to be more in
value by far than those of the whole army opposed to them. Mun's
father defended the Standard very valiantly and adventured it among
the enemy, using the point for a pike, and broke off the point in the
body of a dragoon; then he slew many more (some say sixteen, some
but two) with his sword, but alas! at the last his hand was hacked
off at the wrist and the Standard taken, and he was slain. The Parliament men were thereby marvellously encouraged, and pressed forward
until the King himself was in great danger from the flying pistol-
bullets; and the little princes, Charles and James, who watched the
battle from the windows of The Rising Sun Inn, were like to have
been taken, for they were under the charge of the philosophical Dr.
Harvey, the same who discovered the circulation of the blood, and
whose thoughts had wandered from the battle. However, they made
shift to escape on their ponies. In the same fray fell the Lord Grand
Chamberlain, the Earl of Lindsey, whom the King had appointed
Commander-in-Chief of his armies.

When night fell, five thousand carcases of men lay dead upon the
field, of which each party acknowledged but one thousand as its own,
yielding the four thousand to the other. The Earl of Essex lost the
Standard so hardly won, for a Papist who was a captain of the King's
Guard, disguising himself with a deep-yellow, or orange-coloured,
Essex scarf taken from one of the slain, insinuated himself among the
Parliamentarians; where he boldly accosted his Lordship's secretary
(in whose charge the Standard then was) claiming to have taken it
himself, and was indignant that a mere penman should be confided
with so rich a booty. By the loudness of his outcry he forced the
secretary to yield the Standard, and in the darkness ran back to the
King's army and laid it at His Majesty's feet. Then, though neither side
could justly claim the victory, both presumed to do so; but the King
had the greatest advantage, for the Earl of Essex withdrew his bat-
talions to Warwick, and the King possessed himself of Banbury and
the Lord Saye and Sele's own castle, and marched on towards London;
and upon the 29th of October he came riding in by the North gate of
Oxford, at the head of his foot, with sixty or seventy Parliamentary
colours borne before him, which had been taken in battle, and the

drums playing dub-a-dub, and the men exulting. After the foot came a train of great guns and ordnance, twenty-seven pieces in all, which were driven into Magdalen College grove.

The Mayor and Aldermen of Oxford waited upon the King at Carfax, and as they had presented wine to the Parliamentary troopers, so now they presented a gift of money to His Majesty. He lodged at Christ Church with his nephews, the Princes Rupert and Maurice, and the little Princes his sons. The Royal troops were billeted in Oxford and the country about, of whom a company came to Forest Hill, very riotous, and stole poultry and pigs. These rabble heroes also mocked at the curate when he read the service in Church, and were indecently familiar with the women; and some there were who would not pay their score at the inn, alleging that they defended us from the fury of the rebels and deserved to drink free.

Then came regiments of the King's horse, riding through Oxford, but did not stay: they continued towards Abingdon and Reading and London. The arms that had been presented to the Townsmen of Oxford in the muster at Thame were now taken away by order of the King; which were presented to the Gownsmen, so that my brother James had a pike again and marched with the King in the Earl of Dover's Regiment. My brother Richard, together with other gentlemen of the Inns of Court, served in a troop of horse under the Lord Keeper; but an equal number of his fellow-lawyers were briefed by the other parties in the case and entered themselves as Life Guards to the Earl of Essex. My imagination pictured how it would be when my two brothers came to exchange blows with my husband; for I made no doubt but that he would stand with pike charged in the great battle that must be fought in defence of London, whither the Parliament army was now returning by way of Northampton.

After the King had taken Reading, we took heart from news that Parliament was ready to treat with His Majesty and that negotiations were already begun; it was confidently expected that the war would soon be ended. The dreadful slaughter at Edgehill, where both armies had proved their valour honourably and beyond dispute, was by most men accounted a sufficient blood-letting for the nation's sickness, that proceeded from too much grease and store of blood—that is to say, from too long and careless a prosperity. Then came news that Prince Rupert had advanced again and taken Brentford, even while the

peacemakers were still at work together, and that all the trained bands
of London had marched out to Turnham Green to oppose him, under
command of the Right Worshipful Major-General Skippon. These
trained bands presented so martial an aspect that the King would not
allow the Prince to make an infall upon them; he drew his army back
again to Colnbrook, and resumed his negotiations with Parliament
(but to no purpose) and presently retired thence to Reading and
thence again to Oxford; for it was now the end of November, the time
when all honest armies go into winter quarters and sleep like dormice
until the spring. Oxford he girdled around with a chain of outposts,
at ten or twelve miles distance from it, and raised new works in place
of those that the Lord Saye had demolished.

I need not have quailed at the thought of being widowed by my
brothers, for my husband, as afterwards I learned, was not even in the
march to Turnham Green. Though courageous by nature and remembering how the noble tragedian Æschylus had fought in defence of
Athens, his native city, against the Persians, my husband had lately
fallen out with the Captain of his company, a hosier by trade, whom
he considered a mean-spirited fellow, and would serve under him no
longer. Then, having once grounded his pike, he bethought himself
that there was less honour and greater danger by far in modern warfare than in the ancient. Æschylus, in service as a pikeman, was
doubtless quick to catch or turn away the Persian arrows that were
shot at him, using the shield strapped upon his left arm. Yet in these
modern days were not many brave and valiant men shot down from
behind hedges by cowardly musketeers who would never dare look
them in the face? And what man lived of such incredible dexterity
that he could turn aside a pistol bullet with the cheek of his pike?
Thereupon, considering discretion the better part of valour, he resolved not to adventure his life in battle: for, were he slain, who
would be found to complete the divine tragedy *Adam Unparadised*
that lay half-finished upon his table? A poet's life, he contended, was
more precious than that of a hundred thousand husbandmen or arti-
sans, and it would be ungracious to God to spill it wastefully in battle.
And if, as the scripture says, a live dog is better than a dead lion, a
live lion is better than anything; let the dogs die in his stead!

He therefore continued in his accustomed mode of life, except that
he no longer performed exercises in the Artillery Garden, and if he

perfected himself in the postures of the pike, this he did in the privacy of his garden and for the instruction of his nephews, who, like all children in time of war, longed to be soldiers.

Then came the alarm at the approach of the King's Army to Brentford; and the Lord Saye in a speech at the Guildhall roused up the whole City with: "There is no danger but in sitting still. Let every man shut up his shop and take a weapon in his hand! Up and be doing, for the Lord will be with you!" At this my husband yielded up his pike to a serving-man who stood in need of one; and he wrote a sonnet, which he pinned up as a protection upon the door of his house—being sadly assured that the trained bands, who were officered by such base tradesmen as his hosier-captain, would not stand their ground against men of quality, but would break at the first discharge of muskets and save themselves by their good footmanship. Thus, he argued, the City would be left without defence, except for what might be done by a few desperate men in the guard-houses erected here and there in the streets, with posts, bars and chains; which resistance would encourage the Cavaliers to greater fury, and so the whole assembly of two hundred thousand souls or more would be given up to spoilation and rape.

In the aforesaid sonnet he addressed whatever Cavalier captain or colonel or lesser officer might happen upon his house, and besought his protection against the outrages of the rude soldiery, promising perpetual glory for this act of mercy. "Lift not thy spear against the Muses' bower," he wrote, and recalled how Alexander, the great Macedonian, had, at the sack of Thebes, spared the house of the poet Pindar (though he was long dead) and how on another occasion the Spartans, for the sake of the poet Euripides, had refrained from destroying the whole city of Athens.

The assault intended to London was not delivered and my husband took down the paper; and when a neighbour, Mr. Jokay Matthews, drolled to him about it he was greatly offended and determined to prove himself no coward, by entering the Parliamentary service. Nor would he be shaken from his new resolve by the news that the valiant Lord Brooke, with whom he was familiarly acquainted and who was also a writer of anti-prelatic books, was slain by a chance shot discharged from the roof of Lichfield Cathedral. Therefore when the Spring came, and when Sir William Waller was appointed to command a Parliamentary army in the West Country; and when every

preacher in London cursed Meroz * from his pulpit—why, then my
husband went boldly to Alderman Isaac Pennington, M.P., who was
the Lord Mayor of London and Colonel of the White Regiment, and
who held him in great esteem, and proposed himself to be recommended for Adjutant-General in Sir William's army!

Alderman Pennington asked my husband whether, though a skilled
pikeman and well-versed in the writings of such Latin military authors
as Ælian, Polyænus and Frontinus, he had experience of modern warfare? For without, he could not be recommended for so honourable an
appointment, the payment of which was eighteen shillings a day, while
there were zealous officers in Sir William Waller's army who had distinguished themselves in the famous Swedish service, yet held no
higher rank than captain, some of them, with payment of ten shillings.
For the Adjutant-General's place in an army, though below all colonels, is above all lieutenant-colonels. My husband contentiously denied such experience of warfare to be needful; for the Adjutant-
General's office, he said, is not to command, but to be sent abroad
for the conveying and speeding of the General's command to the rest
of the army; he is chosen for his fearlessness, his good address, his
eloquent tongue, his keen discretion and his copious memory; he must
also be one who can manage a horse well, show skill in swordsman-
ship and command instant obedience.

The Lord Mayor undertook (a little doubtfully, I suppose) to speak
with Sir William Waller in the matter; but it seems that Sir William
Waller, who had a difference with the Lord Mayor on some article of
religion—the Lord Mayor being the less precise in his Presbyterial
opinions—was not to be persuaded of my husband's ability, or already
was suited. Then my husband, since he could not obtain a position
worthy of his ambitions (for, esteeming himself inferior to nobody in
anything he undertook, he had hoped from Adjutant-General to rise
speedily to Commissary-General, or to Major-General) disdained the
humble post that was offered him of adjutant in the White Regiment,
and returned to the Muses' bower, or Meroz, until such time as the
men in authority should come themselves to seek his services.

---

* Their text was drawn from the Book of Judges: " 'Curse ye Meroz,' said the
angel of the Lord, 'curse ye bitterly the inhabitants thereof, because they came not
to the help of the Lord, to the help of the Lord against the mighty.'" It was used
to stir the laggards and neuters by the zealous ministers of both factions.

CHAPTER SEVENTEEN

My Husband Sends for Me

I
T IS not my purpose to write a history of the skirmishes, battles and
sieges of the late wars (the memory of which is dismally fresh in
the public mind): I shall strive to make mention of them only
in so far as my own life and those of my friends and kinsfolk were
affected and altered by them.

The King lay at Oxford throughout the winter of 1642–1643, and
made it his headquarters, as being the nearest place to London that
was commodious enough for his purposes. This proved a great inconvenience to the Gownsmen, who were turned out from their customary
lodgings to make room for the officers of the King's Court and Army.
The Court of Chancery was held at the Schools, some parts of which
were also used as a magazine for corn; the Court of Requests was
held at the Natural Philosophy School; the chief magazine for arms
and gunpowder was in New College; the magazine for cloth, to be
sewn into soldiers' apparel and coats, was in the Schools of Astronomy
and Music; and the Rhetoric School was a carpenter's shop where
were manufactured drawbridges for the new fortifications.

The passage of public coaches and carriers' wagons between London and Oxford was suspended, and all letters seized and examined.
I cannot therefore certainly say how many of the messages which my
husband sent to my father, enquiring the reason of my continued
absence, reached our house; but from something which my father let
fall I guess that one at least reached him. For I overheard that he
told my Uncle Jones: "If Mr. Milton is so solicitous for my daughter's
safe return, why comes he not himself to fetch her back, as a bold and
loving husband ought to do?"

My Uncle Jones answered: "Brother, how can he adventure himself
upon the journey, when he has written in so sharp a manner against
the Bishops? He would be apprehended for certain and cast into
prison, and then his case would be a hundred times worse; for, as I

have heard, Provost-Marshal Smith, the greedy prison-keeper at Oxford, exercises insufferable cruelties upon those who are committed to his charge."

"Well," cried my father, "if my wife Nan were to run off to London, then though I had published a hundred scandalous libels against the Parliament and though the guards on the road were never so vigilant, yet should I make shift to seek her out and carry her back with me or lose my life in the hazard."

To which my Uncle Jones coldly replied: "You could do no less, Brother, being a man of honour. For your wife's guardian, her Uncle Abraham Archdale, punctually paid you the £2,000 agreed upon in your marriage contract, which twenty years ago I witnessed, and afterwards there was her legacy of £1,000, which also dropped into your lap. But it seems that Mr. Milton has not yet received from you a penny of the sum promised him in your daughter's marriage-contract, which also I witnessed."

Then angry words were spoken on either side, and my Uncle Jones came never again to our house.

About New Year, 1643, the Mint was brought to Oxford from Shrewsbury, and set up at New Inn Hall which, having been a famous resort of Puritan scholars, was now by them deserted. The coming of the Mint was no cheerful sight for the Heads of colleges and halls, for the plate which had been spared to them by the Lord Saye, on condition that they refrained from using it against Parliament, was now forcibly taken from them by the King, who minted it into money. These Oxford coins were very pretty ones, on which was written in Latin, "Let God Rise up and Let His Enemies be Scattered!" But it was a sad loss to the colleges to be thus deprived of their ancient dishes, cans, cups and flagons. The President and Fellows of St. John's College, being loath to lose the memory of their benefactors, gave the King the sum of £800, the value of their plate by weight, hoping to save it; but His Majesty, while graciously accepting the money, sent again for the plate and turned it into crown-pieces and shillings. All the nobility and gentry of the County were now required to send in their plate, with a promise of repayment when victory should be won, and my father was constrained to send in 3 lb. weight, which included the cup and dish given me at my christening by my Godmother Moulton; but he kept back 9 lb. or 10 lb. of the better pieces, which he hid in the garden under a bed of clove-pinks. From these requisitions the King took in about 3,000 lb. of silver, silver-gilt and gold; but the two mint-masters, of which Esquire Bushell was one, complained how many gilt cups and cans and dishes, inscribed with honoured names, were underneath but base metal, serviceable to be coined into farthings but not into crown-pieces.

A great many soldiers were billeted upon us that winter, fit only for a gallows on this earth and a hell hereafter. They were very drunken, rude, tetchy, quarrelsome, discontented wretches, who did the estate infinite injury by their thieving and by grazing their horses without leave upon our meadows, and by the idle and wanton spirit that they infused into the tenantry. They made our fine house into a nasty common ale-house with their tobacco-smoke and spitting; and a barrel of our good beer would tremble at sight of them. A King's officer requisitioned our three best geldings for mounting dragoons upon, paying my father but £4 apiece, though worth double that sum; and our best team of heavy horses, at a mere £6 apiece, together with the new blue wain, he took for drawing a great brass gun; and three men of our household to be impressed into the Army, besides six or seven of our tenants' sons. By the King's order, none but able-bodied men were to be impressed, and single men rather than married, and serving men rather than house-holders, and mechanics or tradesmen rather than husbandmen. Nevertheless, my father did not strictly observe these preferences, but discarded the toss-pot knaves and other cards that he would soonest spare, without regard to their quality or condition. Horse-thieving was so common a crime in those days that we were forced to put locks upon the fore-feet of our remaining beasts; yet even this was no positive security against their loss. Nor was a man's life valued as formerly, death in battle being every soldier's expectation; and one day in our wood-yard two troopers fell out about a horse-shoe and went into the orchard apart together, and there fought with carbines. One shot the other in the breast and killed him, and was himself wounded in the leg, which ulcerated and within the week he was dead likewise.

In February our hopes were raised again by the arrival of Commissioners from Parliament, headed by the Earl of Pembroke, Chancellor of the University, who hoped to agree with the King upon an accommodation of differences and proposed a cessation of arms. The King received them well, and sent them away merry with a written answer; but since the Prince Rupert had a few days before this taken

Cirencester, which was strongly defended, the King was urged by a majority of his Counsellors to yield nothing; and so the war continued. Yet while the Treaty was in progress, namely from February until the middle of April, there was a lull made in the fighting; of which my husband took advantage to send a messenger to our house. Since he could find no man bold enough to undertake the double journey, the messenger he sent was his servant Jane Yates.

She came to the pantry door one morning in March and asked leave to converse with my father; but, as it chanced, the person who opened to her was Trunco, who bade her wait outside and shut the door in her face, and then came running to me in the pantry-room. "Oh, Mistress," she cried, "here comes that sour-breathed, lying rebel, Jane Yates, who would speak to his Worship your father. Have I your leave to fling her into the swine's trough, for I swear she was hatched in hell?"

"Nay, Trunco," I said, "that were uncharitable. But do not trouble his Worship, who is busy upstairs with his accounts; my mother may perhaps wish to speak to the woman on his behalf."

When my mother heard that Jane was come, she sent for her into the little parlour and there asked her business. Jane answered that she had a spoken message from Mr. John Milton to deliver to Mr. Justice Powell in person, and to none other. My mother told her that she was Mr. Justice Powell's wife, and that his Worship had given orders that the business he was at was not to be disturbed.

"Why, then, Mistress," said she, "I will wait in the kitchen, by your leave, until his Worship shall be at leisure."

"Nay, that you will not," cried my mother. "I will have no canting Presbyterial trash in my kitchen, stirring up trouble and dissettling the servants. If you must wait, you shall do so in the long barn where the soldiers are quartered; I warrant they'll cosset you kindly when Trunco here gives their corporal a report of the manner in which you entertained her in Aldersgate Street—now, won't they, Trunco? Trunco is a slut with a sweet nature, ready always to return good for good or evil for evil, in equal measure; and the corporal utterly abominates all Roundheads, whether male or female."

Jane then consented that, if she were positively forbidden to address Esquire Powell in person, she would give her message to my mother as his accredited agent; confessing that she feared for her chastity among the ungodly soldiers—though, for my part, I thought that no man living (unless he were blind, drunk and mad all in one) would have ventured to be amorous with such a frumpish, daggy creature as she.

"Say on, then, woman!" cried my mother.

"This is Mr. John Milton's message," said Jane. "He has written four times to your worshipful husband, since this past Michaelmas, but has received no answer; and fears lest his letters have been seized; and therefore sends me, as a person to be trusted, to deliver a message by word of mouth and bring an answer to him again; and he requires to know wherefore his wife is not returned to him, as was agreed, and commands her now to come back in my company. As for the money owing to him, he will be content at present with the £1,000 portion (for the other debt may wait a month or two) and requires it to be paid to Mr. Rous, the librarian at Oxford, who has undertaken to convey it to him by the hand of one of the Commissioners for Peace, Mr. Pierrepoint; and he demands that his wife be sent back to him with an assurance from Mr. Rous that the money is already delivered to him."

"And is that all?" cried my mother in a mocking tone. "In God's name, is that all? In his pretty garden-house at Aldersgate Street has your master received no news yet from some servant or neighbour that this country is embroiled in war? How thinks he that his Worship, my husband, can suddenly in these times lay his hand upon so great a sum as £1,000 or that, if he could, he would yield it to a saucy Presbyterial rebel rather than to his Sovereign Majesty, King Charles—who stands in need of every parcel of clipped groats that his loving subjects can scrabble together? Begone, now, lest I be wroth with you, you bleary-eyed, psalm-chanting hussy, and take a stick to your shoulders."

Nevertheless Jane Yates persisted and cried: "Madam, be not unkind to me, for I am come with great difficulty from London, and am but an envoy, as my Master says, not a principal in this matter. If I come not again with a written message, my master will accuse me that I have failed in my trust."

"Trunco," said my mother, "see that this woman is hospitably entertained for the honour of this house, and take no vengeance upon her." Then turning to Jane she said: "My worshipful husband sends his compliments to your Master and his answer to the impertinent message you bring is this: 'Let him scratch himself wherever he may itch.'"

"Oh, Madam!" cried the wretched woman, "I dare not take back such an answer to my Master!"

"And is he so terrible?" asked my mother. "Upon my soul, I pity you! Why do you not find another master? Yet you, who were bold to bring a rude request to one who is not your master, can surely be bold to carry back a suitable reply?"

So my mother dismissed her. Yet my father, when he heard from his bailiff that Mr. Milton's messenger was in the kitchen, and that she complained to have been denied access to him, went down to her. He addressed her civilly in the presence of the bailiff and myself, and gave her another message altogether. This was that, though I had been suddenly sent from London to Forest Hill by my husband without any invitation from himself, yet he was content to have me with him for awhile, and would guard me well until my husband came to fetch me; but that he loved me too well to hazard me, in the company of a serving woman only, between the embattled armies. As for the money, he said, it was to his regret that he could not deliver the same to Mr. Rous, unless with an assurance signed by my husband that not a penny of it would be used to comfort the King's enemies. And he sent his hearty respects and service to Mr. Milton, Senior. He made Jane repeat his words after him, and learn them by rote. When she had departed he called me to his study and said to me: "My son Milton thinks, perhaps, that he can divorce you, and presently marry another; but my message, given before witnesses, will prevent him, I dare swear; for it is a shrewd put-off and a pleasant one."

I asked him: "Pray, tell me, sir (for this is by no means clear to me), what are the grounds upon which a man or woman may plead for a divorce under the Law?"

He laughed a little and then answered: "Why, Mischief, that is a question as wide as the doors of a college library. Nevertheless, I will answer it in a short Latin verse if that will make you any the wiser:

> Error, conditio, votum, cognitio, crimen,
> Cultūs disparitas, vis, ordo, ligamen, honestas,
> Si sis affinis, si forte coire nequibis—
> Haec socianda vetant connubia, facta retractant."

However, when I looked rueful, he was good enough to explain the meaning of the verse, which was that, in Canon Law, the following were impediments that either forbade the solemnization of matrimony, or annulled it when it already was solemnized:

1. If one of the two parties be by error or trickery mistaken in the other's person, name or condition.
2. If one of them be already married to another.
3. If one of them should have taken a solemn vow of chastity before a priest.
4. If they be of consanguinity or affinity within the forbidden degrees of matrimony; or if unlawful carnal knowledge should have brought the parties within such degrees before matrimony was solemnized.
5. If either party in a previous marriage should have been guilty of adultery or incest; or if the man should have christened his own child.
6. If either party should have murdered a priest, or committed a murder in order to clear the way for a marriage.
7. If either party prove to be Jew, Turk, Saracen or such other.
8. If either of the parties should have used intolerable cruel violence to the other; or plotted against the life of the other.
9. If the man be a priest.
10. If the man be impotent * or the wife's nature be deformed, so that they may not know each other carnally.

"Now, there," he said, "is treasure spread for the Canon-lawyer; who can hit upon a flaw almost in any marriage. For if John of Stiles confess that before his marriage to Joan of Noke he slept between the same sheets with her aunt or cousin, or grandmother, why then, John and Joan were of the same affinity, and their marriage is no marriage, and they are as free as the air."

I asked: "But, sir, cannot a woman be divorced for an act of adultery, or for desertion of her husband?"

"Nay," said he. "A separation may be granted, but there lies no action for divorce: that is, neither party is free to marry again, as in the other cases. Nevertheless, the Puritans are pushing for a reform in this matter, and what is not permitted in Oxford to-day, may, for aught I know, be permitted in London to-morrow. Wherefore, since I will not have you whored by your husband's alleging that you have deserted his bed and board, I have injured his plea by the politic answer I returned his messenger. For he cannot deny that it was he that sent you away, rather than you that deserted him."

* This impediment had been pleaded against the Earl of Essex by his two wives successively, and they had been set free; which occasioned many sharp jests at Court and made him the more ready to show his manly valour in battle on the side of Parliament.

Suddenly he asked: "Tell me, do you perhaps desire to return to him, my dear, come what may?"

"Nay, an honest woman has no legitimate desires," I replied. "She obeys the orders of her governors. And if governors disagree, and if she knows not to which of her governors she owes obedience, whether her father or her husband, what can she do but obey always the latest order? Bid me stay, and I will stay."

"Stay!" said he.

I stayed. I was like a dog that has broken free, yet still trails the chain; and that same summer a Royal Proclamation was read at Oxford forbidding, upon pain of death, all commerce with London whatsoever.

1643 was the year in which the King hoped to achieve the subjugation of the Westminster Parliament—for he called an anti-Parliament at Oxford, which met in the Schools—and planned an advance upon London from three several directions. The plan was that the Earl of Newcastle should march from the far North, by way of Lincolnshire; Sir Ralph Hopton, M.P., who had won fame in the German wars, should march from Cornwall in the West, following along the southern coast; His Majesty himself should move out from Oxford as soon as the others had reached an equal nearness to London with himself. The Earl of Newcastle and Sir Ralph Hopton both won grand victories and by the summer, save for two or three seaports, the whole of the West and North were won for the King, and most of the Midlands. The Earl of Essex sought to make amends by a push at Oxford, and there was great alarm in Forest Hill when news came that he had taken Reading; but his army was discouraged by the death of Esquire John Hampden, M.P., accounted the grand champion of popular liberties, who was wounded in a skirmish a few miles from us, and died at Thame; the Earl fell back and presently Reading was regained by the King.

Nevertheless, the Parliamentarians were stronger than we had supposed. For the Fleet was faithful to them; and they wanted not for money to pay their soldiers; and they held Sussex, where are the principal ironworks in this country and where great guns are cast; and they might fetch from overseas what munitions of war soever they could afford to buy. The King suffered from three great inconveniences, beside the want of vessels: first, the want of money; second, that the levies raised by him in one county would not willingly march into another; and third, that there was continued strife and jealousy between his commanders, especially between his princely nephews and his proud English nobles—anyone of whom would rather that the common ship sank under them all than that he should abate a tittle of his dignity in obeying any commands but the King's only. Had it not been for these inconveniences, the King was already the victor. For London, the head of rebellion, was in such a dismal state of dissension and foreboding with crowds running through the streets, and crying for the blood of "that dog Pym" and of the traitors who were against the making of peace, that the King might have taken the City with ease, had he struck at it with a small, willing, well-paid army. But the gentlemen and peasants of the West would not adventure east until Gloucester had fallen, which was obstinately held by one Colonel Massey; nor would the gentlemen and peasants of the North adventure south until Hull had fallen, which had been succoured and revictualled from the sea.

The King therefore gave his army the about turn and besieged Gloucester, which, as he knew from letters that he had intercepted, could not hold out above another fortnight at the longest. He summoned the garrison, but Colonel Massey gave him a humble denial. Then said His Majesty: "If you expect help, you are deceived. Waller is extinct and Essex cannot come." Nevertheless, the inhabitants set fire to the city's suburbs and continued resolute, for they knew that His Majesty had no siege-train with him worth a rush. Then the Earl of Essex marched out of London with General Skippon and his hardy trained bands, who cared not how far they marched, nor how speedily; they avoided Oxford and passed round upon our left hand and reached Gloucester within ten days, and so raised the siege. Yet His Majesty did not much lament, for he had lured his arch-enemy from his strongest post, and was confident to cut his retreat. He moved swiftly, and straddled across the London road at Newbury in Berkshire and so forced the Earl of Essex to battle. This fight proved every whit as hot as that fought at Edgehill; and again neither side could claim a victory, for though the King's horse were twenty times as good as Parliament's, yet General Skippon's London foot stood as fast as stakes and would not be broken, despite that the cannon shot ploughed through their squares and flung the bowels and brains of their comrades in their faces. On the next day, in the morning, when the Earl marshalled his forces for another fight, he found the London road open to him, and home he took his army rejoicing. It was explained at Oxford that the King had wanted powder and bullets, and therefore could not hold his ground.

In this battle fell the Lord Falkland, who was the King's Secretary for State and his most constant persuader to peace: a good man, weary of the times, who foresaw much misery to England, however the battle might go. In the morning of the fight he had called for a clean shirt, saying that if he were slain that day his body should not be found in foul linen. About the same time died his friend, Mr. Chillingworth, god-father to my brother James, who was then Chancellor of Salisbury; he died in the hands of Parliament men and was ministered to at the last by his Schools rival from Merton College, Dr. Cheynell, who had the satisfaction of preaching Mr. Chillingworth's funeral sermon. He threw into his grave that book of Mr. Chillingworth's, *The Religion of Protestants*, against which my husband had spoken, and cried as he did so: "Get thee gone, then, thou cursed book, thou corrupt rotten book, earth to earth and dust to dust! Get thee gone into thy place of rottenness, that thou mayest rot with thy author and see corruption."

The King, being foiled at Newbury, returned to Oxford, and though he knew it not he had let slip his last chance of victory: for the Londoners, being denied coals by the Earl of Newcastle (who held the North) and thus prevented from drowsing over their parlour fires with warm ale and buttered toasts, grew exceeding discontented and bestirred themselves. One of them complained in Parliament that the price of blood invaluable, so gallantly gotten, had been put into a bag with holes; what had been won was wasted by the sloth or folly of the Generals. It was as if this blood, graciously shed, had served only to manure the ground for a new crop of disasters. In this new angry mood they set about to reform their armies from top to bottom, replacing old, lukewarm and decayed commanders with young and valiant ones. What was more, Mr. Pym drove a bargain with the Scots, who agreed to come to his aid and clear the coalfields of his enemies —though only on condition that Parliament should pay them well, and should adopt the Presbyterial faith on behalf of all England and force the Covenant upon every person in authority.

That was Mr. Pym's last act; for he died about Christmas of this year, 1643, and left Parliament leaderless. Of the other principal men none other had either his parts or his patience. Colonel Oliver Cromwell was as yet a person of little account in the Commons, being hasty-mouthed, rude, without eloquence, and a by-word because of his massacre of the Queen's bears, which she had brought from Holland. For, finding the citizens of Uppingham in Rutlandshire baiting these bears upon the Lord's Day, in the height of their sport he had caused the bears to be seized, tied to a tree and shot; which was poor sport indeed. His opinions at this time he cunningly enclosed in a single phrase: "I can tell you, sirs, what I would *not* have, though not what I would!"

In Forest Hill the names of Generals Waller and Skippon and the Earl of Essex were not of so great terror as were those of lesser officers of the Parliamentary service that were garrisoned in Aylesbury and Thame. Forest Hill lay outside the fortifications of Oxford, upon the side turned towards London, and though we had a few strong forts and garrisons covering us towards London, namely, Wallingford, Shirburn Castle, Brill Town and Boarstall House, naturally there were no works joining these places. We could never sleep secure at night, but would start and cry at every creaking of a door; for always we had the suspicion that soldiers might come stealing up under cover of darkness across the debateable land, and break in and ravish or murder us in our beds. The soldiers quartered upon us were not in the least degree vigilant; and that summer, when the barley was cut and cocked, a troop of Parliament horse came stealthily one night just before the moon rose, under the guidance (as we suppose) of Tom Messenger or some other countryman who was serving with them. They carried away, every man, a great sack of barley, cutting off the ears and leaving the straw behind, and were not discovered until half an hour after dawn, when they got clean away.

There was one Major Jecamiah Abercrombie, a Scot, and another, Colonel Crawford, who were sedulous pillagers and much feared by our defenders. Both met their deaths before the war was ended, but they were very terrible to us while they lived and cost my father a great sum of money in the wheat and barley that they carried off that year, and the sheep and cattle that they drove. They had learned the art of pillage, I believe, under the Swedish King. In payment of the soldiers billeted upon us, for whom we found lodging, drink and victuals, my father was given billeting tickets, which would be redeemed (as was promised) "when God shall enable us." A man's lodging was reckoned at sixpence a day, or sevenpence for a dragoon, which amounted to a very large debt when fifty men were quartered upon us for a space of months. Yet the expense was greater by far than the promised payment, for many wives had marched with their husbands, clinging to them like ticks, and these also must be somehow fed. Besides this, there was the grazing, reckoned at three shillings the week for every horse. But already the expectation of payment was so small that often £5 worth of billeting tickets was secretly offered for thirty shillings of ready money, and a year later could be bought at a mere ten shillings.

1643 was the year in which the camp fever came to Oxford, which put us in great affright. This was a sort of plague and very contagious, but with spots in the place of carbuncles, and for sturdy men and women a greater hope of recovery; yet it was a very wasting disease, and in some parishes swept away all old and infirm people as with a broom. The air of Oxford, being reckoned healthy in general, was not to blame; but great crowds of soldiers were lodged in the city, lying twenty or thirty in one room, who filled all the houses with nastiness and filth and stinking odours; for it is not the custom of soldiers to wash themselves or shift their apparel. These men everywhere fell sick together, as it were, by files and companies, and many died, who might otherwise have lived, for want of anyone to attend to their needs; and by the height of the summer the city was more like a lazar-house than a garrison. Sir William Pennyman, the Governor, himself perished of the sickness. The contagion was carried to Forest Hill, with great mortality among the soldiers, and among our servants and tenants; but none of my family fell sick, for Trunco medicined us daily.

Three times in this year the Lady Cary Gardiner rode over to visit us. The first time she was in great distress, for Sir Thomas, her husband, was thought to be slain; but he proved to be alive and a prisoner in Windsor Castle, whence he was enlarged by the good offices of her brother, Sir Ralph Verney, M.P., and was soon exchanged against an officer of the opposing army. However, it went against Sir Ralph's conscience to swear to the Covenant, and as he had offended Mun and all his other kin by opposing the King, so now he offended his new friends in Parliament; and, resigning his seat, he went into exile in France.

The second time that the Lady Cary came, she showed me a letter from Mun in Ireland, in which he wrote that he was in arrears of pay, £600 or £700, and that his soldiers scarce knew how to put bread in

their mouths; and pillage there was none, for the country was fright-
fully wasted. But he was lately promoted a major, and his health was
good, he thanked God.

The third time that she came, it was to tell me that, since a general
cessation of arms for a year had been agreed in Ireland, Mun was
come home.

"I knew it well," said I, "and throughout the Friday and Saturday
of this past week I felt near suffocated by reason of his closeness; and
dreamed of him every night; and by day continually thrust my head
out of the window to see whether he came not riding in at the gate.
But now I think he is gone farther from me again."

"You were right," said she, "though I had not meant to discover the
fact to you. My brother came to Oxford on Friday last and waited
upon his Majesty, who gave him a gracious welcome, and he is to be
a lieutenant-colonel in a good regiment and to serve on the Welsh
Border. But knowing how you were circumstanced, he could not in
honesty come to this house, though the longing to come was so grievous that he could not sleep, and therefore upon the Sunday he rode
away again."

I saw the Queen once or twice while she was lodged in Merton
College at Oxford, which was not many months; for presently she
sailed to France, with an infant daughter that was born to her at
Exeter on the way, and thereafter left the King to manage his own
affairs. The King I saw often in and about Oxford, but had no speech
with him, except once when, riding alone, he met me in the coppices
of Shotover Forest and asked me, stammering, which way the hounds
had run. His dearest delight was in hunting; and had he been one-
quarter part so bold and thorough in the chase of his enemies as he
was in the chase of buck, he would have swept them out of the Kingdom within a week or two.

CHAPTER EIGHTEEN

I Am Persuaded to Return to My Husband

THE year 1644 was a horribly cruel, tedious year, of which I will present but a brief account. The first quarter brought nothing remarkable, except that because of the difficulties of the time, the fewness of servants, the multitude of dragoons and other soldiers quartered upon us (like idle hungry dogs continually putting themselves in our way to trip us up or with their whining or growling to annoy us), the household tasks that in the brave old days had been pleasant enough, I now found exceeding troublesome. Yet I uttered no complaint, for my mother worked as hard as any slave herself, and my sisters were in a like case with me; moreover, as I had learned, much work and much company are far better than to be idle and alone. The soldiers by negligence fired the smaller barn and a great store of mislan was burnt in it, for which no compensation was paid; and Zara began a familiarity with our Captain of dragoons, which my mother hugely misliked, knowing him to be contracted in marriage to an heiress of Worcester, but which she could not prevent because he was become as much the Lord of the Manor as my father, or more, and we were at his mercy if he cared to injure us. Zara was not openly disobedient or wanton; wherefore my father found it within his conscience to use her as an intermediary agent with the Captain, who would sometimes lend him a dozen stout men to help with his husbandry, or with his wood-mongering.

From the sale of wood my father derived extraordinary profits, because at Oxford three times as much firing was needed as ever before, and the price mounted month by month until, at the last, it was sold by the pound weight as though it were cheese, not by the cartload or faggot. He also secured a profitable contract from Sir Timothy Tyrrell to dig china clay from the ochre-pits on Shotover, which he sold in Oxford to the makers of tobacco pipes, who otherwise could obtain none of sufficient fineness.* Yet, notwithstanding his gains, my father reckoned in the New Year of 1644 that, unless he could convert his billeting tickets into land or houses or money, he was the poorer by £1,000 than he had been a twelvemonth before.

In February the Scots, in alliance with Parliament, crossed the Border and though they stubbornly avoided encounter with the King's armies at least they drew off a part of them that otherwise might have been used against Parliament, and they saved the Londoners their coals. In May it was resolved by the Committee of Safety, which met in London at Derby House, that Oxford was to be taken at all hazards and the person of the King thereby secured; which in this war, as in the play of chess, was a piece of final importance. The Earl of Essex and Sir William Waller were charged with this task and pushed forward with a great army, taking Reading once more and pressing upon Abingdon, a chief bulwark of Oxford, which the King's officers now abandoned by a mistake of their orders.

When at Forest Hill, in the afternoon of May 25th, the cry went up that "Abingdon is taken by the Roundheads," my father knew not whether to stay or fly. Our Captain of dragoons, however, began putting the Manor-house and barns in a posture of defence, breaking holes in the walls as embrasures for his guns—his men stood all night in arms, and he ordered my father to depart the place in the morning with all his household. Upon my father protesting that we were as safe in this house as anywhere else, the Captain threatened to speed him with a pistol-shot if he were obdurate. So we made our exodus on foot, with a few of our choicer possessions in one cart and three or four weeks' provisions in another; but fearing to take the nearer way, over East Bridge, we went about by Islip and came in at the North Gate, which was a tedious trudge. Zara had fallen behind our company at Stanton St. John and slunk back to her Captain; and made herself Lady of the Manor in our absence.

Some time before this, my father had bought an old wooden house of four rooms, near New Inn Hall, which he used as a storehouse for planks and boards, with his own wood-yard adjoining. Here, after a

* These pits put me in mind of a confection that we made at Easter time, of sweet pastes and conserves laid one upon the other in layers: for first came the turf, then a reddish earth, then a blue clay, then a yellow sand, then this white pipe-clay, then an iron stone, then (I think) a reddish maum, then a green fat clay, then a thin grey rubble, then the green fat clay again, and last of all the yellow ochre.

removal of those same planks and boards, we lodged for above a fortnight; and very uncomfortably, for we had neither beds nor tables nor
chairs but what we could contrive with sawn logs and pieces of board,
and no more than two cooking-pots for the seventeen of us, and the
chimney would not draw, but filled the room with smoke. The enemy
lay close about the city, where were no more than two weeks' provisions for a siege, and one of the Royal Council durst advise the King
to surrender, saying that the game was up. The Earl of Essex forded
the Isis at Sandford—where I doubt not my Uncle and Aunt Jones gave
him a loving welcome—and with his whole army passed between Oxford and Forest Hill, until he came to Islip Bridge; but there was held
by troops quartered in Islip itself. The King stood on Magdalen College Tower, as this army marched by, and viewed its order and motion; and from the Work at St. Clement's Port three or four great shot
were discharged at the enemy horse as they skirmished on Headington
Hill. There was no soldier slain by this cannonade, but much window
glass in the parish of St. Clement's was cracked or broken. To the
westward, General Sir William Waller forced a crossing of the River
Isis at Newbridge and sent his horse northward from thence to Woodstock; upon news of which the King's guard on Islip Bridge was with-
drawn and it seemed that we were caught in a bag.

The King resolved to avoid check-mate by escape, which he did very
prettily in a night march on June 3rd, carrying with him a great body
of horse and 2,500 musketeers, of whom my brother James made one;
and a train of seventy carriages. He was not discovered, because of a
diversion which he contrived, sending against Abingdon a great part
of his foot and all his ordnance; by which motion General Waller was
deceived and enticed back from Newbridge. To be brief, His Majesty,
got safely away to Worcester and drew the enemy after him so that
Oxford was free again, though Abingdon remained in the hands of
Parliament.

We left our scurvy lodgings on June 12th and gladly returned to
Forest Hill. "Aye," said my father, with a last look about the dirty
storehouse as we went out. "So Sylvester writes:

> The Angels, wonted to Heaven's blissful Hall,
> Made little stay in this unwholesome stall."

In the blissful hall of our Manor we presently found Zara safe and
sound with her Captain, who was no such great kill-cow as he had af-

fected to be; for when he had seen the approach of the enemy he had fetched his company away to Islip. Zara had stayed behind, against his persuasion, to care for the house. She had posted a warning upon the door that the house was not to be plundered, being the property of Sir Robert Pye, M.P.; which paper was respected, and though the Parliament soldiers who passed through the place took fruit from the orchard and garden, and a little wood from the yard to build their camp fires, they did no other damage. The Captain had marched back but two days before ourselves. Thus Zara redeemed her fault in my father's eyes; but my mother railed at her for a whore.

For the rest of that year we had peace, but for constant alarms that enemy horse were seen. There was a skirmish in Forest Hill itself on August 15th: some dragoons sent out from Abingdon by Major-General Browne, nicknamed "the Faggot-monger," riding up suddenly through a morning mist and engaging our own dragoons. There were men hurt on either side with sword cuts, and our tenant Catcher was slain with a chance pistol shot as he fled to our house to be out of the way. He was a brutish, drunken man and no great loss, who once at the Christmas Communion drank all the wine in the cup, swearing that he would have his penny's worth. A few days after this, Goodman Mathadee's little child, the same who had wailed in the Church, was run down by horsemen as he played in the lane and trampled to death; which was of mischance, not barbarity.

In this year there was plague at Oxford; but the camp fever had somewhat abated.

Elsewhere the war was fought disorderly and with varying fortune. In March a part of Mun's regiment was routed in a skirmish—I could not learn where, but I believe it was fought in Cheshire—wherein his Colonel was slain and he himself narrowly escaped with his life. Yet he brought away the greater part of his men into safety and for his good service was made a Knight; and in the same month was appointed Lieutenant-Governor of Chester, which was a position of great trust and honour, whereat my heart swelled with pride on his behalf. On July 2nd, a Sunday, General Cromwell won a great victory over the army of the Earl of Newcastle. He fought this battle among the sodden cornfields of Marston Moor in Yorkshire (where 4,000 men were slain in the space of three hours), and took York, Liverpool and Lincoln that same summer, but not Chester, which Mun held stoutly, though sore straitened. The Earl of Newcastle fled overseas.

I write that General Cromwell was the victor at Marston Moor, though, as is well known, the Parliament army was commanded by the Lord Leven, a Scot; for the Lord Leven himself was driven from the field and few of his Scots did anything notable that day—it was General Cromwell who, though dazed and bewildered from a wound in his neck, yet routed the squadrons of the Prince Rupert and restored the toppling fortunes of his faction. There was this difference between the Prince Rupert's manner of charging and General Cromwell's, that though both held their fire until they were in among the enemy, yet the Prince Rupert rode at full gallop, to be the more terrible, but General Cromwell at a round trot, the better to rally his men, if need should be, for a second charge. To the south-west, not many weeks after this battle was fought, the King himself was victorious at Lost-withiel in Cornwall, over General Skippon, who, being deserted by the Horse, under the Earl of Essex, lost all his ordnance and 5,000 of his 6,000 foot in retreat from that inhospitable county, and all his guns and ordnance. Thus by the close of the year neither Parliament nor King could justly claim the advantage over the other.

Meanwhile in London my husband continually sharpened and shook his pen. He wrote not, as might have been expected, either against the enemies of Parliament or against any faction in Parliament, but, in the same manner as an injustice conceived personally had brought him to inveigh against the Bishops, so now, when he desired to divorce me and found that he could not do so upon any ordinary plea, he raged furiously and neither studied nor wrote upon anything, hardly, but divorce, divorce, divorce. He published four treatises before he had done; which have brought him many enemies, not only among those who love the accustomed forms of religion, but among his friends, the Presbyterians; which is how he came at last to quit his former inclinations and wheel about to his new platform of Independency.*

My husband, I believe, wrote nothing that was strangely new upon divorce—and here I may say that, though his manner of disputation was ever his own, he was seldom the original of any new argument—yet he was industrious in reviving or refurbishing certain old notions

---

* This Independency, a notion that each smallest congregation is sufficient to judge of its own spiritual needs, without admonition or dictation from others, was a heresy first bred at Cambridge University in King James's reign; thence cast opprobriously out and exiled to Holland and Northern America; now brought back and daily getting head.

that had been long put aside or forgotten, and made them seem novel by the crackling vehemence of his oratory. Of these notions the principal one was this, that such contrariety of mind between husband and wife as will blight the peace of marriage is a just and sufficient cause not only for their separation, but for their divorce. This notion had been advanced, though somewhat diffidently, a century before by the learned Divines appointed at the Reformation of Religion to inquire into such matters. Now that there was a grand Assembly of Divines called to Westminster by Parliament, which should order decently all matters of Church Government, my husband doubted not, by casting this doctrine at their heads, to have the law amended for his own convenience and also (as he wrote) to "stroke away ten thousand tears out of the life of men."

He wrote most bitterly against the unreasonableness of Canon Law, which was still in force; for though the bishops who administered it were fast in the Tower, they had not yet lost the name and dignity of their office, and indeed they remained the nominal arbiters of all questions of divorce for three years more.

A copy of the first of these new writings by my husband was procured for me. It was named *The Doctrine and Discipline of Divorce, Restored, to the Good of both Sexes, from the Bondage of Canon Law and other Mistakes, to Christian Freedom guided by the Rule of Charity; wherein also many Places of Scripture have recovered their long-lost Meaning: Seasonable to be now thought on in the Reformation intended.* He had not set his name to this first book, but there was no disguising of his style and manner.

How he roared and ranted against those who would grant divorce for corporeal deficiency, but not at all for deficiency of the mind! And how he groaned against such a luckless and helpless matrimony as evidently he considered his own to be: for he wrote of two carcases chained unnaturally together, or rather a living soul bound to a dead corpse which, by a polluting sadness and perpetual distemper, would abase the mettle of his spirit and sink him to a low and vulgar pitch of endeavour in all his actions. He also wrote of me (though not directly by name) as a mute and spiritless mate, an image of earth and phlegm, who, by the unfitness and defectiveness of my unconjugal mind and the disturbance of my unhelpful and unfit society, had done violence to the reverend secret of Nature and had driven him to a worse condition than the loneliest single life.

As I read I began to pity him in my heart for the awkward stroke that he had dealt himself by his peremptory and lofty dealings with me, and by his policy of considering his own honour and pleasure with such exactness as to leave no time for any consideration of mine. Yet so painfully did he writhe in his own miseries that, unlike the reforming Divines, he showed no pity for the woman's case, but only for the man's; and when he proposed, as a remedy for this unnatural bond of matrimony, that no civil or earthly power whatever should prevent a man from divorcing a woman (whether she so desired or no) or from marrying another more to his liking, I could not but reckon this as ungentlemanly.

That a man indeed has this right, beyond all power of the Civil or Canon Law to annul, my husband thought to prove from the Book of Deuteronomy, where it is written: "When a man hath taken a wife and it come to pass that she find no favour in his eyes, because he hath found some uncleanness in her, then let him write a bill of divorcement, and give it into her hand and send her out of his house." He interpreted the uncleanness as of the mind equally with the body; and held that, though it were fitting that, before a man put his wife away, there should first be a solemn ceremony performed in the presence of the minister and other grave selected elders of his congregation; yet if then the man, being admonished, should solemnly protest the matter to be of natural irreconcilability, not of malice, he should be free of the prohibition which Christ pronounced against light divorce, and the woman must go back and leave him free to marry again.

To those who might object that a man who marries without due inquiry into the disposition of his wife has none to blame but himself if so be he has caught a Tartar, and that he who marries in haste will have leisure to repent it, my husband replied in these words: "But let them know again that, for all the wariness that can be used, it may yet befall a discreet man to be mistaken in his choice, and we have plenty of examples. The soberest and best-governed men are least practised in these affairs; and who knows not that the bashful muteness of a virgin may oft-times hide all the unliveliness and natural sloth which is really unfit for conversation. Nor is there that freedom of access granted or presumed as may suffice to a perfect understanding till too late; and where any indisposition is suspected, what more usual than the persuasion of friends that acquaintance, as it increases, will amend all?" (Here I seemed to hear the good old gentleman, my father-in-law, pleading my cause.) "And, lastly, it is not strange that many who have spent their youth chastely are in some things not so quick-sighted while they haste too eagerly to light the nuptial torch: nor is it, therefore, that for a modest error a man should forfeit so great an happiness, and no charitable means to release him; since they who have lived most loosely prove most successful in their matches, because their wild affections, unsettling at will, have been as so many divorces to teach them experience."

These words of my husband's, when I read them, brought me into a very lively remembrance of him, after that I had put him out of my mind for weeks and months past. Being now older by two years than when he had married me, and having gained a better conceit of myself, I was ill-content that he should portray me as an image of earth and phlegm, and as of a perpetually dismal and sullen temper. In my mind I fancied myself back again in his company and answering his vehement accusations of my earthiness with smiling wit and pithy sayings. And always the same thought returned: "Yet, however loud he may rail and lament, he is still my husband and he and I are indissolubly married with a golden ring, as he knows as well as I; and neither of us may by Law ever marry again in the lifetime of the other. I would to God that this were not so, for since Mun's father is slain, Mun may follow his own inclinations; who is already an officer of note in the King's Army, with just expectations of high preferment. Were it not for this impediment of my marriage, he would assuredly have ridden up from Oxford the other day and asked leave to marry me, and my father would have yielded me to him very cheerfully. Nor am I to be deceived as to my husband's affections: for, I doubt not, he loves me passionately and knows in his own heart how sadly he has mistreated me, yet is too proud to acknowledge his error. He sent me away for two months to punish me; not for two years to punish himself. And I dare swear that no other woman but myself will ever please him; for, however fair of face or rational in conversations she may be, his soul is yet ensnared in the tresses of my hair, and until he has lain with me and had his whole desire of me he must continue like the unquiet spirit, spoken of in the parable, who walked abroad seeking rest, but found none."

This doctrine of my husband's, though (as I say) no new one, was beyond expression distasteful to the Westminster Assembly. When an Extraordinary Day of Humiliation was appointed in London, because of the King's victories in Cornwall, and when upon that day a learned Presbyterian, Mr. Herbert Palmer, was called upon to preach before the two Houses of Parliament, Mr. Palmer singled out my husband's book as the most impudent of any that year published and the most deserving to be burned. In this sermon, preached against Toleration and Liberty of Conscience, my husband was ranked among polygamists and advocates of doctrines so monstrous that no sane person could embrace them.

When this sermon was published, with other tracts, among them one of Mr. Prynne's, charging my husband with libertinism, lawlessness, heresy and atheism, he defended himself very fiercely in his *Tetrachordon* and his *Colasterion*, shooting out his quills like a royal porpentine. Then, when the Stationers' Company complained against him to the Parliament that his *Doctrine and Discipline of Divorce* had been published contrary to the Parliamentary Ordinance which required that no book should be published without a licence, then he turned in rage against this new infringement of his liberty and addressed Parliament with a book called *Areopagitica*, pleading for the liberation of the Press. For my husband was ever conscious of his superior learning and detested that the judgment of his own books, as being either good or bad, should be in the hands of unlearned men of common capacity, with liberty to strangle them at birth after a hasty view.

So I pass on to the New Year of 1645, a year memorable to me on many sad accounts, and a strange one; one which began publicly with the beheading of Archbishop Laud, after a trial for treason that had lasted for four years. That year brought the early stirrings of a third power which, presently, intervening in the dispute between a Prelatical King and his Presbyterial Parliaments of Westminster and Edinburgh, first broke the power of the King and then by threats and main force broke the power of the Presbyterians, too, both in England and Scotland, and ruled in their stead. This power was resident in the English Army of the New Model, which was first formed in the winter of 1644–5, and which in Oxford the wits drolled against as the "New Noddle," consisting of 14,000 foot in coats of Venice red and 7,600 buff-coated horse, and a serviceable train of artillery. As I have already told, it had been resolved in London that the King could not be brought to reason unless the command of the forces of Parliament were taken from the hands of sick, old or irresolute persons, how worthy so ever, and entrusted to the young, healthy and resolute. It was resolved, too, that reliance must be put not in levies compelled to serve for a season, whose only thought was a speedy return to the shop or the plough, but in soldiers of all the year round who would voluntarily make war their profession; and that three ill-clothed, ill-armed and disorderly armies must be reduced into one which should suffer from none of these defects, but might be counted upon to give a good account of itself against any force that the King might bring together.

The Earl of Essex * having lost the confidence of Parliament by his unkind desertion of General Skippon's army in Cornwall, the young Sir Thomas Fairfax, son of the Lord Fairfax, was appointed Captain-General, and General Skippon his Major-General of Foot. There was no officer appointed at first to be Lieutenant-General of Horse, but presently this appointment fell to General Cromwell, as the person fittest to command, though by the Self-Denying Ordinance all Members of Parliament had been required to relinquish their commissions in the service.

General Skippon assisted Sir Thomas Fairfax when he scrutinized the list of officers for their fitness to command. When a choice was made from those of the former armies, a very great number, most of them Scots, who had done long service in foreign parts were set on the shelf; and commissions were renewed to no more than a dozen such. Whereat, when a very great outcry and complaint was raised, General Skippon answered that the Dutch and Swedish services were ill schools for this present war, and that veteran officers were in general without zeal in the service, neglectful of their soldiers, inclined to the abuse and plunder of inoffensive country people, inadvertent of the enemy's motions, and either unwilling or unable to learn that an English war, if it were ever to have an end, must be waged decently in an English fashion. And he said that the fifteen hundred or more veteran officers who served in the Royal Army were so many thorns in the King's flesh or pebbles in his shoe.

Contrary to what has been alleged by the King's party, the officers nominated for the New Model were for the most part noblemen or gentlemen of good birth and attainments; nevertheless, Generals Fairfax and Skippon did not scruple to entrust the command of regiments to men of low birth if they were the fittest for his purpose—as to

* The Earl of Essex died of a distemper about a year later, in his house at London.

Colonels Okey, Pryde and Ewer, whose trades had been ship's-chandler, drayman and servingman, but who had done experimental service and shown their martial skill in a multiplicity of battles and sieges and skirmishes. General Fairfax would not take the commission that was offered him by Parliament, until it were amended: for it ran like all the others ". . . for the Defence of the King's Person. . . ." This he accounted hypocrisy, because a bullet could not distinguish between King and commoner; and that clause was therefore omitted from all the other commissions.

In this Army, which was well-managed, well-paid and victorious in almost every battle that it fought, there sprang up so great an esteem of soldierly qualities, as courage, endurance, cleanliness, comradely love and the like, that uniformity of religious doctrine was no longer considered a matter of chief importance; and when the Presbyterial ministers who had marched with the armies now forsook the military life, as too arduous, and betook themselves to a quieter way, the troops were left to the ministrations of four or five bolder spirits, all of them Secretaries, as Peters, Dell, Saltmarsh, "Doomsday" Sedgwick and the rest, who cared nothing for the smoke of powder or the hum of bullets, and themselves dealt death in battle.

As the martial discipline was severe and regular, and the officers forbade all riot and licentiousness as unworthy of good soldiers, so it was natural that a relaxation and vent of their confined spirits should be found in religious speculation and visions over the camp-fire at night, and in occasional drum-head preachments of the most fanciful extravagance, by sergeants and corporals and common soldiers; whereunto, if they stopped short of plain atheism and disowned Popery and Prelaty, such toleration was accorded that, in the same troop of one hundred horse, one might number sectaries of thirty different schisms, such as Anabaptists, Old Brownists, Traskites, Anti-Scripturists, Familists, Soul-Sleepers, Questionists, Seekers, Chiliasts, Sebaptists, and even Divorcers of the sect of John Milton. Strange it was then that a soldier might with impunity address God the Father in so familiar a fashion that it would make any ordinary man sweat cold and his skin rise into goose-flesh; yet if he were but half so bold with the Lieutenant of his troop or company he would be cashiered by order of a court-martial and have his tongue bored clean through with a red-hot needle.

Some regiments of foot stood fast by their presbyterial opinions (as did their Scottish allies, who tig-tagged about the country under colour of making war); but the horse, who were the glory of the Army, for their hardiness and boldness, were almost every man of Independent judgment and jested against the Presbyters as "Priest-biters" and against the Scots as "Sots" who were always in the rearward in any enterprise. The National Covenant they scorned as a thing imposed upon our nation by these same Sots, and asked sneeringly: "Was the Holy Ghost indeed conveyed from Edinburgh to London in a cloak-bag?" The Assembly of Presbyterial Divines at Westminster was the butt of their sharpest scorns—against "Dry-Vines" and "Dissembly Men."

This new-fangled army came against Oxford in the Spring of 1645, from Windsor where it had mustered; with great store of cannons, shells, hand-grenades, gunpowder, spades, pickaxes and scaling ladders. But first General Cromwell, riding out from Watlington upon St. George's Day (which happened to be a market-day at Oxford) with 1,500 horse, made an assault upon the Earl of Northampton's regiment, that lay at Islip. He came up by way of Wheatley and passed through Forest Hill in the evening, his troopers armed only with pistols and swords, and wearing high-crowned felt hats, buff coats, great loose cloaks, breeches of grey cloth, and calves-leather boots. At the first alarm our dragoons jumbled away from the town—for their stomachs would not serve them to stand it out—and galloped to Islip to warn the Earl. My father was in Oxford at the market with Zara and two of my young brothers, William and Archdale. In his absence, my mother stood at the gate of the house to answer any question that might be asked; but it seems that the Parliament soldiers who had been quartered on us in the first year of the war had given a good report of us, and there was no plundering or other mischief done us.

My mother sighingly exclaimed to me, when she saw the good order in which the soldiers rode, that she reckoned one troop of those plain prick-eared rascals to be worth a whole squadron of the lace-coated Royal horse; and she was justified in this, for the next day in an encounter at Islip, of which we heard the confused roar carried down the wind, a great slaughter was made of the Earl of Northampton's regiment in a chase of four miles, and about 500 horses taken and 200 prisoners and the Queen's Standard. Moreover, Bletchingdon House was seized, and without bloodshed, because of the ladies come there on a visit to the young wife of Colonel Windebank, its commander

(who was the same gentleman who had brought me from London):
for General Cromwell had threatened to grant no quarter if the house
were put to storm.

Colonel Windebank, being set at large, returned to Oxford, where
he was tried by a court-martial and found guilty of faint-heartedness
and shot to death in Merton College, dying very bravely; I think that
had the Queen been at the King's side she would have constrained
him to reprieve the Colonel, forasmuch as what he had done was for
the honour of the ladies, fearing the deep barbarousness of General
Cromwell's mind. Yet, the Parliamentarians in general used their prisoners civilly, as being fellow-Englishmen and Englishwomen, and abstained from unnecessary plunder; whereas, many of the King's officers
and soldiers, notably those commanded by the Prince Rupert, used
indiscriminate barbarities learned in the German wars. They would
strip a man to his skin before they slew him; and when Bolton in
Lancashire was taken, there was massacre, ravishment, and horrid
cruelties, the like of which had never before been seen in England
since pagan times.

This was a new thing, that rebels should be the orderly ones, and
the King's men a rabble; in the days of Wat Tyler and Jack Cade it
had been clean contrariwise. And some of the Parliament men even
denied that they were "soldiers," forasmuch as this word expresses a
man who serves for pay and is content merely to obey his Prince
or governor. And they would by no means be considered as mere
machines, or as having forfeited all right to an opinion of their own
upon the better governing of their country. They were not hireling
troops, they said, nor yet forced men, but volunteers; mostly free-
holders and burghers, not lavishly paid, and often with great arrears
owing, yet content to continue staunchly in the service wherein they
had engaged upon matter of conscience. They were generally of opinion that the duration of Parliaments ought to be limited, but that
Parliament should be regularly summoned; that elections ought to be
better regulated, the representation better distributed; improper privileges and the coercive power of Bishops to be removed (though the
Bishops might remain, for all they cared); the King, of whom they
still spoke with tender, dutiful sorrow, to be restored to his rights,
but with safeguards set upon his abuse of them; the laws to be sim-
plified and legal expenses lessened; monopolies to be set aside; tithes
commuted, etc., etc. I could not hate them, nor could I even laugh at

them for Roundheads, because a great part of them wore their hair long, especially the horse.

My father with his carts and wains was forbidden to cross East Bridge from Oxford to come back to Forest Hill; and my mother was sorely distressed for his safety and in two minds whether to ask for a safe-conduct to go down to him in Oxford (which would have been granted her, I believe), or whether to hold her ground. Now, in the October before this, a soldier of the Oxford garrison, roasting a stolen pig in a hovel in Thames Street, near to the Cornmarket, had set the building a-fire; and the wind blowing strong from the north, all the wooden houses on the western side of the Cornmarket from Brocardo, or the North Gate, to Carfax were burned down. Among these was the store-house that had been our refuge in the year before; and all my father's timber was burned with it. Knowing therefore that in Oxford we had no longer any place to call our own, and that lodgings were hardly to be found, except at excessive charges, my mother decided to remain in Forest Hill. Yet there was danger here also, for we were within range of the great guns of St. Clement's Port; and one day, as I worked in the upper dairy-house, a cannon bullet of nine pounds weight came hissing quite over the roof and fell in the great meadow beyond.

Colonel Sir Robert Pye, the Younger, who commanded a regiment of horse in the Parliamentary service and who in the year before had reduced Taunton to obedience, called upon my mother one day soon after. He drank wine with us in the little parlour and undertook that no harm should come either to our house or our people. With him came one of his captains, formerly a barrister of the Middle Temple and since become famous, by name Henry Ireton.

Sir Robert had been grievously complained against by the Lady Cary Gardiner, when she had last visited us, for it was he who had assaulted and burned down Hillesden House in Buckinghamshire, the residence of her uncle, Sir Alexander Denton. This was the same house where Mun had been received charitably after his disgrace at Oxford University. My mother, who held Sir Alexander in great esteem, could not readily forgive Sir Robert and, so soon as courtesy permitted, withdrew from his presence upon some household excuse. However, Sir Robert did not at once take his leave, but remained in the parlour, and began to discourse with me upon the subject of my marriage. He was no less a Presbyterian now than when, on Twelfth

Night, five years before, my Godmother Moulton had required from
him a speech in praise of Bishops.

"Madam," said he, "your husband, Mr. Milton, in a book he has
written touching the doctrine and discipline of divorce has scandalized many; and has led many astray. Among them, to my own knowledge, is the woman-preacher, Mrs. Attaway, a lace-woman, who has
for some time past exercised a marvellous influence over the multitude
who visit her conventicle in Coleman Street. Well, this woman has
been persuaded by your husband's book, and being married to an
unsanctified husband who 'does not walk in the way of Sion, nor
speak the tongue of Canaan,' as she says, but is an honest soldier in
our army—she, then, courts a fellow-preacher, one William Jenney, a
married man, who falls in love with her. He likewise, finding his wife
not of a matchable conversation with him, divorces her in the manner
recommended by your husband, and leaves her great with child, and
without a penny of money, to feed and clothe her poor children as
best she can. Then Mrs. Attaway and the said Jenney declare themselves man and wife before God, and say that 'Whom God hath joined
together let no man put asunder.' Now they account themselves free
to stain Sergeant Attaway's bed with adulterous sweats; thus two
households are ruined, and two souls almost irrecoverably lost. Oh,
the beasts, were they rightly served they should be whipped home
into their right wits!"

"I am truly sorry to hear of this, your Worship," said I. "But though
my husband has assured me that, being of one flesh with him, I may
in no wise escape damnation if he be damned, yet I cannot in conscience find myself answerable to God for what he may write in his
books."

"Not directly answerable perhaps," he replied. "Yet I believe you
to be the procatarctical cause—I mean that extrinsic cause which,
though unwittingly, excites the principal cause to action. For had you
not removed from your husband upon a quarrel, as the common report is, and been here environed by the sons of Mars, he would never
have brooded upon these matters, nor would his wits have turned to
almost an atheistical frenzy."

"Common report is here more than commonly at fault, your Worship," I answered, "if I be accused of removing from my husband
upon a froward impulse. For, though I confess that my husband had
fault to find with my Forest Hill manner of guitar-playing, yet upon

my word, I did not quarrel with him (as he will himself assure you) but was sent peaceably back to this house for the summer holidays. Then the war ensuing, and my husband being by the King held a traitor, he could not venture to Forest Hill to fetch me back; and my father was unwilling to hazard my chastity between the armies. So at Forest Hill perforce I remain."

"I am glad to hear this account from you," said he, "which I cannot reject for untrue. But what now hinders your return?"

"Two things," I replied. "My father's absence in Oxford, and my husband's insistence that the £1,000 portion promised him in his marriage contract be paid him right down on the nail at the same time when I return to him."

"As to the first hindrance," said he, "though it may seem unkind in you to depart suddenly without a farewell to your father, yet consider this. Your first duty is to your husband, from whom you have been separated by the accident of war: you must now go to him as speedily as possible, lest you incur the charge of wilful desertion, and in this I undertake to assist you. Nay, more, if you are unwilling, I will even command and constrain you to go to him. As for the money, your father is not here, and evidently therefore he cannot send it; and your husband must wait until such time as we take Oxford and fetch your father home. To be sure, I think it unlikely that your father's estate, being caught, as it were, between the upper and the nether millstone, will yield even a small part of the marriage portion agreed upon; however, that fault lies not at your door."

I thanked Sir Robert for his solicitude and kindness but answered: "Your Worship, what you say is true, beyond denial. But I would have you remember that my husband is a very proud, choleric man, and if I were to come to London it is likely enough that he would not receive me again, and then I am utterly undone. For I believe that the small fault that he found in me has ulcerated in his mind and I am become to him a sort of monster, rather to run at with a charged pike than to salute with affectionate kisses."

Then for the first time Captain Ireton spoke. He was a reserved, saturnine gentleman, with a small face like a cat's, and known to my father from the time that he was a Bachelor of Arts at Oxford University, and used to course game with him. When I looked upon Captain Ireton he put me in mind of the old adage, "The cat knows well whose beard he licks"; yet I did not mistrust him on that account, but only

wondered why Sir Robert had discoursed before him so freely upon
a private matter. Said he: "You will pardon my boldness, Mrs. Milton,
but it was I who brought Sir Robert here, not he me. My friend Mr.
Agar, who married your husband's sister and whose step-sons (I learn)
are taught by Mr. Milton, is greatly concerned in this matter. For Mr.
Agar is a God-fearing man and admires your husband in almost every
particular except only as touching his new doctrine of divorce, which
he detests. It seems now that your husband has written in a book,
called *Tetrachordon*, published a few weeks since, that if the Law will
not yield him that right of divorce which he pants after, why then he
gives fair warning of his intention to follow his own conscience: he
declares that the Law, not he, must bear the censure of the consequences."

"That is a very petulant decision," said I, "and will do him no good."

Captain Ireton said again: "I would not have you think, Mistress,
that I am evilly disposed against your husband or would turn your
heart against him. I confess that I agree with him in this matter of
free consciences, and am no Presbyterian, as is Sir Robert here; nevertheless I am always vexed when I see an honest man, for his conscience's sake, performing any act of plain folly. Well, I will deal
freely with you, Madam: your husband has won the admiration of a
Doctor Davis, a Welsh physician, who has a daughter famed for her
wit and beauty and who is ready to bestow her upon your husband,
after he shall have cast you off by a private bill of divorcement; and
though the gentlewoman herself is averse to the motion, she must
obey her father blindly, just as you obeyed yours when he married
you to Mr. Milton. This is very true that I tell you; God knows I lie
not. Now, I am not one to bandy idle compliments, but this lady is not
so fair as you are by one-half, and as for wit, I judge you to be a
woman of spirit and discernment in no way her inferior. To be brief:
Mr. Agar has begged me, if I pass this way, to warn you of what
liquor is brewing in your vat, and to urge your return before your
husband commits a rash act (matching old Lamech, who was the
prime bigamist and corruptor of marriage) and drags a very honest,
pretty gentlewoman into the mire with him. Nor is Mr. Agar disinter-
ested in this: for clearly if your husband brings into his house, as its
mistress, a woman who is no more his wife than the Queen is mine,
it will be to Mr. Agar's sorrow and scandal, and he will be obliged to
remove his two step-sons, your nephews, from your husband's charge."

While Captain Ireton was yet speaking my mother returned, and I said to her very calmly: "Madam, these two officers are come to warn me of my husband's intention to discard me and take another wife, and have chalked out the way I should go. Colonel Pye has been good enough to offer his services in the matter of conducting me safely to London, and will take no refusal. Since, then, I have no wish to be publicly whored, and since I find no impediment to my returning, except only that no marriage-portion can go with me, return I will— by your leave—for I conceive that my duty obliges me to it. Moreover, I can say before these officers what I could not say before our friends of the contrary party: this, that whether King or Parliament be in the right concerns me not, being but a woman, but certain it is that the Army of Parliament is by far the better ordered, the better clothed, the better mounted, and the better disciplined, and cannot but prevail over the King's. I foresee therefore that my father will never recover the money wrung and screwed from him under the name of loans, nor yet the great sum owed to him for the billeting of troops and for the wood sold to the King's Quarter-Master-General; for the receipts that he holds will be worthless paper if the King be defeated. Yet he can hope for no remission of the private debts owed by him—as the great debt he owes to Sir Robert Pye, the Elder—and therefore he will be ruined. If now I return to my husband and contrive to please him, I shall be able, I trust, to provide shelter and food for you if ever you be cast adrift by the King's defeat."

My mother at first made many objections, but at last saw the justice of my reasoning. She gave her consent, upon Sir Robert's solemn assurance that no harm would come to me and that, if my husband rejected me, he would have me brought safe home again. I asked Captain Ireton where I should lodge in London while Mr. Agar prepared a reconciliation between myself and my husband, and he undertook that Mr. Agar would see me well lodged. Then I asked when might I be convoyed to London, and Colonel Pye told me: "To-morrow morning, if you wish, for I am sending two wounded officers to their homes and you shall dress their wounds for them on the way in payment of your fare."

"At your service, sir," said I, cheerfully, but in truth with a sinking heart: for what Captain Ireton had told me about Dr. Davis's daughter put me in a perplexity. It seemed that I would be forced now to pretend more love for my husband than in truth I felt, if I wished to be his wife again; and to do so went against my womanly conscience. Yet I was faced with Hobson's choice: "this or nothing."

When the two officers had departed the house, my mother used me very kindly. "Marie," said she, "you are a better daughter to me than ever I supposed. Go, with my blessing, to that mad dog your husband —who cares not how he bites, nor whom—and let me see whether you cannot charm him back into sanity with good words. I give you leave to tell him that your frowardness in not returning with that sour woman of his, when he commanded you, was forced upon you by myself, and that you now repent grievously, being overcome by the godly suasions of Colonel Pye. My advice to you is this: abase yourself before him; go on your belly like the serpent; eat dust; assuage his wrath with guile. But so soon as ever he has broken his contract with Dr. Davis and has received you to his bosom at last, why then you are at liberty to rise up again, springing upon his shoulders and making bloody his sides with your spurs."

"And may our maid Trunco go with me, Madam?" I asked.

She answered: "With all my heart, though in taking Trunco from me, you rob me again of the cheerfullest and best woman that ever I had."

So I gathered together my ends and awls and packed them in my coffer: everything I possessed except my vellum book, which I left in my mother's charge, but took the key with me. Once more it was good-bye to merry sweet Forest Hill, where I was born, and ho! for that nasty, musty, fusty, dusty, rusty City of London, the birth-place of my husband, which I must learn to love, even against my natural inclination!

CHAPTER NINETEEN

I Am Got with Child; and My Father Is Ruined

I N THE short siege of Oxford at this time undertaken by the Army of the Captain-General, Sir Thomas Fairfax, two great misfortunes happened to my family; whereof I had no intelligence until a year later, and so can keep their discovery until my next chapter. Meanwhile, I may recount that by May 21st, 1645, the city was so straitened that no more provisions could come in; and that General Fairfax's men built at Marston a new bridge over the Cherwell River, whereat Colonel Sir William Legge, the Governor, fearing an assault, was constrained to drown the meadows and to fire houses in the suburbs to make his defence more secure. Yet there were weak places in the circuit of works, especially to the northward, and the sentries were not so wide awake, nor the arms kept in such good order as when Sir Arthur Aston had been Governor.* For Sir Arthur, who was a Papist, had been a very severe, vigilant officer and fined, or confined, his men for drunkenness as though they had been Roundheads, and forbade all tippling after tattoo. Moreover, the citizens, now that they were paid in promises only, not at all in money, and suffered great inconvenience from the soldiers quartered upon them, and saw that the King's cause was tottering, grew restless and showed themselves backward and sullen in the work demanded of them.

However, in the event, the city was not put to the storm; for when General Fairfax learned, a week later, that the King had left Oxford and was gone into the North to raise the siege of Chester (where Sir Mun was hard pressed), he likewise raised the siege of Oxford and followed after him; and not long after, on June 14th, His Majesty was

---

* Colonel Legge had taken Sir Arthur Aston's place after that Sir Arthur, curvetting upon Bullingdon Green to show some ladies his horsemanship, had tumbled off and broke his thighbone and lost his leg by amputation. There was a jest upon this, that when country people coming to market with their wares asked the sentries at the gate, "Good men, who is now your Governor?" and they answered, "One Legge," the country people cried: "Why, is it still he? We had heard that the old whoreson was gone from you."

caught and routed at Naseby, a village near the town of Daventry, from which defeat he never afterwards recovered, though it was by no means the last battle of this war, and though Oxford held out for better than a year afterwards.

Naseby fight was a very hotly-contested one, in which the Prince Rupert totally routed General Ireton's horse on the one wing, and General Cromwell totally routed the horse opposed to him on the other; and the main bodies charged each other with incredible fierceness, coming to blows with the butt-ends of their muskets. The battle-cry in the Parliament Army was "God our Strength"; and in the King's it was "Queen Marie." General Skippon was shot through the side most grievously, the bullet carrying into the wound a piece of his breast-plate and some shreds of his shirt; and General Ireton was run through the thigh with a pike and into the face with a halberd, and his horse shot under him. General Cromwell was also in great peril, being worsted in single combat with a captain of the King's horse, who with a blow of his broad-sword cut the ribbon that secured General Cromwell's headpiece, and then pitched it off his head and would have cloven him to the chin with a second stroke had not his party ridden to the rescue; then a trooper, in the very nick, threw him a headpiece of his own, which General Cromwell catched and clapped upon his head (though the wrong way about) and so wore it the rest of the day. The King himself managed the fight on the other side, very magnanimously and expertly, as was confessed even by his enemies, and exposed himself no less courageously than any other man upon the field; but it was not to be his luck to die in battle.

It passed wonder how few were the slain in so many hours of bitter fighting, front to front over a space of one mile, not above six hundred men of the King's army of 7,500 nor above two hundred men of the New Model army, which was of double the size. This caused the battle to be belittled in comparison with those fought at Edgehill and Marston Moor and elsewhere, for he is generally accounted the best commander who sheds most blood; thus was Pompey styled "the Great" (a title denied to Julius Cæsar), forasmuch as Pompey in his battles had slain or lost more than two million men, Julius only a bare million. In these late wars of our own, by the bye, steel killed far more than gunpowder (though gunpowder caused the more dismay among ill-trained troops); and disease, especially the camp fever and the small-pox, more than both steel and gunpowder together.

The victory at Naseby I heard celebrated with the loud acclamations of the London populace, the ringing of church bells and the whining chant of psalms in the streets and alleys. A few days later the prisoners taken in the ·battle were marched through the City streets, to the number of near 4,000, with a parade of captured standards, which were afterwards hung up in Westminster Hall. I did not care to watch the rout, for my heart was sore for the poor souls and I could not have abided to hear them hissed at and derided in their passage through the streets. When they were secured in the artillery ground of Tothill Fields, Parliament granted them a safe return to their homes if they would undertake to live peaceably for the future. Yet their confidence in the King's cause was such that by far the greater number refused to renege; they were shipped off as indentured servants to the colonies.

I had taken my two wounded officers to their homes in Bishopsgate, each of whom tried to convert me to his religious tenets, one being an Anabaptist who had a broken shoulder, and the other a rank Socinian with a festered foot. The Anabaptist told me, among other things, how many secret well-wishers to Parliament were to be found in Oxford, from the rank of Colonel downwards, who gave constant information to General Fairfax of what passed in the city. Each man would leave his letter at certain houses, thrusting it in at a hole in a glass window as he untrussed in the street; which letters were at once conveyed over the works by men in the disguise of town gardeners, to a certain stinking ditch, two miles off, where an agent of Parliament was watching to receive them. After parting company with these officers I went by water to Westminster, to the house of Sir Robert Pye, M.P., the Elder, the same who held the mortgage upon our Manor. At this house Mr. Agar waited upon me, and made much of me and rejoiced in my return, and told me that his kinsman Mr. Abraham Blackborough had a fair chamber prepared against my coming. Then, with Trunco, I went by coach to Mr. Blackborough's, which was the same house in the Lane of St. Martin's le Grand where my brothers and sisters were lodged three years before this; but we went after dark, because it was intended that no rumour should reach my husband that I was harboured there; and as I was forbidden to show myself at the window, so Trunco was also forbidden to reveal my true name to the servants.

Mr. Blackborough, a pleasantly satirical gentleman, told me that my husband in his daily walk Citywards in the afternoon would often-

times stop at this house to enquire whether any new pamphlets were
come in; for Mr. Blackborough had a passion for buying pamphlets
and my husband found it more convenient to read them at leisure at
Mr. Blackborough's than hurriedly at the book-sellers' of St. Paul's
Churchyard, where he might be rudely told "either buy or begone!"
and where no chair nor table was provided for his comfort. If he came
on the next day, as was hoped, Mr. Blackborough would encourage
him with a talk of a very fair work entitled *Matrimony at Pleasure* and
having particular reference to himself. "When your husband comes
in," said he, "if I find him in a pleasant mood, I will give you the cue
by raising my voice and saying, 'Now, sir, the pamphlet awaits your
perusal!' and then I will leave the stage to you. But, Madam, from his
discourse on a hundred occasions, I judge that he has so fixed an aver-
sion from you, which I might name a passionate disgust—for whatever
small imperfections you may have he sees through a multiplying glass
—that it will be no easy matter for you to achieve a reconcilement with
him. However, in the very excess of his embitteration lies your opportunity: for by long brooding upon the matter he has convinced himself that you resemble the Gorgon Medusa, with snakes for hair, and
vulpine features, and a cold petrifying eye; and therefore the surprise
of finding you to be, in fact, altogether different from his morbid imaginings will make your task not altogether impossible."

"How do you advise me to bear myself towards him?" I asked. "For,
to deal honestly with you, I come back not because I am drawn by
any great love of him, nor because I once erred and now repent of the
fault, but because, to my mind, a wife's fated place is with her husband even though he be a bad one—and Mr. Milton is a better husband, I believe, than many that there are. Besides, as I told Colonel
Sir Robert Pye, I did not leave my husband of my own motion, but
was sent away by him on a two-months' vacation to my father's house.
Then, the troubles intervening, I have now these three years been prevented from returning to him, and he (as I suppose) from coming to
fetch me, merely by the accidents of war."

"That may well be your view of the case, Madam," he answered,
"but you will not find it by any means acceptable to him in his present
mood. For he has been told that your father considers it a blot upon
his escutcheon to have married his daughter to a 'Roundhead traitor';
which name he much resents, from the pride that he has not only in
the great Cause of Liberty, but in the handsomeness of his long hair.

I counsel you therefore to salve the sores of his injured pride by as sweet a flow of repentant tears as you can pump up from the fountains of your eyes, and to abase yourself upon the floor before him as flat as any Welsh griddle-cake; and I advise you, too, to accept submissively any impositions that he may lay upon you in his stiff, pedagogical manner. For, to deal freely with you, while I admire his learning and parts beyond measure, I suspect him to be a very simpleton in domestic affair."

"My mother has much the same opinion of him as yourself, sir," said I, "and has given me much the same advice. I will be guided by you both, and I am sincerely grateful to you, sir, for all your kindness."

Well, the next afternoon at about two o'clock, watching the passers-by from behind the window curtain, at last I descried my husband approaching, with his brisk step and his cane carried at the trail, like a pike. He appeared very cheerful and ran nimbly up the steps of our house to knock at the door.

Presently I heard his foot on the stair, and his remembered voice and rolling discourse sounded from the adjoining room. He was, I think, upon a new scheme, which filled his mind at this time, for the founding of novel military academies where the well-born youth should be trained in all arts and useful sciences as rulers of the yeomanly and proletarian parts of the nation. I overheard him when he shouted and said that the Universities were nurseries of superstition and idleness, almost beyond hope of reformation. Mr. Blackborough was humouring him with "You are right, sir!" and "Very true, sir!" and it came to me that doubtless what my husband had meant, when he wrote of his need for a wife of fit and matchable conversation, was that I had never given him his "You are right, Husband," and "Very true, Husband!" when he expatiated to me at tedious length upon such subjects as these.

While now I waited for my cue, I dwelt in my mind upon all the saddest things that I could recall from histories and plays, as the death of Hector and the blinding of King Lear, to put me artificially into the necessary frame of spirit; but none would serve my purpose, until I remembered my little white spaniel bitch, named Blanche, which was given me on my seventh birthday—how by a carelessness of my own in playing with her she had broke her leg and whined piteously; and how my brother James had put her out of pain by the discharge of his fowling-piece. At this my eyes began to prick and the tears to

flow. Then the door opened seasonably and Mr. Blackborough cried
out: "Now, sir, the pamphlet awaits your perusal. I hope you will read
it with joy; and, what is more, I warrant the pages to be still uncut."

I advanced, with faltering steps, weeping, and with my hands
clasped upon my bosom. My husband gazed at me with astonishment,
taking an eager step towards me, but then bethought himself and
recoiled in dismay. I knelt down submissively upon the mat and
abased my head, so that my hood tumbled off and showed him my
hair. I began to sob persuasively and to mutter broken words, especially "Oh, forgive, forgive me!" which were, indeed, the very ones I
had used to my poor whining Blanche. Then, all together in a knot,
in came old Mr. Milton, and my sister-in-law, Mrs. Agar, and the
Widow Webber, mother to Mr. Christopher Milton's wife. They had
waited together in another room, and now unanimously pleaded with
my husband, begging him to forgive me who was so young, so fair,
and so contrite. Only Mr. Blackborough stood a little apart from the
rest, with a sour-sweet grin as he watched the scene played out. The
old gentleman begged my husband not to take it ill that I had left the
promised portion behind me; for this was no fault of mine, and if he
dealt honestly with me, he might be sure that my father would in the
event deal honestly with him.

My husband stood amazed and irresolute, but they all wept with
me, even the old gentleman, and he could not harden his heart when
his father wept. He raised me up from the floor and took me in his
arms to comfort me, but did not yet kiss me. Then the company stole
away, on their tip-toes for silence, one by one, and left us together.

I begged my husband to assure me that he had forgiven me, and I
put the whole blame for my frowardness upon my mother, as she had
desired me to do, and continued with my facile weeping until he said
at last: "It is God's will that I should forgive you. It comes not easily,
so enormous is the wrong that you have done me, so hateful your
ingratitude. Yet who can stand against the commandment of God?
Therefore: 'Woman, I forgive you!'"

"You will receive me back as your wife?" I asked in low, choking
voice. "I am still a maid, and have learned my lesson, and will render
you every obedience from this time forward for the remainder of my
life."

He answered, recovering himself: "I will take you back presently;
but not yet, for I must have time to make proper preparation, and to

be assured that you are sincere in your repentance, and that you are
not come here maliciously to father on me the brat of some licorish
Cavalier captain or sergeant-major."

"I am content to wait," said I, drying my tears with my handkerchief. "I will wait twenty years, if only you will receive me back at
the last."

Then he set upon my lips a kiss of love and hate intermingled, and
recalled his kinsfolk and told them of his reconcilement with me. They
rejoiced and praised his wisdom and magnanimity, and took their
leave of us in marvellous contentment. I was astonished at my own
facility for play-acting, and hated myself as an abject, a wretch, a
plain liar, and shrank conscientially from the grave, ironical congratu-
lations of the good Mr. Blackborough.

My husband told me that he had lately undertaken the education
of seven more boys, besides the five that he already taught (and not
the small fry of the parish, neither, but the sons of noblemen and gentlemen of merit) who would lodge with him. Wherefore, since he was
resolved to have his bedchamber to himself and only to admit me into
it upon occasion, there would for a while be no room for me in his
house. However, he said that he had already found a house more suitable to his purposes, namely one of twelve rooms situate in the Barbican, a street that leads out of Aldersgate, where he proposed to settle
at Michaelmas. He commanded me to wait patiently for three months,
and undertook that if I pleased him by my demeanour, and if the
Widow Webber (with whom I should lodge in the meanwhile at her
house in St. Clement's Churchyard, off the Strand) gave him a good
report of me, then he would sign an Act of Oblivion, and enter into a
firm treaty of peace with me.

Yet I believed that it irked him to abandon his grand design of marriage with Dr. Davis's daughter (who was pointed out to me in the
street one day, and was, I own, far handsomer of feature than I), and
the more so because she flouted him—for he hated to be flouted or
crossed; however, abandon it he did, and resigned himself to a renewal of marriage with me.

Thereafter he wrote no more upon divorce, declaring that he had
written enough to serve his purpose, and wished to be remembered
by posterity for other books, not for these only. Instead, he busied
himself with his *History of England from the Earliest Times*, written
after the pithy model of Tacitus's histories, and with the collecting of

his poems, in English, Italian, Greek, and Latin, for their publication.
It was wonderful how jealous he seemed that no verse that he had
ever written should be forgotten, not even his two or three college
exercises on the theme of Gunpowder Plot, and the two elegies on
dead bishops of which Mr. Pory had spoken, and the rhymed translations he had made, while yet a schoolboy, of the Psalms of David. Yet
upon the title-page, when the book was printed, appeared a modest
quotation from an Eclogue of Virgil's:

> Bind me the green field-spikenard on my brow,
> Lest ill tongues hurt the bard who is to be!

His meaning was, that the spikenard should be stop-gap until he had
earned the laurel or green ivy by his grand dramatic poetry.

To Trunco he was kind. Some months before my return to him, he
had found Jane Yates to be treacherous and a petty thief of pewter
and linen, and when he learned that she had sold some of the books
from his library to a bookseller in Little Britain he suddenly dismissed
her, though upon the old gentleman's plea for mercy he did not have
her committed for trial. Then, after one Mrs. Catherine Thomson had
managed awhile for him, not very well but honestly at least, he employed Trunco in his kitchen, and at a good wage when he found how
much money she saved him every month by her wise management,
and how much relish she gave even to simple meats by her judicious
dressing of them. For before she came, the hardiest of his pupils had
dared to complain openly of the victuals set before them.

The Widow Webber treated me no less affectionately than if I had
been Thomasine Milton, her daughter, who since Reading was taken
by Parliament had gone with her husband to live at Exeter. Mr. Christopher was then a Commissioner of the King to sequester estates of
Parliamentarians; and the widow herself secretly favoured His Majesty,
which was a prime cause of her showing kindness to me, for she knew
that my family were of her opinion. By my husband's desire, she kept
me pretty close in the house, not allowing me to go out by myself even
so far as the baker's shop that lay four doors away—yet she contrived
always to give me pleasant employment, so that I should not brood,
and when I went out walking with her she took me often into the
houses of her friends, who were livelier company than I had hoped to
meet. They all consented that London was become horribly dull: no

theatres, no horse-racing, no bear-baiting, no masques, even the suburban maypoles pulled down, the churches made as gloomy as jails,
the mercers' and drapers' shops in mourning, hardly a chaise to be
seen in all Hyde Park, the whole Town dead after nine o'clock at
night. Money I had none, and it irked me not to have so much as sixpence to lay out upon coloured ribbons which the pedlar with a stealthy
glance about him (because of the Ban and Anathema put by the
Church upon all pretty toys) drew out from his pack to tempt me
withal.

My husband came to the house almost every day and usually
brought books suitable for my reading, and discoursed with me pleasantly; but never passed a night with me in my chamber. I found him
far less severe than before in his notions of how a husband should
rule his wife. "The wife," said he, "is not to be held as a servant, but
to be received graciously into her husband's empire; though not
equally; yet largely, as his own image and glory." And, in a book, he
had even written that where the wife exceeds her husband in prudence and dexterity, and he contentedly acknowledges the same, why
then, let the wiser govern the less wise, as is natural!

While I was with the widow I had the sad intelligence that Captain
Sir Thomas Gardiner, the Lady Cary's husband, was slain in a skirmish
near Aylesbury. She was then with child, and great hopes were held
that she would bear a boy to perpetuate the line; but it proved a girl,
and the poor Lady Cary is ever since slighted and despised by the
Gardiners as having failed them.

Chester was again besieged, after an intermission of some months,
but Sir Mun held it steadfastly for the King. In September the Prince
Rupert surrended the city of Bristol to General Fairfax, a little too
easily, which earned him the King's severe displeasure. In the same
month his Majesty, going up to the relief of Chester, was routed before the walls with sad loss. Then, though the garrison was much dismayed for lack of powder and provisions, yet Sir Mun would not yield,
and there was much praise given him by the Widow and her acquaintances for his staunchness. At last I heard it confidently reported by a
young gentlewoman that Sir Mun was lately married; but who his wife
might be she knew not. This news struck me with a dull pain, yet
somewhat reconciled me to my condition. I supposed the wife to be
Doll Leke.

I dreamed of Mun, on the last night before I was taken to my husband's new house in the Barbican. He was lying alone in his bed, and looked very sorrowfully at me, and asked me: "How, sweetheart, can you hope for happiness now? Or how can I? Yet one day we shall meet again, in spite of all, and be happy together."

I will make no particular account of my bridal night, except to say that my husband omitted none of the concomitant pleasures prepared for me on the former occasion, not even the gold dust upon the coverlet; and that my mother was right, perhaps, when she denied he-virgins the right to wed any but widows. However, he had his will of me and I did nothing to displease him, and so great was his self-love that he could remark no absence of love in me while I was submissive to him. He commanded me to keep silence while he caressed me, lest by any loose or unlucky word I might break the spell and profane the sacred rite of which himself was priest and I the willing sacrifice.

Enough of this. He got me with child soon enough, and then caressed me no more, but made me sleep apart from him. He required me, for love of him, to accept a strange new course of life. I must lie at night upon a mattress of straw, not upon feathers, and eat coarse food, and wash myself only in cold water, and read no books but such as told of battles and dangerous enterprises. He also made an armoury of my bedchamber, bringing in swords and pikes and pistols, the walls he hung with red and pinned over with many escutcheons; and he took me often to watch the exercises in the Artillery Garden and in St. Martin's Fields. This was not from any unkindness in him, but from a maggot that he had. For he hoped by these artificial means to beget a son, renowned for his hardiness, who would become a great Captain-General; and that thus an old prophecy might be fulfilled, which was translated from Greek into Latin by one Gildas, in the time of Claudius Cæsar, to the effect that all the world should be subdued at last by the British race. This prophecy, beginning:

> *Brute, sub occasum Solis,*

and ending:

> *. . . Ipsis*
> *Totius terræ subditus orbis erit.*

he wrote out fairly in great letters on a board nailed to the foot of my hard bed; where I could not help but learn it by heart. Our son should be named Arthur, and therefore over the head of my bed hung a great A, embroidered in gold thread upon a silken flag of St. George. In this fancifulness of my husband's I humoured him; and with what result will presently appear.

The Barbican was a somewhat noisy street; but the schoolroom where the boys were taught lay at the back of the house, so that their studies were not much interrupted by the cries of fish-wives, pudding-wives and sellers of brooms, the singing of balladists, or the altercation of carters and coachmen. I was now at last entrusted with the management of the household; and contented my husband, who was good enough to tell me that Trunco and I together made a good team for his plough. Despite the prodigious rise in the cost of fuel and provisions of every sort, it cost me somewhat less (proportionably to the increase in the number of the household) to keep the house in food, drink, soap, candles and firing than it had cost Jane Yates, for all her ostentatious splitting of farthings. My husband now brought me little presents of sober-coloured silk and fine linen to wear when I had finished with my child-bearing, and once, for present use within doors, a silver brooch with garnets made in the form of a sword; but never would allow me to choose anything for myself in the shops, unless it were shoes or stockings or underlinen.

The boys were very good boys and soon came to treat me almost as their mother. Henry Lawrence and Cyriack Skinner (grandson to Sir Edward Coke the lawyer) and the young Earl of Barrimore were my favourites of the dozen that we had with us. My husband taught them to be good swordsmen, and also perfected them in all the locks and gripes of wrestling, and sometimes took them out with him upon excursions to see places of interest and to exercise themselves with rowing upon the river. He was become sparing of the ferule and stick, now that he was resigned to matrimony with me. We had excellent good neighbours, chief among them being that same Earl of Bridgewater, a former President of Wales, at whose castle at Ludlow my husband's masque of *Comus* had been performed; with whom dwelt his daughter, the Lady Alice Egerton, who had been the Lady in the piece, and Mr. Thomas Egerton his son; all of whom used me very civilly. And also in The Barbican, by chance, dwelt Mr. Henry Lawes the musician, who had composed the music and played the part of Thyrsis in the same masque: a gentle, considerate and well-beloved person to whom my husband about this time addressed a sonnet, "Harry, whose tuneful and well-measured song, etc." Thus I heard much music about this time. Yet my husband would not let me be present when soft or languorous airs were played or sung: for the sake of our unborn son, said he, I must rather hear the martial Doric strains that brace the mind, than those of Lydia that enervate it. Our child would be born, as he reckoned, toward the end of July, under the sign of Leo, which favours great captains, like none other in the Heavens.

The sonnet to Mr. Lawes came too late to be included in his book of poems, when he published it at the New Year of 1646; but among the other sonnets I found one evidently addressed to Dr. Davis's daughter (though not by name) as a virgin wise and pure who had shunned the broad green way that leads down to destruction. This piece circumspectly promised the gentlewoman not marriage but a place at the marriage-feast when the bridegroom, with his feastful friends, should pass to bliss at the mid-hour of night; so I found no fault with it. My husband, whenever he writes a sonnet (and he has written no poem of greater scope since I have been with him) keeps a superstitious custom. For first he washes himself from head to foot and puts on clean linen and his best suit, but no sword; then with a cup of clean water in his hand he goes into a room that is well swept and bare of any furniture but a chair and table; where, having locked the door and commanded absolute silence throughout the house, he makes, I suppose, a religious invocation, drinks of the water and sets to. On the door of his room is pinned a warning paper, on which, enclosed in a laurel-wreath, is written the name of the Muse Calliope to whom he owes service.

Christmas was forbidden by Parliament to be kept in London for mince-pies and plum-porridge and holly-boughs were considered papistical idols; and my husband himself was content to let the feast pass by, for he said it was a great interrupter of study and business. Ah, but what a cold New Year led in 1646! On December 8th, at the new moon, it began to freeze and continued bitterly cold until the next new moon, the ice being of a wonderful thickness and no water running in the pipes, so that we had to buy water by the bucket at a high price; and for three weeks we were without coals and would have been without wood, too, but that the Earl of Bridgewater gave my husband leave to root up an old decayed elm from his garden; which, as a wood-monger's daughter, I showed the boys how to reduce to billet wood with saw, beetle and wedge. Then day by day it thawed and by night it froze again, and the roads were terribly glancy for a month or more, so that it was a danger to walk; yet my husband bade me not to fear, so that our son should be born hardy. On the third day of February he took me out to hear martial music played at some muster of troops in St. Martin's Fields, but I got no further than the gate of our house and then I slipped upon the ice and fell, and could not rise. I was in great fear lest I should miscarry, for a miscarriage, they say, brings no less painful a labour than a birth, and with nothing to show for it after; but this I was spared, though there were shudderings in my belly, and I suffered no greater visible hurt than a swollen ankle. My husband would not let me lie abed, but bade me wrap my ankle in cold, wet rags and so hobble about until I could walk again; which was to instruct our son in fortitude.

This third day of February was the day that Mun for lack of provisions, and of powder for his ordnance, was constrained to yield Chester, after a brave defence and upon honourable conditions. He marched his garrison out with colours flying, drums beating, matches alight, bullets in the soldiers' mouths and bandoleers filled with powder. He was permitted to sail for Ireland, to join with the Lord Lieutenant, the Marquis of Ormonde, to whom the King had entrusted the task of combining the Confederate Papists in his interest against Parliament.

In England the war drew to a close with the surrender in March of Sir Ralph Hopton's Cornish Army. Already in many parts of the country one verily might have believed himself in Ireland, the war had so impoverished the people. The King's soldiers had almost starved those with whom they quartered and were half starved themselves for want of pay. They were become desperate, and raged about the country, breaking and robbing houses and passengers, and driving away cattle before the owners' faces. Even their officers became abominable plunderers, and one who deserted to Parliament gave as his reason that when complaints came he was ashamed to look an honest man in the face: for it was truly as bad to him as a bullet. The Parliament soldiers, being by comparison well paid, seldom resorted to knavery, and therefore their cause was the more highly esteemed by the country people and prospered accordingly.

The King began once more to negotiate with the Westminster Parliament; but his demands were great and unacceptable. It was already debated by the Commons what rewards in rank and money should be given to the leaders who had brought them the victory; for only a few castles and garrisons remained still in the King's hands. In April came Mr. Christopher Milton and his wife from Exeter, which was at last surrendered to Parliament. He had lost all his fortune except a house in Ludgate of an annual value of £40 per annum, for which he compounded, and went to live at the Widow Webber's, my husband supplying him with a little necessary money until he could support himself by his exercise of the Law. In May, when I was in the seventh month of my account, came news that Woodstock Manor-house was stormed and the King fled from Oxford, in disguise as the servant of one of his gentlemen and that he was gone into Scotland, there to place himself at the disposal of the Scottish Parliament. With his loving Scots, he said, he had no quarrel that could not be patched.

Then Oxford was again closely besieged and in June the King wrote from Newcastle, permitting the Governor to yield on honourable terms: for he feared for the safety of the young Duke of York and his nephews the Prince Rupert (whom he had forgiven for his loss of Bristol) and the Prince Maurice. But Sir Thomas Glemham, the Governor, remained obdurate. General Skippon was charged with the construction of a stronger work on Headington Hill, and other works were raised all about the city. At first there was firing of great shot on both sides, of which several from Oxford fell in and about Forest Hill, and one killed Mr. Robert Hicks, a Nottinghamshire gentleman, as he rolled bowls upon our Manor-house green. But presently it was agreed to refrain from such dangerous work, lest the ancient churches and colleges of Oxford should suffer injury, and antiquity be slighted.

Sir Robert Pye the Elder sent an urgent message to my father, desiring him for his own advantage to leave the Manor-house and take refuge in Oxford before the siege should begin. For if that were done, then his son, the Colonel, might take possession of the Manor, by the terms of the mortgage; and this he had a right to do, seeing that the arrears of interest were not yet paid nor the principal sum returned. Thus the estate would not be sequestered by the Parliamentary Commissioners (as it would otherwise be); and Sir Robert undertook to act as a good neighbour to my father, and secure all the goods in and about the house and to yield all back to him, so soon as ever the times changed. Upon a distant noise of cannon, my father withdrew in a great hurry from the house and left the keys to be given to Colonel Pye, and fled to Oxford with all his household; where they lodged in an open cattle-shed in Beef Lane, for want of better accommodation, until, towards the end of June, the Governor was persuaded to surrender the city.

The terms allowed by General Fairfax were mighty generous, the garrison to the number of 7,000 men being suffered to march out with arms and baggage; and though the estates of all the Cavaliers taken in the city were to be sequestered, yet the owners were permitted to compound with Parliament; that is to say, by paying a fine not to exceed two years' revenue of an estate, it might be restored to them, and meanwhile they might live there as tenants of Parliament, so long as they behaved peaceably.

However, my poor father had little profit of this generosity. On Sunday, June 28th, a week after the articles of surrender were signed, he rode out of Oxford and came to the door of the Manor-house and knocked for admittance. An old blowsy-faced man put his head out of a window and with pistol cocked and levelled, demanded his business.

"I am Justice Richard Powell and this is my house," said my father. "Pray, who are you?"

"I am Lawrence Farre, servant to Sir Robert Pye the Elder," he answered, "and this is his house, it is not yours."

"Has no message been left for me either by Sir Robert the Elder or by his son the Colonel? Or by Mr. John Pye?"

"None, sir," he answered. "The young Sir Robert passed this way on the 15th day of this month, for he was in the church at Halton that day when Colonel Ireton married the daughter of General Oliver Cromwell; but he gave me no instructions except to guard the place against thieves and intruders. Now he is ridden off with his regiment again."

"I trust that you have proved worthy of his confidence in you," said my father.

"I trust I have," replied Farre, "for not a soul has come in but four persons, with a warrant from the Committee for Sequestrations in the County of Oxfordshire, sitting at Woodstock; three of whom were but clerks who made out the inventory and put a price upon your goods; but the fourth was a gentleman, a member of the Committee itself, and he oftentimes complained that they had put too high a price upon some piece, and then they brought it down low for him. He had a brother outside, whom I would not admit because he had no warrant, though he was the true purchaser of the goods and took them off——"

My poor father cried in a faltering voice: "Oh, what is this you say, good man? There were goods purchased and taken off?"

"Oh yes, indeed, Sir," said Farre merrily. "They have stripped the place clean; and I thought it great pity that my master Sir Robert were not here to bid, for it all went dog-cheap, there being only the one bidder, namely Mr. Thomas Appletree on behalf of his brother. Nay, I would allow none else inside the house, for those were my orders, to admit none without a warrant. Sir Robert would no doubt have liked to buy the carpets and chairs, the tables, the bed-steads, chests, court-cupboards and standing-presses at the price they fetched, or double: for then he might have rented the house at a better advantage. And the linen he might well have bought for his own use."

"They took all, you say?" my father asked, as one stupefied. "Oh, the buzzards! How was it conveyed away?"

"Why, Sir, upon four carts of yours that were also bought, and your great wain, and your two old coaches. They also drove off the pigs and sheep and cattle and some poultry from the backside, and took away the grain and the hops and some parcels of boards; but they had no conveyance for the timber, for which they will come again. The price agreed upon, I recall, was £335, for which Mr. Appletree the brother paid twenty shillings of earnest-money to the chief clerk."

"Oh, but when was this forced sale?" asked my father. "Upon what day?"

"Why, upon the Monday of last week," he answered, "the twenty-second day of June."

"But that was after the signing of the Articles of Surrender," cried my father, "when by General Fairfax's conditions these goods could not be lawfully sequestered, unless I refused to compound."

"That is no fault of mine," said Farre. "I had my orders and my orders I obeyed, and the gentleman, Mr. Appletree, was very civil to me and gave me ten shillings as a gift despite my severity towards his brother. Now, sir, begone, for I have nothing for you here. The house is empty but for my own bed and cooking-pot, and if you would make complaint, you have your redress at Law, I dare say."

Now the value of the goods thus sold in hugger-mugger was, with the high prices then ruling, at least £900. Yet there was worse news to follow. For in my father's absence the Parliamentary soldiers had pastured their horses, some three hundred in number, in our two great hay-fields and about the very time that they should have been mown; and all was eaten up by these horses, and Farre had not accepted the grazing-tickets honestly offered him by the officers, declaring that it was none of his business; and now the regiment was ridden away.

Our Wheatley lease-lands were sequestered also, which put my father in a dreadful fear lest his careless dealings in regard to them should come to the light. Here I must tell what I have lately learned about these lands, the lease of which (as I wrote before) my father had lately pledged to his cousin Sir Edward Powell, for a loan of £300. The lease was held from All Souls College since 1626, the year of my birth; and in 1634 my father had renewed the lease, but without surrendering to the College the paper thereby voided; and four years after that, he had assigned the new lease to one Richard Bateman, in return for £200; and in the year following, being at his wits' end for money, he had assigned the old and voided lease to one George Hearne for a term of thirty-one years, in return for £340, and Mr. Hearne had also kindly rented him the land at £40 a year. This was not honestly contrived, but he had hoped soon to pay back Mr. Hearne the money and so wipe out the fraud. Two years later yet, thinking that he might as well be hanged for stealing a sheep as for a lamb, he went again to All Souls College (which has a long purse and a short memory) and there bribed a clerk of accounts to shuffle the College papers for him; after which, making no mention of the lease that had been renewed for him in 1634, nor of his dealing either with Mr. Bateman or Mr. Hearne, he brought back to the College the old and voided lease (which he still held) made in 1626, and prayed for a renewal of it, which, on the payment of a small fine, the new Warden cheerfully gave him; not knowing that the lease had already been renewed in 1634. It was this quite worthless paper that he pledged again to his kinsman Sir Edward Powell in return for £300; so that, in all, he had profited £840 from a parcel of land that was never his own, besides its natural yield in produce.

As for the other freehold land at Wheatley, this was sequestered too; and here lay further trouble. For my father had not revealed to my husband (who had a prior claim upon it from the old debt upon statute-staple) that it was mortgaged to one Ashworth upon a ninety-nine years lease. Worse still, all the timber lying in the yard at Forest Hill, in value £500, being that which the brothers Appletree had bought but not yet removed, and also a great deal more lying in the

coppices of the Forest and in Stow Wood, was robbed from my
father by Parliament itself. For a humble petition was made by the
inhabitants of Banbury, who complained that one half of their town
was burned and part of the church and steeple pulled down, and
"there being some timber and boards at one Mr. Powell's house, a
malignant, near Oxford, they desire they may have these materials
assigned them for the repair of their church and town."

This petition was at once granted. Thus my father was stripped
bare, and having quarrelled with my Uncle Jones, and the Archdales
and Moultons being all either slain or dissettled and ruined by the
war, he had no friend to whom he might turn; and reckoned his position as desperate. There was nothing for it: his belly cried "cupboard"
and therefore he must come to London and eat dirt-porridge at the
Barbican.

CHAPTER TWENTY

My Child Is Born; and My Father Dies

O N THE evening of July 4th in that year, 1646, I sat sewing linen clothes for my child, with the window open to let in the cool breezes from the North. In the Barbican a ballad-singer sang a ballad that I knew well from childhood:

> Richard Cœur de Lion, erst King of this land,
> He the lion gored with his naked hand.
> The false Duke of Austria nothing did he fear,
> But his son he killed with a box on the ear.
> Besides his famous acts done in the Holy Land. . . .

The song breaking off suddenly, I looked up from my sewing and saw a cart drawn up at the next gate to ours; on which were heaped two or three trunks, a cloak-bag or two and some pieces of furniture, with a man in a soldier's coat seated in a leathern chair, as driver. Beside it stood nine or ten other persons, most of them children, very ragged and dusty, of whom one, a young woman, wore a yellow visor-mask. This young woman was questioning the ballad-singer, who pointed to our house; whereat the driver made the horse go backwards until the cart was over against our own gate. Two men lifted the soldier down from the chair, and when I pitied him that he could not walk, suddenly my heart stopped for I recognized my brother James, and the slatternly crowd with him were the remainder of my family. Being nearsighted, I had not known them at once, because of their travel-stained and dusty apparel.

The misfortunes that had come upon my family in the second siege of Oxford, were now suddenly for the first time presented to me. For on June 3rd, 1645, in the very early morning, there had been a party of horse and foot sent out over East Bridge to surprise the Parliament Guard at Headington Hill, which they did, falling in upon them pell-mell with their swords, slaying fifty and taking nearly a hundred prisoners; but in the confusion my brother James, who was one of those who sallied forth, was shot in the base of his spine by a bullet of more than an ounce weight, which though it had lost its force to enter yet cost him the use of his legs beyond hope of recovery. And another great misfortune was this: my two brothers and my sister Zara, in the crowded lodging where they were, above a hatter's in Penny-farthing Street, all fell sick together of the small-pox. William and Archdale were not marked by the disease beyond what is common; but Zara's face was so fearfully ravaged that ever since she has worn a visor-mask of white or yellow gauze, to spare the eyes of her acquaintance. Once again my mother had cause to lament the dissolution of the nun-neries—for what other bridegroom but the Lord Jesus Christ Himself, she asked, would be loving enough to accept as wife a woman with a face like a leper's?

Trunco went to open the door and saluted my parents lovingly. Then she ran to my husband to announce their arrival, and "Oh, Master," said she, "if I may make so bold—I pray you be compassionate to these poor gentlefolk, not only for God's sake, but for that of my mistress. She is now so near her account that if you show the least hardness to her parents and kindred, though they have treated you never so ill, she may cast your child untimely, which were the greatest sorrow in the world."

My husband, whom Trunco had found walking up and down upon the lawn in the backside, smoking his pipe and reading a book, dashed both pipe and book upon the turf, and asked: "Does your mistress know that they are here? Almost I would rather have Bridewell and Bedlam spew out their scum upon me than that this should happen. Say not a word to her, and I shall send them away quietly, if I may, without her knowledge."

But when he ran into the house he found me already downstairs embracing my mother and weeping for sorrow of James's plight and Zara's, while questions were bandied to and fro like tennis balls. What else could he do then but make them welcome, and send for refreshment, and commiserate their misfortunes? After a while, when he saw their condition, he offered them an asylum until they could put their affairs into better order: for these were the school vacations and all the boys, except Ned and Johnny Phillips, were dismissed to their parents' homes until Michaelmas. My father had grown haggard and old in this last year, and lost a number of his teeth. He behaved to my husband like a dog who fears that he has earned a whipping, but, being rewarded with a bone instead, is unhappy and grovels along the ground. But my mother was a Moulton and kept a proud carriage. Said she: "Well, Son Milton, I acknowledge myself mightily mistaken in you. I assured my poor Dick that we had nothing to hope at your door, and that he wasted his labour and exposed us to insult by making application. Yet he counted upon your generosity, and for once he was right; and I beg your pardon sincerely that I misjudged you. For myself, I confess that had I received from any person so saucy a message as I sent you by your servant, I should never have forgiven it, no, not this side of the grave. Well, I sincerely thank you for your generous spirit and while we abide under your roof I undertake that we shall sing small and huddle away into a small compass and disturb you very little or not at all."

My husband made no reply, but merely ordered Trunco to sweep the rooms and fetch water for the travellers. Presently he excused himself and returned to his book and pipe. During the three years of my absence from him, he had grown to be a rank smoker. Without tobacco he could not settle himself to his writing and if none of the better sorts—as Bermudas, Providentia, Shallow-Congo and the like—could be procured from the shops, he would be content with an infernal Mundungo; and if even Mundungo failed he would fain, I believe, have cut strands of hemp from a bell-rope and smoked that. He excused the nasty practice on the ground that tobacconing settled the stomach better than any cordial julep of anise, or infusion of lime flowers, that I offered him instead. Yet it was a very dear medicine to take, when Bermudas stood at sevenpence an ounce, which was a husbandman's daily wage.

I was overjoyed that I would have my mother by me at my lying-in, for if my husband had any intention then of exposing me to some extreme trial of hardihood, she would prevent him. I truly believed him capable to send me out on a cart into the fields by Highgate or among the windmills of Hampstead, when the first pains came upon me, to be delivered without any midwife's aid under a hedge or in a ditch of stinging nettles—and this not from any unkindness to me, but all for the discipline of his martial son. He had told me one day that the ancient Latins were wont to harden their children when they were young by laying their heads in cold running streams, whereof the weaker ones perished. "Well, sir," said Trunco, who overheard him, "let foreigners do as they please, I care not. But in England I war-

rant that would be adjudged wilful murder, at any crowner's inquest."
And at another time he said to me, offhand, eyeing my belly: "There
is a beast in the Riphaean Mountains beyond Russia, called the rossomakka, whose female brings forth by passing between two trees
grown close together, and so presses her womb to a disburdening."
What? Would he make a rossomakka of me?

I remember that I had a great longing for honey and sugar-works
and such-like, and one day I told my husband: "It is ill to refuse a
breeding woman, who has a pica, lest she miscarry." But he laughed
at that for an old wives' tale, and I must continue on my common
soldier's ration of one pound of bread and a quarter of a pound of
cheese, with salads in season and a few cherries. Yet he allowed me
plentiful milk, so that I should have abundance for the child when I
came to suckle him; and Trunco secretly brought me a parcel of
candied green citron to nibble, which was the sweetmeat that I loved
above all others.

My husband promised me, as a glorious thing, that so soon as ever
our son was born he would make my name famous to all posterity in a
tailed sonnet. The honour of a poem he had already conferred upon
three women, who were these: an Italian singer, Leonora Baroni of
Mantua, with whom, it seems, he had fallen in love for her voice during his tour in Italy; and Mrs. Catherine Thomson, an old devout gentlewoman, who, when he had dismissed Jane Yates, kept house for
him awhile, accepting no reward, from admiration of his writings and
pity of his case; and the Lady Margaret Ley, wife to one Captain
Hobson and daughter to the Earl of Marlborough, a witty woman a
few years older than himself, at whose house he was constantly entertained during my absence from him. It was the Lady Margaret who
had persuaded him (by her wise management of Captain Hobson)
that a woman could rule a shallowling husband without unseemliness;
and who by her liberality of friendship, when he stood in most need
of friends, had constrained him to put off all his contentious scorns
and open his heart to her like a flower of the sun. He and she would
have made a pretty wedded couple, but that she was the elder by an
inconvenient number of years. After my return she was cooled of her
affection for my husband, saying that he had returned like the dog to
his vomit, and abused him roundly that he valued her earnest warnings and dehortations not a chip.

To come to the matter of my lying-in: I was long in labour, near three days, and my husband was distracted, fearing lest the child should die; but born it was at last, on July 29th, which was the monthly fast, at about half an hour after six o'clock in the evening; and it was a girl. My husband was not so mad as to put any blame on me for this error (holding that a child's soul and sex is conveyed in *semine patris*), but was utterly disconsolate for the space of near a month and did not write me my sonnet after all. The child was christened Ann, after my mother and also after his sister Mrs. Agar, and so the letter A that hung above my bed was justified, though not perhaps the laurels. Nan seemed a brave child and prodigious like my husband in feature (which likeness has persisted); but presently I found that she had one leg shorter than the other by an inch or two. This deformity I attributed to my fall upon the ice, and Trunco was of opinion that had my husband allowed me to lie abed for awhile, rather than force me to go on my swollen ankle, the child would have been born straight-limbed. But neither of us durst say a word on the matter to my husband, who never looked kindly upon the child. He would not allow me to be ceremoniously churched after my lying-in, and even on the day that the child was born he refused the midwife to say her formal prayer, but commanded me instead to give humble thanks to God in my heart that I was preserved for His uses. Nor would he suffer my child to be baptized: for, he said that, having diligently searched the Scriptures through, he could find in them no ground at all for the practice of infant baptism, and that except he were convinced for the warrant of such an act by the word of God, why, he held it downright sin to perform it. Upon my objection that a child that was unbaptized was regarded by the common people as unlucky and as a certain prey for the Devil, he answered that what vulgar fools might prate together was unworthy of a wise man's attention. Wherefore the child remains unbaptized to this day.

When I was up and about again, my husband required that other lodgings should be found for such of my brothers and sisters as could shift for themselves: for their comings and goings disturbed his studies. So this was done.

My brother Richard, being a lawyer, was easily settled, for never within memory had so many petitions been drafted, or particulars drawn up, or certificates sworn, or lawsuits set on foot; and old Mr. Milton kindly put him in the way of business. James was uninstructed in any trade or profession, his education having been interrupted by

the wars, but Mr. Blackborough gave him employment in his library
for a small wage, to put the books and pamphlets into order that were
jumbled and tumbled together in heaps, and prepare a catalogue of
them; and afterwards James worked for a book-seller, reading the
manuscripts brought to the shop and advising him upon their merit.
James never complained of his misfortune, but was reserved in
speech, and could in no wise be reconciled to my marriage, my husband and he being so antipathetic. My brother Archdale was taken in
by my Uncle Cyprian Archdale, while John and William, being then
sixteen and fifteen years of age and sturdy boys, decided to follow the
profession of arms. About Christmas they enlisted in the Parliamentary
cavalry, Mr. Agar then recommending them to his friend General
Ireton, whose esteem they soon won, and were promoted by him to be
inferior officers. My sweet sister Ann was sent for by my Aunt Jones to
Sandford, and I saw no more of her until her marriage, not long since,
with a gentleman named Kinaston. Zara remained in the house and
cared for the three remaining children, Bess, Betty and George; she
had turned very devout and I hardly knew her, for her thoughts were
all upon Heaven—I believed her to be a secret Papist, for so her Captain had been, who was slain in the siege of Oxford by the wind of a
cannon bullet.

Now here I must tell how my father attempted to settle his debts
with my husband, whom he favoured above all his other debtors. He
confessed a present inability to pay him my marriage portion, but did
not repudiate the obligation, and promised to pay a part when the
goods unlawfully seized from him by Mr. Appletree should be restored.
He also sent off my brothers John and William to Forest Hill, to recover the silver buried under the clove-pinks in the garden, which,
while Farre slept, they dug up and brought home safe. This silver he
sold privately in Cheapside, excepting only my christening silver,
which I had again for my own, and gave the money to my husband.
He also gave him a sum of money, lately paid him by a Berkshire gentleman, for a great quantity of hurdles sold him before the war; as
also some Parliamentary billeting tickets and grazing tickets which
could be redeemed; so that of the £500 debt there was but £320
left owing.

My father then drew up a paper, giving particulars of the estate remaining to him, which he sent in to the Committee for Compositions,
sitting at Goldsmiths' Hall, and desired to compound; and he said that

when the matter was settled and he had paid the fine, which could not well be large, then my husband could enter upon the Wheatley freehold, now worth £80 a year, and so recover his £320 within four years. However, he dared not reveal that this land had also been mortgaged to Mr. Ashworth on a ninety-nine years' lease, and that this mortgage was elder by nine years than the one given to my husband; and that though the principal sum lent by Mr. Ashworth had been repaid in 1642, to defeat the demise, yet the arrears of interest unpaid amounted to £400 or thereabouts.

He took to his bed in September, being in great distress of mind, because every day he expected his unlawful dealings to come to light, and the disgrace to overwhelm his children as well as himself. In December the Committee, reckoning his estate as still comprising not only the goods at Forest Hill stolen away by the brothers Appletree, but also the timber bestowed by Parliament itself as a free gift upon the citizens of Banbury, and taking no cognizance of his just debts, fined him in the sum of £180; and unless this were paid, they would seize all the goods remaining to him. Whereat he finally lost heart. He refused food and pined away before our eyes, lying in bed all day, in a feverish distemper, with violent sweatings. When I went to his bedside he appeared uneasy in my company, and wept often, accusing himself of having used me unkindly, and would not believe me when I assured him that I had no grudge or complaint against him.

What troubled his conscience more than anything, I believe, was that he had been obliged to take the National Covenant as a Presbyterian before he was permitted to compound. It appeared now clearly that he was a Papist still at heart; for on the day after Christmas, when my mother and husband were both out of the house, my sister Zara smuggled in a disguised priest to perform some rite over him, which I suppose to have been the sacrament of extreme unction, for he appeared most wonderfully comforted. His fever abated, and though he found himself every day grown weaker, yet he was not exceeding sick and died very peaceably a little after midnight in the morning of New Year's Day, 1647.

My father left a will bequeathing to my brother Richard the Manor-house of Forest Hill (though it were no longer his own) with all the household stuff and goods and timber there remaining, and the houses and lands at Wheatley, freehold and leased (the charges upon which were four or five times their value, though he did not confess this, neither)—"besides," as he wrote, "all the other of my real estate in the Kingdom of England and Dominion of Wales" (which was mere fantasy). From this grand legacy my brother Richard should first satisfy my mother in the matter of her jointure, before he paid the other various debts, among which mention was made of my marriage portion. For it now proved that the eldest claim of all upon the estate concerned my mother's jointure of £2,000, which my father at his marriage received from my grand-uncle Archdale, and undertook by bond to lay out in lands for her, that were to be of the yearly value of at least £100 per annum; yet this he had neglected to do. As for the lands at Forest Hill (which also were no longer his), these he bequeathed to be divided among his children, namely, one-half to my brother Richard and the rest equally among the rest of us. He appointed Richard to be his executor, but if he shrank from it, then my mother was to undertake the charge; and he earnestly desired them not to have any difference concerning this will. To Sir Robert Pye the Elder he left twenty shillings to buy a mourning ring as a token of love.

When my father was buried, my husband could no longer allow my mother and Zara and the three children to remain in our house, for he said that they stunned him with their noise. Well, I could not blame him, for it was his house, not theirs. But, because of the burning of so many towns and villages, London was crowded with fugitives and lodgings were hardly to be found except at an exceeding high price, especially for poor widows with young children. Yet my mother found two dirty rooms at last in a mean house and street of Westminster, which was sadly distant from Aldersgate, and I feared that I should seldom see my family thereafter. They departed our house on January 30th.

This was the very day that the Scots, upon a promise of £200,000 and the present payment of an equal amount in coin, withdrew their army from England, and freely surrendered the person of King Charles to Parliament, though he was their King no less than he was ours. The securing of the King's person was the prelude to an open quarrel between Parliament and the Army. For now that the Members of Parliament, being for the most part Presbyterians, had secured their object, they were minded to disband the Army, or at least whatever part of the Army was not of the same way of thinking with themselves, for they needed yet a few regiments of horse and foot for service in Ireland. But the soldiers, now that they were victorious, desired the fruits of their victory and refused barren laurels. Their demands were these following. First, the securing of their arrears of pay, and due provision for such of their comrades as had been disabled in the war, and for the widows and children of such as had been slain or had otherwise died in the service. This was no great thing to ask, forasmuch as the pay of the common soldier for his hard and perilous service was but a penny a day more than the least of my father's husbandmen; and though Parliament was a better paymaster than the King, yet a common soldier was sometimes owed £5 or £6, or as much as £10. Next, in religious matters, the Army demanded such perfect liberty of conscience that if any man wished to worship the sun or moon, like the Persians, or the very pewter-pot from which he drank his beer, none should prevent him—for this liberty was the single religious tenet by which all were united. Lastly, the greater part of them desired the abolishment of the House of Lords, and for England to be governed by a single House of Representers, which should be elected by the whole people, and not by the burgesses or potwallopers of a few boroughs only.

Parliament tried to carry matters with a high hand, ordering the disbanding of most of the horse and nearly all the foot, with only six weeks' arrears of pay and the removal of every officer who would not conform to the Presbyterial Church Discipline, with other indignities. It was also voted by them to enlist a new army for service in Ireland, at a good rate of pay, under the same Presbyterial command. The Army quartered in Essex roundly refused to be disbanded; whereat the Generals Cromwell, Skippon and Ireton were sent out by Parliament to be mediators. Yet when they found how determined were the common soldiers to follow their new course, esteeming themselves The People and therefore the masters of Parliament, and how all the officers sustained them, except for a very few Presbyterians (as Colonel Richard Graves and Colonel Sir Robert Pye, who were among those appointed by Parliament to have charge of the King's person), they threw in their lot with the Army, and so did General Fairfax. They showed little displeasure, or none at all, when Cornet Joyce with a few bold horsemen rode to Holmby in Northamptonshire, where the King was kept prisoner, and stole him from Parliament: for it was known that the Presbyterians were treating privily with the King against the interest of the Army in general and of the Independents in particular. Then, having put His Majesty into a safe place, the Army under General Fairfax began slowly to march towards London.

Parliament itself was affrighted and willing to treat with the Army —for where the sword is, there is power; but the Presbyterial London popular (encouraged by General Massey, he who had held Gloucester so staunchly against the King, and by General Browne the Faggot-monger) raised an uproar and forced Parliament to make opposition. Then General Fairfax marched upon London with speed, as if against a town held by the enemy, and these were great days for my husband: for the Presbyterians, his enemies, were over-awed, and made a most cowardly show. They boldly shouted their war cry "One and all" whenever the Army was reported to be halted; but "Treat, Treat!" whenever it was reported to be on the march again. At last the Tower was yielded peaceably to General Fairfax, and he and his men marched through the city in orderly fashion with laurel wreaths in their hats. Parliament behaved very obligingly to them, and set aside the Bishops' lands and a large part of the estates forfeited by delinquents to be sold to pay their arrears. The men were encouraged by their success and began to ask: "Who were the first Peers of England but William the Conqueror's colonels? Or the knights but his captains? Or the gentry but his common soldiers?"

My husband during this time had written a sonnet against the Presbyterians, as Forcers of Consciences, in which he declared that the new presbyters were worse than any of the bishops whom they had driven out; and in many other ways he showed himself very hot against them. Yet this was the same John Milton who, not six years before, had written:

So little is it that I fear lest any crookedness, any wrinkle or spot should be found in Presbyterial Government that I dare assure myself that every true Protestant will admire the integrity, the uprightness, the divine and gracious purposes thereof, and, even for the reason of it (so coherent with the doctrine of the Gospel, besides the evident command of Scripture), will confess it to be the only true Church government.

We now employed Tom Tanner, a man-servant, to run messages, and to do work about the house not proper for women. His true name was Fly-fornication Tanner, but my husband renamed him plain Tom. He was a dismal Presbyterian who called himself "a mere winter's dust" and "a worm five foot long" and was continually blessing God for His mercies and rolling his eyes back into his head to show the whites. Trunco and I found his discourse terribly tedious, especially as he was always confessing to us the infirmities of his flesh—one day a quinsy, and the next a *flux hepaticus,* and the third a common pleurisy, for each of which in turn he begged our extemporate prayers; and, when these were successful, he stood blessing and praising the Lord like a lunatic. But my husband would often divert himself by asking Tom Tanner, when he came back from a meeting at the Church of St. Anne's, Aldersgate, what he had heard.

Tom would make answer: "Oh, Master, I heard a most godly preachment, which truly I would you had been there to hear!" And once he added: "For it would have lifted your soul out of its vile body."

"How now, Sirrah?" cried my husband. "Do you dare call my body vile? Have a care, have a care!"

"Nay, Master," said Tom, "you are a very handsome, proper gentleman, which is God's providence to bless you, but my meaning is that the preachment——"

"Come now," my husband said, in interruption, "what was the text?"

"The text, Master? What, the text?" Tom replied. "Why, it concerned a king of the Jews who took a pen-knife and cut the pages of a book and cast it upon the fire; and our minister, who is wondrous eloquent, undertook with the same pen-knife to cut into ribbons——"

"What, the same pen-knife!" cried my husband with mock gravity. "Was it yet extant?"

"I know not whether it was an Extant pen-knife or a Sheffield one," says Tom, "but the preacher used it to cut to ribbons those idolatrous poets now living among us who seek to adorn their verses with the names of heathen gods and goddesses, and with lewd tales of nymphs and such."

"He should have kept that knife to cut off his own ears, trimming them as close to the head as Mr. Marginal Prynne's, who first guided your foolish young preacher's feet into this way of knavery."

"Oh, Master, that I should ever hear you speak evil of that godly man, the Reverend Christopher Love, M.A., our minister," said Tom, "who is a wonderful comfortable preacher to all poor wretches who labour under soul concern: for he speaks from the very bottom of his heart, blessed be the Lord's name!"

"Ay, Tom," said my husband, "I warrant your Reverend Cupid preaches from so deep down in his body that the words incontinently break out by a short cut. But come now, how was the text divided?"

"Why, Master, the preacher took his little pen-knife——" began Tom.

"What, the same little pen-knife," cried my husband, in affected surprise. "Was it not blunted by being awkwardly dashed against the adamantine hardness of certain immortal poems?"

He continued so to tease poor Tom, absurdly imitating the Welsh ding-dong of the minister's voice, and ridiculing the fooleries of his congregation, that Tom found it grievous and left his service at last.

The Presbyterial discipline, which had been instituted according to the Scottish model and imposed upon all the parishes of London, my husband found most incommodious to him. However, his house in the Barbican happened to lie within the Parish of St. John Zachary, which was a prime reason why he had removed thither, and the minister was one William Barton who stood under an obligation to my husband, which was this. The old manner of chanting the Psalms of David, in plain-song, just as they stood in the Psalter, was to be abolished as papistical, and they were now to be rendered into verse and sung as prick-song hymns. To this end the Reverend Barton had made a careful metrical version of the Psalms (in rivalry to Mr. George Wither's tuneful but careless one and the out-worn version of Sternhold and Hopkins), and my husband had mended some of the verses for him, and had also prevailed upon the Earl of Bridgewater and other noblemen of his acquaintance to recommend this book to the House of Lords in preference to that published by Mr. Francis Rous, M.P.* which the Commons naturally favoured. When the Lords were by this means persuaded, the Reverend Barton, frankly telling my husband that "one hand washes the other," protected him from an uncomfortable inquisition into his religious beliefs: answering for his doctrinal soundness to the elders of the Parochial Court, and (I believe) assuring them that he had at last done with his pamphlets upon divorce and had signalized his change of heart by receiving me back into his bosom. However, my husband would not hide behind any minister's cassock, as he said. He wrote out a plain confession of faith for the Reverend Barton to show the Triers, but wrote it in the Aramaic tongue which (though our Saviour is not recorded to have spoken in any other, and therefore it was the best possible for my

* Not Mr. John Rous, the librarian of Oxford, to whom my husband at this time wrote a Latin ode.

husband's purpose) he was confident to be clean above their capacity
to understand as also above the Reverend Barton's.

Now that the Army was in control of affairs, my husband had little
cause to fear the presbyters, and upon his removal this year to a new
house in High Holborn, which lay in the parish of St. Andrew, he
boldly avowed himself an Independent. When one day Mr. Agar
brought General Ireton to our new house, the minister was soon informed of the visit and learned to treat my husband with awe. For
General Ireton, since his marriage with General Cromwell's daughter,
had become a man of very great note; and General Cromwell loved
him so much that, it is said, hearing one day that the estate and town
of Ireton in Derbyshire was owned by a Captain Saunders, he made
him Colonel of a regiment, to flatter him into the sale of this place,
which he wished to give to his son-in-law. When Colonel Saunders
was stubborn and would not sell, the regiment was taken from him
again.

The reason for our new change of dwelling was this. Two months
after the death of my poor father, there died in our house that worthy
old man, Mr. John Milton, Senior, who was always the least trouble
imaginable, and left my husband a good sum of money in rents and
the like, so that he found it no longer needful to keep so large a swarm
of pupils. He would seek out a smaller house and dismiss all his boys
but one or two of the older ones, who would be of more service than
vexation to him: for lately he had been troubled by his left eye,
which he had strained by overmuch reading; and these remaining
pupils might read aloud to him, and also make digests of books that he
could not himself find the time to peruse.

My husband, though he had recommended the Reverend Barton's
version of the Psalms above that of Mr. Rous, considered that he could
outgo both; and seeing that these Psalms were designed to be sung
in Churches every Sunday, by the whole population of England, for
a thousand years or more, he thought it pity that, merely for the Reverend Barton's sake, he should be denied the glory of composing these
verses himself. For not only had he a better ear for the music and
harmony of words than any man living—and this I say without fear
of contradiction—but he was a scholar of the Hebrew and would trans-
late from the original. Mr. Agar encouraged him in the labour, and
asked him for samples of his translation, and suggested that (if the
Lords and Commons could not agree as to which was the better of the

other two) my husband's superior version might be urged upon them,
by General Ireton or some other, as a third and best choice.

Our new house, which we entered about Michaelmas, 1647, was a
pleasant one, opening upon Lincoln's Inn Fields; and in it my husband busied himself for two or three months upon these Psalms. He
sent about translations of nine of them, copied into a book, and if
none was found to press them upon Parliament, this was perhaps because they were too nobly and perfectly composed: for, as I told my
husband, the Presbyterian naturally seeks and holds to what is but
second-best, holding it presumptuous in himself to love perfection.

In this year of 1647 provisions were at a rate as had never before
been in our days—beef 3d. a lb., butter 6½d. a lb., cheese 4d. a lb.,
candles 7d. a lb., sugar 1s 6d. a lb. and everything whatsoever propor-
tionately dear. It was a time of great sickness and illness, more fevers
than ever I remember (especially the spotted fever), plague again
abroad in London, little sun, much rain, the fruit rotting on the trees,
and so many cattle dying from the infected grass that milk was scarce
to be got. There was a song that ran often in my head about this
time, called *The World Turned Upside Down:*

> Good men, I'll tell you news that's right:
> Christmas was killed at Naseby fight.
> Charity was slain at that same time,
> Jack Tell-Truth too, a friend of mine.
>   Likewise did die
>   Roast beef and mince-pie,
> Pig, Goose and Capon no quarter found.
>   Yet let's be content
>   And the times lament.
> You see that the world is quite turned round.

In this November, with my mother's consent, my husband entered
into possession of our freehold property at Wheatley and Mrs. Elizabeth Ashworth (relict of Edward Ashworth, who had the elder lease),
being left friendless and in poverty by the cruelties of war, could not
eject him. For, as the phrase is, present possession is nine parts of the
Law, and he could show his statute-staple bond, which was elder than
her lease, in justification. The rents that he took in were £80 a year,
and of these he allowed my mother the third part customarily due to
the widow, namely £26 13s. 4d. This was all the money that she had
for her livelihood, except for the few shillings a month which my

brother Richard allowed her, and a few pence from poor starved James, and once a sum brought her as a free gift by our former tenants and humble acquaintances of Forest Hill, who loved her dearly, as Tomlins of the Mill, Boys of the brick-kiln, Martin the Woodman, Goodman Mathadee and Tom Messenger, who himself brought the money, near £15, with a letter and account. As executrix for my father, my mother was now sued in several courts of justice for divers debts due to divers persons, £2,000 or £3,000 in all—and was in no way able either to satisfy these or to provide a decent subsistence for herself and Zara and the three little ones. She even was reduced to working like a mechanic, agreeing with a pedlar to make him nets for kitchen-service, to boil herbs in, and with a hosier to make women's night-waistcoats of red and yellow flannel. I gave her my christening silver to sell for her needs.

My husband could do nothing for my mother, he said, because his own household and acquaintance must be first considered. And though in one way or another he was worth £250 a year, of which he spent £80 at least upon books for his library, and put by £50, what could I say or do? He owed no regard to my mother, who had never treated him with the civility due him. Moreover, my promised portion of £1,000 had not been paid and would never be paid; and I had borne him a crippled Ann to vex him, not a stalwart Arthur ("King once, and King again to be," as he had hoped) who should glorify and perpetuate his line. And how would my poor child make a good match, with her lameness, unless he provided for her a handsome portion? These thoughts vexed me continually so that often I lay awake at night and could not sleep.

I used to hide beneath my skirt lumps of cheese and brawn saved from my own ration and give them privily to Zara who came to meet me in Lincoln's Inn Fields. My husband would not suffer me to visit my mother in her lodgings, because when once he went there himself upon business he judged the air to be infected, and would not have me exposed to the plague.

However, Trunco came to my mother's relief. There was an honest man who fell in love with Trunco, for she was still a good-looking woman, though near thirty years of age, and it so chanced that his father, a distiller of strong waters, had died and left him his distillery on Ludgate Hill. This man did not understand the stilling business, for he had been at the wars, a cannoneer in the artillery train, but was now discharged, having lost an arm when a great gun burst its breech. Trunco therefore, giving notice to my husband that she would leave him, married her distiller upon condition that he should be the master in name but that she should have the real management of the business and a third share of the profits. It must not be forgotten that before she came to us she was a brewer's wife at Abingdon, and had managed his accounts. Her skill was such that in the first two years she put near £400 in her purse, though the distillery was in a poor way when first she entered into possession of it; and in the New Year of 1648, so soon as she married, she allowed my mother, in grateful recompense (as she said) for her kindness when she was herself in distress, two indifferent good rooms in her husband's house, with commons of beer and bread. I missed Trunco's company sadly, but would not have had her do otherwise than marry, and was content to see her thrive as Goodwife Fairacre, which was now her name. She had good clothes and fine linen and a brave little footboy, dressed in a plush jerkin, plodding behind her with a gilt-leaved prayer-book when she went to Church on Sunday.

CHAPTER TWENTY-ONE

I Speak with Mun Again

IT WERE vexatious to recount every event in the three-sided quarrel
that now ensued: the King playing off the Army Sectaries, in
whose custody he lay, against the Presbyterians of London and
their Scottish allies, and at the same time gathering up his broken
forces for another attempt to impose his own will (and the rule of his
Bishops) upon both parties when their leaders should have extirpated
one another. Bishops were still his maggot: he might yield in all else,
but here he took his stand. It is said that one day, about this time, he
cast a bone between his two spaniels that followed him, and laughed
to see how currishly they contested for it; which some thought that
he intended as a representation of that bone of contention he had cast
between the parties, namely the promise of his royal favour. For it
was generally believed that without a monarchy the country could
not possibly be governed; wherefore the King himself repeated oftentimes to the Army Grandees: "You cannot be without me, I say: you
will fall to ruin if I do not sustain you." These were anxious and uncertain times, hardly any man obliging his neighbour with the loan of
a shilling, or daring to give him more than "good-day" or "perhaps we
shall have fine weather to-morrow," so mistrustful were all become.

I read no diurnals or pamphlets of news and paid little heed to
the talk about me, so that what might be happening in Ireland to Sir
Mun, whom I supposed to be serving still with the Marquis of Ormonde, I could not venture to guess. It had happened to me that, from
the night when I first lay with my husband, I found the bond of sympathy between myself and Sir Mun slackened or cut through; I no
longer either dreamed of him or was aware of the accidents of his
life, and if ever any unaccountable pain or sorrow or happiness stole
upon me I could no longer confidently say as before: "This happens
also to my Mun."

I was become a City wife, a mere droiling drudge, accustomed at
last to the noise and stench and smoke of London, sometimes gossip-

ing idly with neighbours, never riding out or taking other exercise, my body growing fat, my cheeks yellowish, my eyes dull. As for my hair, I confined it under a hat or cap, as did the other City wives, because thick hair worn loose in London grows very foul, especially in the time of choking fogs. Gaudy apparel I no longer wore, at my husband's desire, but gowns of plain cut and sombre colour: for he told me that it was against nature for the female to go more bravely clad than the male. "Witness," said he, "the peacock's tail, the lion's mane, the robin's breast——"

"Ay, husband," said I, for I had learned the art of indecently racquetting back his words, "and the stag's antlers!"

In the City in those days it was generally accounted a sign of reprobation, either in man or woman, to be seen with bright eyes and rosy cheeks, and a heinous fault in a minister or a matron—damnable in a widow. The proof of grace and respectable godliness lay in a haggard countenance and pallid lips. Many a man of a naturally sanguine complexion has been clapped in the stocks only for looking fresh on a frosty morning. Well, I was in the fashion now. Says I to myself: "Marie"—for I was still Marie to myself—"you are come halfway already to the dark grave. It is time you turned devout and interlarded all your speech with 'if God will' and 'the Lord be thanked' and 'if the Lamb show me mercy.'" Yet I seldom went to Church, the services being so strange and my husband neither commanding me to attend, nor himself hardly ever attending. The only words he spoke to me on the matter were to forbid me to receive the Sacrament of our Lord's Body at the hand of a Presbyterial minister: for the Triers, those grave elders appointed to examine persons for their fitness to receive, asked questions that were immodest and impertinent enough to make any honest woman blush. He doubted not but they would seek occasion against him, by pumping me for what I knew of his habits and opinions.

My little Nan was a dull child, and though I desired to love her, I could not, which made me wonder; for Nature, I had heard, teaches every mother to love her child. I was patient with her, but she was long learning to walk because of the deformity of her left leg. My husband was very surly with the child, because she often cried in the night, my milk not agreeing with her; and when she learned to prattle, she stammered. What was worse, though Trunco would have fitted her with a clog to raise her lame foot from the ground equally with the other, my husband forbade it, prophesying that Nature would in the lapse of years compensate for her error by stretching out the short leg. However, in this he was mistaken, for when Nan learned to hobble her body grew more and more awry, and one shoulder was driven up higher than the other.

My husband was never wanton with me either in word or act, nor ever lay with me but with the express intention of procreation, and that very seldom. I thought it a mighty silly distinction that he made between lawful procreation and natural concupiscence; which in effect are as alike as one caraway-cake is to another. Always a few days beforehand he cast an astrological figure to assure a fortunate result, and then solicitously prepared my mind with music and poetry. He prided himself upon the exactness of these figures, the art whereof he had learned from Mr. Joseph Meade (author of *Clavis Apocalyptica*), a senior tutor of his College at Cambridge, and he laughed at such dabblers in astrology as William Lilly, William Hodges or John Booker. Yet he acknowledged Hodges to be good at crystal-gazing and Booker at curing sicknesses by constellated rings and amulets. Lilly he praised because, though a man of mean education, he had written *Christian Astrology*, a book confounding the Presbyterians who held astrology to be of the Devil and no true science; and because he was a useful instrument to General Fairfax, who employed him to keep up the spirits of the soldiers by seasonable prophecies.

For myself, I never had any patience with the stars, which evidently are sly, cozening creatures, saying one thing when they mean another. When I spoke my mind upon them to my husband, he was exceeding angry with me; he thrust my Bible into my hand and commanded me to read out aloud the scripture about the star that guided the wise men to Bethlehem. And he said: "O woman of intemperate and unbridled tongue, do you not see now that a loose word spoken against the holy study of Astrology is as a stone contumaciously flung in the face of God Himself, that will rebound back into the caster's face?"

I answered: "I am truly sorry, Husband, if I have spoken amiss; but I cannot find in this scripture that the Wise Men cast any astrological figures. For they seem merely to have followed their hooked noses, and a moving star; as any unlettered person might have done."

That my husband companied with me seldom, not above twice or thrice a year, I held no hardship, for I was not of a hot and passionate nature; I wanted no more children of him, who had made my former pregnancy so needlessly hard for me. I suckled my child so long as ever I could, for this is held good against conception; and also medicined myself on occasion with the smut of rye, which is used by the women of the Town.

My neighbours, I could see, pitied me, yet some avoided my company because I was never seen in Church, and because it was known that Nan had not been baptised, nor I churched. And often I would overhear how they spoke behind my back, to such as knew me not, with words like these: "Hist, Gossip, see, see! Mark you that little mincing gentlewoman with the proud head who carries the crooked child—that is Mrs. Milton!" Or: "That is John Milton's Manacle—have you not heard of Mr. Milton the Divorcer? For all she looks so sickly I dare say that she has not the physiognomy of Grace. She will burn, Goodwife, doubtless she will burn. Yea, it is lamentable sure she will burn."

My husband seldom took any physic, but like all scholars and schoolmasters and clerks, who from long sitting are customarily bound in the bowels, he used Calabrian manna, which is good for purgations. He suffered also from flatulency, because he was always in haste. He himself confessed that such was the impetuousity of his temper that no delay, nor quiet, nor care, nor thought of almost any thing else, could stop him till he came to his journey's end in any undertaking or study. Thus, though he was in general punctual to the table, he oftentimes came to it like one in a trance, especially if he were engaged in some sharp polemical writing, visibly raging in his mind and jotting down notes in a little book pulled from his pocket. At such times he ate abstractedly and violently; yet every fool knows that a meal that is not eaten graciously and at leisure will always breed wind. He drank little beer or mead or wine, for he said liquor made him drowsy. Yet neither did he drink water, considering that it hurt the digestion to wash down victuals with water, yet neglecting to drink any between-whiles.

I warned him once that, if he did not swill out his guts more generously, they would grow foul, and breed the gout. He laughed at me and asked, for what did I take him? Was it for a cheese-vat or a cider-cask?

"No," said I, "and I will not be so saucy as to amend the proverb, which says that 'one may lead a horse to water but cannot make him drink.'" And I asked him: "How is it that you complain of the headache, yet crouch all day in your library with the windows fast shut and so foul an inspissation of the air, from the fumes of your pipe, that I cannot see across from wall to wall?"

He answered: "The windows are shut against the noise of children playing in the fields, and I drink tobacco to fortify me against domestic misery."

"Oh, that I were wife to King Nebuchadnezzar!" cried I.

"Why so, Addlepate?" he asked.

"Because," said I, "Nebuchadnezzar was no more mad a croucher than you, yet by his eating of grass, like an ox, he had a sweet breath at least."

"Bless me!" he cried. "Will you never leave your vitilitigation—your perverse termagant humour of wrangling and reparteeing?"

One afternoon, early in February, 1648, which was a resplendent day, as warm as May, I felt that suffocation of my spirits, I could scarce breathe. I must go out of the house, come what might, for a breathing-space; though my husband, who had taken his two nephews riding into the country, had commanded me to stay close within doors lest there should come a message for him. I went out, with Nan in my arms, into Lincoln's Inn Fields, where because of the fineness of the weather there was a concourse of lawyers and other citizens at the bowling green. So soon as ever I went out, my heart began to lighten and the dismal vapours to disperse. Then looking shrewdly about me I soon distinguished the cause: for before me, about a quoit's cast away, stood Sir Mun, leaning against a tree, with meagre cheeks and a deep sword-scar upon his brow. He was not watching the play, but gazed fixedly at me.

As I came towards him, he swept off his hat and, said he: "Mistress Milton, your humble servant."

"Be covered, Servant," I answered. "You look not so well conditioned as when last I saw you." For the rich clothes that he wore were old and stained and patched.

He was silent for a while and then he said: "By God, I wish with all my heart that we were both in happier plight."

I began to weep a little, looking down at my worn house-gown and the little dirty brat in my arms.

Then he broke out passionately: "Oh, Marie, Marie, how is it that neither of us is yet dead? What excuse have we for life? That you truly love neither your husband, nor yet your child, is plain and evident; yet doubtless you are a good wife, for the honour of matrimony, and pass as a kind mother. As for myself, I no longer truly love either the King whom I serve nor the cruel profession of arms to which I am committed; yet am a most loyal subject, for the honour of kingship, and pass as a valiant commander."

"It is not so easy to die, dear heart," I answered, "without sufficient cause. My time is not yet, nor is yours, and who can say certainly whether that *Metempsychosis,* in which you once instructed me, be fantasy or truth? While we both yet live, it is something to know ourselves bound together in the same faggot of Time, though lying wide apart. When the bundle is broke and we burn severally, then perhaps we are lost to each other for ever more."

"That can never be," said he hastily. "Mun shall never lose his Marie, nor Marie her Mun. Yet the dark shadow of your husband falls between us; who is a devil, else he had never intruded upon our company; and who from ambitious greed has laid hands on what is not his, except by legality."

"This Devil has scorched his fingers," said I. "He is not happy in his plunder."

"That I doubt not," said he, "and therefore I would carry you with me into France to-morrow—when I sail from Tilbury with the morning tide—but that legality, like chastity, is unassailable. John Milton loves you not, you love him not in return, yet he possesses you by a claim that no honest man would dispute, and will never yield you up, merely from scrivener-bred stubbornness. To be sure, at the Court in France, I could readily procure you a divorce from him, pleading on your behalf a difference of faith; for you married him according to the old Liturgy and he is now, as I hear, turned Levitical Jew. Yet then myself to marry you would go point-blank against my conscience —and against yours."

"Aye," said I, "for I would be a plain whore if I lay in one bed with you to-night, when last night, upon a lucky conjunction of planets, my husband had his marital will of me. And what of Doll Leke, who is reported to be your wife?"

"I have no wife," he answered. "Yet my case matches yours, for I have lain with many women in these last two years, since I heard of your return to your husband; and I could not use you in the same manner as I have used them, even were you to command it. If you ran to France with me, it would not be for carnal acquaintance."

"Could it be otherwise?" I asked. "I am no deaconess of the primitive Church, neither are you a deacon to lie chastely a-bed with me in Satan's despite. Yet I would not wrong a husband who once, against his own inclinations, was persuaded to receive me kindly back into his house after long absence. Nor have I any just complaint against him, for he never raised a violent hand against me, nor abused me in any other way by which he could be held accountable to God. He also fed and comforted my father and mother and my whole family when they were distressed: nor did he defraud my mother of her thirds, when she was widowed. He acts righteously, though without love as you and I know love to be. He has a devil, just as you say, the devil of legality, the same which plagued the Jews to tithe mint and rue, with other follies: but this devil must have his due, or he will howl and run stark mad and hurt both himself and us. True, he has once or twice reproached me without a cause; but then so have I disobeyed him, more than once or twice, and pretended to be the fool that I am not. The truth is that, setting the hare's head against the goose's giblets, neither of us has dealt more than commonly ill with the other. I could not leave him now and come with you: he would ululate like an Irish wolf with the hurt to his esteem, how little soever he may love or value me."

"Yet his kindred and friends would earnestly press him to sue for a divorce from you," said Mun. "And your desertion of him would be a cause to satisfy any one of the new presbyterial Courts that are set up. I verily believe that it would be a kindness to him were you to cut the knot after this fashion."

"Sweet Mun," said I, "you understand me perfectly, but you are mistaken in John Milton. Were I to desert him and company with you, he might indeed win the Presbyters' permission to divorce me for adultery; yet that he should be forbidden to divorce me at his own pleasure on account of the defects of my mind and spirit, but earnestly pressed to divorce me because of a vulgar adultery, this would indeed drive him frantic. Oh, but why do we beat upon the bush? There is nothing good harboured in it for us. Our happiness lies not at the end of the divorcer's road. It is now too late for me to come to you, as both of us know and acknowledge."

He nodded his head and said slowly: "You are right, it is too late. Yet I have thus reasoned with you because of the pain of seeing and speaking with you as through the bars of a prison window when to-morrow I must die. Marie, you and I are married in the spirit, and we passed our bridal night under the bells, which is a bond insoluble; yet what have we to show? Almost I could envy your husband that poor dull infant in your arms, whom you carry not as a treasure, but as a nasty burden."

I began to weep again, and when Nan laughed in my face I grew angry with her and slapped her so that her laugh changed to a screech; then I was sorry and kissed her, but that made her screech the more, until I pacified her with a comfit.

Suddenly it was again with Mun and me as it had been under the bells: we spoke together in a curious riddling language of our own, in which we disclosed to each other deep concepts which were never before so clear to either mind, and imaginings of such rare subtlety that we seemed as ghosts communing together upon the nature of the wind or of the lightning. Presently the grass of Lincoln's Inn Fields vanished away, and all the houses and players at bowls with it, and he and I stood alone, as it seemed to us, on a sedgy bank by a cold river where waterfowl swam and herons waded.

I know not how long we conversed there; but at last the spell waned, the river receded, the several houses shuddered back into their places, the clack of bowls sounded again, and from beyond the houses came the hoarse noise of the parish bellman crying his proclamation against the casting of garbage into the streets.

We parted after a few words more, but without any kiss or other salutation: I placidly taking my child back to the house and Mun sauntering off towards the bowl-game. His last words to me were: "And that I shall never see you again in this life, it is but a way of speaking—as upon New Year's Eve, in my childhood, I would stand at the open door (when the clock wanted but one minute for midnight), and cry to my tall brother Ralph: 'Good-bye, sweet Brother, for I am off on a journey and shall not be back with you again until next year!'"

My husband returned wearied by his unaccustomed jaunt. He asked: "Has anyone called at the house? Is there any message or letter come for me?"

"No," said I, "I have no news for you, except that we are short of coals, and the merchant again has delivered none to us, though three days ago he made you a faithful promise of three or four chaldrons at least. The child is asleep. Are you ready to eat your supper?"

"Supper?" said he. "Nay, not for another half hour at the least. We must not be unthrifty of daylight: I yet have time for a chapter or two of a dangerous book that the Council requires me to examine. Yet will I eat an apple. Come, wife, make haste: first draw off my muddied boots for me, and then bring me my worsted slippers and a rough-tasted apple. Why do you stand and gape?"

"There are no apples in the house, either sweet or rough-tasted," said I, bending down to pull off his boots. "Would you eat a medlar?"

"A medlar!" he shouted. "A medlar! Are you indeed such a pudding-head? Are you ignorant that of all fruits the medlar alone is no friend to the bowels, but contrariwise, is costive in the extreme? An apple, I said; I will have an apple or nothing!"

"Mercy on us," cried I, "is it so with you, indeed? Here are merry lines to enliven your Comedy of Paradise:

Adam: I will eat an apple, bring me a rough-tasted apple!
Eve: Husband, you know full well that God hath forbidden us apples. Will you not eat a medlar instead?
Adam: A medlar, a medlar, puddinghead! Are you ignorant that medlars are costive in the extreme? An apple, I said, I will have an apple or nothing; though I be damned for't. Am I not master here? There is nothing in all the world so good for a weak stomach as a rough-tasted apple.
Eve: Be damned then, greedy guts, and pluck one yourself, though it prove a Sodom apple.
Adam snatches an apple from the tree. A horrid thunder. Enter an Angel with a drawn sword.
Adam: Oh, pardon, good your worship, it was no fault of mine. This woman tempted me.

Come, Husband, why do you stand and gape? Here are now your worsted slippers. Must I draw them on for you as though you were a child?"

He mastered himself and played mum-budget, refraining from a back answer; but in such a scornful haughty manner as I scarce ever saw the like. Then shuffling his feet into the slippers he went off to read in his study. I could judge from his gait that he would punish my sauciness by perfect silence for three days and three nights.

Now I might again be private. Yet this had been so smart a return to my dirty life of cat and dog, that my afternoon's meeting with Mun seemed like a dream—and not in a manner of speaking only, for I sincerely doubted whether a dream it were—a mere shining dew-hung cobweb of my fancy. I confess that I had fallen into a pleasant custom of forging imaginary dialogues between Mun and myself, and knew not whether this was likewise forged. What proof had I that I had indeed met him by the bowling-green? "Oh," I cried, "who cares for what is real or what is unreal? These are but words." There was a student of Trinity College at Oxford who disputed with a learned Doctor upon a point of logic touching the reality of appearances. The Doctor said: "The fox wagging his tail and seeing its shadow upon a wall, held that it was a horn: was that a real horn or no?" This positive student replied: "Aye, a real horn it was." Then the Doctor fell into a little passion and cried: "Well, if it be a horn, a real horn, then toot it, you fool, you!" "Sir," replied the student, "if I were the fox, so I would, I warrant you, and make a great noise, and cause your head to ache withal."

Mun was come from Ireland some months before this upon the Articles of Peace signed between the Marquis of Ormonde and Parliament. For the Marquis had yielded up to Parliament the towns and castles that he held in Ireland, rather than entrust them to the native Irish Papists, with whom he was at variance; fearing lest they might call in Spanish or French soldiers to garrison these strongholds, to the lasting injury of our country. The Marquis was now arrived in France, whither Mun also went after he had seen me; but presently, upon a motion of the Confederate Catholics, as these Irish were styled, he returned to Ireland from France to conclude a firm alliance between them and the King's party of Protestant Prelatists. Sir Mun sailed in the same ship, which sailed too late: for when at last they were able to land at Cork, in September, 1648, they could no longer assist in prosecuting the design intended by the King, which was to levy war against the English Army, from England, Scotland, Wales and Ireland at one and the same time.

Indeed, the Second Civil War was already over and done with. There had been riots and tumults in the streets of London, with the roaring cry of "For God and King Charles," and the discharge of muskets, which put me into great fear; but the troops that were quartered in Whitehall and about Charing Cross proved equal to their task of suppression. More than this, the Kentish rebellion was bloodily subdued by General Fairfax, and the Welsh rebellion at Pembroke by General Cromwell; the Scottish army of Presbyterians, invited across the Border by their English fellows, was defeated in a three-days' battle at Preston by Generals Cromwell and Lambert; and Colchester, in

Essex, the last English town to hold out for the King, was surrendered before the end of August. Nevertheless, when the King was already a close prisoner of the Army, and brought from the Isle of Wight to Windsor Castle, whence he would find it hard to escape, the sword was rashly drawn in Ireland, for a Cause already ruined.

My husband exulted mightily at the victory at Preston, where 8,000 English Sectaries had routed three times their number of Scottish Presbyterians, who had come (as they declared) to "put down that impious Toleration settled by Parliament contrary to the Covenant": for he said that the shame of the two Bishops' Wars was at last wiped out, and proof given that, whereas perfect Liberty of Conscience enables soldiers to fight with intelligence and comradely love, the coercive discipline of presbyters confines, imbecilitates and stultifies even the most martial spirit. And he told me that the Scots on the even of the battle had weakened their forces by a purge of all officers whose imperfect orthodoxy might, as was feared, bring down God's judgment upon the whole array, among whom were their most capable and resolute commanders.

The Scottish prisoners were brought to London and there sold as slaves to the agents of the Barbadoes planters, at five shillings the head.* My mother laughed heartily when she saw the poor, naked, scabby creatures marched through the streets of the City: for those who had sold their own King into slavery, she said, deserved no better themselves. My brother James pitied them; yet he held that the Barbadoes planters would be found better masters than ever their own mad Lords and ministers had been: for so strictly had the planters abstained from any fratricidal discords during the late troubles that for a man to call another "Cavalier" or "Roundhead" was an offence, and he was bound in satisfaction to give a dinner of pork and turkey to all who had been within hearing.

(Yet even this island Paradise has lately been set by the ears, many young English Royalists flocking there, and two Devonshire gentlemen making themselves masters of all the islands in the King's name; so that Parliament has been obliged to send a fleet to recover them. Some men will never learn when they are well off, nor what a marvellous great consumer of public treasure and pestilent breeder of domestic miseries is Civil War.)

---

* Yet the Welsh prisoners taken at Pembroke were sold by General Cromwell at but one shilling the head; which was strange in a man of Welsh descent, to value the Scots as having each man the worth of five Welshmen.

CHAPTER TWENTY-TWO

I Watch the King's Execution

M Y HUSBAND addressed a commendatory sonnet to the Lord General Fairfax, in which he prayed him, when he had concluded the war and crushed the hydra-heads of new rebellion, to set his hand to the task of reforming the government of England, and of so clearing our public faith from the shameful brand of public fraud that no new occasions for rebellion should arise. But this sonnet and his metrical Psalms were all the poems that he now wrote, and his grand design of *Adam Unparadised* was still laid aside. One day I asked him what was the reason that he did not take it up again, since he had hoped to make it the instrument of his immortality. He would not answer for a while until I twitted him, saying: "With that poem, husband, you are like St. George—always in the saddle, never on your way!"

Then indeed he broke out hotly: "A divine poem such as this can be penned only in times of civic grandeur, and by a poet who is domestically at ease. How can I write while rogues prate in Parliament, while beneficed wretches bellow nonsense from their Presbyterial pulpits, and while God yet curses me with so unhelpful and brawling a mate as yourself? Almost it is enough some days to turn me Atheist, for I cannot think but that I have deserved better of God."

"Ay, Husband," said I, "you are a very nonsuch of patience, a perfect Job; and like Job, I hope, you will one day be rewarded for your fidelity and healed of your grievous boils. Yet you may thank God for one thing, that you have no child dancing morrices in your belly, such as I have."

For these were miserable times for me, with constant keckings and vomitings throughout the spring and summer, which continued until the beginning of October. It was a very lively child, whereas Nan had lain torpid.

My husband, being daunted by the failure of his first attempt to beget a great captain, had abandoned the project; yet now he was encouraged by a nativity that he had drawn (according to the rules and practice of Cornelius Agrippa, with the additions of one Valentine Naibod) and set for the night when he ceremoniously lay with me. He expected that this time he would verily beget a son who would be a famous diviner, a mathematical Merlin. He therefore ornamented my chamber with the signs of the Zodiac and of the planets, and with curious mathematical figures whereof I understood nothing but which, he said, it was not needful that I should understand forasmuch as they would work upon my son through the medium of my eyes. On this single work he spent a month or more, until he had it settled to his satisfaction, putting aside his other tasks the while. He also altered my diet, commanding me to eat watercresses, as much as I could stomach; for in an old poem watercresses had been written of as the food of Merlin, and also (I know not why) I was to eat fish and eggs in place of beef and bacon.

Yet once more only the initial letter could be saved of this nativity: on October 25th, 1648, which also was a fast day, in the morning at about 1 o'clock, was born not Merlin, but my second daughter, Mary, who is so much myself in repetition that almost the birth might have been parthenogenous. Mary is brisk, headstrong and agile, a very Turk to her playmates; and now at the age of three, when I write this, promises to grow a head of hair the equal of mine. My husband took the birth of a second daughter very ill. He could find no fault with her except that she was of the female sex; nevertheless, he accused me of a settled determination to oppose his wishes and interests.

About this time he was overcome by a new maggot. For he had seen how in Europe such scholars as Vossius, Grotius, Heinsius and Salmasius were courted and flattered by potentates and cities as worshipfully as poets had been in the time of Petrarch. Pricked by a grand ambition, namely, for Miltonus to be accounted the greatest scholar of his day, he was writing at the one time three several books of huge labour and erudition.

As for the tide of public affairs, this flowed to his liking. He was exceedingly content with the manner in which the Independents of the Army had settled their accounts with the Presbyterians in Parliament. For on December 6th of this same year Colonel Pryde (who had been a drayman before he was promoted to be an officer), coming one day into the House of Commons at the head of his soldiers, with

a list in his hand, extruded all the members who were Presbyterians
or otherwise displeasing to the Army. Where was then the National
Covenant that the whole country had been obliged to swear for the
sake of the Scots? It was cast away like an out-of-date almanac.
Among members extruded were Sir Robert Pye the Elder, Sir William
Waller (once the hero of the Army and styled "William the Conqueror"), General Massey the defender of Gloucester, Mr. Prynne the
crop-eared martyr, and others of the same quality; these were hag-
gling with the King upon the articles of a new treaty (spoken of as
the Treaty of Newport) and would still concede to him what no single
regiment of the Army counted him worthy to receive. In the Army,
where victory had worked upon the soldiers like bottled ale, it was
now openly affirmed that "whosoever has drawn his sword against his
King must fling his scabbard into the fire." Then the remaining members, nicknamed the Stump or the Rump, who were Independents
and favourably disposed to the Army, proceeded in their hardy project. They would convert England into a Republic and, to this end,
dare bring the King to trial on a charge of conspiring against his own
subjects. Yet General Cromwell so ordered the matter that every member felt himself conscientially absolved of his allegiance to the King.
He stood up and told them that any man who moved this business of
his own design was the greatest traitor imaginable; yet since Providence and Necessity cast it upon them all, Almighty God, he hoped,
would bless their counsels. The day upon which the King's trial was
ordered was the very day whereon, seven years before, he had come
to this same Parliament to demand the five members who had defied
him.

"Aye," said my mother, bringing me the news from Westminster—
she would call upon me in the afternoon while my husband was out
walking—"for Parliaments are perishable commodities: after a year or
two they turn sour and begin to stink. Here is a Parliament that stinks
to high Heaven."

This 1648 had been a strange, sad year. January had passed without
any frost hardly, or any wind, but with a flattering sun smiling down
continually, so that fruit trees and hedges budded out and the goose-
berry trees in our garden had little leaves to them. "That is pretty to
admiration," said Trunco to me, "yet for this we shall pay later, or I
am no weather-wise farmer's daughter." The spring entered pleasantly
enough, but suddenly at the latter end of April came terrible frosts

that nipped the trusting shoots and blackened them. In the country-side the rye was blasted when it was already in the ear, and much other grain with it. Summer was wonderful wet, with rain almost every day, which sometimes fell in deluges and rotted the hay and laid the corn flat. What grain could be cut would not dry, but sprouted in the shocks, and what could not be cut grew rank and would not ripen and was choked with weeds and either smutted or mildewed. Summer glided into winter, with but a short interlude of autumn sunshine, such fruits as had survived the frost again rotting dismally upon the trees. I was glad for my poor father that he had been spared the cares and distresses of this season. By Christmastide provisions in our market had risen to double or more the customary prices: beef stood at fourpence a pound, butter at eightpence, cheese at fivepence, wheat at eight shillings the bushel, sugar not to be had.

Then ensued a very disagreeable black New Year, made horrible by the trial of the King. From this awful undertaking many leaders of the nation hung back: all the noblemen who still attended the House of Lords; and the Lord General Fairfax; and of the Commons, even after Colonel Pryde's Purge, not a few, among whom were Alderman Pennington and General Skippon and other brave commanders of the late wars. However, General Cromwell, with Ireton his son-in-law and Mr. Serjeant Bradshaw and fifty or sixty other resolute men continued with the settlement of this matter, though there were no precedent in English history for the judicial trial of a King upon any charge, let alone the capital charge of High Treason.

General Ireton came to our house on the day following the Purge, namely December 10th, and pleasantly asked my husband what writings he had in hand. My husband replied that he was engaged upon one great work, already oftentimes interrupted, namely the *History of England from the Earliest Times;* and upon another, a grand collection of Latin words, with a record of their occurrence in the best authors, to constitute a *Complete Dictionary;* and upon a third, the compiling of a *Body of Divinity* or *Methodical Digest of Christian Doctrine.*

"These are huge, deep, exceeding important and most honourable works," said General Ireton, "and I wish you a favourable issue to your industrious labours. Yet cannot you lay them aside for a few weeks to attend to an immediate matter? We who are in power have need of your pen, which is the firmest and boldest in England, to jus'

tify the resolution we have taken to bring Charles Stuart to trial for
his life. If you serve us well, I undertake that you will be honoured
according to your deserts: for it is a very noble and necessary task
that we shall set you."

"I write to no man's dictation," answered my husband, "yet if you
have need of a pamphlet upon the tenure of Kings and Magistrates,
showing how they are accountable to the people over whom they are
called to sit in judgment, why, I shall be as rejoiced to write it as I
hope you will be to read it. For I believe, with you, that it is lawful
for any who have the power, to call to account a wicked King and,
after due trial, to depose him or put him to death. This can be learned
from the Scriptures, from the cases of Ehud and Eglon; of Samuel and
Agag; of Jehu and Jehoram. Tyrannicide also among the Greeks and
Romans was an open doctrine and a deed of heroic virtue performed
in a hundred cases. What more flagrant names are preserved among
the Greek records than those of Harmodius and Aristogiton, or among
the Romans than those of the two Brutuses? To be sure, Julius Cæsar,
whom the second Brutus slew, was less tyrannical than any of his suc-
cessors in the Imperial line and deserving of mercy on many accounts,
yet he was a tyrant for all that, and Brutus was commendable for his
act, and the more so because Julius was dear to him, a second father.
To come to our own history, beginning with the historian Gildas——"

Here General Ireton, who was pressed for time, encouraged my
husband and told him clearly there was no need to persuade or tempt
him to a task which he was so capable and ready to accomplish. "But,"
said he, "let the work be put speedily in hand, for I can assure you
that this trial will not be protracted like those of the Earl of Strafford
and Archbishop Laud."

So my husband worked at the pamphlet very assiduously, putting
his other writings wholly aside until he had perfected it; and took it
to the printers on that fatal day, January 29th, 1649, when the sentence
was pronounced by the King's judges.

The King had been wonderfully surprised when he was brought to
trial at Whitehall and at first seemed to take a light view of the matter, and would not remove his hat in token of respect of his judges.
He argued ironically with Mr. Serjeant Bradshaw, the Lord President
of the Court (which met in the Painted Chamber), that it was absurd
for a King to be tried by his subjects; and when Mr. Bradshaw asked,
did he plead guilty or not guilty, he replied that before he could

answer he must have law and reason quoted for his appearance before this novel court of justice. He proved so stubborn that the Lord President ordered the Sergeant "to take away the prisoner"; and the King was led out, disputing still. He rested his case, it was said, upon the Law and Custom of England, as also upon the words of the prophet Ecclesiastes, "Where the word of a King is, there is power; and who may say unto him, what dost thou?"

When my husband heard of this defence he snorted like a horse and, said he, "As touching the text in the Book of Ecclesiastes, the Prophet here asks a question but vouchsafes no answer; so also when the Psalmist asks, 'Why do the heathen so furiously rage together?' the matter is left unresolved. Yet to this question of Ecclesiastes, the God-fearing man will spontaneously answer: '*I myself* may say to the King, "What dost thou?"' As for the other matter: those entrusted with framing the Law and Custom of England have never yet been constrained to take cognizance of so rare and uncommon a case as that of a King who ignobly levies war against his own Parliament and people; yet, if one has dared to do so, a perjured traitor to his people he must plainly appear in the eyes of every person of discretion."

His Majesty having refused to plead, it was threatened that for his contumacy he must be adjudged to have confessed to the crime wherewith he was charged. He continued to dispute the authority of the Court, and was again removed. In his absence, witnesses from every part of the Kingdom testified to divers of his acts in levying war, from the raising of the Standard forward. On the third day the King was recalled and permitted to speak in his own defence, but not in challenge of the Court's jurisdiction. However, he would not speak, but made a request to confer with the Lords and Commons before sentence were read. This request was refused him, as tending to delay; besides, in the New Year the House of Lords had been abolished, and the Commons, or what remained of them, not above one-eighth part of the whole, had taken all the power into their own hands.

Then the sentence was read: which was that "the said Charles Stuart, as a tyrant, traitor, murderer and public enemy, shall be put to death by the severing of his head from his body."

The King would then have spoken something, but it was too late; he being accounted dead in Law immediately after sentence was pronounced. His plea was refused and he was led away.

Here was a woeful alteration in His Majesty's fortune, who not

many days before had taken careful thought for his melon-ground at
the royal Manor of Wimbledon; which rarity, as my husband told me,
was very well trenched and manured and admirably ordered for the
growth of musk-melons and melon-pompions, with borders, herbs and
flowers valued to be worth £300. His Majesty was destined never
again to taste of ripe, sugared musk-melon, or with his silver knife to
strip the velvet from that delicate, yellow peach, which he loved,
called Melocotony. Yet still he would not believe that this was any
better than a stage-show, until it happened that as he passed out with
the guard from the Painted Chamber, some soldiers puffed tobacco
smoke his way and no officer forbade them: which had never happened to him in his life before, and convinced him suddenly of the
peril in which he stood. For he was as queasy in his stomach when
tobacco was drunk about him as his father King James had been, who
wrote a book against the habit.

On this same day the King was permitted to say farewell to his children, the Princess Elizabeth and the Duke of Gloucester, the others
being abroad: and the Princess wept very sore when the King told
her what was threatened him. He also warned the little Duke (not
believing that England would ever be proclaimed a Republic) against
consenting to be crowned King in his stead; for that would be to rob
the birthright from his eldest brother, the Prince of Wales, and in the
end he would lose his own head too. "I would rather be torn into little
pieces," the child answered.

On the next day, which was a Tuesday, my husband, who had risen
even earlier than was his custom, came to my room at about half an
hour after five. He bade me rise and put on warm apparel and walk
out with him to Westminster, where we should see a sight never before seen in England; and we must be there early before the crowds
thickened. I took my Mary with me to suckle by the way, and as we
went down the dark streets towards Westminster we ate bread and
cheese. It was a clear night, very cold and frosty, and my husband
forgot for a while his low opinion of my wits and discoursed proudly
upon our country, England: how when she had cast off this devilish
incubus of monarchy and risen from sleep and rubbed her eyes, she
would find herself free and great—yea, far greater than the Athenian
or Roman republics, despite all their wealth of brave commanders,
learned scholars, wise counsellors and notable poets. He said that the
ancients fell short in two things principally: first, that they had a false

and delusive religion, and second that they depended for their welfare upon the unwilling labour of slaves, whereas slavery and serfdom in England were long abolished, and every man here was free, unless perhaps he were bound and confined by his own follies. Then he began to speak rhapsodically of his own part in this glorious revolution, how his pen would confirm what the sword had won, and how a hundred generations should remember him and praise him that he had refreshed their souls with the sweet wine of liberty.

He took great strides and twirled his cane as he spoke, and I could scarce keep pace with him. My child was but three months old, but she was a fat little wag and I had swaddled her well in a fleece, which made no light burden. "Oh, Husband," I cried, "my legs and arms ache. I envy you the liberty whereof you speak so sweetly."

He groaned and recited some Greek or Hebrew verse against my inopportune speech and said: "Confess, all the while that I poured out my heart to you, were you not thinking of to-morrow's flesh-dinner, whether to buy pork or salt-beef, and what herbs to choose for the sauce, and whether there will be leeks in the market?"

"Some person in our household must think of these things," I answered. "And if your purse will no longer bear the expense of a good cook's wages, but only of a snivelling little cook-wench, why then, this person is myself."

We continued in silence, but since, for shame, he could not carry the child for me, as being a gentleman not a common citizen, he was considerate enough to slacken his pace a little. When we came to the neighbourhood of Whitehall Palace, we heard a distant hum and chatter, like a great flock of starlings roosting in a bed of reeds, and the torches and lanterns turned the darkness into day. The crowd was already dense around the Palace, where a scaffold was erected in the open street by the Banqueting Hall, and my husband blamed me for walking so slowly that others had taken up their stations ahead of us. But by good luck we fell in with my brother John, who was now an officer in General Ireton's own troop, and he offered to escort us to a commanding station; the which he did with loud cries of "Make way, there, citizens, in General Ireton's name," whereat the crowd parted on either side of us as the Red Sea parted for Moses when he led the Israelites out of Egypt. We found ourselves standing not many paces distant from the foot of the tall scaffold, which had a railing about it, almost a yard high, with the axe and block in the middle; but we would not see this engine by reason of the black cloths hung upon the railing. Then John saluted us, and departed.

Several men stood upon the scaffold already, wearing black masks, for the task before them was so odious that none durst show his naked face; and the chief executioner and his assistant wore sailors' trousers to disguise even the shape of their legs. The chief executioner was remarkable for a grizzled wig and a grey beard which, when daylight came, had a false aspect. A company of foot-soldiers and a troop of horse were posted about the scaffold to prevent escape or rescue; we stood close to the foot-soldiers.

I listened to the soldiers conversing together, of whom one asked the other: "Comrade Sim, is this not an awful business? Does your heart quail abominationly, spite of all the strong waters that you have taken, and the strong prayers you have offered up?"

"Yea, Comrade Zack," answered Sim, "but I hope I shall not flinch from my way of duty—no more than did certain Roman soldiers of old, whom their duty bound to consent in a business more awful by far than this—those I mean who with their swords restrained the mourning crowds at Golgotha. Are we not every whit so stout-hearted as Romans? Lift up your heart, Zack; you showed yourself a bold enough man at Newbury five years since, by the river. I would not have done what you did, no, not for five hundred pound and a jolly wife, that I would not."

Says another: "Why, Zack, what did you then? Was it in the battle? I never heard tell that you showed yourself to advantage in the set-to that day? Come, the story!"

"It was a witch for whom I was executioner," said Zack, "for I take no account of witches, and fear them not, being born a Sunday's child. I confess that my Sergeant praised me and declared that I acted manfully that day."

"Ay, so he did, I warrant," cried Sim. "Those were the times before the reformation of our armies, while we yet lagged at our ease on the march and neglected our commanders. Zack and I were loitering by the way, in gathering nuts and black berries, and disputing together upon some point of doctrine, I know not what, and there were four or five other idle fellows not far from us. Well, Zack in jest pursued me with his sword and I ran from him and climbed up into an oak-tree, convenient for climbing; and I pulled myself up to the top branches and there defied him. It happened, as I waited in a crotch of the tree, that my thumbs began to prick. I looked through the leaves towards the river, being there adjacent, where I espied a sight of horror: there was a tall, lean, slender woman treading of the water with her feet with as much firmness as if she trampled upon the high road. I beckoned softly and called to Zack to come up, which he did, and another with him, and we watched through the leaves of the tree, nor could all our sights be deluded at once——"

Here Zack took up the tale: "Yet she was not walking upon mere water, but sliding on a small plank-board washed over with the water, to which when she came to the bank she gave a push with her foot and back it steered like an arrow to the opposing bank. Then we climbed down hastily, and the other man with us espied Reuben Kett, our Sergeant (who was come back to rebuke us for straggling), and acquainted him with what we had seen. The Sergeant began to sweat, yet he commanded that we search the wood and lay hold on her straight. The others shrank back, but I encouraged Sim and told him a charm sovereign against witches, which was to thrust his hand in his breeches-pocket and there salute the camrado who enlisted with him. Then he and I, running through the woods, found the same woman seated upon a fallen log, doing nothing, but staring before her. Straitway, I seized her by the arms, demanding what she was, but she replied no words unto me, so I hauled her before the Sergeant, who questioned her long. Yet she replied no words to him neither, feigning deafness. Then he shouted and said to her: 'You are an apparent witch, and we shall deal you death!' whereat she laughed in his face."

"Nay," said Sim, "you are mistaken there, Zack. She laughed not until afterwards, when the Sergeant chose Pious Hitchcocke and Frank Yellows as good marksmen to dispatch her. Then I was chosen to set her against a mud bank by the river, a charge of which you may imagine, good child, whether I was not reluctant. Nevertheless, I performed my duty somehow, and these two gave fire and shot at her, from a distance of not above two pikes' length; but with deriding and loud laughter she caught the bullets, one in either hand, and tossed them back again, to their huge amazement and terror. Then Sergeant Kett prayed to God to give him strength, for he was as weak as a rush, though in general a middling bold fellow and a powerful preacher——"

"That I deny," cried Zack. "He never moved us by his preaching, and was a very Levite, so stiff he was in his observances. I remember he would not suffer us to eat blood-pudding or hare's flesh even in a necessity."

"Well," said Sim, "whether he was Levite or Sodomite makes no matter; for he prayed aloud for strength, and strength flowed upon him, and he let off his carbine close to her breast. Yet the bullet rebounded like a child's ball and took off his leathern hat for him, whereat the witch, though speechless still, yet laughed in a contemptible way of scorn. Then was Zack only not dismayed; for which steadfastness I honour you, Zack. Zack told the Sergeant that to pierce the temples of the witch's head with steel would prevail against the strongest sorcery imaginable; and straitway Zack was her executioner, were you not, Zack, with your capped Sheffield knife? Yea, you made no more of despatching this vermin than if she had been fox or rat."

"Spoke she aught before she died?" asked a soldier. "Did she prophesy? Come, Zack, I know well she prophesied. What did she say before you showed yourself so manful?"

Zack looked at Sim and Sim looked at Zack again. Then Sim said: "She spoke at the end, but only to tell him, 'Nay, Son, it is not much to murder a mad old woman, it is nothing to quail at—but will not your scalp crawl and your bowels be turned to water on the day when you consent in the murder of an anointed King?' "

When Sim had said this, there was silence for awhile in the ranks of the soldiers.

In the civil crowd about us there began to be much mockery and ribaldry, but upon indifferent matters, not upon the great overshadowing event of His Majesty's execution, of which none spoke but in whispers.

A carpenter's wife stood not far from me and the carpenter with her. She had a waggish wit and jeered continually at him in dulcet tones, he answering little or nothing except now and then: "In God's name, Good Puss, cannot you hold your peace?" or "Your prattle is unseasonable, my little pig's eye!" This woman spoke to me and said: "Hearken now, Gossip! When this dear husband of mine comes home drunken, which is not very often, not above seven nights a week, and blasphemes against the Lord and stumbles upon the stairs—what think you that I then do to him? Riddle me that, Gossip! Do you suppose, Gossip, that I ever speak him a foul word? Nay, nay, I would not so for anything. Instead, I cause his bed to be made very soft and easy that he may sleep the better, and by fair glozing speeches I coax him into bed and draw off his boots for him and stroke his head gently a few times, until he settles upon his lees."

Here a little black-eyed serving-wench, standing beside me, interrupted and answered for me, saying: "Why, shame on you, Madam, for humouring the wretch! Ah, you weak and willing slaves, you are traitresses to your sex. Must all wives crouch in your manner to their currish and swinish husbands? Devil take me, if I do the like when I marry my Master: for if he behaved himself like a swine, so would I use him like a beast."

"How! You marry your Master, wench?" cried a seller of brooms. "When is your bridal morning? May I be your brideman and pull the garters off your smooth white legs?"

"For that you must wait a day or two," replied she, "until my Mistress dies."

Then two or three asked her, of what was her Mistress expected to die?

"Why, of what else but jealousy?" she answered. "For yesterday she saw my Master's shirt and my smock hanging close together upon a line, and she has taken to her bed with the mortification of it, and will not touch a morsel of food."

"Ah women, women, have done with your chatter," cried a tarry sailor. "You do nothing to recommend marriage to a lively bachelor such as I am. I believe that a good woman is like the single eel put in a bag among a thousand stinging snakes; and if a man luckily gropes out the one eel from all the rest, yet has he at best but a wet eel by the tail."

At this a bearded old man with a hare-lip, who, for aught I know was a decayed coachman or the like, coughed and said: "Ay, as an honest bishop once dared to tell Queen Elizabeth to her face, in a preachment before her: women for the most part are fond, foolish, wanton flibbergibs, wavering, witless, without counsel, feeble, careless, rash, proud, dainty, nice, tale-bearers, eavesdroppers, rumour-raisers, evil tongued, worse minded, and in every way doltified with the dregs of the Devil's dung-hill."

"Was it indeed a bishop said that?" cried the serving-wench. "Then, by God, it is small wonder that the bishops have said their last goodnight. Gorge me that, Goodman Hare-lip, gorge me that!"

Presently they all began to sing together, to the tune of *"Ragged and torn and true"*:

It never should grieve me much
  Though more Excises were:
The only tax that I grutch
  Is the farthing a pot on beer.
I never would grieve nor pine
  (Whatever you say or think)
If they doubled the price of wine——
  For wine I seldom drink.

I found it exceeding cold, waiting for the dawn to come, and I thought I should faint; but the serving-wench, who had played truant, as she said, to see avenged the death of her three brothers (the eldest of whom fell at Taunton in the siege and the two others at Preston)— she charitably relieved me of the burden of my child for an hour or more. And she held up the child for the crowd to see and cried laughing: "See what a goodly child I have now brought forth! Ah, wait until I bring this sweet child home to my Mistress and ask pardon for my fault. If I find her risen from her bed she will fall down in a fit again and die within the hour!"

"And then I will be your brideman," cried the seller of brooms.

The sun rose and shone upon a vast multitude of people crowding the street from the scaffold as far back as to Charing Cross, and in the other direction almost to the river's edge by the Abbey of Westminster. My child, that had been wakeful and mewling, slept again. Presently there went a stir through the crowd that the King was come, but it was a headless rumour and there we stood a pretty while longer, until we heard the distant noise of drums and the roaring of the crowd as the King came walking through the Park from St. James's Palace to Whitehall, with a guard of halberdiers before and behind. It is said, he walked fast and shivered for the cold. Then ensued another delay, for two hours or more, while we continued in our stations. Word went through the crowd that Parliament was passing an Act to forbid the proclamation of any new King, and that the execution must wait upon this. My husband was reading a book that he kept propped upon my shoulders, and seemed insensible of what went on around him; and I heartily wished myself home in my kitchen with a cup of warm caudle on my lap and my feet thrust up against the embers. Yet there was no escape, and if anyone fainted he was kept upon his feet by the pressing together of the crowd, which stank a good deal.

At last there was a mingled murmur of awe, commiseration and sullen hatred, and my husband put away his book. The King appeared at the middle window of the Banqueting Hall, from which the glass had been removed, and walked upon the scaffold. He wore the ribbon of the Order of the Garter, and also the jewelled Order of St. George. He looked earnestly upon the block and complained, as we thought, that it was too low, being only six inches high. Then he came up to the edge of the scaffold, with a proud, glooming countenance, to make a speech; but, seeing the vastness of the crowd, he thought better of it and addressed only the persons assembled on the scaffold. However, we could hear the greater part of what he said, for the crowd kept silent, except for coughing.

His Majesty's speech lasted for about ten minutes, and was very much below what might have been expected of a King about to die, being both disputatious and incoherent. He did not think fit either to rail against his murderers, or to ask God's forgiveness for them; but read us a lecture, declaring that a subject and a sovereign are clean different things and that the people have no share in Government, though he desired their liberty and freedom as much as did anybody else. He styled himself "The Martyr of the People".

Twice he saw a gentleman go near the axe, and each time he broke off his discourse with "Take heed of the axe; pray, take heed of the axe, for that may hurt me!" He feared, as some supposed, that the axe might be overset and the edge spoilt, so that the blow struck would be a ragged one; but, as I thought, he rather reverenced in the axe a power mightier than his own. What was best in this speech was a confession of his base behaviour in the matter of the Earl of Strafford's trial, yet this might have been Englished more precisely and honestly: for he did not speak the Earl's name, saying no more than that an unjust sentence that he had suffered to take effect was now punished by an unjust sentence upon himself.

Then when he had finished speaking, old Bishop Juxon, who had once been Lord Treasurer * and was no longer even a bishop, but only the King's chaplain—he looked astonished and came forward a pace and reminded His Majesty that he had spoken nothing of religion. The King thanked him most heartily for the reminder, but said no more than that, in truth, all men knew that he died a Christian according to the profession of the Church of England as he found it left him by his father. When he had done, he took a white satin cap

* He was the first to impose ship-money as a tax upon inland towns.

from the Bishop and pushed his hair all within it, the chief executioner helping him. Then he unclasped his dark cloak and gave it to
the Bishop and also the George from about his neck, and took off his
doublet and laid his head down upon the block. There went a buzzing
whisper among the soldiers that it was the very same bright execution
axe, brought from the Tower, that had served to behead the Earl of
Strafford. The crowd was silent.

I could not espy His Majesty's face as he lay there, because the
corner of the scaffold was interposed; but through a chink in the hangings I saw him give the signal with stretching out his hands, and then
the axe swooped down with a true aim and I saw the head leap past
the chink.

The executioner's assistant took the head and showed it to the
crowd, which gave a single sighing gasp and stood silent again, for as
long as one might say the Lord's Prayer slowly over.

This silence was first broken by my husband, who declaimed in a
high voice these words which he had himself translated from a play
of Seneca:

> . . . There can be slain
> No sacrifice to God more ácceptáble
> Than an unjust and wicked King.

"Silence, you brawling fart-bag!" cried the sailor, raising his great fists
at him, the tears rolling down his cheeks. "No more of that; lay off, or,
by God, I'll ram you into the roadway! Have you no bowels, Master,
have you no bowels? It troubled David that he cut but the lap of
King Saul's garment; how much the more should we not be distressed
and troubled? We have lost our King; he is beheaded, do you not
see?"

The broom-seller and the old coachman threatened my husband also
in their own manners; but he looked contemptuously at them and
answered: "Why, rogues, if you loved your King so much, why, then,
did you hold back? Why did none of you raise a finger to rescue him?
Why did you let him die, without protest uttered? Did you fear these
few soldiers?" And to the women who wept he said scornfully: "Aye,
'you daughters of Israel, weep over Saul, who clothed you in scarlet
with other delights!' For this King Saul bathed your gowns in the
blood of your husbands and your brothers!"

Then came two troops of horse to disperse the crowd, the one from

Westminster, and the other from the Strand, and caused a general affright. We were swept along the streets by the press, and some persons who fell were trampled and smothered. My husband and I were driven apart, but the kind serving-wench kept me close company, and we took refuge at last in a little entry by the Church of St. Martin's-in-the-Fields, and waited there while I suckled my babe, waiting for the streets to be a little thinned.

In this entry stood nine or ten other people, not remarkable, and one sturdy blue-eyed fellow, with a crooked nose and mouth, who wept. He seemed to be a merchant, but that he wept inconsolably, his thumb stuck into his mouth, like a two-year-old child. After a while I knew him through his disguise, and "Oh, Mr. Archie Armstrong," I cried, "do not lament so sorely, I beg. It cuts my heart; and yet I cannot help but laugh."

He only bawled the louder, with thick Scottish words intermingled with his cries, of which the sense was a pitiful forgiveness of his poor Master—who upon the scaffold had plainly confessed to the unjust sentence that he had suffered to be carried out upon his Fool, who was kicked from Court only for speaking truth! Then he began to rail vehemently against Archbishop Laud; but another Scot who stood by him cried: "Whist, man, for wee Laudie has paid the piper, ye ken!" So he said no more, yet continued weeping.

I had shed no tears while I stood under the scaffold, nor did I afterwards as I betook myself home; but that night when I was a-bed I wept sore. I had indeed neither loved the King for his virtues, nor commiserated him during his captivity; but now I wept for the loneliness that overcame me when I considered that an ancient lofty pillar, the golden pillar of monarchy, was rudely knocked to the ground. What daughter is so undutiful that she grieves not when her father dies, be he never so besotted, tyrannical or fraudulent in his ways? He is dead, and he was her father. So, when a King dies, the nation mourns; yet ordinarily when a King dies, a King is born and the nation again rejoices. Now there could be no rejoicing; for Kingship was wholly abolished, and a foolish King had died a knave's death.

CHAPTER TWENTY-THREE

Evil News from Ireland

M Y HUSBAND's pamphlet was set on sale about two weeks after this, at three shillings a copy, and enjoyed a pretty sale, though it scandalized many. In one diurnal that was shown me these words were written against it: "There is lately come forth a book of John Melton's, a libertine that thinks his wife a manacle, and his very garters to be shackles and fetters to him; one that, after the Independent fashion, will be tied to no obligation to God or man," etc., etc. This railing accusation, and others like it, did no harm to the book, but rather caused more men to buy it, from curiosity. However, another book, which had the start of it by four days or so, spoilt its market, selling in prodigious fashion at fifteen shillings a copy.

This rival book was first published by one Royston, for whom my brother James was a corrector of proofs, and was named *Eikon Basilike, The Portraiture of His Sacred Majesty in His Solitudes and Sufferings.* It became a sort of Third, or Newest, Testament in the hands of the Royalists. My brother James, when I went to his lodgings with my mother on the day following the King's death, had told me something of this book, which purported to be written by the King himself. But James, though he had seen notes written in His Majesty's own hand upon the copy sent for printing, judged it to be a forgery made by some chaplain or other; for this was a flowery pulpit style, not the King's own crabbed, nervous one. When I told my husband what I had heard, he pricked up his ears and asked me whether I knew at what printing-house the book was set up.

I answered that I believed that it was at Mr. Dugard's.

Then he said: "Good, good. I believe that Mr. Dugard also does jobs for my friend Mr. Simmons, next the Gilded Lion in Aldersgate Street, who is to publish my new work. I shall desire Mr. Simmons to look into the matter and make a report to me upon it."

Well, it is not yet discovered who was the true author of this book. Some have accused a chaplain, the Reverend Symmons; some Dr.

Gauden, Bishop of Exeter; some Bishop Hall's younger son. But at least it is agreed by all save Royalist zealots that the author was not His Majesty.

Mr. Simmons came smiling to our house a day or two later with some manuscript pages of the book, which were supposedly prayers written by the King in his captivity. My husband read these and scoffed, saying that they were well enough botched, but written only to catch the worthless approbation of an inconstant, irrational and image-doting rabble.

He mused awhile to himself and then suddenly, with a chuckle, he said to Johnny Phillips: "Johnny, take down from the shelf the third book of Sir Philip Sidney's *Arcadia* and bring it to me quickly."

Johnny brought him the book, whereof my husband turned the pages over until he found what was required, namely the prayer of the afflicted Pamela, overheard by one Cecropia who listens at the door. He told Johnny merrily: "Here is a holiday task for you, Boy— to convert this maiden's prayer into one for the use of a devout King."

Johnny took away the book to another room, while my husband made us an harangue upon the pious forgery of writings, how it was endemial among the clergy since the most ancient times. Presently Johnny returned with the prayer, decently made over, only a few slight changes having been needed for its conversion, such as the omission of the name of the virtuous Musidorus, beloved of Pamela. Then, when it was solemnly read out, my husband and Mr. Simmons laughed heartily and Mr. Simmons took the reformed prayer without a word said, but winked and huddled it among the other prayers, and put on his hat again and went out in haste.

When the book was printed, those copies that came from Mr. Dugard's house, though not the others, contained the intruded prayer. My brother James was rated for this oversight by Mr. Royston, and would have lost his employment, but that Mr. Simmons, when I told him what was doing, called upon Mr. Royston and took the whole blame upon himself. Mr. Royston was good-humoured enough to laugh at the trick, and presently Mr. Simmons and he did business together with this very book: for Mr. Royston feared that it would soon be forbidden by the new Government, as indeed happened in the middle of March, and Mr. Simmons, confident of the favour of the Government, for which he was become chief printer, agreed to buy from him a moiety of the right to publish the book. Printers are thick as thieves, and care not a button what they print, so long as it will not lose them their ears or set a brand upon cheek or brow. Mr. Simmons was not molested, as it proved, and of the fifty editions of the book that were cast off from the presses within a year, twenty or thirty brought money into his till.

My husband was vexed that the counterfeit *Eikon Basilike* engrossed the whole attention of an innumerable of readers. He himself was almost the only writer of note to stand up boldly in defence of the Regicides; for throughout England there crept a palsy of guilt for what had been done, with a dread for the ensuing punishment. What the King had been in his natural person was clean forgot: now, for regret of his person politic, he was remorsefully cried up as perfect man, perfect King, Saint, Martyr, all but Christ. Then it began to be asked whether this execution of the King, after sentence by an arbitrary Court of Justice, would not prove a most dangerous inlet to the absolute tyranny of the Army Grandees? For if they might take away the King's head against all the rules of Law, how much the more easily might they not in like manner chop off the head of any nobleman, gentleman or inferior subject? It would be "the longest sword take all" and we should presently fall to murdering and butchering one another until we were all destroyed.

There was also great roaring heard from all the Kingdoms of Europe, where it was thought that the English had gone stark mad; and passionate tears were shed by the Scots who had sold him, when they considered that the same stroke of the axe had beheaded at once a King of England and a King of Scotland. In February, at the Cross of Edinburgh, they proclaimed the exiled Prince of Wales as Charles II, and not by the title of King of Scotland only, but impertinently made him King also of England and Ireland. As for Ireland, to the incongruous League forged by the Marquis of Ormonde, between fugitive Cavaliers (most of them Arminians of the Church of England), and the Confederate Irish Papists, were now added Scottish Presbyterians of Ulster whose fearful sufferings at the hands of the Irish Papists ("those bloody Tories" as my husband called them) had been a prelude to the war. In Ireland also the Prince was proclaimed Charles II.

My husband by the writing of this new book, *The Tenure of Kings and Magistrates*, estranged from him his brother Christopher, and the old Earl of Bridgewater, and many other of his former friends. Yet the friends that the book made were more useful and powerful than any of these, as will appear.

In the Republic of England, Kingship was abolished, and the House of Lords with it; and Government was by a Council of State, composed of noblemen, knights and gentlemen, to whom the stump of Parliament yielded advisers and comforters. But how long this Government would prevail against its internal and external enemies was doubtful, though the Lord General Fairfax, General Skippon, Alderman Pennington and other notable men had consented to serve in the Council under the Presidency of Mr. Serjeant Bradshaw.* The two leading spirits in this business were Generals Cromwell and Ireton. General Ireton is dead in Ireland of a fever, not long since, but General Cromwell lives yet: that bustling, busy, fierce, red-nosed, loud-voiced sloven, who can read men better than he can read books; who cants with godly ministers, jests with ribald soldiers, can be solemn and reserved with men of quality—and all this without hypocrisy; who weeps often, does cruel deeds, plays the buffoon at table, goes to Church like a turkey cock, with red flannel about his neck, humbles himself before God, is a most loving father and friend and commander, never looks ahead more than three steps, yet has these three measured out to the one-hundredth part of an inch.

General Cromwell is said to have perused my husband's book, *The Tenure of Kings and Magistrates,* and to have admired it exceedingly; but it is more likely that only General Ireton read it through, and marked a passage or two for his father-in-law's reading. However that may be, very soon after the Council was in session, namely on March 14th, which was a Wednesday, two cloaked gentlemen came to the door with a guard of two halberdiers, and inquired after my husband. They put me into a fright, because I took them to be officers sent to arrest my husband, but I bade them be seated while I fetched him from upstairs, where he was at work upon his *History of England.* He came down with his sword in his hand, for he had declared that he would rather die than be confined in prison; but he soon thrust the blade back into its scabbard when he recognized the two gentlemen. They were members of the Council of State, namely, Mr. Bulstrode Whitlocke, an eminent lawyer, and Sir Harry Vane the Younger.

---

* My husband could call Mr. Bradshaw "cousin", his mother having been of that family—or else another of the same name.

Sir Harry was a man of extraordinary parts, whom my husband about this time had honoured with a commendatory sonnet. His face had something in it beyond the natural: every feature gave the lie to the rest, yet he was not by any means unhandsome. Were I a witch, there stood the man I would choose to be the Devil of my coven; who had soot for marrow, as was said. He had resided for some time in America where, at the age of but five-and-twenty, he was elected Governor of Massachusetts Colony; which appointment he had lost by his favour to a woman preacher, Mrs. Hutchinson, whom the Colonists hated for her usurpation of the priestly function. I would have stayed, from curiosity, but was sent out of the way, this being business of importance.

When the two Councillors were gone again, my husband, trying to cloak the excitement of his spirit, told me that I must begin dismantling the rooms and packing our coffers, for we were to change house.

"What again, Husband?" cried I. "This will be the third time in three years that you have changed your house."

"Aye, Wife," he answered in rare good humour, "you and I will grow expert in the business of removal. Each time less platters will be broken, less books lose their covers, less hats and scarves will be left hanging on nails behind the chamber doors."

"Where is our new house?" I asked.

"That I know not yet exactly," he answered, "but it will be somewhere conveniently near to Whitehall Palace. Perhaps Mr. Thomson, brother to the gentlewoman who managed for me in your absence, will receive us in his house next the Bull Tavern by Charing Cross."

"You have accepted an appointment under the Government?" I asked again. And I thought, but did not say: "The Fiend sent two affable emissaries, Belial and Demogorgon, to tempt you; and you fell."

"Why, yes," he answered, "I am to be Secretary for the Foreign Tongues. It came upon a motion of Lieutenant-General Oliver Cromwell, who praised my book to the Council."

He even disclosed to me what salary he would be paid, which was fifteen shillings and tenpence halfpenny a day; but I knew that he would never alter his mode of life, whatever increase of wealth accrued to him, except perhaps to buy more books. If he had been paid £10,000 per annum, and sugar had risen to 1s. 8d. a lb. (where it stood now), he would have declared that sugar at 1s. 8d. was not worth the eating. Yet upon books and music and perhaps a choice marble statue or two, he would have grudged no expense.

"What will your duties be, Husband?" I asked.

"The writing of Latin letters to Foreign States and Princes in the name of the English Republic," he replied, "and now and then I will be desired to undertake the writing of a book in defence of our new liberties. This is a great new thing that a Secretary of State should be chosen for his learning and his handiness with the pen, rather than for his subserviency to Court doctrine. King Charles had a Chief Secretary, the Lord Conway, whom he accepted as a legacy from King James, that was a notable falconer and a devoted creature of the Duke of Buckingham's, yet could neither read nor write."

"But what of your *History of England?*" I asked, "and your *Latin Dictionary?* And your *Methodical Digest of Christian Doctrine?* However will these works be finished?"

"Why," said he, "they can wait awhile, and indeed now that Ned, at his step-father's insistence, goes up to the University, I cannot easily continue with the *Digest* or *Dictionary*, for John has neither Ned's parts nor his industry."

"I hope," said I, "that our new house will have a garden where I can take the air, and where our children can tumble together on the grass."

"Mr. Thomson's house opens into Spring Gardens," he replied, "but that is no place where I should allow my wife to resort, being now become a haunt of cut-purses, harlots, and idle soldiers. However, on pleasant days you may go with the children into the Whitehall Palace Gardens to which doubtless I shall obtain a ticket; there the company is more select."

"That will be delightful," said I, "if you will hire me a strong young wench to carry our Nan. She cannot go so far as the Palace on her lame foot, as you know well."

"You should have considered these inconveniences when you bore a crooked child," said he. "I am no fool: I know how it comes about that children are born crooked. Say no more lest I accuse you directly of having tried to make away with my child while it was yet in your womb. Had Nan been the son that I expected, and had you so maimed him, I would cheerfully have procured your hanging."

"May God pardon you for that accusation, Husband," said I. "For upon my word, I cannot find it in my heart to do so."

He smiled frostily at me and "You are too free with the name of God, Mary," said he, "and you may leave Him out of this matter. But when my daughter Ann grows to riper years and inquires of her neighbours: 'How came I to issue warped from my Maker's hand? Was He then wroth with me?'—do you not suppose that they will answer and say to her: 'Nay, child, that was your mother's wicked doing: it comes not of God'?"

How could any person dispute with such a man? I told him: "Then the long and short of the matter is that, because you are to be paid near sixteen shillings a day by the Council, our poor babies will be shut up in a noisy lodging-house in a stinking street and never refresh themselves with grass and flowers."

"What is good enough for me," he answered, "will surely be good enough for my wife and daughters? What I earn for myself is no business of yours; and if your father had paid me punctually the £1,000 he promised me, you could have had any wench it pleased you to hire."

Oh, that £1,000 portion! How closely it was clamped upon his mind! He flattered himself that he had a perfect command of his passions, like the Caspian Sea that neither ebbs nor flows; yet one night about this time he and I had high words together in bed, it is no matter upon what. I could not sleep and, about an hour before dawn, I slipped out of bed and went to the hearth. There I blew softly with the bellows, and lighted a piece of paper at the embers and so lighted a candle-end; and took from my needle-box which lay on a bye-shelf a pocket scissors to trim my nails withal; and then came softly gliding back into the bed, shielding the candle-light with my hands, for fear of waking him. But he being very suspicious, and a light sleeper, saw me creeping towards him with the scissors and candle. He startled up and wrestled with me and snatched away the scissors, which were a very good pair made in Woodstock, and flung them out of the open window. Then he exulted, crying, "Ah, Delilah, Delilah, daughter of the Philistines, here is a Samson who sleeps with one eye open."

I began to laugh and weep in the darkness, for the candle was out, and said to him: "Why, Esquire Samson, may I not trim my nails in bed without suffering so fierce an assault from you? You have bruised my wrists and wrenched my thumb and spilt hot grease upon my foot and thrown away the scissors that I prize. Whatever will you do next, pray? Did you fear that I was come to cut off your heartbreakers and so annul your holy masculine virtue? God forbid that I should ever lie in one bed with a lisping she-man!"

All that he would answer was: "You shall be punished for this, you naughty Lamia, you Creeping Cockatrice of Forest Hill!" Yet on the next day I heard no more of the matter; and I think he had repented his suspicions, for towards evening I found another scissors laid in my needle-box, as good as the pair he had thrown away. This was to my profit, for unknown to him I had already recovered the other scissors too, which was caught on the twig of a tree and hung there prettily.

We moved to Mr. Thomson's, who provided us with three upper rooms: one large room in the backside for my husband's books, where he also slept on most nights, one small room for John Phillips, and my room, of middle size, with a closet for the children to sleep, which looked out upon the Strand. In my room we took breakfast and supper together and entertained company. My husband told me that we had now no need of servants, forasmuch as Mr. Thomson would supply our needs, and that all my work would be to care for the children and keep his clothes in repair.

It is exceedingly awkward for a country-bred gentlewoman with two helpless babes to be the guest in a London lodging-house, where the servants are surly, the kitchen removed from her room by six flights of steep stairs and two long dark corridors; the yard where she must wash her linen forever full of coaches and waggons and drunken ostlers—an overflow from the Bull Tavern next door—and nowhere to hang the linen but on a line below the window. My husband rose early and worked at his private business until he breakfasted at seven, after which he went to his work (to Derby House at first, but thereafter to Whitehall Palace). I saw him not again until supper, for he took his bread and cheese with him in a satchel.

John Phillips remained in our rooms all day, busied with the task set him by my husband; and wrote a little book of his own upon the quick and easy teaching of Latin, which was afterwards published by Mr. Royston. John began to show me attention beyond the ordinary and was eager to run errands and do little services for me, and would even mind the children while I was away in the kitchen, though he was no lover of children. But presently a coolness arose between us, for I found that he had conceived an adulterous passion for me, and would fain have lain with me, had I let him. When one day he showed me some amatorious verses he had written, and confessed that I was the Berenice whose hair was celebrated in them, I clouted his nose for him, so that it bled (so vexed I was) and tore his poem to shreds. Yet I could not find it in my heart to blame him, for he was now almost a grown man and, by the vigilant strictness of my husband's care, prevented from ever cooling his intemperate heats in a riotous gaudy-night. Also, he was too much thrown in my company, and knew that I fadged not well with my husband and was restless in my mind. I feared that he would play virtuous Joseph and represent me to my husband as Potiphar's wife; but he was not ill-natured or revengeful and, since I did not complain against him to my husband, he held his tongue likewise. He offered me his services no more, however, and preserved a haughty silence towards me, and shut himself away from me in his room; so that I lived a very lonely life at Thomson's, except for Trunco's visits. Trunco on two days of the week would fetch me and the babes to her husband's house, where there was a little private garden, and where I could converse with my dear mother and with Zara, and sometimes with my young brothers, if they were excused from military duty. My mother would never come to Mr. Thomson's, because of her detestation of my husband.

The Latin letters that my husband wrote for the Council of State were only a small part of his work. He was also set to write a tract against the unnatural league in Ireland made by the Marquis of Ormonde; which he did. And, a more important task, to write a book in answer to the *Eikon Basilike;* at which he worked for the better part of the spring and the whole of the summer ensuing. But the heaviest labour assigned to him was to assist the Council in the suppression of books and pamphlets hostile to the new Government: of which there were a very great number published, of three several sorts, namely the Cavalier sort, the Presbyterial sort, and the Levelling sort.*

* The Levellers, of whom the chief was one Lieutenant-Colonel John Lilburne, were dissatisfied with the new Government, which they considered too tender and forbearing of old evils: they held that every Jack was as good as his master, and would have swept away all privileges of rank and wealth whatsoever. The same Lilburne wrote a book entitled *England's Old and New Chains*, in which he contended that the Army Grandees, as Generals Cromwell, Ireton and the rest, had broken the old chains of monarchy indeed, yet fettered England with new and stronger ones. He raised a mutiny in the Army, but General Cromwell put it down, shooting one of the Levellers as a scarecrow to the rest.

Now this was a transformation: my husband who had written his *Areopagitica* as a trumpet-blast against the licensing or muzzling of the Press was now himself become (with Mr. Frost, the Principal Secretary of State) a Censor of the Press; and was required to chastise with scorpions the printers and authors of unlicensed books whom King Charles and the Presbyterians had chastised with whips only! How he compounded with his conscience in this business, I know not, for I had not the hardihood to inquire; but I think he was of one mind with those Jesuits who held that evil deeds are well done if good from them proceeds. Moreover, he had written the *Areopagitica* chiefly in protest against the licensing of his own wise books by fools; and here was a horse of another colour—he, a wise man, was required to license the books of fools.

As for his answer to the King's book, which he called *Eikonoklastes* (or the Portrait-breaker) he answered it fairly enough for the most part; but he told Johnny Phillips that any stick was good enough to beat a mad dog withal, and since he knew the book to be a forgery, and a dangerous one, he scrupled not to take advantage of the merry trick that he had played upon Mr. Royston in the matter of Pamela's prayer before he had any thought of writing an answer to the book.

Now he wrote:

"From stories of this nature, both ancient and modern, which abound, the Poets also, and some English, have been in this point so mindful of decorum as to put never more pious words in the mouth of any person than of a Tyrant. I shall not instance an abstruse author, wherein the King might be less conversant, but one of whom we well know was the closest companion of these his solitudes, WILLIAM SHAKESPEARE; who introduces the person of Richard the Third speaking in as high a strain of piety and mortification as is uttered in any passage of this book, and sometimes to the same sense and purpose with some words in this place. '*I intended,*' said he (King Charles in the preceding part of the *Eikon*), '*not only to oblige my friends, but mine enemies.*' The like saith Richard, Act 2, Scene i:

> "I do not know that Englishman alive
> With whom my soul is any jot at odds
> More than the infant that is born to-night.
> I thank my God for my humility.

Other stuff of this sort may be read throughout the whole tragedy, wherein the Poet used not much license in departing from the truth of History; which delivers him [Richard] a deep dissembler, not of his affections only, but of Religion.

"In praying, therefore, and in the outward work of devotion, this King, we see, hath not at all exceeded the worst of Kings before him. But herein the worst of Kings, professing Christianism, have by far exceeded him. They, for aught we know, have still prayed their own, or at least borrowed from fit authors. But this King, not content with that which, although in a thing holy, is no holy theft—to attribute to his own making other men's whole prayers, hath, as it were, unhallowed and unchristened the very duty of Prayer itself by borrowing to a Christian use prayers offered to a heathen God. Who would have imagined so little fear in him of the true all-seeing Deity, so little reverence of the Holy Ghost, whose office is to dictate and present our Christian prayers, so little care of truth in his last words, or honour to himself or to his friends, or sense of his afflictions, or of that sad hour which was upon him, as immediately before his death to pop into the hand of that grave bishop who attended him, as a special relic of his saintly exercises, a prayer stolen word for word from the mouth of a Heathen woman praying to a Heathen God, and that in no serious book, but in the vain amatorious poem of Sir Philip Sidney's *Arcadia:* a book in that kind full of worth and wit, but among religious thoughts and duties not worthy to be named nor to be read at any time without good caution, much less in time of trouble and affliction to be a Christian's prayer-book? It hardly can be thought upon without some laughter that he who had acted over us so stately and so tragically should leave the world at last with such a ridiculous exit as to bequeath among his deifying friends that stood about him such a piece of mockery, to be published by them as must needs cover both his and their heads with shame and confusion. And sure it was the hand of God that let them fall and be taken in such a foolish trap as hath exposed them to all derision, if for nothing else, to throw contempt and disgrace in the sight of all men upon this his idolized Book, and the whole rosary of his Prayers: thereby testifying how little He accepted them from those who thought no better of the Living God than of a buzzard Idol, that would be served and worshipped with the polluted trash of Romances and Arcadias, without discerning the affront so irreligiously and so boldly offered him to his face.

"Thus much be said in general to his Prayers, and in especial to the Arcadian Prayer used in his captivity: enough to undeceive us what esteem we are to set upon the rest!"

He also accused the King, upon hearsay evidence, of the horrid crime of conspiring with the Duke of Buckingham to poison his father, King James (whose catamite the said Duke had been) that he might sit on his Throne, and of rewarding the deed with half his kingdom.

Meanwhile, in April of this year 1649, General Cromwell was chosen to go to Ireland, against the Marquis of Ormonde's power. He was appointed Lord Lieutenant-General and General Governor, at £13,-000 a year for three years. In May he went to Oxford, to a University already purged of all Heads of Houses, Fellows and scholars who having favoured the King would not change their colours—three hundred in all; and there with the Lord General Fairfax he was created a Doctor of Law. A number of his officers, some of whom, it was said, could hardly sign their names, much less construe a simple Latin sentence, were created Masters of Arts. In July, dressed in a suit worth £500, he drove off from Whitehall to Bristol, where his army of 12,000 men was assembled. He was in a coach drawn by six Flanders mares, with eighty officers as his life-guards, among whom was my brother John. General Ireton commanded under him.

"Ah," cried my mother, who was with me when I watched his departure. "He is become like the Devil who cries 'All is mine.' God give that he may never return to England, neither he nor any of his self-seeking murderous crew, but leave his bones in a bog." This was the prayer of a great part of the citizenry of London, and there was hawked about a "Last Will and Testament of General Cromwell" which read:

In the name of Pluto, Amen: I, Noll Cromwell, *alias* the Town-Bull of Ely, Lord Chief Governor of Ireland, Grand Plotter and Contriver of all Mischiefs in England, Lord of Misrule, Knight of the Order of Regicides, Thief-tenant-General of the Rebels of Westminster, Duke of Devilishness, Ensign of Evil, Scout-master-General to his Infernal Majesty, being wickedly disposed of mind, of abhorred memory, do make my last Will and Testament in manner and form following . . . etc., etc.

My mother had been incensed at the creation of Masters and Doctors at Oxford. "This Crum-Hell of yours," she cried, "this copperfaced Nod-Noll who was cast out from an inferior University, as unfit to proceed even to a bachelor's degree, and who proceeding to an Inn of Court frittered his time away at the tavern and bawdy-house, and came away with nothing decent accomplished—that such a wretch as he should by reason of his military crimes be honourably entertained at Oxford University, and presented with a Doctorate at Law—oh, it makes the blood run up and down my veins! What knowledge of Law has His Noseship, except it be how to override, pervert and destroy all laws? He has crucified this Kingdom upside-down!"

When it was noised about that my husband was become a little Grandee and that he conferred every day with three or four great Grandees, he was continually waylaid by persons of his acquaintance—

for the most part by Royalists whose estates had been sequestrated —and begged to speak a seasonable word for them in this matter or that. But he always denied them, saying that he knew nothing of the business and was sure that the Commissioners would do their duty, without any prodding or prompting from himself. When these importunate people, women for the most part, found that they could not get his ear by direct means, they came to Thomson's and tried with tears and little presents to use me as an instrument of persuasion. I dared not accept anything, and plainly told them that if I were to plead any cause with my husband, this were the surest way to lose it. There was one lady who thought that I had rejected the present that she offered as not being handsome enough, and came again with marvellous jewels. I should dearly have loved to accept them of her, for my husband gave me no ornaments of any worth: but I told her that she was wasting her labour, for how could I make use of such gifts? If my husband reckoned them to be a bribe, he would rail at me and command me to restore them; and if I did not acknowledge them to be a bribe he would conclude them to be the fee of adultery.

One day came a tasty present, a basket of little white peaches, which came addressed plainly to me, and of which I ate. Unlike Eve, I offered no fruit to my husband, but ate all myself, except for what I gave my little Nan, and cast the stones out at the window. Yet I regretted my greed, for on the third day comes Sir Timothy Tyrrell's lady, who was Archbishop Usher's daughter, with a tale of injustices committed by the sequestrators at Shotover, and other complaints, I know not what; and she reminded me of the bridal gifts of buck and game that my husband and I had from Sir Timothy at our wedding; and at last she asked would not my husband speak a word to the Lord President Bradshaw, etc.? I grew angry and said that the buck had been eaten and given thanks for, long ago.

"Very true," said she, "but what of the white peaches?"

"A basket of little peaches came to me without plea or condition attached to them," I replied, "and had I known that they were intended for a bribe, I should never have eaten of them."

"Well," said she, "I trust you are not simpleton enough, Mistress, to believe that in these days peaches are given away for nothing?"

"No," said I, "I am not; but I fear I can give your Ladyship no better reward for them than my thanks and sincere praise for their excellence. I had not eaten a peach since the second year of the war, and then one only, for the soldiers of Sir Timothy's own regiment stole the rest."

My mother was continually urging me to speak to my husband about the unjust seizure of our household goods at Forest Hill, and of the bestowal by Parliament upon the citizens of Banbury of timber which was not in its gift. She herself would not speak to my husband, because her soul loathed the books that he wrote; but she instructed me in my duty as his wife and her daughter, which was to see justice done. I therefore did speak to him, but he answered that what he would not do for one person he would not do for another. Then, though I told him that it would plainly be to his own benefit (for he still harped upon that one string of my unpaid marriage portion) to put my mother in the way of recovering what was by Law due to her, all he would answer was: "Wife, I am deaf of that ear."

The most persistent of pleaders was Mrs. Royston, wife to Mr. Royston the printer who was put into Newgate Jail for the publishing of books against the Government; for there was now a very severe Act against the printing of seditious or treasonable pamphlets, books or diurnals. Even a person who bought such a book or paper was liable to a fine of 20s., and all ballad-singers and hawkers of books and papers, whatsoever, were forbidden to ply their trade. This Mrs. Royston continually beset our lodgings and followed my husband every morning to his work, were the weather never so foul or rose he never so early; and every night she waited outside the Palace gate, against his return; but made no plea of him, only saying each time, with a curtsey, "I am Mr. Royston's wife; you remember the unfortunate Mr. Royston." At last her importunity conquered him and one day he spoke to the Lord President and Mr. Royston was released from Newgate upon an assurance of good behaviour.

It was while we were in these lodgings that my husband got me with child for a third time; but now he had neither leisure nor inclination to supervise my diet or order the conditions of my life, but left it to Nature, and prayed to God to give him a boy.

It was here too that I first noticed that he was losing the sight of his left eye: for he began to blunder in his gait and by experiment I found that I might make signs to him, or reach him dishes, as I sat on his left side at table, and he would not know what I did. But he said nothing to me on the matter, since with the right he yet had clear enough vision; until one day he told me that our lodgings must assuredly be damp, for the candle had always a misty iris of coloured light about it. I told him that I saw no such iris, and Johnny said the same. Then he confessed that a gross mist had for some time clouded the left part of his left eye, and objects seen only through that eye appeared smaller; and now there was a light mist in his right eye too, and both eyes, when he read before breakfast, ached and refused their office.

We warned him that he must omit some part of his work, if he wished the mist to be dispelled; but he refused to do any such thing. Nor when I recommended plaintain-water to him as sovereign for weak eyes would he accept of it, but asked humorously of what women's university was I a Doctor of Physic? He worked the more assiduously, even on Sundays, when he continued with his *Methodical Digest of Christian Doctrine;* and wholly intermitted his accustomed exercise of afternoon walking. So it was that, eating and drinking voraciously but without any relaxation of mind—for he would now bring pen and ink to table—he was much troubled with the wind, and with binding of the bowels. The gout also had fastened on him—for without exercise the noxious humours continue within the body to poison it, and are not cast out at the pores as sweat—and he grew splenetic and evil-tempered and lost five or six of his teeth, having until then a perfect array of teeth. Yet the work was so much to his liking that he made no complaint and is still a very proper man, with no wrinkles upon his skin, and a fresh complexion and lustrous hair which he combs while he reads. He looks nearer to thirty-four than to forty-four, which is his true age. As for the gout, he said (about this time) that it was a salutary distemper, being a known prophylactic or protection against virulent diseases: a gouty man seldom dies of a sudden fever, and though the gout may kill him in the end, yet he can expect to live long.

As the price of coals and provisions continued high, so other prices rose conformably. Nothing that we used, ate, drank or wore was free from taxes. There was an excise of 1d. a gallon put upon salt, and our cups, spits, washing-bowls, powdering tubs, pots, kettles, hats, stockings, shoes, and all wearing apparel must pay our public debts incurred in the wars. These taxes were imposed by Parliament, and put me in mind of the outcry raised, in the brave old days, because the King had levied ship-money, a trifle by comparison, without consent of Parliament.

It was in these same lodgings that the blow was struck from Ireland that I thought at first had slain me; but I live yet, as this writing proves, though indeed I am not the brisk Marie Powell (or Mary Milton) who wrote such hot and intemperate sentences in the vellum book, which I have again by me. Let this evil news from Ireland close this chapter; then I shall write one more and make an end.

In August of this year 1649 a report reached England that Colonel Sir Edmund Verney, Knight (my Mun) was slain near Dublin, in a sally by the Parliament men of the garrison; but in my soul I knew it for false, though the details of his death and burial were very exact. Then on September 15th, as I was out walking with Trunco, and within sight of Thomson's, whither I was returning, I cried out suddenly "Oh" and sank to the ground; but little Mary, whom I carried in my arms, escaped hurt. It was as though a sharp knife were driven into my heart.

Trunco called upon some by-standing women for help and together they took me into our lodgings and carried me upstairs and laid me on my bed, where for three days and nights I continued as dead, in a trance. What things I did and saw in that trance are out of natural law and improper to be told here; only let me confess that I spent those three days with Mun, a lifetime of happiness it seemed, so that when I awoke again I would not believe that so short a time had in truth passed.

My husband had been fearful lest I should miscarry, for I was in the fourth month of my account, and so cheat him of the son that he again expected. But I rose sound in mind and body, very hungry, and informed of secrets so great that I warrant my husband would have sold his whole library of books to learn them.

In October he came upstairs one evening and asked: "Were you not once acquainted with Sir Edmund Verney, lately Colonel of a regiment in Ireland?"

"Yes, Husband," I answered composedly. "Colonel Verney was the only man that ever I wholly loved, or that ever wholly loved me. Yet, since you will certainly press me upon this point, he never knew me carnally during the whole of our acquaintance."

My husband was silent and astonished for a moment and then he said: "This is an honest confession; and I am content to know that the power to love is not wholly lacking in you, as I had supposed; and being your husband I do not loathe to bring you news of your lover's death. Now, it may be, there will be no more of this unmarital romantic perverseness."

"It is no news to me," said I. "He was stabbed to the heart, as I have known since the middle of last month."

"Then you were misinformed," said he, "for the news only came in to-day. The Lord General Cromwell has written a dispatch to Mr. Speaker Lenthall, in whose company I happened to be this afternoon when he broke the seals."

"Nevertheless, I knew it perfectly," said I, "at the very instant that Sir Edmund was slain. And I can tell you more: that it was at Tredah that this took place, and that Sir Edmund surrendered to General Cromwell and was promised quarter, and was walking in his company when an old acquaintance comes up to him, one Captain Ropier, a cousin of the Lord Ropier's and 'Sir Mun,' says he, 'I fain would have a word with you,' and then he draws a tuck and stabs him to the heart. And I can tell you more," said I, "yet do not ask me more!"

My husband knew not what to say, for I spoke the evident truth. Yet he told me of General Cromwell's letter, who was persuaded that "this mercy of Tredah" as he called it, was a marvellous great mercy, a righteous judgment of God (for the officers and soldiers of the garrison were the flower of the army); and who gave all the glory to God. My husband added: "The Lord General writes positively that Lieutenant Colonel Verney was slain at the storming of the town, not murdered afterwards as you pretend."

"Ay," said I, "for I make no doubt but that it lies upon his saintly conscience."

It passed wonder how barbarously the English soldiers conducted themselves in Ireland, even against their own countrymen, when in England their decent orderly behaviour had been an example to the world. There was a scholar of Christ Church, Thomas Wood, a tall, black swarthy fellow, who was a friend of my brother James, and often walked out to Forest Hill in my youth, to play the buffoon about the house. He became a trooper in Captain Sir Thomas Gardiner's company and a stout soldier; and presently was made a lieutenant. He returned after the First Civil War to Oxford and there made up his arrears and was created a Master of Arts; and afterwards turned his coat and obtained a major's commission in the Parliament Army, and was at the storming of Tredah.

From him, when presently he returned to England, James had an account of the massacre: how, in revenge of the losses that General Cromwell's men had suffered in two attempts to storm the works, 3,000 at least of the garrison, besides women and children, were put to the sword after they had surrendered. Thomas Wood also witnessed the death of Sir Arthur Aston, the Governor, whose brains were beaten out with blows of his own wooden leg, and his body thereafter hacked into pieces, as though he were an Agag. There was fierce dispute among the soldiers for this leg, which was reported to be of gold; yet it proved to be wholly of wood.

He told James that when his men were to make their way up to the lofts and galleries of St. Peter's Church steeple, and up the stairs of the strong round tower, next St. Sunday's Gate (where the enemy had fled), some of the assailants catched up children and used them as bucklers of defence. But the enemy in these posts were not to be dislodged and General Cromwell himself ordered the Church steeple to be fired with a great bonfire made of the Church seats, which was done. Then was heard a lamentable cry from the midst of the flames above their heads: "God damn me, God confound me, I burn, I burn!" And presently steeple, men and bells came all down together at once. And after they had burned or killed all in the nave and chapels of St. Peter's Church, near 1,000, with a great many Papist priests and friars, whom they knocked on the head promiscuously, they went down into the vaults where a few of the choicest of the women had hid themselves and plundered and murdered these too, and Major Wood confessed that he, too, had his part in the plunder, though not in the murder.

Major Wood was not by when Mun was slain, but he confirmed the treacherous manner of it, and it grieved him almost more than anything that passed that day, for Mun and he had been comrades together in many battles and sieges on the King's side. A few months ago he himself died in the same town of Tredah, of the flux, and is buried in the very Church where this unnatural business was done.

CHAPTER TWENTY-FOUR

My Husband Buys Fame at a High Price

SINCE Mun's death I have lived somewhat more harmoniously with my husband; for once my secret was told him, my frame of spirit became understandable, and though he loves me no better, yet he has showed me more indulgence, for which I have punctually repaid him by a studied civility and care. In November of the year 1649 the Council awarded him large, airy, well-furnished rooms in Whitehall Palace, in the part which lies towards Scotland Yard, which I found more convenient by far for the accommodation of my children than Thomson's had been. They gave upon a pleasant private garden and had before been occupied by Sir John Hippesley, M.P. In these rooms at about half-past nine at night, on March 16th, 1650, was born my third child, a son, who was named John after his father; him I love with a wonderful love, that I have never had for either of my daughters. Nor do I love him, as might be supposed, because he is a boy and they are girls, for in general I have ever preferred girl children to boys, as being cleanlier and more loving and more mannerly. Nay, the reason that I love this boy is—

This reason, however, I will refrain from disclosing as yet; for I knew it not certainly myself until the child could walk and prattle and until his features had formed clearly. I will write of other matters and leave that to the last.

First, of my mother and her affairs. In November, 1649, she employed Mr. Christopher Milton in a suit for the recovery (from the Committee of Sequestrators for the County of Oxfordshire) of the household goods and timber stolen from us three years beforehand at Forest Hill; and in June of the next year the Commissioners for Relief upon Articles of War signed a decree in her favour, declaring that a violation of my father's rights had been made, and that therefore the Committee of Sequestrators, namely Mr. Thomas Appletree and his crooked-minded fellows, were answerable for the whole amount of the loss.

Now, my mother had learned from Tom Messenger, when he came to her with the present from our former tenants, that Lawrence Farre, Sir Robert Pye's servant, had lied that day when my father came to him at the Manor-house. The truth was, Mr. Thomas Appletree's brother Matthew had purchased all the goods for the sum of £335, paying earnest money of twenty shillings, but had removed no more than what had been valued at £91 11s. 10d. His intention was that when he should have sold these goods in London, for three times this amount, and thus earned ready money to pay for another load—forasmuch as the twenty shillings that he had paid down was almost all the money he had in the world—why, then, he would come back again. But on the day that my father had come to the house only the choice furniture and hangings from the little parlour and the hall had been removed in the carts; together with the grain, hops, wool, planks and suchlike in the wain. The remainder of the furniture and hangings had been left (as also the coaches, for the lack of cattle to draw them) and all the timber except that which was afterwards taken off by the citizens of Banbury. Farre lied to my father from a fear that he would try to break into the house and violently seize some of his goods again, for which loss Farre would be called to account by the Sequestrators. A few days later Farre reported to Sir Robert Pye the Elder what had been done; whereat Sir Robert was angry, for he perceived that the sale was fraudulent, and gave Farre an order that not another thing was to be removed from the house or yard. When, therefore, Matthew Appletree returned with the carts to fetch away a second load, he was told by Farre to go about his business quickly because the fraud was discovered; and he made off at once, leaving the carts behind, and did not return.

All the goods remaining in or about the Manor-house (where Goodman Mason, one of our tenants, was in present occupation) now came, by the aforesaid decree of the Commissioners for Relief, into my mother's possession, subject nevertheless to the fine of £180 which had been imposed on my father's estate when he compounded. Matthew Appletree was also ordered by the Commissioners to pay back to the estate the sum of £91 11s. 10d.—though it should have been at least £250—which he had unjustly taken, and then he should be given back his twenty shillings of earnest money. Yet this rascal resisted the order and did not pay back the money, and continued to make excuses until, at the end of that year, the power of the Court that had ordered payment lapsed, and so he could laugh at her. Moreover, my mother was powerless to take back the goods awarded her, for she had not even so much as ten pounds in ready money to pay towards the fine. Besides, she considered the fine an extortion, for it was calculated upon an assessment of the estate that was too heavy by far, even were the wrong righted that had been done (by Parliament itself) in the matter of the timber awarded to the citizens of Banbury.

There was another vexation: that in August of this same year, 1650, was passed an Act which touched all persons who, by virtue of a debt or mortgage, had since the outbreak of the Civil War entered upon the estate of any delinquent, for which no composition had been made: by this Act they were ordered to compound themselves, paying such sums of money as would have been paid had the delinquent remained in possession. This was a means of annulling a deal of neighbourly kindness: for often a Parliament family would pretend to hold a mortgage on an estate and would take possession for awhile, so that their Royalist friends and kinsmen might be spared the expense of compounding; and afterwards the pretended bond was torn up and the rightful owners invited to return. This Act seemed likely to help my mother; for since my husband had taken possession of the Wheatley freehold upon a mortgage he was obliged to compound, and was ordered by the Commissioners to pay a proportion of the fine fixed upon my father's whole estate, namely £130; after which he might remain in enjoyment of this property until both his original debt and the fine of £130 had been wiped out by the moneys brought in, namely £80 a year. Thus (as I understand the matter) my mother was left to pay no more than £50 for the recovery of the Forest Hill goods, namely one-tenth of their value of £500.

My husband when he compounded pleaded to be allowed for the "widow's thirds" of £26 13s. 4d., which until then he had paid to my mother from the rents that he collected. But in the Order which fixed the fine at £130, the Commissioners made no particular mention of the widow's thirds, and my husband therefore discontinued the payment of them; for he said that it was unjust that, when he paid a fine which was beyond reason heavy, he should also continue to allow my mother the thirds, having been granted no relief on account of them. Yet, as my mother said, he had come off lightly, forasmuch as the legal fine upon the Wheatley freehold ought to have been £160 (being two years' rents at £80) rather than £130; and, since in any event my husband would recover this £130 within a few years, as well as the remainder of his debt, she held that the Commissioners had, in fact, tacitly granted him the relief for which he had pleaded, and that he therefore should in equity continue to pay her the thirds, which she depended upon. My mother put this argument into writing, and gave it to me to show my husband, which I did. But all that he would answer was that if he were ordered by the Commissioners to pay my mother the thirds, and if this amount were remitted from his fine, then he would do so, but not otherwise. The fine of £130 had come upon him very inconveniently, he said, and deprived him of any income from the estate for near two years.

I said to him: "Husband, this is truly hard. My mother is a widow with four orphaned children wholly dependent upon her."

"Aye, you are right," he answered. "They are the widow and orphans of a fraudulent Welsh rascal."

"My father was a good father to me," I answered. "I love his memory and will not hear it defamed."

"Ah, will you not?" said he. "Then I wish you were as loyal and loving a wife as you are daughter!"

"These thirds are the only money upon which my poor mother can depend for her livelihood," said I, "and it is unreasonable to expect the Commissioners to make mention of them; for it is not yourself that pays the fine, but the estate; you will not be the loser in the end. They fix the fine upon you, for why? Because you are in possession; and, whereas you can afford her this pittance, she cannot live without it."

"How do you know that I can afford it?" he asked. "What if I say that I cannot so? I wish to hear nothing more upon the matter. My answer to your mother is a plain 'No.' "

When I told my mother what he had replied, she was near frantic, having counted upon the £26 13s. 4d. as a means of securing £500. For with a loan of £25 promised by my Aunt Moulton, who though living in poverty still had a few jewels to sell, this sum would have been sufficient to pay the remainder of the fine and also her coach fare to Forest Hill, where she might then reclaim all her goods and sell them at a fair price. But now, until the fine were paid, what could she do? Acting upon my brother Richard's advice—for Mr. Christopher Milton would have no finger in this pie—she presented a petition to the Commissioners, praying them to order my husband to pay the thirds, to keep her and her children from starving.

The Commissioners, examining their former decision, found that there had been no order made to my husband to pay the thirds, and instructed her to go to Law with him if she were not satisfied. This she could not do, for she had no money wherewith to prosecute, and besides, she feared what my husband might do to me in revenge. Thus she continued in poverty, and so continues to-day. It is very hard, as I have plainly told my husband. I have even dared remind him of the duty owed to the fatherless and the widow; and all he answers is that the scripture forbids him to defraud any such, but does not order him to defraud himself on their account.

Of what has happened to my brothers and sisters since 1646, the year in which I last wrote of them, I will say no more than that I have lost my brother William, a captain in the Parliamentary service under General Monck, who was killed in Scotland by a musket shot, I know not at what place; and that my dear brother James writes for a diurnal that is very bitterly set against the Government, and I fear daily to have news of his imprisonment; and that my sister Zara is married. During her poverty Zara became the saintliest of women, and one day implored my forgiveness for all the unkindness that she had done me; which I granted willingly, for I had been no good sister to her, I fear. Then she asked leave from my mother to go to France and there seek a nunnery, which my mother, however, would not grant; and Zara resigned herself in obedience. But a captain who had been blinded in the war, Richard Pearson, a Papist, fell in love with her gentle voice and good deeds, and married her; he has but £100 per annum, but we consider it a fortunate match indeed, for he is a gentleman of nine or ten descents, and of a cheerful heart.

For myself, I am not the same woman that I was before the birth of my son, and so great a harm the little rogue did me in his coming forth that Trunco, who was my midwife, told my husband bluntly that if ever he companied with me again, and got me with child, he would find himself a widower when my nine months were out. I cannot walk now but with a stick, and to drag myself upstairs and down again is a misery. Yet I will not pretend to unhappiness. My husband has hired a good country woman to help me with the children; and he is contented with the love that I bear for our son John, whom oftentimes he dandles upon his knee, singing quaint songs to him; and at the same time as he bought a coral for John, with silver bells, to cut his teeth upon, he gave me as a gift a gold ring with three pearls in it.

My husband is now at once the proudest and most pitiful of men, because of all that has happened to him since he was appointed Secretary for the Foreign Tongues to the Council of State. He writes smooth letters in Latin for the Council in answer to letters addressed to it in the German, Dutch, French, Spanish and Portuguese tongues—for all these tongues he understands well enough to converse in them with Ambassadors on behalf of the Council. Until a few months ago he still examined suspected papers and books for the Council and reported upon them; and for a year or more he wrote anonymously for *Mercurius Politicus,* a diurnal that comes out on the Thursday of every week, over which he was set as Censor and licenser. There was one piece of his published in this *Mercury* that made a stir. He wrote it upon the case of the Reverend Love, minister of St. Anne's in Aldersgate, who last year [1651] plotted with the Scots and the exiled Presbyterians, Colonel Graves and the rest, for the suppression of the Council of State and the proclamation of King Charles of Scotland as King also of England. When he, with his crew, were apprehended and convicted of treason, all the Presbyterial ministers of London pleaded for his pardon. But my husband in this *Mercury* approved the sentence of death as just and exemplary, and General Cromwell had him executed upon Tower Hill as a scarecrow. Ah, how bitterly poor Tom Tanner must have lamented his godly minister!

The maker of this news-sheet, which flies every week into all parts of the nation, is one Marchamont Needham, a scurrilous fellow, sometime usher at the Merchant Taylors' School, who scribbled for Parliament against the King, but, when the King was beheaded, against Parliament; he was afterwards put into prison, whither my husband was sent to reason with him and persuade him to change his coat again. The writers for the diurnals are most of them for sale, and at no high price. During the late wars any meritless boasting Falstaff might puff out his own fame by a little money paid to the publisher of a *Mercury* or *Intelligencer.* For this practice one Sir John Gell was a bye-word, who kept the diurnal-makers in pension, so that whatever was done against the enemy in his own county of Derbyshire, or in neighbouring counties, was attributed to him as a matter of course. Yet what is read in print is by the vulgar taken for Gospel; wherefore it is the Council's policy to engage at a good fee all the most industrious writers of the day, even those of scandalous life and conversation, so be it only that they have the knack of persuading the people that white or grey is smutty black; and, on occasion, that smutty black is angelic white. The Council is very lavish with gifts where there are good services to be rewarded: conformably with the proverb that they who steal a sheep will give away the trotters for God's sake. If a man do but stir his hat to them, he shall not lose his labour. Mr. Needham is become a great crony of my husband's; I cannot abide the fellow, with his leering looks and faithless heart—for what is to recant but to cant again?—nor can I understand how my husband can be so little squeamish, unless it be that he himself has so often turned cat-in-pan, from Prelatist to Presbyterian, and from Presbyterian to Independent, that he sympathises with all others of restless conscience.

Now both at home and abroad the reputation of the Council has grown prodigiously. The Lord-General Cromwell has subdued Ireland as it never was subdued before, so that whole provinces are now sheer wilderness; and, upon the Scots inviting their new King Charles II into his Kingdom, this same Cromwell invaded Scotland and won the famous battle of Dunbar; and last year, upon King Charles's conspiring with the English Presbyterians for a revengeful invasion of England, he won the yet more famous battle of Worcester, in which the Scots lost 14,000 slain or captured, against an English loss of no more than 200. Since then it is hard for most Englishmen not to own pride in such an army; and the Princes and States of Europe, that at first abominated the crime of the mad English, have learned a new respect for them; for the Council carries matters with a high hand in all its dealings. However, King Charles escaped from the battle of Worcester, not very gloriously, and while he lives his Cause lives too; though Scotland, having surrendered to General Cromwell's arms, is now incorporated in the Commonwealth of England, and Sectaries of all sorts flourish like weeds in the gardens of Presbytery.

Aye, General Cromwell is become our chiefest man. The Lord General Fairfax, already before the victory at Dunbar, resigned his Captain-Generalship, for being married to a Presbyterial wife it went against his conscience to invade Scotland, the home of Presbytery: he lives retired among his books and orchard trees on his fair estate of Nun-Appleton in Yorkshire, and I think it will take a sharp and long screw to draw him thence again. Wherefore, as the balladists sing:

Our Oliver is all in all,
Our Oliver is all in all,
   And Oliver is here,
   And Oliver is there,
And Oliver is at Whitehall.
   And Oliver notes all,
   And Oliver votes all,
And claps his hand upon his bilboe
O fine Oliver! etc.

Even to my husband, who is chary in his praises, Captain-General
Cromwell appears to be the greatest commander in the history of the
world; and Captain-General Cromwell, for his part, has come to think
very highly of my husband and has complimented him to his face as
the first writer in all Europe: and so he is regarded by very many
people besides, since his conquest of the great Salmasius.

Who has not heard of Salmasius, *alias* Claude de Saumaise, until
latterly regarded as the only literate prodigy of his day, the greatest
scholar since Aristotle? To deal freely with you, I had never heard of
him myself until my husband was commissioned by the Council to
write a book against him; but I am a woman and never was sent to
the University; and besides, his fame was more resonant on the Continent of Europe than in this island. But I warrant that my husband
knew his name and fame: indeed, he had praised him in pamphlets
written while he was yet a Presbyterian. Salmasius had published his
first treatise in 1608, the year of my husband's birth, at the age of but
twenty. In 1629 came his masterpiece, a folio of eight hundred closely
printed pages, being an edition of the encyclopædic history of Solinus
Polyhistor, with profuse augmentations, in the form of learned Latin
glosses upon every chapter; so that Solinus himself seemed a mere
stammering puny by comparison with his new tutor. This book was
greeted with such marvellous praise by all the scholars of Europe, or
such at least as were not jealous of his reputation, that he was beset
by letters from rival Universities, offering him professorships and other
honours, with promise of high fees, and drenched with countless
panegyrical encomiums. He was sent for by the learned men of Leyden, Utrecht, Padua, Bologna, Upsala and Oxford, and by the Pope
himself (though Salmasius was a professed enemy to the Papacy, having been converted in Germany to the Reformed Religion) who wished

to redeem him by gifts and flattery; and the French King was also jealous that he should remain in France.

The Dutch won this tug of war, for they made the highest bid at the auction, offering him a professorship which took precedence of all others at the famous University at Leyden, and carried a public salary. At Leyden he would find a better library than in any popish University, and also Messer Elzivir would publish his books, who was the best printer in Europe. Wherefore, Salmasius accepted this offer, writing that there was always greater liberty in a Republic than in a kingdom; and at Leyden for eighteen years or so he continued, writing massive books upon antiquities, religion, philosophy, Law, astrology and I know not what beside. Such admiration did these books excite among the learned that the French King longed to have him return to his dominions at whatever price; and when he courteously declined, yet sent him the badge of knighthood as a free gift and honour. To him, as to the acknowledged oracle of learning, the man of vastest knowledge then living, persons of every condition and quality flocked from all quarters, seeking enlightenment for their doubts and difficulties.

This Salmasius seems to be a man not unlike my husband, fretful, keen-minded, proud, unwearying, subject to headaches, quarrelsome, always crouched before a book with pen and paper beside him, forgetful of nothing that ever he has read, always holding a greater store of book-learning in his mind than he can find time to void out again in the form of other books. In three things only he differs from my husband—he is not a poet; his fame has made him something careless; and he is ruled by a termagant wife.

Salmasius had been in no wise unaware of what was passing in England and had inquired closely into our affairs. He was consulted both by Royalists and Parliamentarians upon the differences that divided them, and had pronounced against the intermeddling of Bishops in temporal affairs, though he would not have Bishops abolished, root and branch. However, he was abhorrent of Sectaries and Schismatics, and it was hoped by the Scottish and English Presbyterians, and by the English and Irish Prelatists and Papists now in exile, and by King Charles II himself, that he would write against those who had executed his late Majesty and had seized the government of England and Ireland. A fee of £100 was offered to Salmasius by King Charles from his scanty store, which Salmasius graciously accepted—tempering the wind to the shorn sheep—and by November, 1649, his book was written and printed, with the title, in Latin, of *The Royal Defence*. It began rantingly thus:

Of late the horrid rumour smote and sorely wounded our ears, but more our minds, of the parricide committed among the English, upon the person of their King, by a nefarious conjuration of sacrilegious persons. Whomsoever this hideous news assailed, on the instant, as if he had been blasted by the stroke of lightning, his hair upstarted and his voice stuck in his gullet. . . . Ay, the Sun himself in his perennial circling has never looked upon a baser or more atrocious deed . . . worthy of universal hatred and invective are the authors of this prodigious and unheard-of deed, and most worthy moreover to be pursued with fire and sword, not only by all Kings and Princes in Europe who rule by royal right, but also by the magistrates of every well-framed and honestly-minded republic. For these factious fanatics not only delight in assailing the thrones of Kings, but endeavour to subvert every power not by themselves created, desiring and intending nought else than a revolution and an overturning of all that is fixed as well in the Church as in the State; and with such endless lust of further innovation as may win for themselves the licence to govern all and yield obedience to none . . .

Salmasius then inquired into the rights of Kings, as written of in the Old and New Testaments, maintaining that even tyrants are sacrosanct and inviolable to their subjects, and answerable to God only; and, with copious citations and quotations, carried the argument through all ancient and modern history. To this he appended a brief history of Kings in England, satisfying himself that they were in no wise dependent upon Parliaments; and at last came to the climax of the work, the horrid trial and execution of King Charles, with a marvellous eulogy of his virtuous life and character. This was his conclusion:

It was the soldiers of the Independents alone, they and their officers, all inhabitants of the Kingdom of England (for this pestilence of Independency is not to be found either in Scotland or in Ireland), and who are in number not one man in a hundred of the English people, these, I say, by a parricide so unutterably violent as never can be expiated, deprived the three Kingdoms of their one King, and him of his life, for no other cause than their whoring after a perverted faith which abhors regal government and detests Kings.

This was the book which the Council called upon my husband to answer, and he was the very man for the purpose; for here was ground that he had long made his own, into which Salmasius had trespassed. When my husband was given this commission, he was like a boy that has been lent an axe by his father, with leave to cut down a certain tall, rotten tree. How he rejoiced, swinging the axe through the air; feeling the blade with his thumb and then grinding it yet sharper at the oiled stone; striking the haft upon the ground to make the head sit the firmer; then tapping the bole of the tree, here and there, for sounds of hollowness, and marking upon it with chalk the line where to make his hacking strokes, so that it would fall easily and along the very line that he intended for it. Throughout a whole year my husband worked at his answer, in all his leisure time allowed him by the Council, shutting himself in his library, with bread, cheese, beer, tobacco, and candles, and forbidding any disturbance or interruption whatsoever, though the Palace caught fire or villains burst in to ravish me or slay my children. His was no easy task: for, having orders to pursue Salmasius like a beagle through every one of his twelve chapters, not leaving any matter of importance unanswered, he must find and examine the original context of each citation and redargue the opinions derived therefrom, with fresh citations from the same authors and others, ranging from Homer to Hottoman, from Sulpicius Severus to Sichardus, from Gildas to Guiccard.

My husband found this work very hurtful to his eyes, being forced to write the book piece-meal, and to break off almost every hour to rest them a little. Yet never was a man more earnest in a task than he then, faithfully returning clout for clout, objurgation for objurgation, mud-bullet for mud-bullet, filth-ball for filth-ball. Salmasius (he wrote) was a dunce in Latin grammar; he was also a hireling mourner at a funeral, who canted and shed crocodilian tears; he was a beetle, blockhead, liar, slanderer, slave, apostate, devil, turn-coat, sheep, weevil, ignoramus, French vagabond, Judas Iscariot, and a long-eared ass bestridden by a virago. That King, whom Salmasius lamented (he wrote) had been a swinger who used in the playhouse to wanton with the women of his Court, and in public places to fondle the bosoms of virgins and matrons, as also their more secret parts; a monster who had also been nasty with his father's own catamite, the Duke of Buckingham, the very instrument by which he had poisoned his father; a base pretender, moreover, to royal lineage, forasmuch as his grandfather was David Rizzio, a wanton Italian music-master, the paramour of Mary, Queen of Scots.

The Republican form of Government (my husband wrote) was by God thought more perfect than Monarchy, though He gave leave to the Jews at least to change one form for another and denied not the right to other nations. The Army (he wrote) had shrewder and truer insight into affairs than had the men in Parliament, for they had saved by their arms what the others nearly ruined by their votes. England (he wrote) had never had a King that was not, by Law and Custom, liable to be judged by his people for any crimes committed against them. Thus he concluded:

I have no fear, Slug, of any war or danger that you could contrive to conjure up for us among Foreign Kings with your hasty and insipid eloquence; despite your playful report to them that here we use Kings' heads for footballs, that we play with crowns as with spinning-tops, and make no more of an imperial sceptre than if it were a fool's staff. The fool's staff comes to you, Vain Dolt, for.thinking to persuade Kings and princes into war against us by such trumpery argument. You write mighty tragically in your peroration; as Ajax you crack your leathern whip, crying: "Oh, the injustice, the impiety, the perfidy, the cruelty of these men I will proclaim to Heaven and to Earth, and, proving their guilt upon them, will assuredly send them with my curse down to latest posterity." Ha, ha! Do you, then, a witling, a sot, a mouther, a pettifogger, born only to transcribe or steal from good authors, do you indeed imagine that you are able to write any book of your own acceptable to posterity? Nay, Fool, the coming age will wrap you in a bundle of your own fusty writings and consign you to oblivion: where you shall lie everlastingly, unless perhaps this late book of yours be taken up one day by readers so studious of my Answer to it, that they are led to knock the dust from its covers.

This answer, the *Defence of the English People,* was published by Mr. Dugard, who had been released from Newgate Jail on condition that he changed his colours and aided the Council. Newgate is an eloquent preacher: she turns hearts to repentance almost more speedily even than that droll prevaricator, the Reverend Hugh Peters, General Cromwell's chaplain, converts Presbyterians in search of fat livings and University Fellowships to his own reckless form of Independency.

My husband is become friendly enough with Mr. Dugard, an excellent printer, who was also formerly Master of the Merchant Taylors' School. When another printer stole the copyright of one of Mr. Dugard's books (upon a disease called the Rickets) my husband brought a complaint before the Council and had justice done. But latterly his friendship for Mr. Dugard, who prints whatever he can sell, has led him into trouble; for, in a heedless mood, he licensed him to print a book which, upon a petition of ministers, a Committee of Parliament examined and found "blasphemous, erroneous and scandalous," and ordered copies of it to be publicly burned in London and Westminster, under direction of the Sheriffs. This book, which was written in Poland, denies the Trinity, the Divinity of Christ, the Divinity of the Holy Ghost, and the twin doctrines of Atonement and of Original Sin, averring them all to be gross and pernicious fallacies. My husband could not well plead unawareness of what was printed in this blasphemous book, forasmuch as some years beforehand he had made some very sharp observations against such licensers as set their *imprimatur* upon books they had not read; nor could he approve the doctrine. By what shuffling and compounding he escaped censure I know not, but I believe that he represented this book as a laughable and harmless monstrosity, a signal proof of human aberrancy, a reduction to absurdity of unscholarly speculation. Yet against such opinions as these there had been an Act passed with very severe penalties for their promulgation, banishment if the offence were repeated and death if the banished blasphemer returned to our shores.

To come to the *Defence of the English People.* It had made a wonderful hit, yet not in England so much as in the Universities of Europe, where the scholars are grown weary of Salmasius (nicknamed by them "The Awful Man"), and rejoice to see him put to shame. For this notable Goliath had by his careless confidence left so many chinks showing in his armour, that my husband scorned the use of a sling-stone to sink him in cowardly fashion after the manner of David; but had come against him armed with the customary weapons of a scholar-warrior and had beaten him at his own sword-play, piercing him through and through; and had, as it were, given the finishing stroke with Goliath's own tuck. For my husband quoted against Salmasius words published four years before in Salmasius's renowned book upon the Papacy: there he recommended the rooting out not only of the Pope but of the whole hierarchy of bishops, which had ruined kings and princes with their miserable tyranny; and here for a fee of £100 he execrates the Parliament of England because it has done this very thing—and he even uses the same arguments in favour of Episcopacy that there he confuted: namely, that Bishops are necessary and desirable to prevent the sprouting of a thousand pestiferous sects.

Now it happened that Salmasius was away from Leyden at this time. He was fallen into disgrace with the Dutch, who now sought an alliance with England and who, upon a complaint of our Council of State, forbade the further publication in their territory of Salmasius's *Royal Defence.* Yet he was gone from Leyden haughtily, upon an invitation from Christina, Queen of Sweden, who loves scholars and has made a collection of them at her Court, like so many curious living jewels—Freinsheim, Vossius, Heinsius and the rest. Without Salmasius, her necklace was incomplete; but now that Salmasius was come too, (dressed in scarlet breeches, with a black hat and a white plume) with leave from the Curators at Leyden University, she was well content. She had that year entertained as her tutor in philosophy the most renowned philosopher of the age, Mounseer René Descartes, but he was lately dead, from the inclemency of the Swedish climate. Salmasius, fearing to suffer a like fate with his fellow-countryman, spent most of the winter snug a-bed in a splendid apartment of the Royal Palace at Stockholm, where the Queen frequently visited him, and consulted him upon matters of great importance. Often, when Madame Salmasius was out taking the air, she would shut the doors and wait upon him as a servant, plumping his pillows for him, mending his fire, or warming up a caudle. It is said that one day, coming in suddenly, she saw how the great scholar hastily thrust a little book under his bolster. "Ah, my good Sir Claude," said she, "do not hide away that precious little book." He, making some uneasy excuse, denied it to her; but she was a Queen and out from under the bolster it must come. It was a nasty, fribbling, lecherous little book, and the Queen gave it to her Maid of Honour, the Lady Sparra, to read aloud; which she did, stammering and blushing. The Queen laughed heartily the while and complimented Salmasius upon the grand promiscuity of his reading.

It was at Stockholm that Salmasius was shown a copy of my husband's book, but the Queen had read it beforehand and being highly delighted with it could not satiate herself in praising it to her Court; for she clearly dotes upon the clangor, the sweat and the dust of literate conflict, and cares not who vanquishes whom, so long as lusty blows and keen thrusts be given and exchanged. "I wonder, now," said she, "whether this regicide Miltonus would consent to tarry awhile in our Court. He would be a great ornament to it, I dare say, for both in learning and invective he seems a match for any man living."

Yet she continued kind to Salmasius, who was madded with rage and vowed to send Parliament and my husband together to the Devil, so soon as ever he was sufficiently recovered from his long sickness to undertake the task. "That will be delightful, dear Master," the Queen answered, laughing prettily. "I warrant you will slice that English pig into rashers for broiling on your coals, and my hope is that our town of Stockholm will have the honour to print so splendid a work."

This account I heard from my brother James. My husband had asserted that Salmasius, when he was publicly humiliated by the *Defence* (of which several editions have now been sold, and translations published in French and Dutch) was scorned and sent away by the Queen; yet I prefer to believe with my brother that the Queen had pity on him, and that his departure from Stockholm soon afterwards was upon an urgent summons by the Curators of Leyden University. He has not yet made an answer, though the book lies upon his stomach like a raw, undigested gobbet of meat. His rivals grin and nudge one another and say: "The Awful Man will never recover from the stroke that the English Regicide dealt him in his guts!" Salmasius at one time gives out that he scorns to answer so currish and scurrilous an upstart, and at another that he will sufficiently demonstrate his absurd pretensions to learning by a mere citation of the errors in quantity and accidence committed by him in his Latin poems.

Every foreigner of note resident in London, whether ambassador, envoy or agent for any foreign Prince or State, has now either called upon my husband to felicitate him upon his wonderful book, or has done so upon a casual meeting. The Council, not to be behindhand in its compliments, voted my husband the sum of £100 as a reward for his labours; but this he refused, lest Salmasius should in his answer reproach him for having accepted the very same fee which he had hypocritically reproached Salmasius for accepting. My husband reckons £100 a paltry recompense of his tremendous labour; he would have either £1,000 or nothing.

While we lodged in these rooms in Whitehall—of which my husband was once nearly dispossessed by an Order from the Council to remove "all unnecessary persons from the Palace"—an allowance was made to him for a weekly table at which to entertain foreign ambassadors and agents. I was never present at these dinners, but my husband gave me leave to save him expense by ordering the drinks myself and dressing the meats in our own kitchen; for the Palace kitchens are sluttishly managed. This contented me, for it was many years since I had dressed delicate food for persons of discerning taste, and I ate and drank plentifully myself of what was left over. My husband won much fame by this table; though to him one dish is hardly to be distinguished from another except by sharp and biting sauces.

Four or five answers were written to my husband's books. Of one my brother James brought me a copy; it named my husband a frigid and severe Censor for his reproach that his late Majesty had in public touched the naked skins of beautiful women—was the King not handsome and young, and was his touch not also bestowed upon the wretched and scrofulous? The writer sneered at my husband as a sour Puritan who, besides adding "Divorce at Pleasure" to the other scandalous doctrines of the Independents, had put away a sweet wife from jealousy. This stirred my secret laughter; I did not show the book to my husband.

In December last we removed from Whitehall Palace, and took a garden-house in Petty France, in Westminster, next door to the Lord Scudamore's and opening into St. James's Park: this was upon a quarrel with our near neighbours in the Palace. The gentleman, an officer of the Life Guards, was exceeding noisy. By day he continually exercised himself with his friends in fencing and wrestling, and by night they sang roaring choruses together, with psalms and drinking songs intermingled. He also had two or three lively and undisciplined children and a wife who twanged a guitar and sang very high and screamingly, quite out of tune. The partition walls being but of lath and plaster, the vexation was great. My husband had also complained of the frequent interruptions of his work by idle persons, come to the Palace upon some other business, who were desirous of meeting and discoursing with him. In our new house, as not in our former lodgings, there is room for Ned Phillips, who has returned from Cambridge dissatisfied with the severe government of his college by the Reverend Goodwin, its new head. My husband has urgent need of Ned, as well as of John, to be hands and eyes for him; for why? My husband is now gone stone blind.

The physicians warned him, when he consulted them upon the dimming of the sight of his left eye, that if he would not leave off reading for a year at least, he would lose the sight of the other also.

But, being ordered by the Council to write against Salmasius, he would not heed them, thinking it a fair bargain to purchase the applauses of all Europe at the price of his remaining eye. This eye he doctored with lotions and issues and seatons recommended to him, which made the matter worse: for there was a running between the nose and the corner of the eye which seemed to betoken an Ægilops, but proceeded doubtless from weakness, not from any purulence. Things that he looked upon began to swim to the right and left so that he stumbled upon his feet like a drunken man; and at night, when he lay down to rest, a copious light dazzled into his head out of his shut eyes. Now, he says, there is a constant and settled darkness before him, by day as well as by night, of the colour of wetted wood ashes. Only by rolling his eyes can he let in a little chink of light at the corners. It is hard to believe him sightless, for his eyes are not changed in aspect, though they stare horribly. Nor does he complain, for he declares his conscience clean of any sin, the atrocity of which might have brought this calamity upon him; and he has won the fame he sought—for, if Salmasius were before the greatest scholar of Europe, it follows that the conqueror of Salmasius must be the greatest scholar of the whole round world.

The other day by chance I espied the Reverend Robert Pory walking in the street. He limped from a wound that he had got in the siege of Colchester. I know not what his business or profession may now be, but he was not in black clergy apparel. He seemed prosperous enough and was still much of a chuckler. When I told him, "My husband, John Milton, is blind," he answered, not unkindly, "Why, I am sorry for that. Yet John will not consider himself beyond measure afflicted, for as a poet he will find himself in choice company. And, now I think on it, this fate was not obscurely prophesied him by some Angel or other spirit whom at Cambridge he ceremoniously invocated: namely, that in the noon-day of life he would make one with Homer and Tiresias."

I asked: "What? Did my husband truly invocate Angels? Was that not superstitious in him?"

"Nay," he answered, "for the Collect that is read upon Michaelmas Day allows of praying to Angels."

My husband comforts himself philosophically that God looks with particular care and favour upon the blind; and that He is wont to illuminate their gross darkness by an inner and far more excelling light; and that He curses all who mock or hurt them. Now is come the time to win that epical fame which he has so long coveted and brooded upon. Even my continuance with him will not, I believe, restrain him from his project: for to-day he called John Phillips to read out to him the opening lines of *Adam Unparadised* and mended a word or two, to keep his hand in. (Johnny is become a great rogue and rake-hell, now that his uncle cannot well control his goings-out and comings-in, but that is no business of mine, for he does not pester me at least.)

I have had three children by my husband and the fourth is in my womb, which will be born in a month's time from now. The third child, the boy, he has never seen since he was a few months old, and then only dimly. This is well, for little John is no Milton (or Melton) either in body or in feature: nay, upon my word he is pure Verney, he is the very spit and image of my poor murdered Mun!

How came this about? For I never lay carnally with my love. There are Doctors who hold that in the third or fourth month of gestation the child's soul is born. Think you it possible that Mun, dying, bequeathed his soul to my child—to the end that he might continue with me, and love me legitimately and be by me cherished and beloved? Yet what you think I care not.

Yesterday, my husband sent for the little boy, who is now near two years of age. He talked to him in simple words and said merrily: "How are you named, my little one? Let me tell you! You are not Jeremiah nor Jeroboam nor Jehoiakim nor yet Jambonius Justinianus: you are my son John."

J is a hard letter for a prattler's mouth, and when my husband said: "John! Repeat it after me: 'Hey Diddle Dumpling, *my son John!*'" the child looked up into his face and answered: "Son Mun."

"Nay, Child, not 'Mun,'" cried my husband, "Mun is nothing. Say 'My son John!'"

The child looked earnestly at him, hunched his shoulders, straddled his feet apart, and with very great fury and boldness shouted out again: "Son Mun!"

My husband was vexed and cried again: "Nay, nay, Child, you must obey your Father. You must say the word aright after me. You are named *John* after your father *John,* who was named after his father

John. What is your grandfather's name? What is your father's name?
What is your own name? They are all the same—*John!* Say 'John!' "

The child, seeing how my husband stretched forth his hands to seize
him, escaped and ran away from him shouting: *"Son Mun, Son Mun!"*
and held out his arms to me to be kissed.

THE END

Epilogue

MILTON wrote in his family Bible (now in the British Museum), on the blank page opposite the first chapter of *Genesis*, where he had recorded the births of his first three children:

"My daughter Deborah——"

Then another hand added to his dictation:

"—— was born the 2d day of May being Sunday somewhat before 3 of the clock in the morning 1652, my wife hir mother dyed about 3 days after. And my son about 6 weeks after his mother."

Edward Phillips, who in 1694 published a life of his uncle, wrote that little John's death was caused by "the ill-usage or bad constitution of an ill-chosen nurse." Yet Deborah survived.

Four years later Milton married a second wife, Katherine Woodcock of Hackney. Very little is known about her. This is the wife whom in a sonnet he called "my late espousèd saint." She died in February, 1657, and her five-months-old daughter Katherine died six weeks later.

He continued, despite his blindness, to work for the Council of State, though at a reduced salary. Probably he wanted to go to Sweden as British Ambassador and there replace Salmasius in Queen Christina's affectionate esteem: he certainly wrote her a panegyric in his *Second Defence of the English People* which is so adulatory that it cannot be easily explained otherwise. But if he had such a plan, he was disappointed, for on June 16th, 1654, three weeks before the book came out, the Queen abdicated the throne. Salmasius had lately died "it is thought of a broken heart." Milton accepted £1,000 from the Council of State as a reward for his *Second Defence*, written against a Scot named More who had taken up the cudgels for Salmasius. The following autobiographical passage occurs in this book:

"Let us now come to the charges which were brought against myself. Is there anything reprehensible in my manners or my conduct? Surely nothing. What no one, not totally divested of all generous sensibility, would have done, he reproaches me with want of beauty and loss of sight.

"'A monster huge and hideous, void of sight.'

"I certainly never supposed that I should have been obliged to enter into a competition for beauty with the Cyclops; but he immediately corrects himself, and says, 'Though not indeed huge, for there cannot be a more spare, shrivelled, and bloodless form.' It is of no moment to say anything of personal appearance, yet lest (as the Spanish vulgar, implicitly confiding in the relations of their priests, believe of heretics) anyone, from the representations of my enemies, should be led to imagine that I have either the head of a dog, or the horn of a rhinoceros, I will say something on the subject, that I may have an opportunity of paying my grateful acknowledgments to the Deity, and of refuting the most shameless lies. I do not believe that I was ever once noted for deformity by anyone who ever saw me; but the praise of beauty I am not anxious to obtain. My stature certainly is not tall; but it rather approaches the middle than the diminutive. Yet what if it were diminutive, when so many men, illustrious both in peace and war, have been the same? And how can that be called diminutive, which is great enough for every virtuous achievement? Nor, though very thin, was I ever deficient in courage or in strength; and I was wont constantly to exercise myself in the use of the broadsword, as long as it comported with my habits and my years. Armed with this weapon, as I usually was, I should have thought myself quite a match for anyone, though much stronger than myself; and I felt perfectly secure against the assault of any open enemy. At this moment I have the same courage, the same strength, though not the same eyes; yet so little do they betray any external appearance of injury that they are as unclouded and bright as the eyes of those who most distinctly see. In this instance alone I am a dissembler against my will. My face, which is said to indicate a total privation of blood, is of a complexion entirely opposite to the pale and the cadaverous; so that, though I am more than forty years old, there is scarcely anyone to whom I do not appear ten years younger than I am; and the smoothness of my skin is not, in the least, affected by the wrinkles of age.

"If there be one particle of falsehood in this relation, I should deservedly incur the ridicule of many thousands of my countrymen, and even many foreigners to whom I am personally known. But if he, in a matter so foreign to his purpose, shall be found to have asserted so many shameless and gratuitous falsehoods, you may the more readily estimate the quantity of his veracity on other topics. Thus much necessity has compelled me to assert concerning my personal appearance. Respecting yours, though I have been informed that it is more insignificant and contemptible, a perfect mirror of the worthlessness of your character and the malevolence of your heart, I say nothing, and no one will be anxious that anything should be said. I wish that I could with equal facility refute what this barbarous opponent has said of my blindness; but I cannot do it; and I must submit to the affliction. It is not so wretched to be blind as it is not to be capable of enduring blindness. But why should I not endure a misfortune, which it behoves every one to be prepared to endure if it should happen, which may, in the common course of things, happen to any man; and which has been known to happen to the most distinguished and virtuous persons in history. Shall I mention those wise and ancient bards, whose misfortunes the gods are said to have compensated by superior endowments, and whom men so much revered, that they chose rather to impute their want of sight to the injustice of heaven than to their own want of innocence or virtue? What is reported of the Augur Tiresias is well known; of whom Apollonius sung this in his *Argonauts:*

> " 'To men he dar'd the will divine disclose,
>   Nor fear'd what Jove might in his wrath impose,
>   The gods assigned him age, without decay,
>   But snatched the blessing of his sight away.'

"But God Himself is truth; in propagating which, as men display a greater integrity and zeal, they approach nearer to the similitude of God, and possess a greater portion of His love. We cannot suppose the Deity envious of truth, or unwilling that it should be freely communicated to mankind. The loss of sight, therefore, which this inspired sage, who was so eager in promoting knowledge among men, sustained, cannot be considered as a judicial punishment. Or shall I mention those worthies who were as distinguished for wisdom in the cabinet, as for valour in the field? And first, Timoleon of Corinth, who delivered his city and all Sicily from the yoke of slavery; than whom there never lived in any age a more virtuous man, or a more incorrupt statesman; next Appius Claudius, whose discreet counsels in the Senate, though they could not restore sight to his own eyes, saved Italy from the formidable inroads of Pyrrhus: then Cæcilius Metellus the high priest, who lost his sight, while he saved not only the city, but the Palladium, the protection of the city, and the most sacred relics, from the destruction of the flames. On other occasions Providence has indeed given conspicuous proofs of its regard for such singular exertions of patriotism and virtue; what, therefore, happened to so great and so good a man, I can hardly place in the catalogue of misfortunes. Why should I mention others of later times, as Dandolo of Venice, the incomparable Doge; or Boemar Zisca, the bravest of generals, and the champion of the Cross; or Jerome Zanchius, and some other theologians of the highest reputation? For it is evident that the patriarch Isaac, than whom no man ever enjoyed more of the divine regard, lived blind for many years; and perhaps also his son Jacob, who was equally an object of the divine benevolence. And in short, did not our Saviour himself clearly declare that that poor man whom he restored to sight had not been born blind, either on account of his own sins or those of his progenitors? And with respect to myself, though I have accurately examined my conduct,

and scrutinized my soul, I call thee, O God, the searcher of hearts, to witness that I am not conscious, either in the more early or in the later periods
of my life, of having committed any enormity which might deservedly have
marked me out as a fit object for such a calamitous visitation."

[*Translation by the Rev. Robert Fellowes.*]

As Secretary for the Foreign Tongues, Milton supported the Lord
Protector Cromwell, whom he styled "our chief of men," in all his bold
acts, from the rude abolishment of what was left of the Rump Parliament (the "take-away-that-bauble" episode), to the un-English attempt at governing England by regional major-generals. Not being
required to do so much office work as formerly, Milton found time for
his own writings. As John Phillips wrote in 1686:

"Nor did his darkness discourage or disable him from prosecuting, with
the help of amanuenses, the former design of his calmer studies. And he
had now more leisure, being dispensed with, by having a substitute allowed
him, and sometimes instructions sent home to him, from attending in his
office of Secretary.
"It was now that he began that laborious work of amassing out of all the
Classic Authors, both in Prose and Verse, a Latin Thesaurus to the emenda-
tion of that done by Stephanus; also the composing of *Paradise Lost;* and
the framing a *Body of Divinity* out of the Bible: all which, notwithstanding
the several calamities befalling him in his fortunes, he finished after the
Restoration. As also the *British History* down to the Conquest; *Paradise
Regained, Samson Agonistes, a Tragedy; Logic and Accidence commenced
Grammar;* and had begun a Greek Thesaurus; having scarce left any part
of learning unimproved by him."

John Phillips was a journalist. Just before the Restoration he had
turned Royalist and wrote of Milton's *Eikonoklastes* as a blasphemous
libel, though previously he had written vigorously in defence of it.

Oliver Cromwell died in 1658. His mild son Richard succeeded
him. The Restoration took place in 1660. Milton's life was then in
danger, but though he was for a while in custody he was not hanged
and disembowelled as Hugh Peters and the rest were: he merely lost
all the money he had invested in Government funds. Jonathan
Richardson relates (1734) that Milton's life was saved by the inter-
cession of Sir William Davenant, the noseless Poet Laureate whose
life Milton himself had similarly saved in 1651, when Davenant was
captured on the way to America.

Richardson also writes:

"After all it is to be observed that the pardon which secured Milton to us was that of the Parliament, into whose hands the King had committed the affair, and who did as they thought fit; in some points, no doubt, complying with the Royal intimations in other ostentatious of their zeal and then most remarkably fashionable loyalty. Though the King had expressed his desire that the Indemnity should extend to all who were not immediately guilty of the murder of his father, and had said it mainly in his speech of 27th July, yet that restriction was far from being punctually observed. The interest that saved Milton was therefore made to, and was effectual with the Parliament, or rather the Legislature; the nation forgave him, though they little knew how well he would reward their clemency by his future writings, chiefly *Paradise Lost*. And what made this clemency the more remarkable is that this very year, whilst his fate was in suspense, the old controversy was raised up with bitter invectives. Salmasius died some year before, whilst he was preparing a furious reply. This work, though imperfect, was now printed; but Milton's fortune and merit withstood this malicious attack.

"'Twas enough that Milton was screened from being excepted in the general pardon, his life and person were then safe, his two most obnoxious books being sacrificed in his stead, which was the most that his friends could hope for. Bishop Burnet's conclusion of what he says on this head I will add. 'Milton had appeared so boldly, though with much wit and great purity and elegancy of style, against Salmasius and others, upon that argument of putting the King to death, and had discovered such violence against the late King and all the Royal Family, and against monarchy, that it was thought a strange omission if he was forgot, and an odd strain of clemency if it was intended he should be forgiven. He was not excepted out of the Act of Indemnity. And afterwards he came out of his concealment, and lived many years much visited by all strangers, and much admired by all at home, for the poems he wrote, though he was then blind, chiefly that of *Paradise Lost*, in which there is a nobleness both of contrivance and execution, that, though he affected to write in blank verse, without rhyme, and made many new and rough words, yet it was esteemed the beautifullest and perfectest poem that ever was writ, at least in our language.' This passage is put in this place entire, though the latter part of it refers to what comes after. I will only further observe, that had the Bishop known this story of Sir William Davenant, he would not have been one of the wonderers at Milton's escape. How many things appear unaccountable, merely because ourselves cannot account for them. The wisest men fall into this folly in some degree every day of their lives.

"Secured by pardon, Milton appeared again in public, and in a short time married his third wife. He was now blind, infirm, and 52 years old. He had several dwellings in the remaining part of his life. One in Jewen Street. This was in 1662, and about 1670 I have been told by one who then knew him, that he lodged some time at the house of Millington, the famous auctioneer, some years ago, who then sold old books in Little Britain, and who used to lead him by the hand when he went abroad. He afterwards had a small house near Bunhill Fields, where he died, about 14 years after he was out of public affairs. Besides those dwellings Elwood says in his *Own Life*, 'Himself took a pretty box for him in Giles-Chalfont (Bucks) for the safety of himself and family, the pestilence then growing hot in London.'

"His time was now employed in writing and publishing, particularly *Paradise Lost*. And after that *Paradise Regained* and *Samson Agonistes*. The last of these is worthy of him, the other of anyone else. If it be true that he preferred this to the first of the three, what shall we say? . . .

"Well it was for him that he had so fine an amusement, and a mind stored with rich ideas of the sublimest kinds: for besides what affliction he must have from his disappointment on the change of the times, and from his own private losses (and probably cares for subsistence, and for his family), he was in perpetual terror of being assassinated. Though he had escaped the talons of the Law, he knew he had made himself enemies in abundance. He was so dejected he would lie awake whole nights. He then kept himself as private as he could. This Dr. Tancred Robinson had from a relation of Milton's, Mr. Walker of the Temple. And this is what is intimated by himself:

> " 'On evil Daies though fall'n and evil tongues
> In Darkness, and with Dangers compast round,
> And Solitude . . .'

"His melancholy circumstances at this time are described by an enemy, in what my son found written in the spare leaf before the Answer to *Eikon Basilike*:

"Upon John Milton's not suffering for his traiterous book when the Tryers were executed, 1600.

> " 'That thou Escapd'st that Vengeance which o'ertook,
> Milton, thy Regicides, and thy Own Book,
> Was Clemency in Charles beyond compare,
> And yet thy doom doth prove more Grievous farr.
> Old, Sickly, Poor, Stark Blind, thou Writ'st for Bread,
> So for to Live thou'dst call Salmasius from the Dead.'

"If this writer had known of the terrors mentioned above, he would have been glad to have added to his other miseries this which was equal to all the rest put together—if he can be said to be miserable who could write *Paradise Lost*. . . .

"It has been seen that he was tormented with headaches, gout, blindness; and that though he was a gentleman, and had always enough for a philosopher, he made no show, nor had the affluences of fortune, perhaps was sometimes a little straitened, at least his family was not easy, how much soever himself was, only on their accounts. He had other domestic vexations, particularly that uncommon and severe one of the affront and scorn of a wife he loved,* and the continuance of it for some years, and this without allowing him time to know what conjugal happiness was. Many of his choicest years of life were employ'd in wrangling, and receiving and racquetting back reproach, accusation and sarcasm. Which though he had an arm and dexterity fitted for, 'twas an exercise of his abilities very disagreeable to him: as it must needs be to one accustomed to praise, as he was in his younger years, to one ever labouring to deserve esteem and love, to find himself laden with obloquy and hatred by a great part of mankind, and even by many of those from whom he had a right to expect and demand the contrary.

"I have heard many years since that he used to sit in a grey coarse cloth coat at the door of his house, near Bunhill Fields, without Moorgate, in warm sunny weather to enjoy the fresh air, and so, as well as in his room, received the visits of people of distinguished parts, as well as quality. And very lately I had the good fortune to have another picture of him from an ancient clergyman in Dorsetshire, Dr. Wright. He found him in a small house, he thinks but one room on a floor; and that up one pair of stairs, which was hung with rusty green, he found John Milton, sitting in an elbow chair, black clothes, and neat enough, pale, but not cadaverous, his hands and fingers gouty, and with chalk stones. Among other discourse he expressed himself to this purpose; that, was he free from the pain this gave him, his blindness would be tolerable.

"Music he loved extremely, and understood well. 'Tis said he composed, though nothing of that has been brought down to us. He diverted himself with performing, which they say he did well on the organ and bass viol. And this was a great relief to him after he had lost his sight.

"In relation to his love of music, and the effect it had upon his mind, I remember a story I had from a friend I was happy in for many years, and who loved to talk of Milton, as he often did. Milton, hearing a lady sing finely, 'Now I will swear,' says he, 'this lady is handsome.' His ears now were eyes to him."

Paradise Lost was the epical version of the play *Adam Unparadised,* and when he published it in 1667 he got a £5 advance from Simmons (a son of the Aldersgate Street publisher) on every edition of 1,300 copies, to sell at three shillings a copy. This was good payment for an epical poem in unfashionable blank verse, for money was worth about five times what it is to-day. He was paid the second £5 in 1669.

Edward Phillips wrote about Marie's daughters:

"By his third wife Elizabeth, the daughter of one Mr. Minsha of Cheshire (and kinswoman to Dr. Paget), who survived him, and is said to be yet living, he never had any child; and those he had by the first he made serviceable to him in that very particular in which he most wanted their service, and supplied his want of eyesight by their eyes and tongue. For though he

* Marie; not Katherine or Elizabeth. [R. G.]

had daily about him one or other to read to him, some persons of man's estate, who of their own accord greedily catched at the opportunity of being his readers, that they might as well reap the benefit of what they read to him, as oblige him by the benefit of their reading; others of younger years sent by their parents to the same end; yet excusing only the eldest daughter by reason of her bodily infirmity, and difficult utterance of speech (which to say truth I doubt was the principal cause of excusing her), the other two were condemned to the performance of reading and exactly pronouncing of all the languages of whatever book he should at one time or other think fit to peruse; viz. the Hebrew (and I think the Syriac), the Greek, the Latin, the Italian, Spanish and French. All which sorts of books, to be confined to read, without understanding one word, must needs be a trial of patience almost beyond endurance; yet it was endured by both for a long time. Yet the irksomeness of this employment could not always be concealed, but broke out more and more into expressions of uneasiness; so that at length they were all (even the eldest also) sent out to learn some curious and ingenious sorts of manufacture that are proper for women to learn, particularly embroideries in gold and silver. It had been happy indeed if the daughters of such a person had been made in some measure inheritrixes of their father's learning; but since fate otherwise decreed, the greatest honour that can be ascribed to this now living (and so would have been to the others, had they lived) is to be daughter to a man of his extraordinary character. . . .

"He died in the year 1673,* towards the latter end of the summer, and had a very decent interment, according to his quality, in the church of St. Giles, Cripplegate, being attended from his house to the church by several gentlemen then in town, his principal well-wishers and admirers.

"He is said to have died worth £1,500 in money (a considerable estate, all things considered), besides household goods; for he sustained such losses as might well have broke any person less frugal and temperate than himself; no less than £2,000 which he had put for security and improvement into the Excise Office, but, neglecting to recall it in time, could never after get it out, with all the power and interest he had in the great ones of those times; besides another great sum, by mismanagement and for want of good advice."

Milton had lost his most valuable property, the Spread Eagle in Bread Street, where he was born, in the Great Fire of 1666.

Late in life he won extraordinary fame for his poems, his champions being John Dryden, the Poet Laureate (who had Milton's permission to turn *Paradise Lost* into a rhymed opera) and Andrew Marvell, who honoured him as the new Tiresias. Their opinions outweighed that of Edmund Waller, who had been at Cambridge with Milton: "The old blind schoolmaster hath published a tedious poem

* This should be 1674. [R. G.]

on the Fall of Man. If its length be not considered as merit, it hath no other." In the reign of Charles II Milton was also regarded as the leading authority on Divorce, and consulted by great personages in the matter of the Lord Roos Divorce Bill, which the King personally helped through Parliament because he wanted to divorce his Queen, who was barren.

Milton left a nuncupative will, in which he said:

"The portion due to me from Mr. Powell, my former wife's father, I leave to the unkind children I had by her, having received no part of it; but my meaning is, they shall have no other benefit of my estate than the said portion and what I have besides done for them, they having been very undutiful to me. All the rest of my estate I leave to disposal of Elizabeth, my wife."

This will was rejected by the Prerogative Court of Canterbury when the daughters brought a suit against the widow, and they were awarded one-third of the estate to be divided among them, the widow getting the remaining two-thirds; it was clear to the Court that the marriage portion was a hopeless debt. During this suit, Elizabeth Fisher, a maid, testified that when she told Mary Milton (the daughter who so closely resembled her mother) that Milton was to be married again, she replied "that that was no news, to hear of his wedding, but if she could hear of his death, *that* was something." It also appeared in evidence that to keep themselves in pocket-money the girls had secretly sold books from Milton's library to the ragman who called at the door.

The widow, who had beautiful golden hair and had been twenty-four when she married Milton in 1663, paid off the daughters cheaply at £100 each. This bought Ann (the deformed one) a husband, a "master builder"; but she died soon after in childbirth. Deborah had already married Abraham Clarke, a silk weaver of Dublin: she had children and grand-children who emigrated to Madras, where Milton's line seems to have petered out. Mary did not marry, and was dead by 1682, when her grandmother, Ann Powell, died, worth £343, leaving £10 each to Deborah and Ann. Marie's sisters had all married. Mrs Powell left £50 each to:

Anne Kinaston, wife of Thomas Kinaston of London, merchant.
Sarah [Zara] Pearson, wife of Richard Pearson, gent.
Elizabeth [Bess] Howell, wife of Thomas Howell, gent.
Elizabeth [Betty] Holloway, wife of Christmas Holloway, gent.

But there is no bequest to any of the brothers except Richard, which was an annulment of a £180 debt he owed her, and it may be supposed that the rest were dead, some perhaps killed in the Commonwealth wars, some swept away by the Great Plague of 1665. Richard was a successful lawyer, one of the Readers of the Inner Temple, and at the Restoration managed to secure a new probate of his father's will and recover the Forest Hill Manor-house and land from the Pyes. The house was pulled down about 1850. But St. Nicholas's Church still stands and has not been wholly ruined by Victorian church-restorers.

Lady Cary Gardiner made a happy second marriage with one John Stewkely; she outlived her contemporary, Marie, by fifty-two years, dying at Islington in 1704, much mourned. Robert Pory was one of the Prebendaries of St. Paul's in the year of the Restoration. Christopher Milton turned Roman Catholic, was knighted in 1686, and became Chief Justice of the Common Pleas: his line is long extinct. The Rev. Luke Proctor appears to have continued as curate of Forest Hill until 1663, when he was succeeded by a man named Foster.

The double-dealing of Richard Powell, Senior, came out a few years after Marie's death, in a case heard at Oxford in the Chancellor's Court. All Souls College were the defendants, charged with allowing the Wheatley lands, which they had leased to Richard Powell, to be deceitfully mortgaged to Sir Edward Powell after they had already been mortgaged to Messrs. Bateman and Hearn. The decision absolved All Souls and incriminated:

"Richard Powell the lessee, who wittingly deceived himself that he might cozen * Sir Edward Powell. . . . Now deceit is a crime and a body without a soul (although it be All Souls) cannot be guilty of a crime, and so not be charged to pay damage or any way punishable for a crime. And therefore if any suit would have lien it must have been against some natural persons of that body; but to charge them as a body politic, there is no colour."

* A pun. Sir Edward Powell was his cousin.

Appendix

I

THE SEQUESTRATION OF THE GOODS OF RICHARD POWELL, ESQUIRE, AT FOREST HILL (JUNE 16TH, 1646)

RICHARD POWELL

A copy of the Inventory, with the prices of the goods as they were appraysed the 16 of June, 1646.

In a trunke of linen, as followeth:

1 paire of sheetes, 5 napkins, 6 yards of broad tiffany, 3 paire of pillow beares, 1 hand towell, 1 hollan cubboard cloth, 1 remnant of new hollan . . .	£0 16	0

In the backside:

240 pieces of tymber, 200 loades of fire-wood, 4 carts, 1 wane, 2 old coaches, 1 mare colt, 3 sowes, 1 boare, 2 ewes, 3 parcells of boards . . .	156 12	2
In the wooll-house, hoppes at	2 0	0
In the common, 100 butts at	60 0	0
One bull	1 10	0
Mr. Eldridge hath in his hand as much tymber as he was to give Mr. Powell for it	100 0	0
At Lusher's farme, the piece of corne in the great field at	42 0	0
The broad meddow eaten up by the souldiers . .⎱ One greate ground eaten upp . . . . .⎰	not praysed.	
One ground called Pilfrance, at	10 0	0
More, 1 piece of wheate	6 13	4
Mr. Powell hath at Forrest Hill 16 yard land which⎱ was usually sett at £8 or £9 yeare, and the tith of⎰ all the field	not praysed.	
Mr. Powell hath at Wheatley 1 house and 3 yard land free land and 3 yard land and halfe upon lease . .	£477 0	0
Wee have in money	£23 0	0
32 pieces of silver, 2 little silver spoones, 1 broken silver spoone, 1 clock bell, at	2 0	0
15 quarters of mastline at	14 0	0
5 quarters of malt	5 0	0
6 bushells of wheate	1 2	0

In the studdy or boyes chamber which should have followed next after
    the little chamber over the pantry:
  1 bedstedd with greene curtaines and vallons laced,
    1 feather bedd, 1 feather bolster, 1 paire of blanketts,
    1 yellow coverlid, 1 old horseman's coate with silver
    buttons, 1 great chaire, 1 great chest, 2 court cub-
    boards, 1 standing presse with drawers . . .   2 13 0

Sold unto Mr. Matthew Appletree all the goods in this inventory appraysed, that is to say the household goods:

	£	s.	d.
In the hall	1	4	0
In the great parlour	7	0	0
In the little parlour	3	0	0
In the kitchen	1	4	0
In the pastry	1	10	0
In the pantry	0	10	0
In the bakehouse	3	6	0
In the brewhouse	3	6	0
In the upper daryhouse	1	12	0
In the seller	1	15	0
In the stilling roome	1	1	0
In the cheese-presse house	0	12	6
In the matted chamber	4	16	0
In the chamber over the hall	2	18	0
In the chamber over the little parlour	3	15	0
In the two little chambers over the kitchin	1	0	0
In the servants' chamber	2	0	0
In the little chamber over the pantry	3	3	0
In the studdy or boyes chamber	2	13	0
In Mrs. Powell's chamber	8	4	0
In Mrs. Powell's closet	2	9	6
In the roome next the closet	1	10	0
In the roome over the washhouse	7	9	0
In Mr. Powell's study	1	14	0
In the same roome more linen	0	16	0
Malt, mastlin, wheate, a clocke and bell	22	2	0
In the backside: 4 hogges, 2 ewes, 1 mare and fold, 3 parcells of board, 240 pieces of tymber, 200 load or thereabouts of firewood, 1 wayne, 4 carts, 2 coaches	156	12	2
Wood lying in the common, 100 butts	60	0	0
In the wooll house, hoppes	2	0	0
A bull	1	10	0
	£310	12	2

Sold these goods, the 16 of June, 1646, by us whose names are under written, for the sume of three hundred thirty and five pounds, unto the abovesaid Mr. Appletree, and paid the same time to John King, in part of payment, the sume of twenty shillings, and the rest to bee paid at the delivery.

JOHN WEBB, RICHARD VIVERS, JOHN KING.

Witnesse [*then follow the marks of witnesses who could not sign their names*].

	Vera copia ex^t,

Vera copia ex^t,

27 Feb. 1650–1.   T. PAUNCEFOTE, Regr.

I make oath this as a true copie,

T. PAUNCEFOTE, R.M.

[*Side Note*].
In the first Cart.

1 Arras worke chayre.	1 Tapestry carpett.
6 Thrum chayres	1 Wrought carpett
6 Wrought stooles	1 Carpett green with fringe.
2 Old greene carpetts	3 Window curtaines.

II

RICHARD POWELL'S COMPOSITION PAPERS AT GOLDSMITHS' HALL, 21 NOVEMBER 1646

A Particular of the reall and personall Estate of Richard Powell, of Forrest Hill

He is seised of an estate in fee of tythes of Whatley, in the parish of Cudsden, and three yard lands and a halfe there, together with certayne cottages, worth before these times per annum £40 0 0

This is mortgaged to Mr. Ashworth for ninetye-nine years for a security of four hundred pounds, as appeares by deed bearing the 10th of Jann. in the 7th of King Charles. } A demyse of 99 years defeated by a pay-mente of £400, the 30 of Jan. 1642; arrears unpaid.

His personall estate, in corne and household-stuffe, amounts too 500 0 0

In timber and wood 400 0 0

In debts upon specialityes and otherwise owing to him . . 100 0 0

He oweth upon a statute to John Mylton 300 0 0

He is indebted more before these times by specialityes and otherwise to severall persons, as appears by affidavit . . 1,200 0 0

He lost by reason of these warres three thousand powndes.

This is a true particular of the reall and personall estate that he doth desire to compound for with this honorable Committee, wherein he doth submitt himselfe to such fine as they shall impose according to the Articles of Oxford, wherein he is comprized.

RICHARD POWELL.

Recd. 21 November, 1646.

4 Dec. 1646

These are to certifie, that Richard Powell of Forrest Hill, in the county of Oxford, Esquire, did freely and fully take the Nationall Covenant, and subscribe the same, uppon the fourth day of December 1646, the sayd covenant being administered unto him according to order, by me,

WILLIAM BARTON,
Minister of John Zecharies, London.

Probat. est.

[*Dorso,*]—Richard Powell, of Forrest Hill in the county of Oxford, Esq. took the oath this 4th of December, 1646.

THO. VINCENT.

8 Dec. 1646.

Richard Powell, of Forrest Hill, in the County of Oxford, Esq.

His delinquency, that he deserted his dwellinge and went to Oxford, and lived there whiles it was a garrison holden for the Kinge against the Parliamente, and was there at the tyme of the surrender, and to have the benefit of those Articles, as by Sir Thos. Fairfax's certificate of the 20 of June, 1646, doth appeare.

He hath taken the National Covenant before William Barton, minister of John Zacharies, the 4th of December, 1646, and the Negative Oath heere the same daye.

He compounds upon a Perticuler delivered in, under his hand, by which he doth submit too such fine, &c., and by which it doth appeare:

That he is seized in fee to him and his heirs in possession of and in the tythes of Whatley, in the parish of Cudsden, and other lands and tenements there of the yeerely value before theis troubles, £40.

That he is owner and possessed of a personall estate in goods, and there was oweinge unto him in good debts, in all amountinge unto £600; and there is £400 more in tymber, which is alledged to be questionable.

That he is endebted by statutes and bonds £1,500. He hath lost by reason of theis warrs £3,000.

He craves to be allowed £400 which, by a demise and lease, dated the 30th of January, 1642, of the lands and tenements aforesaid, is secured to be paid unto one Thomas Ashworth, gentleman, and is deposed to be still oweinge.

Fine at 2 yeeres value, £180.

[*Signed*] D. WATKINS,
JEROM ALEXANDER.

III

MILTON'S PETITION TO THE COMMISSIONERS FOR SEQUESTRATION AT HABERDASHERS' HALL

25 Feb. 1650–1

To the Honourable the Commissioners for Sequestration at Haberdashers' Hall

The Petition of John Milton

Sheweth,

That he being to compound by the late Act for certaine land at Whately, in Oxfordshire, belonging to Mr. Richard Powell, late of Forest-Hill, in the same county, by reason of an extent which he hath upon the said lands by a statute, did put in his Petition about the middle of August last, which was referred accordingly; but having had important business ever since, by order of the Councell of State, he hath no time to proceed in the perfeting of his composition; and in the meantime finds that order hath bin giv'n out from hence to forbidd his tenents to pay him rent; he therefore now desires he may have all convenient dispatch, and that the order of sequestring may be recalled, and that the composition may be moderated as much as may bee, in regard that Mrs. Powell, the widow of the said Mr. Richard Powell, hath her cause depending before the commissioners in the Painted Chamber for breach of articles, who have adjudg'd her satisfaction to be made for the great damage don her by seizing and selling the personall estate divers days after the articles were sealed. But by reason of the expiring of that court she hath received as yet no satisfaction, and beside she hath her thirds out of that land which was not considered when her husband followed his composition, and lastly the taxes, free quartering, and finding of armes, were not then considered, which have bin since very great and are likely to be greater.

And your petitioner shall be ready to pay what shall be thought reasonable at any day that shall be appointed.

(Signed) JOHN MILTON.

25 Feb. 1650–1.

Mr. Brereton is desired by the Commissioners to perfect his report in Mr. Milton's case by Tuesday next.

A. S., E. W.

[*In the margin, in Milton's own hand*]

"I doe swear that this debt for which I am to compound according to my petition is a true and real debt, as will appear upon record.

"John Milton."

Jur. 25 Feb., 1650–1.

IV

MRS. ANN POWELL'S PETITION, 16TH JULY, 1651.

To the Honourable the Commissioners for Compounding, &c.

The humble Petition of Anne Powell, widow, the relict of Richard Powell, of Forrest Hill, in the county of Oxon, deceased,

Sheweth,

That the petitioner brought £3,000 portion to her late husband, and is now left in a most sadd condition, the estate left being but £80 per annum, the thirds whereof is but £26 13s. 4d. to maintaine herselfe and 8 children.

The said estate being extended by Jo. Milton on a statute staple for a debt of £300 for which he hath compounded with your honours on the Act of the first of August, and therein allowance given him for the petitioner's thirds, yet the said Mr. Milton expects your further order therein before he will pay the same.

She therefore humbly prayeth your honours' order and direction to the said Mr. Milton for the payment of her said thirds, and the arreares thereof to preserve her and her children from starving.

And, as in duty bound, &c.

ANNE POWELL.

To be read next petition day, July the 14th, 1651.   S. M.

16 July, 1651.

[On the fly-leaf of this petition are the following notes]

Mrs. Powell,—By the law she might recover her thirds without doubt, but she is so extreame poore she hath not wherewithall to prosecute, and beside, Mr. Milton is a harsh and chollericke man, and married Mrs. Powell's daughter, who would be undone if any such course were taken against him by Mrs. Powell, he having turned away his wife heretofore for a long space upon some other occasion.

This note ensuing Mr. Milton writ, whereof this is a copy.

Although I have compounded for my extent, and shall be so much the longer in receiving my debt, yet at the request of Mrs. Powell in regard to her present necessitys I am contented as farre as belongs to my consent to allow her the 3rds of what I receive from the estate, if the Commissioners shall so order it that what I allow her may not be reckoned upon my accompt.

[In the margin, Mrs. Powell's note, 16 July, 1651]

The estate is wholly extended, and a saving as to the 3rds prayed but not granted we cannot therefore allow the 3rds to the petitioner.

Glossary

abecedarian	one who is still learning his **A B C**
account	period of pregnancy
acrimonious	acrid
aegilops	ulcer in the inner corner of the eye
Anabaptists	a sect that considered it necessary to be rebaptized
anothergates	otherwise
antics	grotesque figures imitating the antique
anti-Scripturists	a sect that denied the final authority of the Scripture
armiger	entitled to a coat-of-arms
atlasses	Eastern silk-satins
Auriga	charioteer
avence	herb bennet
Aqua-Mirabilis	"The wonderful water prepared of cloves, galangals, cubebs, mace, cardamums, nutmegs, ginger and spirit of wine, digested 24 hours, then distilled"
bagnio	a Turkish-bath establishment which was also a brothel
battle	battalion
Bezoartis	a preparation against poison, made from the livers and hearts of vipers, etc.
blind buzzard	a wilfully ignorant person
brawl	a sort of cotillon
breeching	beating on the breeches
brown-bill	a halberd or battle-axe with the blade stained brown, usually with ox-blood
budge	stiffly grave
buff-coat	a soldier's coat of stout buff-coloured leather
buffle-head	a person as stupid as a buffalo
butt	tree-trunk with its branches lopped off
buzz	rumour
camp-fever	typhus, complicated by relapsing fever
cashiered	paid off from the Army. (Not necessarily discharged with ignominy)
cat-in-pan, to turn	to be a political turn-coat
caudle	warm spiced gruel, mixed with wine or ale
chaldron	36 bushels
to cheek	to grasp the pike by the cheeks, or side-pieces, and bring it to the ready, as if about to lunge
Chiliasts	a sect that "expected the Millennium any day soon"
the claps	gonorrhea
clerk-ale	a feast for the benefit of the parish clerk
clip	hug
coat and conduct money	a tax to provide soldiers with service coats
coat card	court card
cocker up	pamper
collop	slice of meat for frying or grilling
commons	rations
compound	come to terms with

concoct the surfeits	digest the excesses
copula carnalis	coition
corky	dry as cork
costive	constipating
coven	a group of twelve female witches, with a male devil
culgees	figured Indian silks
to cry "cupboard"	to ask for food
cupped	bled with a cupping-glass
cuttanee	East Indian linen
daggy	bedraggled like a sheep that has lain in muck
deboshed	debauched
dehortations	exhortations against something or someone
deliration	delirious speech
demise	the expiration of a title to property
diurnals	journals
dividual	separate
to doltify	make doltish
to droil	to labour
to droll	to joke
house of easement	earth closet
elicampane	horse-head
endemial	endemic
ends and awls	a cobbler's odds and ends
ex animo	voluntarily
extended	seized upon in satisfaction of a debt
extrude	to remove forcibly
fadge	agree
Familists	a "monstrous and horrible sect that held religion to be based on Love rather than Fear"
ferule	a flat ruler with a pear-shaped end and a hole in the middle to raise blisters; used by schoolmasters
fescennine	bawdy
fico	fig
to firk	to move briskly
flaggy-haired	with lank, wispy hair
flibbergib	a flighty gossip
fliperous	flippant and frivolous
flux hepaticus	discharge from the liver
Fogo	volcanic fire
Fortune	Company of soldiers
fossilia	ancient objects dug up. (Not necessarily fossils)
frammer	hurdle-making instrument, rather like a wrench
fribbling	petty
to fub	to take down or outwit
fucus	cosmetic paint
gaggling	cackling
galliard	a lively dance in triple time
gerfalcon	male falcon
gillyflowers	carnations or pinks
gingerline	of the rich brown colour of gingili
girdlestead	waist
gitterning	playing on the gittern, a sort of guitar
glabrification	making smooth or bald
gloat upon	cast amorous glances upon. (Not in the modern sense of gazing with lustful satisfaction)
glooming	gloomy-looking
gloze	explain away deceitfully

goddamme blade	a swaggering gallant
gorge me that!	swallow that!
gorget	piece of armour protecting the throat
green-geese-pie	pie made of freshly-killed geese (i.e. not pickled or smoked)
gricomed	syphilitic. (A nobleman or knight was said to be "gricomed", whereas a citizen "suffered from the Neapolitan scab" and a serving man "had the plain pox")
grutch	grudge
gust	appetite
heart-breakers	a man's long side locks
Hiera Picra	"sacred-bitter": a drug of aloes, honey and canella which "purges choler from the stomach"
hinnies	mules dammed by an ass and sired by a horse
Hocktide	a festival celebrated on the second Monday and Tuesday after Easter, when rents were paid
hogen-mogen	high and mighty. (A Dutch term)
to huddle	to jumble away into concealment
hugger-mugger	hole-and-corner secrecy
hydromel	Russian mead
Ibis	"this foul bird feedeth upon watersnakes and useth his beak for a clyster-pipe. Wherefore the poet Ovid, taking example from the poet Callimachus, cast this word satirically at an author whom his soul loathed"
to imbecilitate	to weaken
impostume	a swelling
indifferent good	fairly good
indurated	hardened
infall	assault
issues	artificial ulcers created to cause a discharge of matter
Jacobus	gold coin of King James I
jakes	latrine
jauncing	bouncing
jaunt	a fatiguing journey
jennet	small Spanish horse
John apples	apples ripe about St. John's Day (June 24th)
jointure	dowry
jump right with	fit in with
junto	governmental clique
keck	retch
kill-cow	a person of great importance
kind, against	unnaturally
Lamia	a vampire witch
lapides sui generis	stones of distinct variety
lardons of lard	slices of pork or fat bacon for enriching a pie
leaguer	the camp of an army investing a fortress
leash of hawks	three hawks
leet-ale	festival at the time of the annual Manorial Court of Record
lick-dish	servile person
licorish	lustful
logger-head	"one whose wit is as little as his head is great"
losel	ruined or worthless
lozenge figure	diamond shape: used for enclosing a woman's coat-of-arms where a man would use a shield-shape
to make legs	to bow ceremoniously

to make the beast with two backs — to have sexual intercourse

malignant — an enemy to Parliament—but the Royalists occasionally used this same word against the Parliamentarians

manna — the crystallized juice of the manna-ash

mantling — drapery or leaves fastened to a helmet to keep off the sun; now shown in coats-of-arms as ornamental scroll work

mastline — like "maslin," "mesclan," etc., a different spelling of "mislan"

matches — lengths of perpetually-smouldering wick used by musketeers for touching off their muskets, or by cannoneers for their cannon

maw — crop of a fowl, honey-bag of a bee

melon-pompion — large pumpkin-like melon

mislan — rye and wheat mixed

Mithridate — a compound drug invented by King Mithridates of Pontus to protect him against every sort of poison; also used against infectious diseases

mittimus — warrant for commitment to prison

mixen — manure heap

montero-cap — a Spanish hunter's cap, with ear-flaps

morion — steel helmet without any face protection

Mundungo — tobacco that has gone mouldy

musk-melon — a small sweet melon

muster — a parade of soldiers, or a parade list

nappy — heady

Natura Naturata — the passive as opposed to the active principle of Nature

nimmed — pilfered

niny-hammer — a conceited fool

nuncupative — given by word of mouth

Obs — objections in a logical dispute

obsequious — obedient. (Not necessarily in the sense of being servile)

officiously — dutifully. (Not in the sense of being a nuisance)

Old Brownists — followers of Robert Brown, an Elizabethan clergyman, the "Father of Religious Independency"

oyster, choking — a damaging retort

panagories — popular festivals

pelting — wretchedly trivial

phlegm — one of the four "humours" which were held to rule the constitution of the body. Phlegm made one apathetic and *phlegmatic*. The others were Blood, which made one lively and *sanguine;* Yellow Bile, or Choler, which made one petulant and *choleric;* Black Bile, which made one gloomy and *melancholy*

pica — an unnatural longing by a pregnant woman for a particular food

poaching — making "poches" or holes in the ground

points — tagged laces

the popular — the mob

pot — familiar name for a morion, or steel cavalry helmet

powdering-tubs — pickling tubs

praysed — valued

prevaricator — a joking quibbler

prick-song hymns — hymns with formal written music

privileged men	college servants and the like who, though not University students, were reckoned with the Gown, not the Town
procatarctical cause	external cause
prolusion	introductory drama
propria quae maribus	a Latin verse written by Lilly the Grammarian to help boys to remember the gender of Latin nouns
puny	freshman or novice
Questionists	a sect of sceptics who believed only in liberty of conscience and liberty of prophesying
quintain	a swinging target for lance practice: anyone who did not hit it squarely was apt to be unhorsed
rabbits	young rabbits. Full-grown ones were coneys
raddled	daubingly marked
rebus	a punning picture, e.g. the Abbot Islip's personal rebus in Westminster Abbey shows a little man falling from a tree, "I slip"; also two eyes and a lip, "Eyes lip"
to redargue	to go back over an argument
to renege	to break one's oath or principle
rossomakka	the Russian maccarib, i.e. reindeer [?]
ruck	the slower-moving mass in a retreat or race
ruddle	red dip for marking sheep
ruffler	swash-buckler
ruffles it	swaggers
running-battle	a country sword dance
sack-posset	warm drink made with dry Spanish wine
sand-caster	sand-pot used before the invention of blotting-paper
scout-master	intelligence officer
scrivener	law-stationer, who also gave legal advice and arranged loans and mortgages, etc. He stood in much the same relation to a lawyer as an apothecary did to physician
to scum up	to froth up
seaton	a twist of silk or other material inserted in a wound to keep it open and thus maintain an artificial issue
Sebaptists	a sect that believed in self-baptism
Seekers	a sect that held that no perfect Revelation had yet been granted to Man, but ecstatically looked for one
Sergeant-major	Major
sequestration	official confiscation
several	separate
shallowling	a superficial person
sillabub	a drink of milk warm from the cow, curdled with sweet wine or cider
slip-coat cheese	cream cheese
slouch	slovenly fellow
slubberdegullion	a slobbering person
smooty	smutty
snaggle-toothed	with teeth jutting irregularly
snail-water	a drug distilled from snails, as a remedy against consumptions and hectic fevers
snap-sack	knapsack
snibbed	snubbed
to snuff	to sniff disdainfully

Socinians	followers of Lælius and Faustus Socinus, sixteenth-century theologians who held that Jesus was Man, not God
Sodom-apple	a Dead Sea apple
Sol	solution to a logical problem
soosies	fabrics of silk and cotton mixed
Soul-sleepers	a materialistic sect that denied the existence of the soul
spooner	spoon-maker
spud knife	a cheap knife
to stand perdue	to be in ambush
stilling-room	distillery
stock-fish	salted cod
stomach, without	unwilling to face something
sublunary	earthly
swinger	rogue
tabor	drum
tailed sonnet	a sonnet with six extra lines
Tangerine	of Tangiers
tenter-hooks	crooked nails fastened to the edges of cloth to prevent it shrinking after it is milled
thrum-chair	chair with a woven seat
thwartly	contradictorily or perversely
tire-woman	lady's maid
Tories	Irish bandits
tormentil	sept-foil
to tote	to peep
town bull	the bull provided for serving the cows of a township
train-oil	whale oil
Traskites	a sect who held that the Sabbath should be celebrated on Saturday
trot	hag
tuck	a rapier
turk's cap	tulip
ululate	howl
untruss	undo one's breeches
vapouring	talking nonsense
Venice red	scarlet
verbenas	leaves and twigs used in religious ceremonies
vitilitigation	recrimination
whifflers	armed attendants who clear the way for a procession
whirret	smart blow
whored	made a whore of, by a false or repudiated marriage
wisses	knows
witling	a person who thinks himself witty
yawl	bawl